Praise for The Red Rose of Romance and War

"John Yates takes the bare bones of his family's wartime history and fashions it into a rollicking adventure and romance that turns, as so much of real life does, on the chance of a moment."

—Ian Kirkwood, Newcastle Herald Journalist

"Fascinating historical facts, a close-up look at the terrible conditions in the trenches during World War 1 and a beautiful love story! I found it gripping from start to finish."

—Gwen Grant, Melbourne

"In recent years there has been a resurgence of interest in the First World War as more writers seek out the personal battlefield and wartime stories of the Australian Digger, none of whom are with us today. This is the author's first book but it isn't your average debut novel.

John Yates is the son of the late Wilfred George Yates, who as a 25 years old bush worker enlisted in the Australian Imperial Forces as an infantryman and served alongside Joe Maxwell on the Western Front during WW1. Lt. Maxwell was undeniably one of the AIF's most courageous and decorated soldiers. On another level it is the story of a young soldier's first experience of love while recuperating in a London hospital.

The story of Lance Corporal Wilfred George Yates is a good read."

—David H Dial OAM, Military Historian

THE RED ROSE
OF ROMANCE & WAR

JOHN A. YATES

ISBN: 978-1-63950-359-9 (sc)
ISBN: 978-1-63950-360-5 (e)

Writers Apex

Gateway Towards Success

8063 MADISON AVE #1252
Indianapolis, IN 46227
+13176596889
www.writersapex.com

Contents

"Wilf Yates"

Chapter 1

As the stretcher bearers were loading Wilf into the horse-drawn ambulance, Lt. Joe Maxwell stopped by, gripped him on the shoulder, and said, "Hurry up and get back onto your feet, mate. We need every bloke available to keep this unit viable. We've already lost too many good soldiers to this dreaded trench foot, plus other wounds and worse."

"I'll do my best, Lieutenant, but you make sure and look after the rest of the lads while I'm gone. I want to see them all here when I return."

As the stretcher bearers gave Wilf's stretcher the last push into the holding rails on the carriage, the sound of a new shell attack caused the usual commotion, and men scattered back to the security of the trenches.

The calm voice of Maxwell could be heard yelling, "Take cover, men."

The ambulance driver was anxious to get the horses moving out of harm's way, although where that happened to be was anybody's guess. As the horses were driven along what appeared to be an old track, it seemed that the Huns (Germans) were observing their movements and redirecting their fire close by. That was not the case at all because shells were falling over a wide area of this once fertile farming land.

Wilf, being flat on his back, could not see the devastation around him. He had been living in this environment for what to him seemed like years; he knew what it looked like.

The inescapable stench of the dead horses and donkeys along both sides of the track penetrated inside the canvas walls of the ambulance, overpowering any smell coming from Wilf's trench-foot infection. Under normal conditions, the pungent smell of trench foot was bad enough, but the smell of the dead animals was worse.

There were three other soldiers with Wilf, all with the same disease of the feet.

Eventually, he knew they were moving further out of range of the enemy artillery fire. They soon arrived at a Regimental Aid Post, where they were transferred into a motorised ambulance; this vehicle held eight soldiers in various stages of pain.

Wilf couldn't tell what was wrong with all of the men, but two of them had lost legs, and another was heavily bandaged around the head; only his nostrils and one eye were showing. A caring nurse had been assigned the difficult job of keeping him alive for the first leg of the journey to Blighty (England).

The ambulance was again underway at last, but the journey was hardly smoother. The roads were much better, enabling the driver to travel faster. However, the vehicle swayed about more noticeably, making the nurse's task even more difficult.

Wilf wondered what prompted a young girl to willingly give up a life of relative safety at home and come to this hellhole called the Somme. The nurses had to put up with such trying conditions in order to offer life-saving care to men from all around the world. He thought about the marvellous job they all did.

The constant swaying kept up for nearly an hour before they arrived at a railway siding. There were a lot of instructions being shouted by marshals to a rabble of ambulance drivers as they arrived.

The drivers were anxious to discharge their precious cargoes into the care of orderlies and nurses. It was their job to load these men onto the waiting railway carriages for further travel to the harbour. There would be a different lot of nurses waiting there to load their new charges onto the waiting vessel for the journey across the English Channel to hospitals scattered around London and beyond.

Wilf found it impossible to sleep during the ambulance journeys, mainly because of the bumpy, swaying ride. Once on the train, it was certainly smoother, but now the extreme pain from his feet was enough to keep him awake. He felt like he was an imposter in such company when he considered his condition, compared to the terrible plight of most other wounded soldiers around him.

Once the wounded and sick men were loaded onto the boat, the mood of the men changed dramatically. To them, it seemed like they were nearly home and out of harm's way. Most did not realise the danger of the many German submarines lurking in the channel, waiting for a chance to sink Allied vessels travelling in either direction.

If soldiers were in any condition to sing a song whilst being shipped across the channel for hospital treatment, the song was always "Take Me Back to Dear Old Blighty." The words of this song must have added at least an extra 15 per cent chance to the soldiers' recovery rate, even before they arrived at a hospital.

Chapter 2

The military ambulance arrived at the King's College Hospital at two in the morning. Wilf was carried by stretcher into the ward to be greeted by Nurse Davis. Wilf was sound asleep and unaware of his surroundings as the orderly handed Wilf's record card to Nurse Davis, which she immediately read: *Wilfred George Yates, number 6414, Lewis Gunner of the Eighteenth Infantry Battalion, Second Division of the Australian Imperial Force.* He was twenty-five years old, five feet ten with brown hair and blue eyes. His occupation was described as a Teamster (Bullock driver). He enlisted in Sydney and sailed for England on the *Suevic* in 1916.

After arriving in England, he did extensive training on the Salisbury plains, served in France and Belgium, and was deployed in the trenches around the town of Ypres in Belgium. He was suffering with trench foot and had been withdrawn from the front line and shipped off to England for recovery.

Nurse Davis helped transfer Wilf into a regular bed and noticed from his appearance that he was a wiry, outdoor worker whose body was extremely fit and strong, even for an Australian Digger. Ann had already cared for a number of Diggers in this hospital but was unaware of where the name Digger came from.

She was a nurse with considerable experience looking after injured and sick soldiers from the Western Front. She was five feet four and of slender build, with high cheekbones and blonde hair that was always pulled back and covered under her nurse's cap whilst on duty.

Nurse Davis proceeded to record Wilf's details in the ward register, at the same time making sure he was comfortable. She leaned over the bed and said, "Wilf, can you hear me?" to which he nodded. "I know it's very late, but would you like something to eat or drink?"

"No, I just want to sleep," he replied weakly. He was worn out from the long journey.

Wilf slept well during the night until woken by the day-shift nurse who came to attend to his feet. She also brought him some nourishment, after which he went back to sleep again. Just after dark, he was awakened by the night-shift nurse, Nurse Davis.

"Wakey wakey," she said. "I need to take care of your feet. I'll be back in a few minutes, so you can think about having something to eat." She went away to get the implements needed.

Wilf stirred, and by the time Nurse Davis came back, he was feeling somewhat aware of his surroundings and said, "Yes, I would like something to eat—and a drink also, please."

"How about I arrange a sandwich and a cup of tea for when I have finished bathing and massaging your feet."

"It sounds good to me, thank you."

She caught the eye of the tea lady on the other side of the ward and made arrangements for a sandwich and tea in about half an hour's time.

Nurse Davis proceeded to put in place a large bowl and a jug of hot water and said, "Are you feeling well enough to sit up?"

"Yes, I think so. I'm feeling pretty good after that great sleep. How long was I asleep?"

"You've had about eighteen hours all told since you arrived."

"Have I really? I must have been tired. That ride in the ambulance was a nightmare, although I did sleep a little on the boat."

"Tell me about yourself. Where do you come from, and what made you come over here to this horrible war?"

"Well, I'm from Australia, as you probably already know. I've always been a bullock driver, and I joined up to see the world."

The conversation continued while the nurse first bathed his feet and then massaged them for some time.

During his time in the hospital, Wilf's stay was made not only more tolerable but also exciting because of the daily contact he had with Nurse Davis. Her hands were so gentle, massaging and bandaging his feet daily. Her gentle touch would even linger and caress his body, bringing soothing balm, or so he imagined.

Wilf was smitten very early during his four-week stay in the hospital by this gorgeous, blonde-haired nurse who asked Wilf to call her Ann. Ann's skin was so soft and fair, unlike most Aussie girls whose skin was browned by the strong Australian sun.

As soon as Wilf was able to sit up and write, he asked Ann to find some paper and pencil so he could write to his mother. Wilf was very close to his mum and wrote:

> *Dear Mother,*
>
> *Your most recent letters have not caught up with me yet, as I have been shipped back to England with trench foot and am currently in the King's College Hospital at Denmark Hill, London. I am being very well cared-for by some wonderful nurses.*
>
> *You will be glad to hear that trench foot is not an injury caused by bullets or shrapnel. Trench foot comes about because a lot of our time is spent in ankle- to knee-deep, putrid water, sometimes twenty-four hours a day, sometimes for weeks on end.*
>
> *The condition is first noticed as blackened feet with white, spongy, swollen flesh similar to frostbite. It is believed to be caused by germs bred in the filthy water of the trenches. The germs enter under the toenails, causing the feet to become discoloured and giving off a*

terrible odour of putrid flesh. Amputations are necessary for bad cases. Mine are not that bad.

Each soldier whilst in the trenches is required to rub his feet twice daily with whale oil, on issue. It is a pitiful sight to see men screaming with pain, struggling back along the duckboards in the freezing cold with their feet wrapped in sandbags. Swollen feet do not fit into boots very well.

I know it sounds terrible, but they shipped me out before my feet became too bad. They tell me that I could be over here for five or six weeks; you will be pleased about that, I am sure.

Please give my love to the rest of the family. I will write again soon.

Love you, Mother.
Wilf

Ann took every opportunity available to call by his bed. One of her colleagues told Ann that the other nurses on her shift deliberately did nothing for this Aussie patient in bed number 32, to allow Nurse Davis to have the extra time with him. Ann was such a real honey that other nurses and the doctors treated her as a special and dedicated nurse. Her special exuberance and sparkle did not go unnoticed and was appreciated by those around her.

After four weeks in the King's, Ann came to Wilf one afternoon as he sat out on the veranda enjoying the sunshine on his feet. She said, "I have some good news and bad news for you."

Wilf said, "You had better give me the good news first."

"I have just spoken with the doctor, and you are to be discharged from the hospital in two days' time. That will be Saturday, and you will be discharged for two weeks of rest and recovery."

"That sounds marvellous to me. So what's the bad news?"

"Well, you mightn't think it's bad news, but I'm going to miss you when you're gone."

"Well, I'm going to miss you too, so that part is bad news for me too. However, can't we see each other away from here?"

"That would be great. I'm off for two days, this Saturday and Sunday."

"Well how about we go for a picnic this Saturday to celebrate my discharge from hospital?"

"Lovely, that couldn't have worked out better. I would've been very disappointed if you hadn't asked me."

"I was trying to pluck up the courage to ask you sometime, but this has worked out just wonderful. How about I arrange for a picnic basket to be ready when you're discharged at about ten o'clock? Your discharge time would normally be nine o'clock, but they're never on time."

"Where will we meet?"

"Right over there outside the main entrance," she said, pointing to the large doors on the other wing.

Just then, another nurse called for Ann's assistance, so Wilf was left on his own to ponder his good fortune.

Wilf had already learned that Ann was twenty-three years old, born February 29, 1894, a leap-year baby. She had studied hard during training, throwing herself into her job as a nurse so seriously that dating was something she had not had time for.

Chapter 3

Wilf was discharged at nine fifteen with plenty of time to sweat and pace, waiting for the appointed meeting time. Completing the necessary paperwork prior to the release of a patient had not been the problem that Ann had suggested it might be. He had never known forty-five minutes to take so long. Even a three- or four-hour artillery bombardment was not as painfully long as this wait.

At ten o'clock, Wilf was waiting out in front of the main entrance as arranged. He felt a great sense of excitement as he leaned upon the walking cane that had been supplied by the hospital. His feet felt quite good, but the cane was there just in case.

He watched with anticipation as Ann came out of the double glass doors and walked in his direction. This was the first time he had seen Ann's hair down. It was shoulder length and bounced as she walked towards him. She was carrying her hat and a small picnic basket. As she came closer, he could detect the sparkle in her eyes. Her face beamed like sunlight filtering through the foliage of trees in a rainforest canopy back home in the bush.

Wilf could tell that Ann was a reserved person. This suited him. The attraction they had for each other was nearly enough to cause them to fall into each other's arms as their hands touched in a more formal manner.

Neither spoke for a little while until Ann offered a quiet hello to break the ice. Wilf was so stunned at the sight of this wonderful creature offering her hands to him that he could manage little more than a gasp. *Hello* and *Ann* were two words that just wouldn't come out.

Wilf had his kitbag to shoulder, which was going to be a real pain to take on a picnic, but there was no alternative.

"I have no plans of coming back to the hospital today, so let's see how we go." As she put on her hat and tied the ribbon under her chin, Ann said, "Let's head in this direction towards the river." They headed off along Denmark Hill Road towards Camberwell Green.

This eagerly and longed-for event for both of them was too sacred and special to spoil with words. Wilf savoured this moment of time in silence. He had been dreaming about this event for the last two days and sensed that Ann was feeling the same way.

Ann broke the silence saying, "You must remember that the doctor has released you into my care ahead of normal time, so this is why we're taking our time."

"I'm thoroughly enjoying the experience," he said as Ann guided him onto Camberwell New Road, past Kensington Park and The Oval, heading towards Vauxhall.

"Wilf, I think if you're a cricket fan, you would have heard of The Oval. That's it right there."

"I have indeed; I've read of The Oval a number of times. This is where our boys gave your boys a real thrashing once."

"I think you're right. I shouldn't have pointed it out to you."

Wilf allowed his free hand to touch the back of Ann's hand ever so gently at different times as they walked. Each touch sent a wonderful sensation up his arm; he was not an experienced man in these delicate ways.

They stopped to let a group of excited young boys pass. Wilf said, "I think they must be going to The Oval. It's Saturday, isn't it?"

"Yes, it is. What would you normally do on a Saturday?"

"Well, as you already know, I'm a timber cutter and bullock driver, and I work six days a week with my father in the bush. The only time I ever get to talk with girls is when we go to church on Sundays. That's a three-hour ride each way in the sulky."

"This must be a huge change for you to be so far away."

"It certainly is; it's a much bigger change than I could possibly have believed when I made the decision to enlist."

"We've talked a lot about that change in little snippets at the bedside, but when we get a chance to sit down, I want to hear a lot more."

"I don't think there's much to tell—"

Ann interrupted him to say, "Look, there's a Hansom cab coming this way, and it's empty. I'll hail him because I don't want you do doing too much walking."

The horse-drawn cab pulled alongside, and Wilf helped Ann up into the cab.

"Just continue down to the river please, driver."

"Well this is a new experience for me. Did I hear you refer to this as a Hansom cab?"

"Yes I did. These cabs used to be the way nobility moved around London. There's not a lot left now, with the motorised cabs taking over. The tourists still like them."

They travelled past Vauxhall Station, and Ann said, "We have a choice to make, and there are three alternative destinations coming up ahead. We could turn right at the main Vauxhall intersection along Wandsworth Road. This will lead towards Lambeth Palace and the old Vic Theatre. Or we can go straight ahead over the bridge and into London proper. Or we have a third option to turn left past St. George's Wharf. This will take us past the flower gardens into the park by the river."

"The flower garden sounds nice, but I'll leave that to you, Nurse; you know what's best for my feet."

Lots of words were unnecessary for them to understand the beauty of the day and this very special occasion. Nor was the direction in which they were travelling very important. Wilf was just so excited being with Ann.

"This will do, driver," Ann said as they came to the entrance of the gardens.

They alighted from the cab at the flower gardens. Ann paid the driver because Wilf had no English money.

"Is there somewhere to sit down along there?" he said.

"Yes," said Ann, "under some large, shady trees near the embankment." So that was where they headed.

Wilf didn't really care where they were going; he was just so pleased to have Ann by his side.

They headed down a little lower, along the lush green grass that covered the bank. Wilf took the opportunity to keep hold of Ann's hand, helping them both negotiate the steeper parts of the bank. He felt great satisfaction at achieving this manoeuvre.

Wilf may not have been experienced in these things, but he was careful enough to make sure that her hand stayed closely clasped in his. He had never had electricity in his home in Australia, but the tingling that was running up his arm felt like the electricity he had read about. *Why were people so afraid of electricity if this is what it feels like?* he thought.

Ann said, "I felt very privileged to think I was allowed to walk the streets with an Australian Digger in full uniform by my side for everyone to see."

"I don't think anyone really took much notice, did they?" he said, but he also felt very privileged to have this wonderful lady by his side to guide him.

Now there were just the two of them walking side by side, with no one else around.

Ann said, "Look over there, under that large tree. There's a park seat. Let's go there. We'll have a good view of the boats working on the river."

"Sounds good to me; I'm quite hot in this serge tunic. I'm sure they were made for the colder climates of the Somme. I'm not too sure that anybody actually thought too much about what type of clothing would be most suitable in the various climates and seasons of the war."

Ann noticed he was perspiring and said, "Why don't you remove your jacket?"

"What a jolly good idea." He was only too happy to remove his jacket in this warm spring weather.

"The River Thames is such a large river compared to the creeks and streams I'm accustomed to in the bush. The only river of any size I've seen back home is the Hunter River at Raymond Terrace."

Ann asked, "What's special about that river?"

"I've been going to Raymond Terrace since I was eleven years old, in my first year of work." he replied. "I worked with my father driving a horse team with loads of timber. We walked nearly thirty miles to Raymond Terrace three times each week. The Cedar timber we carry is loaded onto boats for eventual shipment to Britain."

"Why three times per week?"

"It takes us one day to go down, and then we camp out under the stars and cook a meal in our camp oven each night, before making the return trip back to Stroud the next morning."

"That's amazing; people haven't done that sort of thing here in England for a long time."

Ann pointed across the river. "Right over there are some very well-known buildings. I shouldn't bore you with the names because they probably don't mean anything to you."

"Give me some examples?"

"Well that's Pimlico opposite and Balmoral Castle, Tyrell and Hungerford Houses, and then over this way, you can see the Westminster Boating House, Maitland House, and then there's Eagle House right behind."

"Some of the places you mentioned are also the names of places within fifty miles of my home back in Australia."

"Really?" said Ann as she flicked her long hair to one side. "I suppose there must have been some lonely people who settled in Australia, thinking about home."

"I suppose that when the English people came to colonise Australia, they must have named the towns to remind them of home. We certainly have a lot of towns with the same names as yours. I've seen the signs here from the trains when we were on the way to Exeter, like Stroud and Gloucester."

None of the boating activity going to and fro on the water, although quite new to Wilf, was enough to take precedence over the moment. He was enjoying the experience of holding the hand of this angel sitting by his side.

"You have two weeks of convalescence to go before returning to the front. You've been walking like an accomplished walker today, with no obvious problems, but I must remind you that you still need to give your feet lots of rest."

"Thank you, Nurse. I'll do as you say and enjoy it."

"Anyway, I have something planned. I'll tell you about it later."

The activities on the river were the catalyst needed to open up all sorts of topics about each other's past. Only small segments of the past had already been discussed in the short stolen moments together around bed 32 in ward 3 over the last four weeks. They both chatted as though they had done this sort of thing many times before.

Ann pointed out some other places across the way on the Chelsea Embankment.

Wilf said, "I'm amazed how much you know about London. It's such a big place. Are there any places you don't know?"

"Oh plenty. I only know a fraction of the places. Tell me about some of the places you've seen in your travels."

"Well, back home there's not much to talk about; it's very limited. But since coming over here and being on the Somme, I experienced many different parts of Belgium and France when on leave. Most of that time was spent wandering around those towns without a guide, marvelling at the architecture that goes back nearly a thousand years."

"That must be very interesting for you. I want to show you some of our great buildings."

"I look forward to that," he said. "I was particularly taken by the massive cathedral in Amiens. I couldn't fathom how they built such a huge building in the twelfth and thirteenth centuries without all of the new technology available to the workers of the 1900s."

"I've no idea either," said Ann.

"It makes me wonder … How did they cut the stones? How did they lift them up so high? How did they make the stones stay put over the arches? How did they make all the beautiful stained-glass windows? How did they make the bells? The questions just keep on going."

"It is mind boggling, isn't it?" said Ann as she gave his hand a firm squeeze.

Wilf said, "I read about the famous Notre Dame Cathedral in Paris. I've now learned that this cathedral in Amiens, which apparently looks very similar to Notre Dame, is more than twice its size. I also learned that when this cathedral was built, its purpose was to shelter, if needed, the entire population of the town—over twenty thousand people."

"These types of buildings are very common here. London has many huge buildings, so I can see why you're so excited. It's probably because you have none like these back home."

"You're right."

"I want to take you to see some of these great buildings of London, places like St. Paul's, Westminster Abbey, Buckingham Palace, and all the other places that I've planned for you to see over the next two weeks before you return to those awful trenches."

"How are you going to do that when you have to work?"

"I told you before that I was working on a plan. Well, I plan to get time off at the hospital to show you around. I haven't worked out all the details yet, but I will."

"That would be absolutely terrific. I don't know what to say other than thank you."

Wilf was so thrilled to be sitting there with Ann. Sometimes there were long periods of silence. He didn't want to talk about the carnage he had witnessed on the front, but those thoughts kept creeping into his mind. There were places where it was impossible to keep to the duckboards when moving up to the front line. Sometimes one needed to step off the boards to make room for stretcher bearers bringing back badly wounded soldiers. Sometimes there was three feet of mud on either side of the boards, and many times the mud was filled with bodies of horses and men. The bodies stopped the soldiers from sinking all the way down when stepping off the boards. It was not something he wanted to talk about in this situation; it was something he didn't want to even think about.

Ann snapped him out of those dark thoughts, saying, "Well, I think we should eat. I've prepared some curried-egg sandwiches. I hope you like egg. There are a couple of bottles of water there also."

"Curried-egg sandwiches are my favourite," said Wilf. "They actually are; I'm not just trying to be nice to you."

"I'm glad you like them. It's hard to find nice things in these days of rationing. My mother does so well buying things like meat and vegetables, food items that I hear others say they rarely ever see, especially cheese."

Now that lunch was over, there were better things to talk about than food shortages. They were now catching the full benefit of the shade, afforded them by the large tree under which they were sitting.

Ann said, "I want to learn more about Australia. Tell me all about your country and your family."

"My knowledge of Australia at large is quite limited, having grown up in the Dungog and Stroud districts of NSW. I had never even been to Sydney until I boarded the train for the 180-mile journey to enlist in the AIF last year. Thinking about Australia now seems like a whole lifetime away because of all the new things I've experienced over here."

"It all sounds very interesting to me, so keep talking."

"Well, I'm the eldest of six children. I have four sisters, Leila, Ilma, Vera, and Millie, plus my brother, Ned, who is the youngest."

"Are they all still at home?"

"No, my eldest sister, Leila, got married just before I left."

"I assume both your mum and dad are still alive?"

"Yes, they are, and both very well and able."

"Did any of your family go to Sydney to see you off?"

"No, it's too far away, 180 miles to Sydney."

"Oh, that's a shame. So you were on your own?"

"Originally I was, but I did meet a family of seven sisters on the wharf; they took good care of me. I was a complete stranger to them. They came into town from Pyrmont to see off one of the boys from their church. They took turns carrying my kitbag as we marched through the streets of Sydney to the docks at Walsh Bay."

"Oh, that was really sweet of them."

"One of the sisters promised to write, and we have become good pen friends."

Ann didn't reply.

"At Walsh Bay, we boarded the *Suevic* bound for England."

"Tell me—what it was like? I've never been out to sea."

"Well, it's not easy to explain because it was a very emotional experience."

"Okay, I can understand that, but I'll be a good listener."

"Well, I'll try. I left Sydney Harbour in a large ship with thousands of other men who probably were also making their first-ever sea voyage. I had never even set foot into a rowboat before. So you can imagine how apprehensive I was as the ship moved from the dock, pulled by a couple of tugs. There were crowds singing and waving from the poorly lit wharf."

"That would have been a sight."

"The ship turned south into dark, low-clouded, rumbling skies. The ominous blackness caused a silence to settle over most of the men. Maybe for the first time, they realised there was now no turning back. Well, that's how I felt anyway. Maybe we all realised there would be very few silver linings in the storm clouds ahead."

"I'm sure it must have had quite an effect on you."

"Up until then, enlistment had almost been a buzz, but once at sea, the seriousness of the situation took hold. There was no point thinking about whether I had done the right thing or not. Very few of the men, though tired from the events of the day, were keen to turn in. Most of them sat around staring out of the widows into the darkness beyond."

"That sounds quite eerie to me. I don't think I would like it."

"In this early part of the voyage, there were the odd pockets of men trying to keep their minds off the events outside and what lay ahead by playing cards in an abnormally boisterous manner. Eventually, most of those groups folded up the cards, quieted down, and joined the silent majority staring out at the darkness. Maybe the effect of the huge, rolling seas on their stomachs had more to do with their early capitulation rather than their desire to study the darkness and what it held."

"I don't know if I could take it."

"Nobody knows until they face those boisterous seas. The voyage was so rough leaving Australia, nearly every man on board was sick for the first three weeks. I was so violently sick I thought I would die. The thought of death actually seemed quite attractive. Not to mention the rotten rabbit stew served to us that caused most of the men and crew to be sick. It was so bad that two men died."

"I can't begin to imagine how awful it must have been because I've never been out to sea either. Was the ship an old one?"

"I learned on board that the *Suevic* had quite a chequered history. It was first built in 1901 by Harland and Wolf at Belfast for the White Star Line. This was the same builder and shipping line that owned the *Titanic*."

"That's interesting. It survived longer than the *Titanic*?"

"It very nearly came to an early end in 1907, when it became wedged bow-first on the Stag Rock when returning to Liverpool. They eventually used dynamite to separate the bow section from the main part of the ship. They then towed the main body back to the shipyards where they fitted a new bow section."

"Wow, that makes for an interesting saga, and you're now part of the ongoing story."

"There was a lot of talk by politicians in the newspapers before sailing about *these splendid young men who were prepared to sign up to travel to foreign shores to fight for God, king, and country.* I signed up for adventure in a foreign land and to see the world. This was something I could never have contemplated doing without joining the army."

"Keep talking. I'm enjoying this," she said.

"I always enjoyed history lessons while at school learning about the early exploits of the kings of England. I always read the newspapers from front to back even though they were often weeks old before we received them."

"In the army, I receive the grand sum of six shillings a day. This is five times more than I earned cutting and hauling timber. My thinking was, at the time, I would be able to see the world at the government's expense."

"You obviously enjoy history. It was a good plan to see the world," she chipped in, "but I suppose things have worked out very differently than what you ever thought. Although if you hadn't made that decision to join up I would never have met you."

"That's a big bonus for me," he said as he felt Ann snuggling closer into his body. His arm was wrapped around her waist. Ann fitted neatly into Wilf like a kitten cuddling against its mother after being fed.

"Don't mind me chipping in," she said. "Just keep going."

"We had some unique experiences on the boat after things settled down. When we were in the Port of Durban, we watched the native boys dive for pennies thrown by the Diggers from the ship. The ship was moored in the harbour to take on stores for the next leg to Capetown.

"After spending Christmas day in Capetown, we set off the next day for St. Helena where Napoleon had been imprisoned by the British for six years of his life, after his defeat at the Battle of Waterloo."

"Oh, I haven't read about that."

"After a one-day stop at anchor, we sailed for Freetown, Sierra Leone. These destinations were not officially notified ahead to the men, but the rumour mill worked well, and most of the troops knew generally where we were heading."

"Why the secrecy? Who did they think you were going to tell anyway?"

"It was on this leg of the journey that training became serious. We were taken out on deck for gun practice with live ammunition. We had to put into practice the training we had received previously in Sydney—in virtual silence. For me, this was a new and truly amazing experience."

"I'm sure it would be."

"My thinking was that at least I would be able to tell the folks back home that I had experienced the roar of gunfire. Little did I know that this noise could be considered noisy frogs outside our home at night while trying to sleep, compared to the noise that was to come on the front line."

"Oh that must be terrible, Wilf."

"These were all very new experiences for this boy from the bush who had not previously travelled more than fifty miles from home. At home, I only saw other slab bush homes, similar to our own."

"What about your early life?"

"Well, up until I was eleven years old, we lived in a slab hut in the village of Thalabah near Dungog. The family then moved to a new house in Stroud. The house consisted of three rooms with hessian curtains for interior walls and hard-swept earth as the floor."

"Coming from the big city of London, it's hard for me to imagine."

"Not long before I joined up, we moved north to a new area, four miles out of the small village of Craven. This area has more accessible cedar timber.

"The ship eventually arrived in the Bay of Plymouth, sailing upriver to Devonport where we disembarked and travelled by train to Exeter. I did not know at this time that my great-grandfather had left Plymouth to establish life for his family in Australia."

"How did you find out?"

"I wrote and told Mother where the boat came in, and she replied with news of the family connection in Plymouth. Apparently my great-grandfather had a rope-making business there."

"That would have been interesting for you, if you had known at the time and had time to look around a little."

"Yes, it would have been interesting, but we were moved on to Exeter where we were served afternoon tea by the lady-mayoress before leaving again for Salisbury. It was at Salisbury where we were to receive more training."

Ann said, "I've been deeply interested in your story. I feel so privileged to be sharing the day with a man who has travelled so far and experienced so much to serve his country. And then to finish up with him by my side, that's an even greater privilege."

"I think the privilege is all mine."

He hadn't talked at all about what he had been through on the Western Front. Ann had seen so many of the casualties from the front in the hospital. Many of those lives were so shattered emotionally, possibly forever, because of what they had been through.

"I can only admire your inner and physical strength, knowing what you've been through," she said as she snuggled closer to him. "Many others I've nursed would be emotional wrecks for the rest of their lives."

Wilf took the opportunity and kissed Ann on the lips. It was a magic moment for him, and he knew Ann felt the same. He didn't need to be instructed in this procedure; it all happened so naturally.

After some time, Wilf turned to Ann and said, "Now it's your turn. Tell me all about you."

"There's not much to tell you about me. I've always lived in London and have travelled by train to Brighton on a few occasions to stay with my aunt, uncle, and cousin during school holidays. At school, I always wanted to be a nurse and studied hard, and here I am."

"You're not telling me very much, but your overall knowledge of London is pretty good, so I intend to have you share that knowledge with me over the next days. Is that a deal?"

"It sure is, Wilf."

Wilf had his eye on a lovely red rose protruding through the fence of the flower markets. He stood up and without taking his cane walked over to pick the rose. He returned to Ann and said, "I want you to always remember this special red rose as an expression of my thankfulness for the way you cared for me in the hospital."

"Thank you, Wilf. I promise to always remember this special rose because it is so beautiful both in shape and colour. Thank you."

Wilf sat down and wrapped his arm around Ann's shoulder. She took hold of Wilf's other hand and drew it to her body for a long pause as they looked into each other's eyes. No words were needed; just holding each other close was more than enough.

Wilf's hand found its way as if drawn by a magnet under her flowing blonde hair to her soft neck, moving gently and ever so slowly past her ear to her soft cheek. Each time his fingers brushed her cheek, he felt sparks tingle the back of his fingers. Ann lifted her head higher and allowed his hand to move her face closer towards his. She thought she might even cry as her hungry lips quivered. That position was frozen for what seemed to be forever. Their eyes looked deeply past the colour of the respective iris's opposite, into the secretive darkness beyond.

Ann lifted up her face slowly but deliberately, as the warmth of their lips drew closely together. They both found the sweetness and softness of home for what seemed like eternity; taking a breath did not seem necessary in this private world that happened so naturally for them. Their hands explored each other's faces in a way neither of them were accustomed. Not even their dreams were this good.

Ann said, "I don't want this day to ever end."

"Let's make the most of it while it lasts," said Wilf.

They hugged and kissed for a long time.

Chapter 4

The last few hours under the shade of the tree was a wonderful time to remember, hopefully forever. Ann had learned so much about Wild's background. The sun was now starting to creep under the lower branches and making it uncomfortably warm.

Ann said, "I think it's about time you took this leap-year baby home."

"What do you mean?" he replied.

"You must have been sleepy when I told you in the hospital. I was born on February 29, 1894. So as I've technically only had five birthdays, I'm really only five years old, so that makes you a cradle-snatcher, and you shouldn't have me out after dark."

Wilf said, "I will remember that in future. It will save me a lot of money on birthday presents."

"I know from the records that I'm three years younger than you."

"I've no idea where we are and how to get back. If I was at home, my bush instincts would tell me to follow the river. *When in doubt, follow the river.*"

Ann knew exactly where they were and knew they needed to retrace the path trodden by the horse that pulled the Hansom cab from the railway station. They set off at a leisurely pace, soaking up more of this special day.

They walked lazily up the embankment in time to see a motor-cab coming their way. Ann flagged the cab, and they travelled to the station where she purchased tickets.

Wilf said, "I marvel at the way you know where to go and how to purchase the right tickets. It must be very easy for you, but it would be a real adventure and a nightmare for me. I didn't even purchase a ticket to travel from Gloucester to Sydney because all those enlisting for war travelled for free. When the ship arrived in Devonport, we went up to Salisbury for further training. No need for tickets then either."

Ann said, "This is all my pleasure, so let me take charge."

"While you were buying the tickets, I noticed on the board the cities of Stroud and Gloucester. Are they large towns here?"

"They're both great towns here in this country," she replied.

"Back home, the same towns are about thirty miles apart with a combined population of less than fifteen hundred people, with nothing much in between except my family and the village of Craven."

Ann took Wilf's hand and negotiated the path to the train, where luckily they both found a seat together. Ann could sense that Wilf was overwhelmed with this new experience of travelling underground.

Shortly after the train began moving and they were seated, Wilf said, "Well, that was my first experience on the underground. When I felt the rush of air being forced out of the tunnel ahead of the approaching train, it reminded me of a bicycle pump I saw back home. I was so intrigued that I unscrewed the cap to see what made the air rush out the end when I pumped the handle. Today, I imagined that the tube was like a giant pump with the train as the washer pushing out the air."

Wilf was trying to read over another fellow's shoulder that had a newspaper open where a headline mentioned "The Red Barron," but the print was too small for Wilf to read any further. He indicated the headline to Ann and then whispered, "The German Red Barron is well-known amongst the Diggers for his daring aerial exploits over the trenches around Ypres."

The train quickly approached Victoria Station before coming to a stop. "I didn't think the train had a chance of stopping before it got to the end of the station," Wilf said. "I was wrong."

Ann helped Wilf from the train and then guided him to the other train headed for King's Cross.

"The only trains I'd travelled on before this were slow. The train from Gloucester to Sydney took over seven hours, to travel less than two hundred miles. The troop trains around the countryside of England were even slower. They seemed to spend most of the time waiting at sidings for other trains to take precedence."

"What about the trains in France?"

"Oh those trains were terrible, let me tell you. Over there, it's not uncommon to take many hours to travel five kilometres."

"We're heading to King's Cross with about five stations in between. I don't know how many miles, but it should take us about fifteen minutes."

"Do you know the names of each station?"

"Yes I do, but I won't bore you with the details now."

"You are truly amazing."

"Wait till we get to King's Cross Station; they have recently installed a moving stairway to get the passengers from the underground platform up to the street level, without taking a step."

"I can't wait to see that! I can't figure it out." After alighting from the train, they were told by an attendant on the platform that there was a problem with the escalators and everyone would have to use the stairs.

Ann knew that the original stairway had been reconstructed to incorporate the moving stairway. The only other stairs were the cast-iron spiral stairs, rarely used except for emergencies. The treads were narrow, tapered, steel plates mounted around a central pipe. They were steep to climb. She knew that Wilf's feet were starting to swell again and giving him some trouble after his first big day out.

"How are your feet coping?"

"I'll make it okay," said Wilf. He never complained. Why would he with a special lady helping him with every step of the way?

"I'll give them a good massage tonight."

"I'll look forward to that."

The fresh air was welcome as they emerged from the crowded spiral staircase into the street. There were crowds of people rushing about at the end of their day, determined to get to their destination in the shortest possible time.

Ann said, "Don't you just love this racket?" as she took his hand to cross over Euston Road.

The roads were busy with a mixture of horse-drawn delivery carts in various shapes and sizes, squashing their way through the horse droppings. Motorised vehicles had slightly overtaken the number of horses on the roads, but the smell from the manure on the road was still quite strong. Ladies tried to lift the hems of their long, flowing skirts as they danced around the droppings scattered over the road. A couple of sweepers were hard at work doing their best to keep on top of the manure problem, although it was not as bad today as it had been in previous times before the new motor vehicles.

"It's a lot worse when it's raining," said Ann. "It's not too bad today."

Then there were the new commercial motor vehicles and Omnibuses belching out smoke from the exhaust. The noise was a mixture of the motor exhausts, the pounding of the horse's hooves on the cobblestones, and their masters shouting to their horses in the congested traffic. Over all of this noise could be heard the paperboys trying their best to sell their papers. The noise in this busy street made it near impossible to have any discussion as they walked.

They turned into Crestfield Street, and Ann realised holding hands was not good enough; she linked her arm through Wilf's.

"Isn't it good to get away from that busy street?" said Ann.

"It's certainly a very busy street. Those double-deckers with the open tops were something new for me. I've been transported in France by horse-drawn busses as well as the military motor-buses, but those double-deckers are something totally new to me."

"I promise you, we will explore them another day and ride up top in the front seat."

"I'll look forward to that."

They rounded the corner into Argyle Square, which was covered with huge sycamore trees. Ann said, "Let's just stop for a moment and listen to the birds. I think they're happy for us and want us to know."

Ann was silently planning how to get more time off to share with Wilf. She was due to start her Monday shift at three in the afternoon but desperately needed a good reason not to go to work. This was her seventh year at the hospital, including training. She had not needed to have even one day off due to sickness in that time. She had taken off only three days of leave in those seven years, to visit her sick aunt in Brighton.

Ann had a good record and knew she needed to get a message to the hospital in the morning to tell them she had a stomach sickness and needed some time off. She would take the days out of the leave she had accumulated.

Naturally she would not get paid for the time off, but she didn't mind that. She did not feel guilty about planning to say she was sick because it was perfectly true. She was sick—love sick, that is—and the butterflies in her stomach would not settle down. She would ask for one week off for a start and then think about the second week later in the week.

Got it, she thought to herself, *I can ask my best friend, Hazel, to talk to the matron.* Hazel lived nearby and was scheduled to start her shift tomorrow at noon.

As they approached the house, Ann hurriedly explained the plan to Wilf, but now she had even more important things to do. She needed to introduce Wilf to her parents. Ann waltzed into the house on a cloud of air and untied the ribbon from under her chin. She threw her hat onto the couch, along with the picnic basket. Ann knew that her mother would twig to her excitement because she didn't normally make that sort of entry, not ever.

Ann said, "Mother, Father, I want you to meet the most wonderful man I've ever known, Wilf Yates. He's from New South Wales, Australia."

Mr. and Mrs. Davis welcomed Wilf enthusiastically and told him to make himself at home in their house.

Mr. Davis made a spirited and grateful welcoming-speech, saying, "We acknowledge and are grateful for all of the young Australians from the far-flung colony who have sacrificed much to give up the comforts of home and family to come to the defence of the motherland."

"Thank you for your kind words, Mr. Davis. I'm honoured to do whatever I can do to help push back and defeat this awful enemy."

Mr. Davis asked Wilf if he could show him to the lavatory. He took him to the rear door and pointed to the small outhouse, which Wilf found was fitted with one of those new-fangled flushers. It had a storage tank above, which let out a gush of water to flush the bowl by pulling on a chain dangling from above. This was new to Wilf, seeing one in a private home, although he had seen them at the hospital. Wilf flushed twice for the novelty.

Ann and Mrs. Davis prepared the meal, and Wilf chatted with Mr. Davis, who said, "Tell me, Wilf, about the way of life in Australia, and with business in particular. I'm keen to find out how hardware is sold in Australia. Is it sold in specialty stores or just mixed in with general merchandise? The distribution of hardware has become a specialised field in London over the last twenty or so years and has created a whole new demand for such products."

"In the bush where I come from, it's not that specialised, but I'm not sure if it's different in the big cities because I've not been there."

"Oh that's interesting, very interesting."

They discussed many different topics, and then Wilf said, "I saw a headline in a newspaper on the train. It said something about the Red Barron. Do you know what that was all about?"

"Yes I do. I read the article, and it was something to do with the Red Barron celebrating another umpteenth aerial battle; I'm not sure of the actual number. It was on the anniversary of his first combat win back on September 17, 1916. Of course, the article was really old news but had only now been leaked to the British press. The information came from a German plane that had crash landed near Scarborough. A document was found on the plane with the never-before-published information, at least on this side anyway."

"I understand now. The Barron is well known amongst the troops on the front."

Their conversation was interrupted with the announcement from Ann that tea was ready to be served.

As the meal moved on, the conversation became a little more relaxed, with all of them asking questions of Wilf continually.

After the meal was over, Wilf said, "Mrs. Davis, thank you for such a splendid meal. I think that was the best hot meal I've ever tasted. Ann has told me that you are very capable at finding good food in spite of rationing."

"Thank you, Wilf. It is our pleasure to have you here."

"It has been over a year since I tasted anything other than army fare or YMCA canteen food. Although I must say that the food at the hospital wasn't too bad."

Mrs. Davis said, "I'm concerned about where you will be staying tonight. Do you have somewhere to stay?" This was something that had not been discussed today, even though both he and Ann had harboured silent thoughts.

"I've no plans at this stage, Mrs. Davis."

Mrs. Davis was very quick to jump in, saying, "You are most welcome to stay here; we have a spare room for as long as you like."

Naturally, Wilf was overwhelmed with the generosity shown to him and offered a feeble protest. Mrs. Davis would not hear of any objection; it was settled.

Ann said, "You can have my brother Joe's room. He's an artillery officer with the Northumberland Fusiliers. He's already deployed on the Western Front."

Mr. Davis was an erect and assertive man who had a responsible position at H. W. Gooch's Hardware store on Pentonville Road.

Mrs. Davis had the same lovely fair complexion and demeanour as her daughter. She gave a lot of her time to the various guild activities of her church, especially helping to care for the injured troops now recuperating after their return from the front. Wilf could not help comparing the lovely nature of Ann to her mother; it was obviously in the genes.

Mr. Davis said, "I'm keen to learn firsthand information about how you think the war is going."

"Well, I don't think it's going too well at all. However, the troops don't always get the right information, and we have to add two and two together from the bits and pieces we learn from our officers and other soldiers we meet going to and from the lines."

"I can understand that."

"From what I understand, the initial push by the Germans in 1914 was halted by the French, north of Paris. The British Expeditionary Force then slowed them down again at Mons. Fighting took place on the Aisne, causing the Germans to retreat and spread out to both the north and the south to prevent the Allies from outflanking them. This ended in two parallel lines of trenches opposed to each other, now referred to as the Western Front."

"I understand that in general detail."

"The line extends from the Swiss border in the south to the sea coast in the north. The initial failure of the Germans' plan allowed enough time to bring in more British reinforcements to protect the ports of Calais and Boulogne. The German attacks on the city of Ypres, if successful, would have given them a clear path to the channel ports. Hence, it is absolutely necessary for the British to hold Ypres at all cost; they have been doing so at great cost ever since."

"Yes," he said, "we get a lot of news reports about Ypres."

"On the Ypres Salient, hundreds of our troops die on a normal day, but on some days, thousands die, and even tens of thousands in the various battles for Ypres. The Salient is open to attack on three sides at the same time, by a semicircle of German artillery. This area is hated by the British and Australian troops because the Germans occupy all of the surrounding ridges most of the time. Their position enables them to shoot anything that moves down on the low lands. The ridges have been taken and lost many times."

"I've never been to war, Wilf, so it's hard for me to imagine just how terrible it must be."

"Let me tell you, the slaughter of human beings is unbelievable and hard to take, let alone describe. I'm sorry, Mr. Davis, if I seem a little emotional, but that's the effect it has on me, and I'm sure on most other soldiers too."

"I understand, Wilf, and I shouldn't ask you to go further."

"No, I'm over that now. I would love to keep chatting."

They chatted for some time, and after cleaning up and doing the dishes, Mrs. Davis said, "Ann, take Wilf up to the spare room and show him his bed, towel, and the washing facilities."

"I'll certainly do that, Mother, but I think we will go out for some fresh evening air first."

"That would be nice for both of you."

They walked out the front of the house where the street was deserted except for some teenagers playing some game at the far end. The children could only just be picked out in the darkness as they ran back and forth across the street.

They turned right past the Wellington pub next door where a few patrons were sitting outside enjoying the evening air. It wasn't very far, less than one hundred yards to the Argyle Square, where the birds were still making a racket in the trees.

"I know where there's a park bench; hang onto me, and I will guide you there," Ann said. "I brought some old newspaper to put on the seat."

"That was clever of you, I must say."

Wilf could not see the bench in the darkness, but Ann knew its location.

They sat on the park bench in the dark; this was the first time they had been together in the darkness.

As Ann's eyes grew accustomed to the reflected light from the streetlamps, she turned to face Wilf and fumbled for both of his hands, holding them close to her body. She said, "I want to thank you for such a wonderful day. I could never have imagined such a splendid day like this the first time I saw you when you were admitted; you were in a bad way."

"I too had a great day, and thanks to you, I hope there will be many more. The word great does not seem to be a strong enough word to describe my feelings. I'm clumsy with words sometimes."

Ann fixed that problem as she lifted her face towards his and they kissed for a long time.

He wrapped his arms around Ann's body and hugged her close as they kissed. Wilf wasn't sure when to take a breath, but it just seemed to happen even more naturally than earlier that day in the park.

They hesitated for a moment, and Ann said, "How long ago was the first time we kissed? It seems longer than that one in the park this afternoon."

"Well it was today after lunch."

"With so much having been learned about each other, it could surely not be the same day," said Ann as they embraced again.

Finally they made their way back into the house in the light of the moon. Mrs. Davis had left a small lamp just inside the front door. Ann picked up the lamp and led the way up the stairs to the spare room.

Ann said, "I think Dad must have taken your kitbag up for you."

"That's jolly decent of him."

As they reached the bedroom, Ann said, "Should I leave the lamp with you, Wilf?"

"That won't be necessary because I'm not used to such luxury at home in the bush."

Before she turned to leave the room, Wilf drew her close and stole one last kiss in the bedroom doorway. The passion was still there and had been lying just below the surface, on the way home in the train, through dinner and out in the moonlight, waiting to break out at such a moment as this.

Now the dreaming would begin.

Chapter 5

The next morning, Ann was up early and explained to her mother and father about taking some time off work to show Wilf the sights of London. She wrote a note to her special friend Hazel, explaining the plan and asking her to speak to the matron at the hospital when she started her shift at noon. This would be enough time to arrange a relief nurse. She gave the letter to her father and asked him to leave a few minutes early and drop the letter off with Hazel on their way to church. Hazel lived only three houses from the corner of the street where the church was located, so it was very convenient.

Mr. and Mrs. Davis left the house at around eight o'clock. Wilf had still not stirred, which meant that yesterday had been a tiring day for him. Ann knew this was unusual because he was normally up at daylight in the bush, and it was a hard habit to break. She knew from talking to so many patients that while at the front it was different because there was no such timetable of events there. They slept whenever they could, even in the rain and with the never-ending noise of battle overhead. Sometimes sleep evaded them for days on end without any rest at all.

Ann had already bathed earlier and was now concentrating on preparing a breakfast tray for when he awoke. She crept up the stairs after nine o'clock and opened the door, only enough to make a little noise to catch his attention if he was already awake. The noise caused Wilf to turn his head, so Ann went in and said, "Good morning, sleepyhead."

"I had a wonderful sleep and had no idea of the time. It's very unusual for me to sleep in." Ann sat on the edge of the bed, kissed him on the cheek, and brought him up to date with the happenings of the morning. Then she went down and brought up the breakfast tray and left him to eat alone while she ran the bath for him. She knew this would be very soothing for his tired feet. She would give them a massage afterwards.

Ann set up a basin with some massaging oil on the couch downstairs in readiness for when Wilf finished his bath.

While massaging his feet, she said, "The plan for today is to catch the tube into town and visit Westminster Abbey and the Houses of Parliament."

"That sounds great!" he said. "That should give me plenty to write home about."

"I hope so. I hope it won't be too much for your feet."

Wilf got dressed in the only clothes he owned in this part of the world.

"Okay," said Ann, "all ready to go, but without a kitbag to weigh you down today."

"Well, let me carry the basket?"

Ann wouldn't hear of it and said, "No, Wilf, you have your cane to handle. I'll handle the basket."

Arm in arm, they set off down the street for another great day of discovery together.

"I thought we might get some rain, so I made sure to pack an umbrella."

"I think your judgement will prove to be correct."

"I've always lived in London but have never taken the time to learn in detail about the great treasures of London's history, simply because they are there and always would be there."

"I suppose this is typical of most people's approach to historical places in one's own hometown."

"I visited the Houses of Parliament with my school but didn't listen carefully to all that was being said. However, I believe there will be guides at various places. We can either listen to the guide answering other people's questions or you can ask your own."

At the station, Ann again made her way to the ticket office and purchased two return tickets. They entered the station for the Piccadilly Line, just in time to see the train emerging from the tunnel. They did not even have to stand around, but walked straight into the carriage and sat down. The train made a few stops before they made a change onto the Northern Line. They changed again at the Embankment onto the Circle Line, with only one stop before their final destination at Westminster.

Wilf was absolutely amazed and said, "How do you possibly know where you are going? You amaze me. It's too much to comprehend for this boy from the bush. With all of those changes, the journey has taken less than twenty minutes. That will take some explaining to the folks at home."

As they came out of the underground entrance, it was beginning to rain a little, so Ann put up the umbrella. "Link arms and hold your hand tight over mine. With both of us holding the umbrella, it will keep us close together and in step."

"I like this idea and hope it works well," he said as he clamped his hand tightly over Ann's and she led them towards the Thames. "I've no idea where we are, so I'm happy to be led by you."

"We're on the opposite bank to where we shared our first kiss yesterday, and a little further downstream. We're also about one mile away from Vauxhall."

"That was a very special part of London for me," he replied. "I'll never forget Vauxhall."

"Me neither." Ann gave his hand a squeeze, thinking about yesterday. As the pedestrian flow came to a halt, she gazed into his eyes and said, "Do you know what I'm thinking about?"

"I do," he said as they moved off again up the steps to the Westminster Bridge.

At the top of the steps was a large bronze monument with a striking lady driving a chariot with two horses. She was wearing fine, textured, flowing robes and a crown. She held a long spear in her right hand, and her left hand held the reins high to encourage the two horses to rear high back onto their hind legs.

"Who is the lady and what is this all about, Ann?"

"With you being a keen horseman, I thought you would be interested. I've only recently read a book about this great lady; she is Queen Boadicea."

"What made her so great?"

"Queen Boadicea was recognised as Britain's first Christian queen. She was crowned in AD 60 shortly after the Claudian Legions of the Roman Empire had been shattered in battle by the British warrior-patriot Caradoc. He and his joint leader, Noble Arviragus, were eventually captured by the Romans. They changed his name from Caradoc to King Caractacus."

Queen Boadicea monument at Westminster Bridge.

"I always liked history at school, but I never learned about her."

"Caradoc's treacherous betrayal was carried out by some of his previously loyal subjects. This resulted in Caradoc and his family being taken captive back to Rome where they were held under house arrest in the Palatium Britannicum for two years. His time in captivity was followed by a Roman pardon of the British king, which resulted in a strange alliance between the scions of Rome and the British Royals of that time."

Wilf said, "I'm amazed that you have retained all of this information." He gave her a hug.

The Houses of Parliament were directly across the busy road. Ann said, "There is an underground tunnel close by that will take us right under the road to where we want to go." She led off in that direction. Ann put the umbrella down as they descended the steps into the tunnel. She didn't want to break the togetherness-grip that had been keeping them close as they walked in step, as one unit in the rain.

They climbed the steps from the tunnel and were now close to the Parliament buildings. Wilf said, "I can see workmen erecting lots of sandbags around the walls and entrances."

"This is to give some protection to the buildings in the event of an air attack. There have been a number of night air raids, but up till now we haven't had any daylight raids on London."

"The stacks of sandbags are a lot neater than ours."

With disappointment in her voice, she said, "Oh no, the buildings may be closed off to the public, but maybe not. I just noticed some others moving inside, so I think we'll be all right."

The buildings were open to the public, and they moved around the inside of the buildings. Ann said, "How do you like the woodwork?"

"I'm truly amazed at the beauty and grandeur of the buildings, just as I was when I first saw the interior of Amiens Cathedral. Being a timber cutter, I'm naturally drawn to the beauty of the timberwork all around here."

"Isn't it spectacular?"

"I'm amazed to see what can be done to the rough logs by these master-craftsmen after we ship them to England."

Of course, who wouldn't be amazed when both of them could enjoy the beauty all around them whilst at the same time feeling the raging excitement and pure joy within?

After a while, they stopped and listened to the guides telling their stories about the history of the parliament and how Guy Fawkes had attempted to burn down the building.

Wilf said, "I'm well aware of Empire Night and its significance from lessons we learned at school. Even though we had a primitive little school in the bush, we learned a lot of history up until I left school at eleven, especially British history. We always had a bonfire on Empire Night in recognition of Guy Fawkes's attempt to burn down the parliament."

Just then an elderly man recognised Wilf's Australian uniform and his brown slouch hat. He sang out from across the hall, "Good on you, Digger." Wilf tipped his hat in recognition of the salute he received.

"Wilf, why do they call Australian soldiers Digger?"

"I wasn't real sure myself until it was explained to us on the boat one day. The term Digger goes back to the goldfields around Ballarat in 1854. The gold diggers had risen up against the British government of the day, who they claimed were not giving them a fair go."

"Is Ballarat near to you?"

"No, it's down in Victoria, about five or six hundred miles away."

"That's a long way, although I suppose Australia is so big."

"The government was fining the diggers for not always having their prospecting license with them in the slush at the diggings. The police collecting the fines legally received half the money, so about one thousand miners out of a total of twenty-five thousand armed themselves and confronted the police. It became known as the Eureka Stockade and formed part of Australia's folklore."

It was now Ann's turn to show her appreciation of Wilf's knowledge. "You're not so bad at Australian history either," she said.

After about an hour of walking around, they were just about "parliamented-out" and feeling in need of some refreshment. Ann found a vacant bench outside where the water had dried off. The rain had cleared, and the sun was breaking through. They took turns to mind the seat as the other wandered off to the lavatories nearby. Wilf looked on as Ann opened up the basket of food she had prepared. She said, "Curried egg, plus some fruit and a bottle of water?"

"You couldn't have made a better choice, Ann. It looks very inviting to me."

They enjoyed their picnic lunch as Ann planned the next part of the day. "We'll have a look through Westminster Abbey, which is only next door, so it doesn't involve a long walk. How are your feet?"

"My feet aren't too bad at this stage, and the sit down is very welcome." He looked up to Big Ben and said, "I was admiring the clock and waiting for it to strike one. I think it must be slow."

Ann said. "There is no chiming of the clock; it has been stopped since the early bombing attacks on London. Would you like to know about its history? I know a little about it."

"I certainly would, especially from you."

"Well, the clock is the largest four-faced chiming clock tower in the world. The tower was completed in 1858 under the supervision of the architect Charles Barry. It was the last piece of work by the artist Augustus Pugin before his descent into madness."

"It must have driven him mad. Did it?"

"Maybe it did. The tower is 315 feet high, and the clock face measures twenty-three feet in diameter. At the bottom of each face are the words, *Oh Lord, keep safe our Queen Victoria the first.* The main bell measures nine feet in diameter and stands seven feet six inches high."

Wilf was all ears. "How much does the bell weigh?"

"The first bell weighed sixteen tons, requiring sixteen horses to draw the bell to the site, and it took eighteen hours to haul the bell up into the tower. Wait till you hear this. The first bell cracked during trials and was replaced by a slightly smaller bell of thirteen and a half tons, which also cracked because the hammer used was too heavy."

"Wow that is some bell."

"The crack in the second bell was chipped out, a patch was added, and it remained silent for three years during repairs. That same bell is still in place today although it has been turned around at least once to protect the crack."

Wilf said, "Who was Ben, the Ben that the clock was named after?"

"Technically speaking, the clock is not named Big Ben. The tower was originally called The Clock Tower, but I don't know who the Ben was. Today, it's the bell itself that is nicknamed Big Ben, but the tower is part of St. Stephens, North End."

"How in the dickens did you know all of that?"

"Maybe it's because I'm smart! No," she said, "I can't lie. I looked it up early this morning, knowing we were coming here today. I wanted to impress you."

"Why spoil it? I would have believed you anyway."

Ann went on to say, "Nobody seems to know who the Ben was because there was a Ben who helped install the bell and another big Ben, a heavyweight boxer at the time."

"I don't suppose it matters that much anyway."

After nearly an hour break from touring, they set off for the Abbey. There were hundreds and hundreds of monuments, most of which meant nothing to Ann, let alone Wilf, and they passed them over fairly quickly.

Ann said, "There should be a few of particular interest to you. Have you heard of Horatio Viscount Nelson?"

"We learned about Nelson at school. He died at the Battle of Trafalgar."

"Yes, you're exactly right. I'm planning to take you to Trafalgar Square to see Lord Nelson's column." She pointed to the wax dummy of Nelson directly ahead on the end wall of the Abbey and said, "That wax and wooden effigy we are looking at stands a little over five feet tall; this was his actual size. They made a mistake with Nelson's blind right eye and made it incorrectly on his left side. The clothes on the statue are actually some of Nelson's own clothes."

"The uniforms look better than the ones we're issued now."

"Yes, I think you're right."

Wilf said, "There's Sir Thomas Stamford Raffles, the founder of Singapore back in the early 1800s, and there's David Livingstone, the famous Scottish missionary who died in Africa in 1873. There's another, Scott of the Antarctic, and Robert Stephenson who built the first steam engine."

"I think you should be the one bringing me here rather than the other way around," said Ann.

"I only know a few of them really, but they all appeared close together. Here's a familiar name and of significance to most Australians, William Wilberforce. He became a politician in the building next door in 1780, fighting for the abolition of slavery; his work stopped the convict trade to Australia."

"You're really good. I think you should look among the names to see if you have any ancestors on the honour roll." They looked but found none bearing Wilf's family name.

"I'm surprised how similar the Abbey is internally to the Amiens Cathedral in some respects, with both having confessional booths, especially since the Abbey was not a Catholic church."

Ann said, "The Abbey and most of the cathedrals in Britain were originally Catholic churches, prior to the abolition of the monasteries by King Henry the Eighth in 1538. The Church of England was then established, subject to the king of England instead of the pope, but they didn't change the furniture."

"That's a simple explanation and makes sense to me," he said.

By this time, they had done enough walking for the day, and Ann decided to make for home. They headed for the station, and once again Ann produced her tube train magic, guiding them home on totally different lines.

As they sat together on the train, holding hands, Ann could not help thinking about when Wilf would have to leave for the return to the front. How horrible it was going to be when separated from each other after this extremely brief time. They had learned so much about each other and their respective family histories.

She said, "Do you think about returning to the front?"

"I try not to. I try to concentrate on this wonderful and affectionate human being next to me."

"You're so sweet."

"I do think of the safety here in London compared to that hellhole of a place called Ypres. I hope all of my mates will still be there when I get back."

"So do I."

"The one person in our unit that seems to be bulletproof is Sergeant Joe Maxwell. He's such a crazy bloke and takes unbelievable risks, but he still survives each action with a flare of bravery that could not be missed, even by his superiors. The general talk is that he's destined for more bravery awards of some description down the track. There's a good chance he'll be a lieutenant by the time I get back."

"Do you get along with him all right?"

"Oh, he's really a likeable larrikin. He originates from Cessnock, a mining village in the Hunter Valley about sixty miles from my home, and at the time of enlisting, he worked as a boiler-making apprentice at Hexham. Hexham is only about six miles from Raymond Terrace where we deliver the logs to the boats for export."

"Is he a tall bloke?"

"No, he's shorter than me, but when on leave, we go our separate ways. Maxwell likes the grog pretty much, and when drunk, he gets into fights real easy. He has a name for that sort of thing."

Ann sat silently, thinking over what Wilf had said. Then she said, "Time to get up. This is our station."

The moving stairway was operating today, which was good for Wilf's feet as they glided effortlessly from the station platform to the street level. As they moved through the station crowd, Ann held Wilf's hand firmly, guiding him outside into Euston Road, towards her home. Ann was enjoying the experience of this wonderful and exhilarating new world with Wilf. Even the birds flying around in pairs seemed happier and more playful as they went about their spring task of building new nests together.

As they reached the Argyle Walkway, the silence was broken by the shrill of blaring sirens, warning of an imminent air raid. Ann jumped with the sound of the siren screeching from the speaker mounted on the pole nearby in the square. This was the first time she had experienced the sound of sirens up close; the noise was deafening. Her inner thoughts were suddenly drowned as if by a sudden release of water from a dam-wall bursting over her. She was unsure if she should take cover near the walkway or run.

Wilf pulled Ann close so he would not have to shout too much above the din, saying, "How far to your home? It's about a hundred yards, isn't it?"

"Yes, less than that. Can you run?"

"We don't need to run. We have enough time to reach home before any bombs start falling, and I can't hear any planes yet."

Ann could not get over how calm Wilf was in this situation but nevertheless gripped his hand tightly to drag him faster than she knew he should move; her thoughts were for the shelter and safety of home.

They turned the corner around the Wellington Pub. A few hesitant customers were at the front door, obviously trying to make up their minds whether to stay or make a run for it. Ann knew there was no real shelter nearby anyway.

A few neighbours were out in the street showing panic, screaming above the noise of the sirens and the barking of dogs, desperately searching for their unseen children, needing to get them home and out of danger. This was the real thing, not a drill.

They approached the front door as Ann fumbled in her bag, trying to find her key. She had never been in a crisis quite like this before, and although terrified, she was now over the initial shock and handling the emergency quite rationally. Her training as a nurse in the casualty section helped her to handle emergencies at the King's, but this was different.

Wilf, on the other hand, had been subjected to many bombing raids in the trenches. He now took control and inserted the key into the lock and helped Ann inside. He closed the door, took Ann in his arms, and said, "Don't worry, we'll be all right."

"I certainly hope so. I'm not used to this."

The house was empty. Ann's parents had been out most of the day, having left early for the Anglican church on the High Street. They stayed after the service to help prepare evening meals for the troops and were not expected home for another two or three hours.

Ann said, "Dad always said the best place inside the house, in the unlikely event of a raid, would be under the large cupboard in the spare room." Wilf was not so sure about this, but he was the guest and went along with the plan and helped her up the narrow stairs.

"Dad's plan is to tip over the large oak cupboard until it rests on the wash stand—then we can climb underneath." They did this as quickly as they could; it was very heavy. Wilf grabbed his great-coat and climbed underneath just as they heard the first bombs falling somewhere in the distance.

"This is really frightening for me, Wilf."

"I would like to think it would be the last. Remember when we were talking on the train, I said how I enjoyed the safety of London compared to the trenches in Ypres? Maybe things are about to change."

"I certainly hope not."

Wilf covered Ann as best he could with his army great-coat, saying, "You'll be all right; just stay close." The house shook, and some crockery was heard falling downstairs as more bombs burst, this time closer than the earlier ones. The crashing sound of bricks and glass close by caused them to look at each other with special looks they had not previously shared.

The look in Ann's eyes showed fear of what was happening outside. She asked herself, *Why is this happening at this time when life for us is so full of all the happiness and love that I can imagine?*

Wilf hugged Ann even tighter, saying, "We have no control over this evil, but one thing I'm sure of, we will come through this experience."

Ann noticed that it had gone all quiet outside. She continued to hug Wilf so tightly that not even a falling bomb would find enough room to separate them, or so she hoped. The raid did not last very long, but for Ann it was an eternity.

She said, "My lovely, long, black skirt is going to be soiled, but that doesn't matter as long as we are both safe. To be held tightly in your arms was all that really mattered."

"I think so too. It's not like this in the trenches, I can assure you. I think it's all over now anyway." He winced as he stood and moved the heavy cupboard to one side.

Although he was still recuperating from trench foot, Wilf ignored the pain as he hobbled down the stairs at the first sound of the all-clear.

"Maybe I can be of assistance to someone in need. Your skills could also be needed, Ann."

"I'll do what I can. I'm right behind you." Ann scrambled down from the second-floor room. Poor as it may have been, it was still a place to shelter. The three-story building was well built from stone, better than other timber buildings in the area, but still not built to withstand bombs.

As they opened the front door, people began to appear on the street, and voices could be heard calling for help. Screams came from a neighbour who discovered a family member had been injured. Frantic calls were made to enlist the help of others.

Wilf and Ann comforted an old lady with tears streaming down her dust-covered face; she was still half-buried under some timbers from a rear shed where she had taken shelter. Wilf removed the timbers, and Ann checked her over and said, "I think you're all right, dear. Everything seems to be in order, nothing that a nice cup of tea and a bath won't fix." They helped her back into her house, and Ann said, "How would you like me to make you a nice cup of tea, dear?"

"No thanks, love. I can see my daughter coming. You have both been very kind."

Ann explained the situation to the daughter and left the lady in good care.

Emergency medics arrived at the corner to take care of one of the injured in the next street.

One out-of-breath air-raid warden in his late sixties told them that the large drapery shop on Euston Road near King's Cross Station had received a direct hit. The military was still trying to tear away rubble to find victims believed to be trapped inside the shop.

Ann said to Wilf, "Oh my goodness, we just walked past that shop on the way from the station. Do you remember I looked at some of the refinery displayed in the shop window?"

"I certainly do."

Ann said, "That was too close for comfort, wasn't it?"

"I thought we were in good old London, not on the front line."

Once they returned home, standing up the heavy oak cupboard was the most difficult task, and once completed, they sat on the edge of the bed with arms around each other. There was now a strange silence as they looked into each other's eyes.

"I've just been thinking how much our lives are entwined after only knowing each other for such a short time," said Wilf. "Whatever our plans were last month, after this raid it seems they aren't worth much at all. Is our future about to be changed?"

"I can't answer that, Wilf. Maybe some time in the future we will be able to answer that question."

Ann busied herself preparing something for tea while Wilf fetched some firewood from outside and stoked the smouldering embers in the stove to boil the water. He added enough water to the copper kettle sitting on the stove to make a few cups of tea.

"You know, boiling the billy is something I do three or four times a day back home; I'm quite used to this."

"What is a billy?"

"A billy is a tin can used to boil water over an open fire to make a cup of tea. Here you use an iron or copper kettle on the stove."

"I've heard Australian soldiers singing one of your national songs, something about a billy and catching a sheep and stuffing it in a kitbag?"

"No," said Wilf, "that's a billabong. That's totally different. I'll explain that to you another time when you have the time to listen. It's a bit involved."

"Is it an Australian word?" she asked.

"I think so. Until I enlisted, the song had been strangely familiar to me, but not one to be heard much around the bush. Once the boys were issued their uniforms, it seemed that the song came with the clothing and was sung everywhere with great gusto—not always understood and not always in tune."

"I know what you're saying; I've heard them singing the song," said Ann.

"I learned all about the words of the song from one of the officers on the boat who had been a schoolmaster before joining up. He had a wonderful memory and good general knowledge about almost everything. If you remind me sometime I will explain the original meaning of the words to you and how they really fit into the Australian way of life. It's not what most Australians think."

Ann served the quickly arranged meal. They chatted for a while, discussing what had happened that day and where events may be leading. Ann took a lamp, and they tidied up the spare room. The tipping over of the large cupboard had caused most of the dust.

Ann heard a noise downstairs and said, "Sounds like Mum and Dad are home. Let's go down and see what they know." Ann led the way down, saying as she reached them in the living room, "Welcome home. I suppose you know what happened?"

Mr. Davis said, "Yes, we knew there had been a raid, but it wasn't until we got to the station at the Cross that we learned how close it was to home. Is everything all right?"

"Yes, everything's okay; we sheltered under the oak cupboard upstairs and have just finished tidying up the room. Wilf was my strength; he was marvellous."

They were weary from a long day of giving service to the troops, which was always gratefully received. They talked about their experiences of both the air raids on the way home in the bus from the church and the close bombings around home.

Mr. Davis said, "I will have to bring home some sisal tape so we can tape up the windows to protect them from the concussion of bomb bursts."

Mrs. Davis added, "The butcher said rolls of blackout paper are already being distributed to the shops down near the station, so I suppose it will be our turn soon."

"If they come soon," said Ann, "Wilf and I can put the paper up for you."

Wilf said," If you don't mind me saying so, I'm not happy with the temporary shelter upstairs. I would strongly suggest that tomorrow I start digging a shelter in the backyard, based on my experience with trenches and shelters on the front."

Mr. Davis replied, "I appreciate your offer and would be pleased to purchase whatever materials you need. I might have some materials here already but not very much. If you could give me a list of what is required, I will have everything you need delivered by the company's driver midmorning tomorrow. I already have a mattock, a saw, a pick, and some shovels in the shed."

Wilf said, "I will get up at daybreak and check the most suitable position for such a shelter, considering the high surrounding walls of the neighbouring buildings. I will check what you already have and make a list of the extra timber and iron needed for you to take to work."

"I've just thought of an idea," said Mr. Davis. "The company owes me a lot of time. I will arrange with Mr. Gooch to use the driver to help you dig the hole tomorrow."

"That would be great," said Ann.

"When he arrives with the timber midmorning, he can stay and do the heavy digging for you. He's a big strong bloke called Thomo."

"Are you sure it will not be too much for your feet so early?" said Mrs. Davis.

"No, I think it will be okay. Your daughter has done an amazing job. And I've spotted a stool in the shed I can use; I will take the opportunity to sit down and plan from time to time. If it feels too much, I will knock off early. Rome doesn't have to be built in a day. Besides, the soil is very sandy."

Ann said, "Well, it's been a very tiring day for everyone, so I think we should all turn in to make an early start in the morning."

Wilf was up before dawn to take a good look at the backyard. He selected a spot where the trench could be dug to best advantage and visualised in his mind exactly what was required. He would dig the trench to a depth of about five feet deep, three and a half feet wide, and eight feet long. After allowing for the wall timbers and the duckboards underneath, this would be large enough to shelter four people with ease, and six if needed.

Because of the gentle slope of the ground on which the house was built, it allowed natural drainage away from the house down the lane separating the Davis property from the Wellington Pub next door. *Perfect for a shelter*, he thought to himself. He went inside to draw up a plan and make a list of materials needed. He gave the list to Mr. Davis and made some explanations about the structure.

Wilf said, "Do you have an axe available because it would be much quicker for me with an axe than a saw?"

"Yes, I do. It is a relatively new axe and very sharp."

"That will be great." With Wilf's timber-cutting skills and the knowledge he had gained on the front, this job was right up his alley.

Breakfast was cooked and eaten by Wilf with enthusiasm for the job ahead. Mr. Davis had also found some old clothes and work boots to fit Wilf, to save his uniform. Wilf changed and was ready to start work. The tools had not been used for some time but were nevertheless suited to the conditions. By nine o'clock, he had marked out and started digging the first six inches of the hole. He was staying off his feet as much as possible and was pleased to be called by Ann for a cup of tea and a rock cake, freshly baked by Mrs. Davis.

Whilst having their cup of tea, the discussion got around to names. Ann said, "My mother's first name is Margaret, after my grandmother. When I came along, they wanted to keep the name going in the family, so they called me Margaret-Ann. However, my older brother Joe found it too much of a mouthful for a little boy who could only manage the Ann part, so the name Ann stuck. I've always been known as Ann throughout school and nursing."

Wilf said, "Both names are nice and also pop up in our Yates family line."

"Well, isn't that interesting," said Ann. "It's strange how names hang around in families and link together."

"Well, it's time for me to get back to work." Wilf moved outside in his socks to don his work boots. Within half an hour, Thomo arrived with the timbers and other materials from the hardware store.

After a brief chat about the number of Aussies Thomo had noticed over here for the war effort, Wilf explained the plan.

"That doesn't look too difficult Wilf. Until recently I've always worked as a coal miner so this is chicken-feed for me. I will have the hole finished, I think by mid-afternoon."

"That sounds terrific. I'll get on with the job of measuring and cutting the timbers."

Wilf set about cutting the timbers for the base girders required for the side and back walls. These boards needed to be strong enough to withstand side pressure from the sandy soil. He completed the floor externally, ready to drop in when Thomo finished sometime later in the afternoon.

Thomo was a great worker and finished ahead of time. He then helped Wilf to lay down the floor and set the corner posts and top rails.

Wilf said, "You have been a huge help to me today, mate. I'd like to come out to see how you crank up the motor. It looks like a very modern machine."

"It's the very latest," said Thomo. His powerful, big arm gave one swing on the handle, and the engine easily sputtered into life. He climbed aboard, gave a wave, and headed back to the hardware store.

Wilf returned to the hole to think over what had to be done to finish the shelter. Ann came out and said, "You've done very well. Do you think you will finish it tomorrow?"

"I hope so. Thomo was a great help. I couldn't have wished for better."

He packed up the tools and went in for a bath prepared by Ann, and a rubdown.

While Ann was massaging his feet, Mr. Davis arrived home and inspected the shelter. Wilf stayed inside.

They sat down for the evening meal as Mr. Davis came in from his inspection and said, "I've been out and had a look at the diggings, Wilf. I'm amazed how much you have achieved in one day. The sheets of iron were not exactly what you specified, but other than that, everything else was spot on."

"There's no problem with the iron size; I can make do quite well with the alternative size. The iron is only a covering for the roof to keep the water out, and it will be covered with a lot of the soil dug from the trench. The top soil will make good protection if subjected to a nearby blast. But the real credit for the day goes to Thomo; he was great. I couldn't have done it so quickly without him."

"Well, I'm glad it all worked out well. You're doing a great job for us, and we appreciate it very much," said Mr. Davis.

"Thank you, Mr Davis, but I want to stress that the shelter cannot give protection in the unlikely event of a direct or close hit. Nothing short of a deep, concrete structure could do that. This shelter is just to protect those inside from debris flying about from a blast nearby."

"I fully understand that."

"And, Mrs. Davis, that was a delicious meal. I don't understand how you make something so special from so very little. It certainly tasted lovely, especially the way you did the vegetables."

"Thank you, Wilf. I enjoy cooking for my family, and you're included in that."

"Thank you," he said.

While Wilf had been working on the shelter, Ann emptied his kitbag, along with the uniform he had been wearing, and washed and ironed everything. She also sewed on some buttons that were either missing or nearly off.

She said, "You won't know yourself next time out."

While Ann helped her mother, Wilf sat and chatted with Mr. Davis.

"Wilf, tell me what you know about the Germans and their aeroplanes. From what I read in the papers, this raid on king's Cross was the first bombing raid by the Kaiser's flyboys on London in daylight hours."

"Yes, I think you're right. But from what I read in today's paper, daylight bombing raids are not being taken very seriously by a lot of Londoners at this stage. Many gather in the streets to watch these strange planes drop their load of bombs on everyone else's home or business except their own, or so they hope.

"I read in the paper at work that ninety people were killed the other day with another 195 injured, mostly in the Folkestone area. London is not well prepared for this type of warfare, and the government is hurriedly developing new forms of self-defence, on the back of a cigarette packet or so it seems."

"It must be very difficult for your military planners and your government to do the right thing because most of your military is already deployed in France and Belgium, with more still deployed in the Middle East."

"Yes, you're quite right, Wilf. More troops are hurriedly being drafted to defend the homeland. Blackout paper is being distributed to businesses and households to cover up windows to prevent the enemy from selecting easy targets. However, it is believed that most of the future attacks will be in daylight hours."

"This is due to the heavy losses being suffered by enemy planes running low on fuel," said Wilf, "while searching for their home fields in the dark, on their return to Germany."

"I think what you will find, Wilf, is that people at the top don't realise that this war is not like any other before, and our people in particular have had a big problem in accepting that and coming up with enough new ideas to keep in front—or maybe I should say, to get in front."

"I'm sure you're right. Dropping bombs from planes is a new form of warfare, and there are virtually no experienced people to guide them. The bombs, until very recently, were basically what we commonly called 'mills bombs' in the trenches. They made some minor modifications to the firing mechanism and call them bombs. This allows the pilot, who is also the bombardier, to drop the bombs over the side of the plane as he sweeps down low enough to identify his target, before letting the bombs go. The life of these early pilots is not terribly long, as you can imagine, but they are the new glamour boys of the Kaiser."

"Are their planes any better than ours?"

Wilf said, "I don't know how they compare size for size because there are new ones coming out all the time. I'm very much aware of the types of planes used over the Somme. I don't know if they are any better than ours, but they do have a distinctive sound. As a matter of fact, I believe the ones that flew over here the other day were the same as those we now mostly experience at the front."

"Is that right, Wilf? The same planes?"

"Yes, they were, but what was different the other day was to hear the sound of the British planes giving chase. According to what I've since read in the paper, they were British Airco planes. I haven't seen them in France."

"Do the Germans have many larger planes?"

"I'm not an expert on planes, but I do know that German planes now have sophisticated bomb racks fitted inside larger purpose-built bombers, such as the Fokker Eindeckers that flew over here the other day."

"I notice, Wilf, that calls are being made in Parliament for more retaliation from the home defences. Others say that the British Airco DH2s are doing the best they can with limited resources. The German Zeppelins were the initial bombing threat to us here in Britain, but after six were destroyed by ground fire, the last of the fifty raids came to an end. Since then, the Germans have conducted tip-and-run raids with their Gotha GIVs, killing twenty-five civilians in the night raids over London."

Ann walked in and said, "I think you boys have had enough war for one night. I think it's time for bed. You've already had your feet taken care of, Wilf, so you can have a long rest."

Wilf said goodnight to the others as Ann led him up the stairs carrying the lamp.

Chapter 6

The next morning, Wilf was once again up at daybreak and proceeded to plan his next moves so he would be ready to finish cutting the timbers when it was suitable to do so after breakfast, without waking up the neighbourhood.

The roof rafters and side boards were added along with the seat.

He dug a narrow trench sloping away from the door and secured the pipe he had specified under the duckboards.

Ann said, "I know where to find enough small stones to cover the mouth of the pipe to stop the soil from blocking the pipe." She came back with a bucketful and showed Wilf.

"They will do the job perfectly," said Wilf. "I'll give you the job of laying the stones over and around the entrance to the pipe. You'll need about three buckets. Have you got enough?"

"Plenty," said Ann. "I can do that job for you."

Wilf lay awake last night thinking about how to make a secure door, one that could be easily put into place. He came up with a louvered lift door that could be slipped downwards into a bottom channel but could also hold firm at the top. It was important that it could be handled not only by the ladies on their own but also strong enough to withstand a blast of air from an explosion. He was happy with the result and made the door and fixed the iron on the roof. It was pretty well complete.

He called Ann and said, "Now I need both you and your mum to try it out. I want you both inside before I cover the top with soil dug from the trench."

They all entered crouched over and sat on the seat. Ann could tell that her mother was apprehensive about trying out the shelter. It wasn't that bad until Wilf secured the door, with the only light coming through the louvers.

Mrs. Davis said, "I don't like the idea of being in here in the pitch dark."

Ann explained, "We have a very small lamp in the house, which should be hung permanently in the shelter along with some waterproof matches."

Wilf said, "I will locate a special hook inside to hang the lantern."

As they left the shelter, Mavis Buckley, their next-door neighbour, slipped through the small opening in the fence to find out what all the banging was she had heard that day. Mavis was remarkably similar to Ann in height and appearance; even her hair was similar.

Ann said, "Wilf, this is Mavis Buckley, our next-door neighbour. Mavis and I've grown up together, and people sometimes think we're sisters."

"I could have taken you for Ann's sister quite easily. I suppose you want to take a look at the shelter."

Ann said, "Mavis, Wilf is from Australia, and we have become good friends over the last few weeks. I nursed him at the hospital."

Mrs. Davis said, "Have a look inside, Mavis. It is bigger than we need, so feel free to use it with us should we have another emergency."

"Thank you," said Mavis, "that would be good seeing that I'm here on my own most days." Mavis crouched over and took a good look inside.

Fred Buckley was rarely at home, being preoccupied with his work in the navy; he was a second officer on a mine hunter. It was an extremely dangerous job but necessary for the defence of the British Isles. Ann was only two years younger than Mavis but knew from discussions they had in the past that things were not very good between her and Fred. Mavis had already threatened to leave him a couple of times.

Mr. Davis returned early from work to help. "I can't believe it's nearly finished," he said. They all had to do the emergency air raid drill once more.

The only work left to be done was shovelling the soil down around the three sides and on top of the iron sheets. Ann insisted she could help do that, and so with three of them shovelling, it didn't take long.

Once the soil was tapered off on three sides, there was none left over for the garden. Mr. Davis expressed his appreciation to Wilf as Ann looked on with immense pride. It showed on her face and in her eyes. Mrs. Davis could not help but notice this look of satisfaction and was so pleased that Ann—for the first time—had shown a real interest in the opposite sex. She also thought deep down that Wilf was a good catch for her daughter.

Wilf said, "I sincerely hope you will never have to use this shelter, especially with bombs dropping close by."

"That is our hope too," said Mr. Davis as the ladies nodded.

The tools were put away, and the leftover short pieces of timber were stacked with the firewood. They went inside to clean up before sitting down to another lovely meal prepared by Mrs. Davis.

At the dinner table, they had the usual discussion about the newspaper headlines, mostly about the war. Ann said to Wilf, "Providing you are up to it tomorrow, after your hard day in the trench, what would you like to do?"

"The place most people from Australia would want to visit if they ever got to London would be 'to see the queen,' or that's what the nursery rhyme says."

Ann said, "Well that's now settled; we will go to Buckingham Palace tomorrow to see King George V, if he's at home."

Mr. Davis said, "It was only last year I think that the king protested against Germany's war atrocities by renouncing his German name and titles. He dropped the name of Saxe-Coburg-Gotha and adopted instead the name of Windsor, in honour of his castle."

After the dishes were cleared, Ann again massaged Wilf's feet and then said, "I've washed all of your clothes today and will show you where I've put them in your room." She led the way up to Wilf's room.

When inside the room, Wilf said, "I already know where you put my clothes because I saw them after my bath. I think you just wanted an excuse to come up and say goodnight."

"How could you say that?"

"I'm certainly not going to complain, am I?"

Ann said, "I hope not, but I also wanted to say how I'm very grateful that you've taken the time to build the shelter for my parents. Most of the time, I will be at the hospital, but I will feel more confident knowing they have a secure place to go in an emergency." Ann managed to put down the small lamp and didn't give Wilf time to respond with words. Instead, she threw her arms around his neck and demonstrated her real appreciation. The flickering light set the scene to help them forget the hard day behind them. It was some time before his "lady with the lamp" made her way down the stairs. Wilf got changed and climbed into bed.

Wilf lay on his back staring into the darkness, thinking about this new twist his life had taken. He wondered what changes were needed to come about on the front to bring both sides together to stop the fighting. He really wasn't sure what the war was all about anyway. *Something about some Arch-Duke being assassinated in a foreign country*? Neither the killer nor the victim was British, so where was the problem? Nobody seemed to really know what it was about, except to appease somebody's pride. Did anybody really know or care? He dreaded the thought of returning to the front.

After lots of thinking about Ann and the sheer joy they experienced when together, he drifted off for a well-earned sleep.

Chapter 7

Wednesday morning, they headed off again to the station at King's Cross. While Ann purchased the tickets, Wilf looked up to admire the large domed roof with massive curved steel girders over the station. Using his ability for determining the height of trees, he estimated the top to be close to eighty feet high. The glass let in a lot of natural light and plenty of air to accommodate the huge numbers of passengers using the station daily. He was impressed with the large, four-sided clock with a face about five feet in diameter. The large size allowed it to be seen from anywhere in the station, on that level.

Ann returned with the tickets, and they proceeded down the moving stairway to the right platform and boarded the train. They changed at Euston and then four stops to Charing Cross where they walked out into brilliant sunshine, into Trafalgar Square. Right in the middle of the square stood Nelson on top of his column. Hundreds of people were walking around and looking up to the column.

"Nelson was a favourite of most of us boys at school."

"Did they tell you he was as short as we saw him at Westminster the other day?"

"No they didn't, not in our bush school anyway. The main thing I can remember is that he had an illustrious career as a young Royal Navel flag officer. He was best known for his unorthodox navel tactics, orchestrating the defeat of the larger Franco/Spanish Armada at the

Battle of Trafalgar in 1805. It was England's greatest navel victory where he was killed by a French sniper."

"Boy oh boy, your memory is good. You're dead right. To the Royal Family and I think also the British people, he is the most famous of all the heroes of the past."

Wilf pointed to the people feeding the pigeons and said, "I can't get over the thousands of pigeons walking all over the square and on anything else that stops still long enough to be taken as part of the square."

"I wonder why all the military chaps are over there," said Ann. "I counted about fifty of them."

"They are probably something to do with the bombing the other day, stationed here just in case they're needed."

Ann grabbed his hand and pointed. "Look, there's a photographer over there with nobody waiting; let's have our picture taken. I would love to have a permanent record of this special time together."

Wilf said, "That's a good idea; it'll be a record of our first days together in London." He produced his wallet to pay for the photo.

The photographer's assistant positioned them just right so that Nelson was in the background. The photo would be ready at eleven thirty.

Ann said, "Let's wander down to Admiralty Arch, it's not far. We can then come back to collect the photo. I would like to show you Scotland Yard nearby, but I don't think we will have enough time to do that and see the changing of the guard at one o'clock."

They picked up the photo on time and headed off for the bus stop, which Wilf had already investigated and located. They had five minutes to wait for the bus, enough time to pull out the photo. It was a very good one and pleased them both.

Wilf said, "The photo is yours, but I'm disappointed we did not order two prints."

"I'll take good care of the photo and cherish it forever. Maybe we will see another street photographer in our travels, and the next one can be yours, but only if I can have a copy also, please?"

Wilf picked the right number and said, "I think this is the right bus coming now."

She gripped his hand and said, "Don't be worried if I have to do a little jostling. You take your time, but I want to be first up the stairs to make sure we get a front seat."

The bus arrived, and Ann did a little pushing while Wilf paid the conductor for the fare. Sure enough, when he climbed the stairs, Ann was right down in the front seat beckoning him to come forward.

"What an experience this is," he said. "I don't have enough time to look at both sides, and there is so much to see." They went under the Admiralty Arch, past horse guards and so many other places Ann was trying to describe to him.

Unfortunately the trip to the palace was not very long, and they arrived all too quickly and earlier than expected. It gave them time to wander along Buckingham Way to the rear of the palace. They briefly glanced at the gardens as Ann looked around unsuccessfully for some roses, before heading back to get a good viewing position.

Ann said, "There's a low stone wall around the Queen Victoria Memorial Statue. It will be good for you to rest the feet white waiting for the guards."

They found a spot to sit, and the guards eventually arrived, right on time. Ann said, "Oh good, they're being led by the marching band of the Grenadier Guards. They're my favourite. I think, but I'm not sure, that they're the first regiment of the Household Infantry."

"They're very impressive, and the sound is fantastic," said Wilf as he gazed in awe at this very special sight for any visitor to London.

"Do you like them? I always have since I was a little girl. I think they're always exciting to watch."

"Do you mean the band or the guards?"

"Take your pick. I like them both."

Wilf had a big smile of delight on his face as the band came close. He was impressed by what the very smooth or even casual soft-shoed steps of the bands' men as they looked steadfastly straight ahead, as if the crowd wasn't even there. What a moment for him to enjoy, and how he wished he had a camera. The sound of the bagpipes was special for him.

Ann took her eyes from the band to glance at Wilf's face. She could see that he was absolutely enthralled with this new experience.

The guards now came closer, and the sound of the hard boots meeting the cobblestones mixed with the squeak of the leather and could be heard above the sound of the music ahead of them, keeping the time.

Wilf hadn't said a word when the band was close, but to him this was the experience of a lifetime. As the band stopped for the changing of the guard, he said, "That is just so good to watch. Do they do exactly the same thing every day?"

"No, the guard is only changed when the king is in residence at the palace. If you watch closely, you'll see that the old guard passes on verbal instructions to the new guard. I'm sure it's always the same information, but it's purely tradition," said Ann.

"Oh I thought they did this every day. Do they use the same band all the time?"

"No, the bands and the guards are drawn from five different regiments of the Foot Guards in the British Army. I think they come from the Irish, Scots, Welsh, Coldstream, and the Grenadier Guards."

Wilf asked, "Do you know why they're called Grenadier Guards?"

"I've no idea. I thought it was just a name."

"A grenadier was originally a soldier who threw grenades, and for a similar reason, the fusiliers were originally the ones who lit the fuses on the artillery."

"My brother, Joe, is in the Northumberland Fusiliers, but I can't remember him ever explaining where the name came from; maybe I didn't ask."

After the guard changed, they marched off back into the palace grounds, and the crowd cheered in appreciation of the music and the display of precision drill, known all around the world. The crowd started to move off at the same time.

Wilf said, "Well that was really something very special, but my *trip to London to see the queen* has not produced the results hoped for. You would think seeing I had travelled so far she would have come out to give us a wave."

"Maybe neither the queen nor the king is at home."

"Obviously," said Wilf. "Isn't she of European descent?"

"Queen Mary was technically the Princess of Tech of the Kingdom of Wurttemberg in Germany. Although she was born and raised in Britain, after marrying George, she became the Duchess of York, then the Duchess of Cornwall and the Princess of Wales in succession."

"I'm impressed. Where to now?" he said as he took her arm.

"Let's walk along Birdcage Walk and then to St. James Park Lake."

"That's fine by me," he said.

"I'm surprised that you didn't ask why the street was called Birdcage Walk."

"That did enter my mind, but I didn't want to interrupt the beauty around us as we walk along arm in arm in this glorious sunshine."

"Yes, it is rather special, isn't it?" She waited a little while and then said, "I'm disappointed you didn't ask because I do know the answer, so I will tell you anyway. It is called Birdcage Walk after the Royal Menagerie and Avery which was located here in this same place, during the reign of King James I."

"Really, that's a long time ago, but I just love you telling me the answers, especially without me having to ask the questions. I don't want to be a pest asking all the time."

"I love telling you the little that I do know."

"I think you underestimate your knowledge. Was that the same King James who translated the Bible?"

"Yes, it was," she said and then proceeded to offer more of her knowledge on this important subject.

The street was lined down both sides with lush green hedges and overhanging deciduous trees bursting forth with fresh new spring colours.

"Most of the trees are called plane trees. Do you have them in Australia? You're the expert on trees."

"We do, but they aren't natives. Plane trees are known for their flaking bark and resistance to coal-fire pollution, etc. I also noticed some scarlet oak trees and black mulberry trees; they're all bursting forth with new spring colours."

"Yes, aren't they beautiful? I love the way the taller trees make a lovely canopy over the roadway."

They turned off the walkway into St. James Park towards the lake and spotted a nice, shady tree. They sat down and enjoyed the picnic lunch Ann had brought along. After a long rest, they found themselves wandering amongst the entertainers in the park performing for the sightseers. Despite there being a war going on not too far away, there were always plenty of sightseers in this part of London. More than 50 per cent of the men were in military uniform.

They walked slowly through the park watching the various skills being practiced by performers, such as acrobats.

"This must be a good place to hone their skills," said Wilf. "Hey, look, there's an organ grinder with his monkey. I've never seen one of them before."

"Watch and you'll probably see him turn the handle." The entertainer had an elaborately decorated horse-drawn caravan with a small, colourful pipe organ as part of the unit.

They turned towards some even louder music coming from the merry-go-round. Ann said, "Okay, let's get two tickets so you can show me some of your horse-riding skills."

As they approached the merry-go-round, Wilf said, "I'm literally blown away at the sheer beauty of this machine."

"Isn't it really something?" she replied. "Look at all the beautiful horses."

There were five identically carved, prancing horses side by side with golden, flowing hair moving up and down on a spiral pole to the music. The music came from a beautifully decorated pipe organ with colourful, giant art-glass butterflies mounted around the pipes, reflecting the light from hundreds of electric globes. There was a carved heading over the organ that read: Gaviola Fair Ground Organ 1906.

"This doesn't apply to you, Wilf, but if a rider is not into horses, these must be for them." She pointed to the ornate, rocking gondolas and the spinning lovers' tubs. "They're to accommodate the elderly or staid people, and lovers too of course. Each gondola seats four people."

Wilf said, "Thank you, Ann. We should come back one night and try the lovers' tubs."

"Don't tempt me."

Around the perimeter of the platform were highly polished golden rails fixed to spiral posts of the same material, probably brass. They were obviously there for safety.

Ann said, "I don't think I've seen anything so beautiful before."

"I'm sure I haven't either, Ann," he said as he went off to the box and bought the tickets.

They waited for the next ride. Wilf didn't tell Ann, but he was considered to be quite a horseman back home, actually quite a daring horseman. He could ride at full gallop uphill, downhill, and across streams chasing cattle. He would achieve results that others would silently envy and then talk about to others at a later time. He wasn't one to brag about such things but kept those thoughts to himself. Now was not the time for that type of daring anyway.

However, there was another kind of daring. When the merry-go-round came to a stop, he headed for a horse with Ann in tow. He lifted her up and placed her side-saddle on the horse and stood alongside. He was happy to stand next to the horse, gently embracing Ann and waiting for the music to start. There was a vacant horse next to hers, but she couldn't coax Wilf to ride that one.

She said, "I'm really happy because I prefer to have you alongside, holding me on my horse." The music started, and the circular platform moved with the horses going up and down to the music. Wilf was intrigued as he watched the horse move up and down on the spiralled brass pole. The loud pipe organ music blared out from the pipe organ located right behind Ann in the centre of the apparatus. These would be special moments to remember. The ride ended much too quickly for Wilf.

As they alighted from the deck, now stationary, Wilf pointed and said, "Ann, what are all the people doing over there in the far corner of the park? There appears to be a lot of running around."

"I've no idea. Let's go and find out."

As they got closer, Ann said, "It looks like they're having a tug-of-war. Maybe it is a private family party or a social picnic?"

"What are the others doing off to the left?"

"It looks like an egg and spoon race. Yes, that's what it is because I can see them suddenly stop and go back to pick something up from the ground. Do you play games like that in Australia?"

"Yes, we do, and other games like sack races and three-legged races. Do you do the same things here?"

"Yes, all of those fun things as well. Maybe our two countries are not as different as we sometimes think."

"I think you're right," he said. "After all, most of our people came from England and Ireland in the first place. Although we did have an influx of Chinese people coming into the country during the Gold Rush days, but overall there were not that many of them. They seemed to stop when the government introduced the white Australian policy."

"What is that all about?" she said.

"I'm not really sure, to tell you the truth; we don't hear much about it back home. I do know that it started at the same time as Federation in 1901. The plan was to give preference to immigrants from Britain, which meant that coloured people could not come in. The reason you wouldn't hear about it here is because all of the English people wanting to migrate to Australia would have no trouble getting in because they're white. Maybe you would hear more about it in Africa if you wanted to migrate."

They stopped watching that group after a short while and strolled towards the other side of the park, just holding hands and enjoying life together. Wilf said, "I can hear more music; let's head in that direction."

If Wilf thought he had seen the ultimate in beauty back there, what confronted him next was so much better. It was an elaborately decorated pipe organ with countless pipes pouring out even louder music.

Ann shouted above the music to Wilf, "This is huge! I've never seen anything like this either."

"It looks to be about forty feet long. I wonder if they erect it each day or leave it here under guard."

There were eight beautifully carved, bare-topped buxom ladies dressed in various coloured wraparound skirts, each one standing on a small, round stool. The black stools were carved with a colourful head, something like a gargoyle. Other carved ladies either played trumpets or ate grapes hanging from a huge bunch above.

There were cherubs beating long, fine sticks with knobs onto golden bells, in time with the music. Most beautiful of all were the angels with brilliant white wings playing harps.

Above them was something like a rotunda set back into the structure behind four tall marble columns. Inside the rotunda were six carved dancing couples, individually twirling around on an even larger circular platform, bringing all the dancers to the front in time with the music.

As the music slowed, Ann said, "The colours of everything are spectacular; the way they have highlighted them with so much gold, it's really beautiful. I wonder where it was made."

"I did notice a sign over there to the right. It says: Gebr Bruder Waldkirch Germany 1895."

Ann said, "It must have come out of a music hall in Germany."

"Isn't that interesting? While we are over there trying to destroy them, they send everything of value over here for you to take care of."

The music started again as Ann took Wilf's hand and guided him away, saying, "You know, I could get used to this. I just love walking with you and enjoying the sunshine."

"It's a great experience for me also."

They walked from the park around the Ivy Lodge, across Horse Guards Road, appreciating the architecture of the Foreign Affairs Empire Offices, down past No10 Downing Street.

Ann said, "That's where Prime Minister David Lloyd George lives."

"Yes," he replied, "I've read about that place a number of times, and now I've seen it."

They continued past Admiralty House and stopped to watch the constant drill exercises of the guards in front of the gate to Horse Guards, and then they proceeded along to the Victoria Embankment to gaze out over the Thames once again.

They found an empty park bench to rest some weary bones and to do their favourite thing, which was to learn more about each other. Their conversation eventually turned to what they planned to do over the next week, before Wilf returned to the battlefields of the Somme.

Ann said, "There are so many places I want you to visit, like Auntie and Uncle's place down at Brighton by the sea. Like Glastonbury and Stonehenge, Windsor Castle, the Tower of London, Greenwich, and so many other places. There will not be enough time to fit them all into another week."

Tomorrow Wilf had to present himself at the Barracks to visit the doctor to gain a clearance for another week's recovery leave. How he hated the thought of only having one more week to share Ann's company before being parted.

Ann said, "This last week has been such a wonderful week for us to enjoy together, a week we could never have imagined such a short time ago."

Wilf said, "Don't forget that you have only asked for one week's leave from the hospital at this stage."

"Don't worry. I already have another plan in mind."

Wilf said, "But, Ann, you must—"

"Trust me, darling. I will attend to that problem on Saturday."

He said, "I do trust you. I know you will do the right thing, and I love being called darling by you. This is a new experience for me."

The day was getting late as they made their way home. The sun set before they entered the train station for the journey home. This was the first time Wilf had emerged from the station at King's Cross in the dark. They took their time to make the walk home in the dark and actually took a different route along Crestfield Street and then through the Argyle Square Gardens. They made a few stops along the way.

Argyle Square was empty, as was their park bench.

Ann said, "Let's just sit down for a little while and think about our next week together. I want to feel you close to me. This has been a most amazing week."

They enjoyed the silence of the sycamore trees overhead. The birds were doing their thing at this time of the year, flitting around mostly in pairs, obviously enjoying the mating season, constantly calling their partners.

Ann looked up into Wilf's eyes in the barely visible light and pulled him even closer. They kissed for a long and enjoyable time.

Tomorrow would be another great day.

"It is a real bonus only having to go to the Barracks behind the King's," said Ann.

"Better than trying to find my way to one of the many other Hospital Barracks around London."

"It certainly could have been a lot worse," said Ann. "This makes it very easy. It will be just a formality to get clearance from the doctor for another week of recovery leave. That's what they normally do. Hazel told me that they sometimes give an extra two weeks, which would be nice, wouldn't it?"

"It certainly would."

The next morning, they were up for an early breakfast and set off for the Barracks.

The news that greeted them at the Barracks behind the King's College Hospital the next morning shattered their world and broke their hearts.

If they had been greeted by three hundred German tanks and twenty thousand German soldiers with bayonets fixed, about to surround and take over the hospital, it would have been easier to accept. The information received destroyed them both.

Chapter 8

Wilf waited in line to see the doctor for over one and a half hours. A nurse asked him to remove his boots, socks, and putties prior to him answering a range of questions by a junior doctor. He was then instructed to put his gear back on before being directed into the next room by a nurse.

Sitting behind the desk was an elderly senior doctor who sported a very white and wide curling moustache and a small, pointed beard. The doctor said in a shaky voice, "Take off both boots and socks and hop up on the table." While Wilf was removing his boots and socks, the doctor proceeded to read the reports that had been presented to him by the nurse.

The doctor then proceeded to prod and poke at Wilf's legs and feet. After referring back to the report, he stroked his beard with a puzzled look on his face and said, "Put your boots on."

He sat down at his desk to study the report and added some extra details. Wilf by this time had completed the more difficult task of putting socks, boots, and putties back on.

The doctor eventually stood up and said, "From what I read here, your battalion is in France at this time, is that right?"

"Yes they are, Doctor."

"You will be pleased to know that I cannot get over how well your feet have recovered in such a short time. Somebody must have taken very good care of them for you."

Wilf said, "That's good to know." He wasn't sure what to expect next.

The doctor said, "I can see no reason why you cannot resume duty straight away. It will take about three or four days to get back to your battalion, maybe even a week, by which time you will be fighting fit. You can report back for service to these same Barracks on Sunday morning at 0900 hours. The clerk outside in the corridor will have more details for you."

As he dismissed Wilf and handed the report to the nurse, he turned again and said much as an afterthought, "Did you do anything special, young man, to speed up the recovery time?" Wilf was devastated and could only manage to shake his head in the least detectable movement he could manage.

After being given final leave by the nurse, Wilf walked slowly back to the appointed place where he knew Ann would be waiting for him. She knew these things took time, so she had managed to find a paper to read to kill time. After a two-hour wait, she looked up to see Wilf coming. Immediately she knew the news was not good. Wilf sat down alongside Ann and found it very difficult to breathe, let alone break the news. He could hardly manage to put two words together.

"The doctor wants me back on duty this Sunday."

Now it was Ann's time to try to speak, eventually saying, "You can't be serious," as tears started to flow. Wilf hugged Ann, and they sat for a while and wept unashamedly. Eventually Ann broke away and sprung to her feet, pulling on Wilf's hand, saying, "Let's get going, we haven't got a second to lose."

Although Ann was devastated and tears were still falling, she linked her arm through Wilf's, using her other hand to dab at her cheeks.

"I know it's too late now, but I should have insisted that you hobbled in to the doctor's using your cane."

It had been her intention to front the matron whilst in the general area of the hospital to tell the truth about her situation and ask for another week off. If the matron would not cooperate, although Ann believed she would, Ann was prepared to quit on the spot to join the Queen Alexandra's Imperial Military Nursing Service (QAIMNS).

Now there was no need to go to the matron. Ann was expected back on duty at three o'clock on Sunday, after seeing Wilf off.

As it was now lunchtime, Ann decided to visit the tent canteen set up in the grounds by one of the local churches. They both needed a cup of tea to get through this difficult, unexpected period ahead. They bought some sandwiches and hot tea and sat down in the corner so they could plan what to do with the day and a half left for them.

Ann was still teary and wanted just to hold Wilf's hand and stare off into the vacant distance and dream of what could have been. After a brief discussion, they decided to set off in the same direction as they did on their first day together. They couldn't make up their minds as to whether they should go down to the same large tree near the Flower Markets and relive that first day together, or turn right at Vauxhall and proceed along the Albert Embankment towards Lambeth Palace.

They decided to go towards Lambeth Palace where there were many parks along the Albert Embankment. They had no idea how far they would go or what they would find. Ann had never walked along this part of the embankment. The afternoon was a quiet time of contemplation for them as they sometimes enjoyed just sitting or walking together, a lot of that time in silence. There were other times when Ann buried her face in Wilf's shoulder and sobbed. Wilf had great difficulty controlling his emotions and remained silent.

At the end of their quiet afternoon of walking and sitting and talking together, they arrived home via the tube just at dusk to break the news to Mrs. Davis. She was home alone. Mrs. Davis also had trouble holding back some tears as she turned her head away from Ann, who had again released her emotions with Wilf supporting her. His arm was wrapped firmly around her shoulder.

Mrs. Davis said, "I've been reading the paper this afternoon; things are not going well on the Western Front." She didn't say any more but knew that the names of many of the thousands of dead soldiers were being listed every day, with reports of the many hospitals throughout the country now overflowing their capacity with the wounded troops. The stories were unimaginable to her. She located the paper and hid it out of sight so neither Ann nor Wilf could be upset further by reading the terrible news stories.

Mr. Davis came home and was told the bad news by Mrs. Davis as she served the meal she had prepared. As he followed his wife into the kitchen, he said, "I've been reading today's paper on the way home, and things are looking terrible on the front. I've come to like Wilf and have grown to respect him very much in the space of less than a week. I don't like what this war is doing to our daughter."

As he moved back to the dining room, he said, "I want to assure you again, Wilf, that I'm very grateful for the shelter you built for us. I will check it regularly to make sure the water is draining away properly and that the lamp and matches are ready for use." They all chimed in with remarks that they hoped it would never be needed.

Wilf said, "Remember, it's only a light shelter not an underground concrete bunker." To reassure them further, he said, "I read somewhere recently about the chances of someone receiving a direct hit in any large city. They're so infinitely small. I can't remember the exact details, but so far in London, which as you know is one of the largest cities in the world, such casualties are only counted in the low hundreds and not thousands. In other words, a very small percentage of the total population."

Mr. Davis said, "I think I read the same article."

The next day, they waited to see what the weather was like before making the final decision on the destination for their last day together. Ann suggested the boat journey to allow maximum time together. Ann prepared the customary picnic basket, and they left early for the city on the tube and alighted at the Embankment Station. Ann knew this was the best place to board a small steam ferry to travel downstream to Canary Wharf at Greenwich. They could watch the working boats on the Thames, without the need for a lot of walking.

Wilf said, "I'm blown away by the size of this river and the large rise and fall of the tide, which obviously happens twice each day."

"I believe the difference between high and low tide is about eighteen feet."

"Is there any particular stretch of the river where the boats used to moor with the convicts on board? I read they sometimes lived on board for months on end before sailing off for Australia."

Ann didn't know much about this subject, so she went and asked the captain. When she came back, she said, "The boats used to moor in 'the roads' on the Thames around the Woolwich Docks area. He said that's about five miles further towards the sea past Greenwich. I'm sure you know more about the history of the convicts than I do. It wasn't something taught in the British schools like it probably was in Australia, for obvious reasons. You told me that you liked history at school, and you certainly seem to remember a lot of the details."

"Well, in those times, you had a problem over here. The population was exploding in Britain, and the younger ones couldn't find work, so they got involved in crime, especially in the big cities. Did they teach you this at school?"

"Yes, they did. America had been the preferred destination to send your convicts, but after the War of Independence, they no longer wanted anything to do with Britain. This caused the prison populations in the British Gaols to overflow. They had to find extra accommodation for the prisoners, so they made good use of a lot of floating hulks on the Thames."

"Really, you mean old boats used as prisons right here?"

"Apparently so; the convicts could eat and sleep and be taken ashore in the early morning light to work till dark. Over a thousand additional convicts were added to the hulk population each year. Then riots broke out, and the government of the day decided something had to be done to alleviate the problem. So in 1785, they decided to ship them off to a little-known place on the other side of the world called New South Wales."

Another ferry with a lot of young people and some troops on board passed very close, going in the opposite direction. Ann said, "Let's give them a wave." They both stood and waved. The kids returned the wave with lots of cheering.

The ferry moved quickly out of range, and when they sat down again, Ann said, "Keep on going; I'm enjoying the history lesson."

"Where was I? That's right, the first fleet sailed around 1787 with 736 on board plus crew and guards. Between 1788 and 1868, over 160,000 convicts in over 1,000 ships arrived in Australia from Britain and Ireland. This is how Australia first got started; we were a pretty rough bunch."

Ann listened intently as Wilf continued. It wouldn't have mattered if he was making it up; she was prepared to just listen and enjoy being with him. Tomorrow he would be gone, and for who knew how long?

They went ashore and walked up the long slope to the ticket office. Ann enquired about return times and was told they had two hours before the next ferry would be returning.

Ann said, "There should be plenty to see nearby because this is the place where time really began; this is where the mean-time started the world clock."

"What else do you want to see?"

Ann said, "There are so many historic buildings in this town, such as the Royal Palace of Placentia where so many of the Royal Family members have been born. We should also look up the Royal Naval Hospital for Sailors, rebuilt by Christopher Wren."

"You did mention his name before. What did he do?"

"He was the great man of history who built so many of the great buildings and cathedrals of London."

Two hours was not long enough considering that they needed to find some place to sit in the shade to enjoy their last picnic lunch together. They wanted to enjoy each other's company and not talk about the future that they could not control or even understand in this crazy world of war.

After finishing their lunch, they started off to visit some of the sights. Suddenly right in front of them, a matter of only three yards away, a motorcycle slid sideways into a lamppost at the intersection. The rider was travelling way too fast around the corner. Ann immediately jumped into action and rushed to lend him whatever assistance she could.

Ann kneeled down and supported his head on her bent knee, saying to Wilf, "Keep the people back to give him plenty of fresh air. Find somebody who can notify the ambulance station."

He was bleeding profusely from a deep gash on his thigh. She suppressed the bleeding, finding at the same time that his femur was fractured. He was holding his chest, which Ann checked, saying, "He may have cracked some ribs, but I think that's not a problem to worry about now."

He had some nasty abrasions on his face and arms, but these were not serious. Ann made him as comfortable as she could, and with Wilf's assistance comforted him until the ambulance arrived and took over.

Wilf said, "I was very proud to see firsthand how a professional works. You were terrific."

"Thank you, but that wasn't a really bad case. You should see some of them that come in as a result of motor bike accidents; they're a real killer."

"Being from the bush, I've had nothing to do with motor bikes, so this was a real eye-opener for me. I can see how vulnerable the rider is and what damage can be done—and so quickly."

"You have seen a very good reason to stay away from motor bikes," said Ann.

The accident had taken up most of their spare time at Greenwich. Ann looked at the time and said, "I don't think we have enough time to see any of the sights here. We need to head for the ferry."

On the return voyage, the ferry was scheduled to stop at the Tower of London. Ann said, "We won't have a lot of time at the Tower either, but I want you to visit this historic place. It houses a lot of British history, including the Crown Jewels."

Wilf said, "Let's do it." Fortunately the weather was still fine, so they did a lightning tour of the castle and headed for the tube, to arrive home as planned, just as darkness fell.

Ann had asked her mother that morning to make sure the water for the bath was hot. Mrs. Davis had prepared a special send-off dinner in Wilf's honour. This was not requested by Ann, but Mrs. Davis wanted to do something special for this man who meant so much to her daughter.

Whilst waiting for Mr. Davis to come home from work, there was enough time for Wilf to have a bath and a foot massage.

Ann said, "This might be your final bath for some time, who knows. And I don't think you will get another massage, will you?"

"Going on the past, it could easily be two or three weeks or even more to the next bath, depending on how long after arriving in France before I'm sent up to the front. But I can assure you, there won't be any more massages."

Wilf thought a lot about his future at the front while having his bath. The thoughts weren't good at all.

By the time he was dressed again, Mr. Davis arrived, and tea was ready to be served.

Mrs. Davis had gone to a lot of trouble making little, coloured paper decorations by hand. Ann had no idea where her mum had stored the coloured paper because the stores had not stocked such luxuries since the outbreak of war. The table looked a picture with the glasses sparkling in the reflected light from the flickering candles. The variety of colour on the table stood out against the dark background of the wallpaper behind. The wallpaper was a heavy dark green with gold fleur-de-lis set into cream-coloured diamond borders. Wallpaper was not something Wilf had seen back home. Newspaper glued to the timber upright slabs was commonly used to keep out the drafts.

Mr. Davis said grace before the meal and asked the Lord to keep Wilf safe and return him safely, to which they all said a loud amen. It was a sumptuous meal of baked pork, potato, onion, and pumpkin, plus beans, peas, and a homemade apple sauce. This was followed by preserved peaches and custard, and some apple juice had been scrounged from who knows where.

Wilf said, "That was a most delicious meal, Mrs. Davis. How are you able to obtain all of these products in these difficult times?"

She said, "I had to call in some favours from my favourite storekeepers for this meal. Mostly I have to rely on the government-issue cookbook to serve up something edible from the rationed foods available."

Mr. Davis stood up, and the talking ceased. He said, "I ask you all to please stand and raise your glass to this special man who has come so far to do his part for the defence of the Realm. I propose this toast to Wilf's good health and safety in the difficult days that lie ahead for him."

Wilf, although new to this sort of dining procedure, said hesitatingly at first, "I would also like to propose a toast to a very special family, a family that has provided me with a loving and caring home away from home, the Davis family of Whidbourne Street." They all drank together the apple juice, which none of them had tasted for such a long time.

After dinner, Ann went off to have her bath while Wilf and Mr. Davis helped clear the dishes and wash the heavy baking pans from the stove. Mrs. Davis went about preparing a lunch box for Wilf to take with him tomorrow. She had no idea how long it would be before he was provided with his next good meal. Mr. Davis was keen to extract as much information from Wilf about conditions on the front. Wilf kept back most of the horror stories that he did not even want to even think about, let alone talk about on this last night.

Ann came back after her bath and looked radiant yet sad at the same time in the glow of the now flickering lamps. She said, "Mum we are going for a walk. I'm not sure how long we will be. We'll say our goodnights now; please don't wait up for us. I'm sure we will all be up in time to say our farewells in the morning, before I take Wilf to the Barracks."

As they walked out, Mrs. Davis called out, "Don't bother to take a key; I'll leave the door open for you."

After they were gone, Mr. Davis said, "I believe my wife is nearly as upset as my daughter at Wilf's leaving." She put her arms around his waist and buried her face in his chest to hide the tears.

Mrs. Davis said, "Wilf has become like a substitute son. I like him very much."

Their own son, Joseph, was away on the front and was not one to write often. They both feared for his safety. Mrs. Davis spent many long hours through the dark nights thinking about where her son was and what he was suffering in that terrible wasted land of the Somme, just as most mothers of soldiers do. Now she would have another one to worry about.

The weather was cold outside, so they both needed coats, at least at this stage. They set off for their last walk in the dark, less than a couple of blocks away, to the Argyle Square Gardens to say their passion-filled farewells. Saying goodbye in the morning at the Barracks would be totally different and too difficult to contemplate at this time. There would probably be hundreds of soldiers registering for transport. They too would have their loved ones with them to say their goodbyes.

Ann said, "I find it impossible to believe that someone could make my life so happy in such a short time. You have dominated my every waking thought, as well as most of my sleeping thoughts, if I can put it that way."

"You have done the same for me," he said as he drew Ann close to him.

"But I fail to understand, if you can make me so happy in such a short time, why am I feeling so miserable right now?"

Wilf didn't have an answer that he could easily verbalise without losing control of his emotions. Instead, he kissed her more deeply and longer than they had done previously.

It was impossible for them to talk or even think about how they had become so inexplicably entwined together in less than a week. On the other hand, they didn't want to think of what the future might hold for them. The now was the most important thing on which to concentrate and the only alternative. They just melted their entire beings and thoughts together into the one soft, warm cacoon and hugged. They didn't know for how long they stayed in that embrace. Wilf had forgotten to bring his fob watch.

Chapter 9

Early on Sunday morning, they were all up to have breakfast, and Wilf packed his kitbag in the early light. Both Mr. and Mrs. Davis were sombre.

"It's like seeing off our own son," said Mrs. Davis.

Even Mavis Buckley from next door came in to say farewell to Wilf and gave him a big hug. No wonder people thought Mavis and Ann were sisters. Wilf again thanked them for their hospitality, and they in turn told him he would be most welcome at their home anytime in the future, for however long he wished to stay.

Mrs. Davis said, "I hope it won't be too long before you return, Wilf."

He gave Mrs. Davis a big hug and said jokingly, "Here is my army address and home address in Australia in case you need to tell me that Ann has not been taking good care of you."

"Don't worry. I will put it safely in the drop-down bureau that Dad bought for us to celebrate our twenty-fifth wedding anniversary. I know Ann showed it to you; I saw you having a good look at the workmanship involved in the roll-top."

They said their good-byes and walked out. Wilf turned to wave. Ann said, "Let me carry your kitbag for you."

"No, you've got enough to carry with the lunch box prepared by your mum." They walked mostly in silence until Wilf said, "Your mother is such a sweet person. I don't believe I've ever known another person as kind as she is. No wonder you're such an angel; you get it from your mother."

"Thank you for saying that. It's very kind of you."

The journey to Denmark Hill was mostly in silence. There were lots of things they both wanted to say, but words didn't seem appropriate at this most difficult time. As they approached the Barracks at the rear of the King's Hospital, the number of people there was not just in the hundreds as they had presumed. There were already thousands milling about. They, like all others in a similar situation, had difficulty locating the right place for Wilf to report. They were about fifteen minutes late getting through the crowd to his designated position.

Ann said, "Judging by the number of people darting around all over the place, I think most of the others are lost also. There are a lot of people here."

When Wilf knew exactly where he was required to be, he moved away a little to one side and put the kitbag down with the lunch box on top. He turned towards Ann, taking both of her hands in his, and looked into her eyes, but only for a brief moment. Their arms quickly found their way around each other for their last embrace. The tears started down Ann's cheeks. She said, "I don't care if everyone sees me crying." All around them, the same thing was happening with lovers and mothers and sisters seeing off their men.

Ann was crying, and Wilf couldn't find words to express his feelings. His tongue was glued to the roof of his mouth, maybe to hold back his emotions. All he could do was to hold Ann tightly, as if this would prevent any parting. Their lips locked together, finding continuous comfort that blotted out anything else going on around them.

The bugle sounded nearby for the men to fall in, and they were suddenly jolted back to reality as orders were shouted by the sergeant major. Wilf knew this was it. He hugged and kissed Ann for the last time and then picked up the lunch box and slung the kitbag over his shoulder. He gave Ann one last, long agonising look as he found three words that fit together. He mouthed the words without sound. "I love you," he said.

She understood the words perfectly and replied, "I love you too." He turned to make the few steps required to the designated spot to fall in. He couldn't turn around again; he was struggling to hold back a flood of tears welling up inside.

He knew Ann would be emotional and beside herself with grief at having to part in this way. He felt the same way. Nearly everyone else around them was experiencing the same problem, so there was no shame in showing tears.

As he waited in line, his thoughts went back to the wharf in Sydney. That farewell was nothing like this. He had been all alone in Sydney, from the bush, with nobody to see him off. Then the seven Bisset sisters, there to say farewell to one of the boys from their church, befriended him.

The sisters were not even old friends, just new friends he had met in an atmosphere of frivolity. Their names, he could not remember at that stage. There was lots of singing and laughter as they marched along with the boys going off to war. It wasn't a sad parting like this; it was a happy occasion. It was so different from the way he was feeling now.

Ann wanted to follow Wilf, but there were now soldiers on duty already swinging barriers into place to separate the troops from the crowds of people gathered to say farewell to their loved ones. The crowd was pushed away about fifty yards, making it impossible for Ann to keep Wilf in sight. She hung around, hoping to see them march away, but that didn't look likely to happen any time soon.

The sun was high overhead, and there was no shelter, so the crowd started to disperse. Ann decided to walk around to the other side of the hospital grounds where she knew of some trees under which to shelter. She was not due to start work until three, so she had a couple of hours to kill. She sat down on a slab seat under one of the trees, dropped her head into her hands, and sobbed until there were no tears left to cry.

Ann had been smart enough to have a spare set of clothes ready at the hospital last Saturday when she planned to have the first picnic with Wilf. She went to the nurse's quarters and changed after washing her face over and over, trying to remove any appearance of distress. That was not possible, and when she first appeared in the ward, other nurses welcomed her back from her sick leave. Some made comments about the fact she still did not look well enough to return to work.

Then she ran into Hazel. Ann immediately burst into tears again. Hazel knew Ann took off the last week to be with Wilf, so she knew some of the story. Hazel led her away to the seclusion of one of the storerooms where Ann could explain the happenings of the last week.

Hazel and Ann had started their nursing career together after leaving school. Hazel was taller than Ann with jet-black hair. She was slim and a very capable nurse. Hazel had shared her own failed romantic episodes with Ann in the past. Now it was Ann's time to share her romance with Hazel. Hazel listened closely as Ann explained in the space of ten minutes the happenings of the last week. Hazel then had to run and arranged to catch up again at the meal break, but that didn't happen.

Things were chaotic with a new load of wounded and sick soldiers being admitted from the front. Normally when there were lots of new critical casualty cases to be cared for, Ann was able to get on with her job. She could divorce herself from her personal happenings outside the King's and get on with the job in a detached sort of way and bury her thoughts. She could not do that today. Each soldier she saw with horrific wounds needing urgent attention only made things worse. She could not get out of her mind that this could be Wilf at any time in the future, or even worse.

Because of the heavy load of new patients arriving, Ann did not finish her shift until nearly three in the morning. She went back to her dormitory but made no attempt to change for bed. She collected some writing materials from her locker and headed down to the reading room where she could write the words to Wilf that her locked tongue had been unable to express earlier in the day. Ann filled six tear-splattered pages, exposing her heart to Wilf.

Ann was still writing when the sun came up. She had no idea how long it would take for the letter to reach Wilf, but she believed from what he had told her it could be as long as two or three weeks. This was because of the uncertainty of where his battalion would be and the logistics of the army postal division keeping track of sudden, unplanned movements.

Chapter 10

Wilf did not see Ann again after he let go of her hands and turned towards the fall-in area. He wanted to turn again and again as he walked away but was struggling with his emotions; he did not want to make it harder for Ann. Standing around in the sun was not easy to take, especially with myriad thoughts and emotions going through his mind. He had no idea if Ann waited around for long or not. It was nearly another hour before the troops were marched away to the transports for the journey to Folkestone.

There was more waiting around before they were loaded onto the *Victoria*, the ship designated to take them across the channel. Nobody could tell them where they were headed other than back to France and that awful war that nobody wanted.

After a rough crossing on the *Victoria*, he eventually landed at Le Havre. Then followed many hours of standing around, marching, trucks, buses, and trains until they arrived at the Harfleur Station.

Wilf lost count of the hours since he left Ann. He was worn out and tired but very grateful for the lunch box and the bottle of water, prepared by that wonderful, caring lady, Mrs. Davis. His thoughts were with Ann every waking moment; he hadn't slept at all so far.

After two more days of hanging around soup kitchens and many false parades, they were again awaiting orders to move out by train; the rumours said it was to be Amiens. New instructions were received as the rain came down. They were marched to a cattle train around midnight; it was about half a kilometre away, and Wilf's great-coat was soaking wet.

The cattle trucks were absolutely filthy, and the smell, a mixture of cattle dung, human excrement, urine, and vomit, was overpowering. Wilf, being a bullock driver, was fortunate in that the smell of cattle dung was something he could handle. He felt sorry for the clerks, the solicitors, and other white-collar workers with him who had never been subjected to such smells before. Neither had they needed to sleep rough or anywhere other than in their own beds. Travelling in these conditions was absolutely terrible and enough to make many of them sick. The journey was not fast by any means, and they often stopped for longer periods than they spent moving.

On more than one occasion, they stopped alongside another stationary train, heading in the opposite direction. These trains had special carriages equipped as medical vans to transport the wounded soldiers from the front to hospitals along the French coast and across the channel. The sounds of the wounded in pain was so bad that it would be hard for anyone to forget.

The screams of agony on one occasion were so loud and terrifying that it caused a problem in Wilf's cattle truck. One young Canadian soldier was so disturbed that he went berserk and tried to force open the sliding doors, which were always latched on the outside. He did his best to flatten two of his mates who tried to help him. In the end, it took five men to subdue him and bring him under control. It caused a deep silence to fall over the men in his wagon and helped them for a long time to forget the stench that surrounded them.

They restrained him until two military police were summoned to take him under control at the next station. They placed him in handcuffs and led him away. Wilf thought to himself, *Maybe he's the smart one.*

In this period of silence, Wilf spent a lot of time in the darkness reflecting on the stories he had heard from the original members of the Eighteenth Battalion, especially of their experiences in the Dardanelle Campaign. Wilf was one of the reinforcements who joined the Eighteenth in Belgium after that campaign. It was believed by the officers that the

Australian and New Zealand troops were used as cannon fodder by the British generals and absolutely slaughtered on the landing beach, which happened to be in the wrong place anyway.

It was fairly common news in the papers back home before he enlisted, that the Australian government under Prime Minister Andrew Fisher had not been advised in advance of the landing at Gallipoli. The number of casualties suffered was disproportionate to the number of Australian troops deployed.

Andrew Fisher tried hard to get the British government to take him into their confidence and advise him in advance of major battle plans; they refused his demands. Now Wilf could see that the same thing was happening all over again on the Western Front, with no real plan of where the war was heading. At least on Gallipoli they had been evacuated when no progress was being made. Who was going to admit defeat on the Somme? How do you evacuate all of the troops and their support from a place like the Somme? It would be called an even more catastrophic defeat.

The distance from Harfleur to Amiens, according to the rumour mill that circulated from wagon to wagon at each stop, was about two hundred kilometres. However, the journey was to last nearly four whole days. On route, they stopped in Rouen for breakfast, the city where Joan of Arc had been burned at the stake by the British when she was only nineteen years old. Wilf remembered from his history lessons at school that she was a peasant girl who led the French Army to several important victories during the Hundred Years War. That was about as much of the story as he could recall.

This train load was made up of British, Canadian, Indian, and Australian troops. Wilf learned from another Digger who had previously had leave in Rouen that this city had one of the finest cathedrals in France. He pointed it out to Wilf in the distance. The train would not be around long enough to make a visit. He was rather glad about that because it would not be a good feeling to visit such a place without Ann by his side, especially after their visits to the historic buildings in London. He knew it would be like wandering around looking at deserted buildings without a soul or a history to share. He needed Ann to share the experience with him; otherwise, he wouldn't have any real interest.

They arrived at a small town on the outskirts of Amiens called Salouel, where they were told to disembark and bring everything with them. That simply meant their kitbag. More time standing around waiting. Wilf thought that the first army to get organised enough to cut out all of the lost time waiting around would win the war. Eventually they were marched about four kilometres away to a camp, where they were fed and then slept before moving out once again to their respective units.

It was now nearly a week since he had said good-bye to Ann. He had not been in any place long enough to even think of posting her a letter, but his mind never stopped thinking about her and what he would put to paper the first chance he got to write. Being constantly on the move, he had not received any mail from home since before he was shipped off to dear old Blighty about seven weeks ago.

He hoped there would be mail waiting for him when he re-joined his unit. He left for Blighty when they were in Ypres. Would they still be there? Hopefully they were not too far away now.

They were ordered to fall in once more, and as they marched, he thought about the lads in his unit and wondered how many would be missing when he returned. Wilf wondered if Joe Maxwell was still in the land of the living. Surely his luck could not last too much longer, with all the dangerous stunts he performed.

They eventually arrived at the camp in time for a meal and were allocated tents. Wilf fell off to sleep quickly, as did most others, to be awoken at daybreak by the sound of reveille sounded by the camp bugler. While having breakfast, a sergeant major stood up on a chair and said, "For all of the men who arrived last night by train from Harfleur, you are to receive one day's leave today. Another announcement will be made at canteen tonight."

Wilf said to another Digger sitting beside him, "What can you do for a day out here away from the main city other than to catch up on one's letters to folks back home?" Most men did just that, including

Wilf. His indelible pencil, silent for such a long time, was now ready for action.

His first letter was to Ann.

My dearest Ann,

You have no idea how I hated leaving you at the parade ground like I did. I couldn't turn around; I would have made an utter fool of myself. We waited a long time before leaving. I hope you did not hang around in vain in the sun.

The most important thing I want to say is that I love you, so much that it hurts. I don't wish you any hurt, but I believe (or hope) that you are feeling the same way. My hope is that when you receive this letter your feelings towards me will not have changed; mine certainly haven't. I'm sorry that I'm not good at putting into words just how I feel at the time. My whole body aches for you at such times, but my tongue lets me down something dreadful.

I cannot adequately describe to you my feelings for you and how dreadful it was for me to separate the way we did the other day behind King's. I cannot recall such a terrible experience occuring in my life, ever. As a matter of fact, I know for certain that there has never been such a terrible experience for me. You alone have had such a dramatic effect on my life.

The loving care you have shown to me has been quite remarkable in such a short time.

I've heard about other couples being so welded together, but now I know what it is like.

It is hard to think of what lies ahead over here and how I can get through it without you. You have given me such wonderful memories to dwell upon. Like our visits together to the Houses of Parliament, the Abbey, the Thames, and the flower garden near Vauxhall. I hope you will remember the red rose I picked for you. I think it means as much to me as I hope it means to you. Please keep that rose always in your mind.

I'm sure I don't have to tell you that war is a very dirty business. Even the trains have been very hard to handle. The cattle wagons they provide as transport for us over here are really terrible. The only thing that gets me through is to keep thinking about what we have in common and all the wonderful experiences we have enjoyed together over recent weeks. You have certainly changed and enriched my life.

Wilf continued on and filled eight pages before signing off.

He knew there would be letters awaiting him when he eventually joined up with his unit again, probably in the next few days. There would be maybe half a dozen letters from mother, who regularly wrote once a week; she kept him up to date with the family matters at home. His younger brother, Ned, who was working the bullock team with his father in Wilf's place, sometimes put pen to paper and wrote quite long letters. There would be letters from his four sisters and maybe one or two from Teen.

Christina Tivendale Bisset signed her letters to Wilf as Teen; her family called her Teenie. Wilf was quite formal in his letters and addressed her as Miss Bisset. He remembered her as a very beautiful, petite lady with long, brown hair. Wilf had only known her on the wharf at Sydney, but he learned from her letters that she had grey/green eyes, was five feet three inches tall, and was the shortest of the seven sisters. He learned from a letter he received from Teen's sister Alma that Teen was known as the peacemaker in the family because of her lovely, quiet nature.

Teen worked as a seamstress in a shirt factory in Sydney and kept Wilf up to date with the happenings in Sydney. She told him of the huge effort being made by the various ladies' auxiliaries to support the troops in France. She told Wilf about another good friend John Ridley. He was one of the first boys to leave for Gallipoli. He had been wounded at Fromelles and was now back in the action as an officer. Teen hoped they might meet up some time.

In the absence of any incoming mail, Wilf was able to write some long letters, and one of those letters was to Teen.

Dear Miss Bisset,

I'm on my way back to the front after a stint of nearly six weeks in Dear Old Blighty. I wasn't injured but was transported over there with trench foot and spent four weeks in hospital. I'm sure you have heard a lot back home in the papers about trench foot; it's pretty common over here.

After my release from the hospital, I enjoyed a week sightseeing around London, visiting many of the great sights. I will tell you about those sights individually when I get the chance.

You have been very kind to keep me up-to-date with the happenings back in Australia and in Sydney in particular. I will fill you in with some up-to-date information about what some Aussies have been doing over here. Maybe you have already read about this in your papers; I don't think so because it has been kept pretty quiet even here.

A special unit made up of Aussie miners was set up to build a huge tunnel under the German front line. Many of these men are from the Hunter Valley coal mines.

They tunnelled for some seven or eight months under Hill 60, one of the hills on the Messines Ridge. They set off nineteen mines simultaneously along a ten-kilometre tunnel using over one million pounds of explosives, which left craters two hundred and fifty feet deep; the explosion was heard in London over 130 miles away. The explosion killed between 10,000 and 20,000 Germans, either blowing them apart or entombing them in their trenches. Another 8,000 Germans were taken as prisoners.

I'm so thankful I'm not a miner and involved in such a horrible aspect of war. Is there anything worse than war? Multitudes of men, no, millions of men, are thrust into this unbelievable slaughter where men's lives are either ended abruptly or changed forever. Not to mention the devastating effect it has on the millions of people back home, waiting for news that sometimes never comes. I can't imagine in my wildest imagination anything worse.

I really shouldn't write like this, but I suppose you see it every day in the papers.

Teen Bisset

Wilf continued for a couple of pages with other happier news. He then sent his very best regards to her sisters and asked that she keep up the good news of her activities at home.

He finished all of his letters, including another special one to Ann, and had them ready to post when they presented for canteen in a little over one hour. He lay back on his bunk with his hands behind his head and wondered what Ann would be doing right now. He dropped off to sleep and was awoken by the bugle call summoning them to tea, for soup, sausages, cabbage, and mashed potatoes.

The Australian troops were told again by the sergeant major to be ready in the morning after breakfast for shipping out to the front at Ypres. This was to be another train journey of approximately 160 kilometres. The way troop trains travelled, that could be another two or three days away.

The next morning, they were marched to the railway yards, where they boarded more cattle wagons that were in worse shape than the previous ones, if that was possible. There were twenty-nine soldiers crammed into Wilf's wagon.

After two days, they arrived at the Castrea Station at Fletre, where the building next door had been bombed out. As they alighted, Wilf saw for the first time a real tank.

There were twelve identical tanks on a train going past on the way to the front. Looking from the side, each tank looked like a giant, oblong steel box that had been squashed forward by an even larger boot. There were hundreds of large, steel rivets holding the steel plates together. Around the circumference of the tank on both sides were what looked like large rubber bands with numerous parallel slats attached. These slats were obviously the revolving feet that enabled the machine to move forward through mud and shell craters without getting bogged.

Mounted on the side was a large, square steel box with a revolving turret inside. Protruding from the turret was a short-barrel heavy-calibre gun. Wilf wondered why the gun was on the side and only able to cover the side area. It would have made more sense to have it mounted on the front because that was where the enemy would be. He understood that as many as eight men could be cramped up inside the tank. He was an outdoorsman and didn't like the thought of being one of those men inside.

They marched about two miles to the base camp where the Eighteenth Battalion was located, awaiting the draft for the front line. As soon as he had been advised where to find his platoon and had been dismissed, he made his way straight for the postal hut to collect his mail.

It was already mid-afternoon, so he was able to spend the rest of the day reading through the letters. In the past, it had always been his mother's letters from home that he looked for first. She always ended her letters by saying that she prayed every night that God would bring him back safely. He was always assured when he read her letters.

Wilf hoped beyond hope that there would be a letter from Ann, but he was realistic enough to understand that the Army Postal Department didn't work that fast. The news he received from home was all good. Any news from home, short of a death in the immediate family, would have to be good compared to the events on this side of the world. There was not enough time to answer any of the new mail; besides, he had written letters to most of them in the last couple of days.

The sound of battle could be heard quite loudly, so he believed they could be as close as ten to twenty miles from the front line. He proceeded to locate his mates, and the first one he came across was Eddie, who said, "Good to have you back, mate."

Wilf replied, "Can't say the same thing, Eddie. It was hard coming back, very hard."

Eddie said, "We lost three of our mates while you were away."

"Who were they?"

"I'm sad to say they were some of your closest mates, Lawrie, Tommo, and George."

"That's terrible news," said Wilf. "What about Maxwell—how's he doing?"

"Oh, he's okay. You can't beat him. He's been recommended for another medal, the Military Cross on top of his DSM. This latest one is for action just before you went off to Blighty."

Their battalion had been given leave shortly after Wilf left, and as usual, Maxwell had been arrested for fighting in a pub and locked up. When it was time for him to return to camp, some military police arrived at the gaol to take Maxwell into their custody. They returned him to his unit. It was always joked about that this was not the only time he came back to camp this way. Some of the men said, *Just so you can win more medals.* One thing you could not take away from this twenty-two-year-old Joseph Maxwell was his impish sense of humour and winsome smile.

As if on cue, Joe Maxwell came around the corner and saw Wilf and stopped.

"Good to see you back again, Wilf. How's the feet?"

"The problem is they're too good. I had the personal services of a pretty blonde nurse to take care of me."

"I'll bet you did," said Maxwell. "Was she fat, forty, or married?"

"None of those," said Wilf with a glow all over his face. "She was a real beauty."

The next morning, they were up before daybreak and told to be ready to move up towards the front by 0700 hours. It was raining quite heavily and continued all day. They marched about twelve miles north in the rain to a small, deserted town called Steenvoorde. Wilf knew the name of this place well because his cousin Cliff had been buried there only last year.

They arrived about three o'clock, and Maxwell told them to find what shelter they could and get some rest because they were to move up towards the line sometime after 0200 hours. Maxwell directed Wilf to partner Burt, his new mate on the Lewis gun. Before Wilf had been shipped off to Blighty with trench foot, his partner on the Lewis gun had always been Tom Keenan. Poor old Tom had been knocked while Wilf was away and had been replaced by Burt Edwards, whose mate had also been seriously wounded and was not likely to return.

Burt joined the Eighteenth Battalion at the same time as Wilf. He came from Marrickville in Sydney, had black hair, and was short and stocky; he was very powerful for his size. He was very knowledgeable and talkative in many ways, provided he liked you.

They camped in a very old, small, and disgustingly smelly shed that was wet and muddy inside, but at least they were out of the rain.

Rations were distributed to the men in anticipation of them moving to the front line the next day. Each of the soldiers was instructed to thoroughly check his weapon before dark.

Wilf and Burt went out to the horse-drawn ordnance-carrier, collected their Lewis gun, and took it back to the old shed to clean and check it thoroughly. They then returned the weapon to the carrier, ready for what may come tomorrow. The wind had changed, and the sound of battle was much closer.

Burt filled Wilf in on the changed tactics now being used since General Sir John Monash had taken command of the Australian forces. Previously, the Diggers had been lumped in with both British and French divisions. Monash had been pushing for the command of his own troops for some time. The word being spread around the troops was that Monash wanted to coordinate artillery with small arms, infantry, tanks, as well as airpower. In the past, all units did their own thing according to the plan of the French generals. The improvement was noticed among the men, and morale had improved. It did not mean things were any easier, but the new tactics seemed to achieve better results, which were improving all the time, at Fritz's expense.

The number of Germans wanting to surrender had increased. The number of British tanks now in the line was a huge boost to all of the troops. The big increase in the number of Lewis guns was also a big plus. The numbers of men in the battalions were way down, but they had seven times more Lewis guns now than they did in early 1916.

Wilf said, "Looks like there have been some good improvement made."

"I hope so, but I think we should try and get some sleep."

Both were able to get some sleep in the stench and were awoken at two o'clock and instructed to move out.

It was still raining as they helped themselves to some of their rations before falling in. Instructions were given to those on the Lewis guns as to when they were to collect their weapons. Because of the weight of these guns, about one hundred pounds each, the men were spared the heavy burden until the last few hundred yards before they reached the duckboards.

On the way to the trenches, they had to pass through the town of Ypres. On one side of the street was a continuous stream of weary and dirty Australian soldiers returning from the front. On the other side, Wilf's battalion made their way with full packs, single file to the front.

This was the main street of what was once a beautiful city, where not one building was left standing in the entire town. They had to pick their way over rubble of what was once the largest building in town. The Cloth Hall, from what Wilf could see, had been much larger than Westminster Abbey. All that was left standing was one side of the central tower.

Before they reached the outskirts of the town, the men were ordered to halt and have some biscuits and water. Wilf said to Burt, "Could you ever imagine such destruction as this?"

Burt said, "This was not a small town, but it has been completely obliterated by the Huns. I've an aunty who's married to a Belgian. He came from these parts, and he told me a little about the place before I left home; he knew a lot about its history."

"Does he live in Sydney?"

"Yes, near me in Marrickville. He told me that the Cloth Hall was built in the 1200s, and this building had been the central marketplace for the buying and selling of cloth from all over Belgium."

Wilf said, "Why was a town trading cloth so important to the Huns?"

"The Germans realised early that Ypres stood in their way to take the port cities on the coast, so they needed to take Ypres early. They had done the job of destroying the town, but the British and Australian forces would not let them through to the coast. It's a pitiful sight to see now."

Even whilst they were in this totally destroyed town, they were not out of danger, because the Huns persistently shelled the town from a close semicircle of artillery emplacements around the town.

After leaving the town along the Menin Road, they had to take cover in the never-ending rain for some hours until after dark. Darkness would enable them to pass Hellfire corner, a notoriously dangerous intersection constantly shelled by the Germans from their vantage points on the surrounding hills.

They were now very close to the front line trenches, and the Germans kept up a constant barrage of deadly gas. This made the wearing of gas masks mandatory and a major problem in the rain. Wilf found it pretty near impossible to see where he was going. With rain on the outside of the visor and moisture vapour on the inside, caused by the heavy breathing from the load being carried, he couldn't see. He wasn't on his own. Nor was it easy to see the duckboards, as they were covered in dark Flanders mud, blending with the black of night.

"The Cloth Hall at Ypres before the war."

"Australian troops file past the same destroyed Cloth Hall 1917

"Troops negotiating the duckboards"

"An image of despair."

The importance of wearing a gas mask was impressed upon Wilf in his early introduction to trench life. This was when he saw for the first time a Digger convulsing in excruciating agony, shortly before succumbing to an agonising death. This was the result of mustard or phosgene gas from the Hun's murderous attack. However, even gas attacks from their own shells could suddenly turn back on their own men with an unpredictable change of wind.

Finally they were within the saps that led into the trenches. It had been a terrible night making their way with their heavy loads, along the duckboards over the muddy fields, with only the glow of the exploding shells lighting their path. That in itself would have been bad enough, but with Fritz shelling gas, could it get any worse than this? Wilf didn't think so.

Wounded men were given priority as they were carried away from the front line by the constant stream of medics doing a great job. They laboured on in very trying circumstances, also struggling with the added burden of gas masks. There was usually up to a metre of mud containing bodies of both donkeys and men either side of the narrow boards. The duckboards were about twenty-four inches wide, and sometimes in difficult areas, there were two banks of boards side by side. Wilf was used to balancing on greasy planks to fell large trees, but trying to keep his footing on the slippery surface of the duckboards was a challenge.

Stretcher bearers struggling past with wounded men needed both banks of boards to keep their balance on the constantly moving boards, sometimes suspended over, but floating on water. The chains on either side held them together.

The sounds from the wounded and dying men as they went past were not as bad as had been heard on the trains Wilf had passed. Probably they were still shell-shocked at this stage or high on the relief of morphine. One could be heard crying out for his mother. It was hard to imagine anything being more difficult to do than the work of a stretcher bearer. These boys in some instances were desperately overworked, carrying men away from the line, knowing that a large percentage would not make it to the aid station.

Suddenly they were in the pitch darkness of the trenches. Trying to see out of his mask on the duckboards was one thing, but once in the trenches, it was another thing altogether; it was utterly impossible. The trenches here were about six or seven feet deep, plus the side mounds. The sandbags along the top to make the parapet on the defensive side and the parados on the rear side of the trench meant he was down about eight or nine feet deep in this dark tunnel, without a roof for protection.

The men Wilf's lot were relieving were totally exhausted and could not escape fast enough. The incoming officers and NCOs huddled around in a small group to be briefed on the whereabouts of Fritz's positions and where to expect the main thrust from the enemy. It was now the turn of those being relieved to get away for some well-earned rest before they were given leave. Still they had to get out of this hellhole, and nothing around here was certain. It would still be at least twenty-four hours before they could say they were really "out of there." They had held the line for seven days, and it was now up to the new blokes to take over.

The enemy fire was not that bad at present, probably because it was raining heavily. It always seemed to be raining at the front. However, there was some protection given by the rain because once the rain stopped, the artillery started first, and then the machine guns followed, making the noise unbelievable.

Wilf remembered one time at school when a new water tank had arrived and the old one was put on its side. He climbed into the empty tank, and the rest of the school, a total of eighteen boys and girls, found heavy sticks and beat upon the sides and wouldn't stop until the teacher arrived. That sound had been terrible even when he put his fingers in his ears.

But this sound in the trenches was so much worse and went on day and night, and there was no teacher to bring it to an end. Putting fingers in his ears made no difference at all because the sound didn't enter through the ears only; it penetrated every part of his body and bounced around inside, especially his head. He tried not to even talk or mouth words to another in the din of battle. If you did, the concussion from the explosions was enough to slam your mouth closed. If your tongue happened between your teeth at the time, you bit your tongue—and bad. A sore tongue seemed to be a common ailment whilst in the trenches.

The trenches reminded Wilf of a long rut or grave with the ends kicked out. Very rarely did you find an end; it always twisted and turned in a new direction. It was also a rut and difficult to climb out of; some never did.

It didn't take long for the lice to find new fields to invade. They became constant close companions for the duration whilst in the trenches. They soon got into the men's hair and clothing, and no amount of scratching and personal cleaning overcame the problem. The only sure way to get rid of them was to wait until they got back to camp. Whatever the chemical was that they provided for the bathwater, it did the trick.

From time to time, orders were circulated along the trenches that another attack against the Huns was being planned. The words passed from man to man, "We're going over the top at such and such a time." Every man with a rifle made sure there were ten rounds jammed into the magazine as he moved up onto the fire-step. They were either designated to climb over the bags or be ready to give covering fire to those leaving the trench first, before following after those still trying to move forward.

The agony of waiting dragged on, waiting for the signal to go. An officer moved along, issuing the words nobody wanted to hear, "Zero minus five minutes, men." Men would readjust their webbing or their chin strap, anything that would give them a better chance of beating the enemy. Spare socks were already stuffed down the top of their boots to give the blisters some relief.

Mostly going over the bags happened in the middle of the night in the pitch-black darkness with the green-orange muzzle flashes from Fritz's rifles and machine guns trying to kill you. You couldn't see Fritz because he was always hidden below the parapet of his trench with maybe just the occasional top of his helmet showing, silhouetted against the illuminated background glow of the exploding artillery shells.

What was once a proud farmer's field of tilled soil or crops ready to be harvested had changed into an unrecognisable expanse of utter desolation. From the occasional proud tree giving shade to the cattle, there was now nothing but mud as far as the eye could see. Mud and more mud with the once proud trees reduced to splintered stumps.

When the shells landed and all hell broke loose, the gentle undulating fields with leafy foliage were transformed into overlapping craters. These craters were filled with toxic, poisonous, yellowy filth from the explosives, mixed with the remains of rotting carcasses, waiting to claim forever those who fell helpless into its clutches.

Wilf's whole being was impacted by the relentless noise of the eighteen pounders from behind his own line. The shells screamed overhead, pounding the enemy for over an hour. Then the whistles sounded, and men gave bloodcurdling screams as each man, with bayonet already fixed, sprang into action. The bayonets reflected slivers of light from the flashes of exploding shells as the men scaled the crudely made ladders inside the trench. These ladders were placed there in readiness for the attack. Others climbed without the aid of a ladder, scrambling up the impossible slippery walls of the trench from the firing-step position and over the parapet.

The rattle of the machine guns from both sides added to the deafening, thunderous roar, filling the hearts of all those going over the bags with never-before-known, unimaginable, cold-sweat fear.

A lot of men never made it out of the trench because the Huns were also waiting for the sound of the whistles. Wilf knew that when the Huns heard the whistles and screams, they automatically opened fire along the top line of the trenches opposite.

Making it over the bags without being shot was a miracle. Another problem was being knocked off the ladder by your mate falling from above, watching him make a sickening jerk backwards the moment part of his body rose above the parapet. It was hard to avoid a falling body in the darkness.

Getting through the tangled coils of rusted barbed wire was a nightmare. The Huns had machine guns spitting out savage bursts of lead from left and right, providing raking crossfire from both directions. Their withering fire was directed along the wire, especially at the wire openings that the Huns identified in daylight. This unforgettable sight of mates stopping lead or being knocked by shrapnel large and small, silhouetted against the glow of shells bursting near and far, was something that could not be forgotten.

Sometimes shrapnel or bullets piercing a man's body could cause hands to fly into the air, flinging a gun away in the one movement. Others, hit by non-life-threatening metal, simply fell forward from their crouched, running position into a prostrate heap, head first into the mud. There they could drown in as little as a few inches of water, with the weight of a sixty-pound pack on their back pressing them down into the murderous mud. Others fell into a crater, sometimes to be buried forever by the next exploding shell, never to be found, just missing in action with their identity known only to God.

Wilf looked left and right, and all he could see was a moonscape of stumps interspersed with violent eruptions of earth shooting upwards from all that remained of the defoliated forest. The forest was now a sea of black mud with hundreds of bodies from both sides scattered over no-man's-land. Some warriors were draped over the wire like limp, wet sacks filled with meat, awaiting the next agreed truce. Burial parties then went searching for missing mates, provided they could still be found.

The chance of getting any further than your own wire was not good. If you did, then there were belts of the enemy's wire to negotiate. Once through the wire, you were already on top of the enemy's trenches, firing down at anything perceived to move in the darkness.

In the enemy's trench, you faced different types. If you were really lucky, Fritz was more scared than you and took off through his own trenches and saps. Others were temporarily dead; their brains frozen, they lost the power to think. Then there were the crazies who believed the war could be won in hand-to-hand combat; they lunged, slashing wildly with their bayonets from the moment others dropped into their trench. Their bayonets were fixed before they hopped over the bags, and men died on both sides looking into the eyes of their executioner—often both at the same time.

Sometimes for no explainable reason, the fighting slowed, giving the men a chance to have a drink and a biscuit. Wilf looked over the scene and believed some gains were made, but for how long? At least it gave time for the officers to count their numbers and see how many were left. It was not uncommon to lose 60 per cent of the men, either dead or wounded, in an attack like this. The medics were always behind in their work, both answering the cries for help and tendering first aid, or where possible dragging the bodies back to the trenches.

Burt said to Wilf, "You wait and see; within days, it will be the Hun's turn to counter attack and win back his own trenches."

Wilf replied, "They probably will, and more men will die, but for what purpose?"

"There is no obvious purpose that I can see," said Burt. "This is how this war has been played out in these fields since 1914. Over three years to gain the same muddy, corps-filled trenches that have been in our possession previously. How many times? Nobody appears to keep count."

There were some quiet times in the trenches, allowing men to catch up on repairs to the trench walls, duckboards underfoot, and the filling of fresh sandbags. They reshaped the crumbling fire-steps or re-anchored the sheets of corrugated iron over their favourite sleeping shelf dug into the trench wall. The only unorganised sport was rat-shooting, with a never-ending field of targets to choose from.

To clean one's equipment was always important. Very rarely did they get a chance to boil a billy of tea and have a bite to eat of their favourite dog biscuits or bully-beef. But most important of all, there was the need to relieve one's self, if not already done so in the frenzied heat of battle.

All of this, including the eating of food, would be undertaken with the stench of death gripping them by the throat. There were millions of flies taking time-out from the decaying corpses nearby to feast upon whatever they had in their hands, trying to transfer that morsel to their mouths.

When night descended, there were barbed-wire fences to be repaired in the darkness. Wiring parties were appointed to leave the trench on their bellies, moving across no-man's-land under a sickening fog of death. The aim was not to be heard by Fritz, sometimes only twenty yards away.

Wilf found the coils of barbed wire unbelievably heavy to handle, and they gouged the flesh even when handled carefully. These flesh wounds never healed whilst still in the trench.

The heads of the stakes used to support the wire were pre-wrapped with old sandbags whilst still in the trench. This was to deaden the sound of the hammer striking metal when driving the stake into the mud. Fritz would listen for this sound and would respond, immediately setting off a flare with a deep *woomph* as it jettisoned high above into the night sky. The bright glow would illuminate those unprepared below, trapping them like rabbits caught in the light of a torch.

Only seconds were available for the one kneeling with the hammer to drop immediately onto his belly or be picked off by an observant Hun. Staggered gaps were needed between multiple rows of wire belts twenty-five yards wide to stop Fritz from charging through. Fritz identified the wire gaps in daylight and covered them with raking machine-gun fire, night or day when needed. This produced showers of sparks at night as the bullets hit, but it rarely severed the wire.

Wilf was always thankful to get back into the relative safety of the trench, even if the wiring party's excursion was relatively short lived.

There were times during daylight when things were too quiet for Maxwell, and he looked for opportunities to do his stuff. Wilf had heard stories about some of Joe's exploits, but on this occasion, he witnessed his actions firsthand. Joe hid his revolver down the back of his belt and then waved a white rag on a stick above the parapet for some fifteen minutes. When he thought it safe, he gingerly climbed over the bags, made his way slowly through the wire, waving his flag. He approached the enemy's dugout about twenty-five yards away and with his winning smile and demeanour attempted to make conversation.

He casually lit a cigarette and offered one to his opposite number. When he knew he had Fritz's confidence and knew they were sufficiently relaxed, he slowly put down his flag, flat on the ground. Then in the process of rising to his feet, he whipped out his revolver and sprang into action. He was decorated for this action. Whilst Maxwell was thought by some to be careless for his own safety, he always took great care of the other blokes under his command.

How could Wilf explain this sort of thing to Ann or Teen or even his mother? He always had trouble explaining in letters just how bad things were. Even if he did his very best with all the most descriptive adjectives he could muster from his school days, it still didn't do justice to this indescribable hell called the Western Front. And besides, he didn't want to tell them just how bad things really were.

Why put more worry onto the ones you love? It would be bad enough for them reading newspaper reports about someone else's son or father or brother or lover who had suffered under these indescribable conditions. They should not be told about the constant torture of the artillery and machine-gun fire, booming all around while trying to shelter or even sleep in a water-filled, muddy trench. Let alone the dark, rainy nights struggling to breathe inside a gas mask, especially with the enemy in another trench only twenty-five yards away, trying his best to kill you.

The shells the troops dreaded most were the drop-shorts from their own artillery. They made a different buzzing sound as they tumbled end over end and put fear into every man. It was the fear of not knowing whether the tumbling shell would drop short nearby—or even land in your own trench.

His company, as part of the Eighteenth Battalion, held their ground for seven days before they too were to be relieved. Seven days and nights with so little sleep, and what sleep you did get was in water-soaked, smelly clothes under a constant cacophony of ordinance exploding around about them or whizzing overhead, sometimes from both sides.

Just like the previous three years of battle, very little ground had been gained or lost. Tens of thousands of men's lives blown to pieces and their personal effects sent off home with a letter to their next of kin, although not always. The usual effects sent home consisted of a diary, a small Bible, some badges, and an identification disc and chain removed from around their neck. Plus whatever else that man held dear to him that could be carried in his kitbag without it adding too much weight. Other common articles included some touristy artefacts he had purchased while on leave or some trench art that he had been shaping to kill time in the trenches when the enemy wasn't actively doing his best to kill him.

The battalion's relief arrived. They now had to foot-slog back to support camp for a rest and then be transported back to base camp at Fletre, before getting ten days' leave. All Wilf could think about as he trudged through the mud was, *I've survived another battle, and how long before I can get my mail, especially, and hopefully, from Ann.*

The majority of their company had survived this stunt, but many other companies were not so fortunate. The battalion strength was diminishing fast, down to less than four hundred men from over nine hundred at the beginning.

By the time Wilf was allocated a bunk in the support camp, he got very little sleep. He then stood all the way in the back of the truck on the way back to base camp. On arrival, he was allocated his tent, and he was too weary to walk the extra hundred yards or so to enquire about his mail; it would have to wait until morning. Wilf dropped onto his bunk and slept for nineteen hours.

Chapter 11

The barracks weren't flashy, but anything was better than where Wilf had been. After awaking from his long sleep, he needed to get himself cleaned up before enquiring about his mail. The lice were driving him mad; he could not stop scratching. And besides, he couldn't stand his own smell. Nor could he walk very well either; his old football-knee injury was giving him curry. He knew he had no choice, bad knee or not, and set out for the ablutions block for a big scrub-down.

Wilf was aware that he had a heap of washing to be done before going on leave for ten days, but getting hold of his mail took precedent; he could not wait to get his hands on Ann's letters. It took nearly two hours of waiting before he got his bundle.

He believed that if his surname started with an A rather than Y, life would be much easier, with a lot of time waiting around avoided. He was nearly always last in any queue where names were read out in alphabetical order. Eventually, it was his turn, and after catching the bundle thrown to him, he scanned the envelopes quickly. Yes, there were about six envelopes with British stamps.

The letters from England were easy to identify because they were all the same size with a stamp bearing the king's photo, usually all the same red colour. The letters from Australia also had the king's stamps, but the envelopes were different shapes and sizes. He could not wait to get back to his tent to start reading through the pile. There was now a new spring in his step, despite his bad knee.

Wilf eagerly slit open the envelopes as he walked. He bounced onto his bunk and sorted Ann's letters into date order. He identified the earliest letter and then lay back and read.

My dearest Wilf,

How I miss you and cannot wait until you are safely back to our home again and even better still, safe in my arms again after this terrible war ends. There is a very special place waiting for you inside my arms. They're so lonely without you.

How I hated leaving you at the parade ground yesterday. I don't want to distress you too much by telling you how long I cried for after I left you and went back to King's. I will simply say that I love you and miss you so much.

The only way I think I will be able to get to sleep when I finish this letter will be to think about all the wonderful times we have had together. This will probably cause me to cry even more than I'm doing now as I write and cause me to eventually fall asleep. I hope so anyway.

We received a new batch of soldiers last night on my first shift back. A lot of them are also Diggers. My heart breaks every time I see a new wounded soldier. Horrible thoughts flash through my mind thinking it could be you. I'm so grateful that you had trench foot and not some other ghastly, disfiguring injury. One Digger was from your battalion, I think. His name is Arthur Williams. I must ask him when I get a chance if he knows you. Right now, he is not fit to talk to, but he will be okay.

I didn't knock off my shift until nearly three o'clock this morning. Things were quite chaotic, and it made it near impossible for me to keep focussed on my job, thinking always about you.

Dawn is now breaking, but I still haven't told you everything. I don't want to stop writing yet because it brings me closer to you.

Ann's letter continued, but Wilf paused. Sometimes he needed to go back and read some of the earlier details, either to get the sequence of events right in his head or simply because he just loved reading that part over and over; it gave him goose bumps. In a later letter, he read:

Mother and Father are constantly asking for news from you; I think you have truly won both of them. Mavis next door also keeps asking if I've had recent news from you. Things are not good between her and her husband, as I've told you before. I had a day in the city with Mavis on my last day off. We went shopping, but there is not much available in the shops; I think most clothing factories are busy making military clothing.

Dad keeps a good watch on the drainage from the shelter. I can't tell you how many men he has sent over to have a look at the shelter; he is very proud of your handiwork.

Another letter included news of another air raid:

> *On my last day off, the sirens sounded again, and we made our first real use of the shelter. Only Mum and I were home, but Mavis also came running and joined us in the shelter.*
>
> *The shelter was perfect; the door was not difficult to put into place from the inside, and the lamp was just the thing to eliminate the scariness of the darkness. Mavis suggested we should put some magazines in there. She is not normally good in the dark, but she handled the experience quite well. Mum was no trouble at all. It was a little like the girls' day out really. It turned out to be a bit of fun in the end because no bombs dropped anywhere near us that we could hear. It did draw me closer to you though, and the others also asked me to express their thanks to you.*
>
> *Dad convinced Mr. Gooch to build a shelter along the same lines at the back of the Hardware Store, to be used by staff and customers in the event of such an emergency. Thomo was given the job along with the help of another couple of the chaps. He came over here one day to make a couple of sketches because he had not seen the finished job; he was impressed with the simplicity of the door. Thomo was instructed to finish it quickly as a matter of urgency. It is much longer than yours and holds a total of eighteen people comfortably, or twenty-four at a pinch.*

Dad explained to Mr. Gooch that the design was by one of his daughter's patients from the hospital who had firsthand experience building dug-out shelters on the Western Front. Other store owners came to see the finished shelter with plans to do the same thing at their premises. I said they should be called Wilf Shelters because they were simple to build and anyone could build them if they followed your plan. Dad had one of his men make a proper drawing of the shelter, with simple how-to-build construction details. The plan will be made available to their customers along with a list of materials, which they can supply. Dad said Gooch's could do good business out of the shelters, and you should get some reward for your design. When you come back after the war, I will make a special trip and introduce you to Mr. Gooch; I understand he is a very nice man.

Wilf stopped reading for a spell while he took in what he had already read. He felt pleased that the shelter was successful and already used, even though for what sounded like a false alarm. That was the best part.

Ann's letters were filled with lots of news from the hospital and about attacks on other parts of Britain "by those horrible Germans." However, the letters were also filled with Ann telling Wilf how much she missed him and what she wanted to do the next time they were together. Her words were always positive, believing that the war would end soon. Then they could get on with their lives without the constant news in the papers telling of the human slaughter and the reality she knew of only too well at the hospital, the sufferings caused by this terrible war.

There were another three letters from his mother, including some new, warm socks she had knitted, one each from his four sisters, one from Teen, plus another from her sister Alma Bisset, and another six from different friends from around the district and old school friends.

The one from Teen started off:

> *Dear Wilf,*
>
> *Thank you for your last letter. It is always good to hear from you; at least I know you are all right and can share the good news with my family who ask about you frequently and of course the girls at work also. I'm especially glad to know you are safe and doing well.*
>
> *Your last letter told me you were in hospital, had seen some wonderful sights, and were about to return to the front; hearing you had not been injured was a bonus. I look forward to hearing about the special sights you saw in London. I can only imagine what it must be like to see such famous places. When you're back home, which I hope won't be too far off, I think you will be in heavy demand from people wanting to hear of your experiences. I hope you can find the time to write me about some of those places.*
>
> *You will remember, I'm sure, that when I met you for that one and only time, my six sisters and I were there to see-off one of the boys from the church. He departed on the same ship as you. I know you didn't get to meet him on the wharf and probably not on the ship either. I'm sad to advise you that we received*

> *news yesterday to say he was killed in action somewhere on the Western Front.*
>
> *Bad news seems to be happening everywhere these days, and I hope you will be kept safe so we can meet again after your return. Writing is one thing, but to be able to have a chat with you would be special.*

Every soldier needed a friend like Teen to keep up one's spirits when things were not going well so far from home. She continued with details of important happenings at the shirt factory and her church. She asked if Wilf had run into her old friend John Ridley; he was also serving in that same area.

He was also pleased to receive a letter from Teen's sister Alma; she had only written a few times previously. Alma was Teen's closest sister, just two years younger. She was quite a wag and was always pushing Teen to the fore, and in the middle of the letter, Alma wrote:

> *I want you to remember that I was the one who carried your kitbag to the wharf. However, Teenie is the middle of us sisters and for a very good reason. That's because she is the one with the most caring and good-natured personality. Teenie is the one who always acts as the peacemaker in our family. She steps in and prevents quarrels that can sometimes happen in large families, especially those comprising seven girls.*
>
> *I suppose Teenie has told you that our mum is a Scot of strong character, and she needs to be. Our father, who we never see, took to the drink in a big way and left Mum to bring up us seven girls on her own. I think she has done a magnificent job.*

He finished reading his mail just as the bugle sounded for tea. Wilf folded the letters; no doubt he would return to them again when he had time to spare. There was not enough light left to start writing letters after tea, so he would wait until they arrived at their new location at Hazelbrouck in two days' time; tomorrow had to be washing day.

He was not sure yet which towns were being allocated for leave. He did know that tomorrow they would be given their ten days' leave to do whatever they wanted. Wilf's first priority was to spend the first day writing letters.

The next morning, the trucks arrived to take them to the station and the train journey to Hazelbrouck. From there were three choices to be made. No1 was to Bethune where there were lots of pubs; many of the blokes couldn't get there quickly enough. No2 was to Amiens where Wilf had already been, and No3 was to Beauvais. This was further away and closer to Paris. He wasn't sure if he would get to Paris, but it sounded good. He selected Beauvais.

The other reason for Wilf to choose Beauvais was that it was closer to Peronne where they were required to report after their leave. They did not necessarily always go back to the same place but to where the planners in head office decided they were needed most. It was always harder to find his own way back to the Battalion; another good reason for choosing Beauvais.

On the way, their train passed through a large town called Bethune, and they crossed over the Bray-Sur-Somme. Looking out over the river, he wasn't sure if he was upstream or downstream from the battlefield but could not stop thinking how much blood would be mixed with the water if the river was downstream.

The journey was about one hundred kilometres in total, but they seemed to travel faster and more often than on his last journey. They arrived just at dark and were advised, among other things by the marshals, that the YMCA was right next to the station; that is where Wilf headed.

The YMCA was the foremost volunteer agency providing support in many different ways to the troops. Mainly this support was to the soldiers on leave, but they also had mobile soup and tea kitchens up close to the front line. This resulted in many casualties amongst their people, and medals were awarded to those prepared to go the extra mile, helping the troops in dangerous situations. Wilf headed to the desk and enquired about accommodation, which they were happy to offer. He had a good meal and an early night. He was still feeling the after-effects of his time at the front and the journey back. He slept well and rose later than was normal and enjoyed a relaxed breakfast.

This place was so quiet compared to the noise of the camps and of course the roar of the battlefield. It seemed just like the place of refuge it was meant to be. There were many different types of activities available, including quiet reading rooms with an abundance of reading material available. There was a writing room with all Wilf needed to catch up on his letters. Postal services, games rooms, entertainment in the concert halls, chapels with padres for those needing counselling or just wanting to talk. Most important of all, the canteens were always open.

After breakfast, Wilf headed to the writing room with his stack of mail to spend the day writing. However, when he looked at the bright sunshine outside, he decided it would be better to be outdoors today because two fine days in a row in this part of the world were not common.

When he returned from his day out, he immediately started his letter to Ann, telling her about his visit to the cathedral and other places of interest. He was pleased with his earlier decision to spend the day outdoors because it rained hard all the second day. He spent the rest of the day writing letters to home, and after finishing, decided there was enough time to get to Paris and back over the next few days before reporting for duty again. This was a journey he had never envisioned making, but here was the opportunity right now. He checked the details at the support desk and set off the next morning to see Paris.

Chapter 12

Ann came home in search of a letter from Wilf as she now often did. Mrs. Davis saw her coming and rushed to the front door saying, "You're going to be happy, Ann. I'm already happy knowing Wilf must be okay because his hand-writing is on the envelopes; there are a few letters from Wilf."

So excited was Ann ripping open the first envelope that she nearly ripped the letter inside. There were many pages.

Mrs. Davis said, "You read the letters while I get you some tea." Ann trembled with excitement as she moved into the lounge room to read the earliest letter first.

My dearest Ann,

How I have missed you. It was so good to get back from the line safely once again and to find your letters waiting. I love reading your letters and do so over and over.

I miss you terribly and wish I could be there with you. I'm currently on leave in Beauvais, and every waking thought is about you. My love for you grows stronger each day. I hope you are well and so too your mother and father. Please tell them I also think of them; they're such special people.

Earlier on, I was not keen to visit any of the famous Cathedrals without you, but I looked at it a different way and decided to make the visit and then describe my visit in detail to you. I was told at the YMCA desk the most important building of historical significance in town is the Cathedral of Saint Peter de Beauvais. So today I visited this place, and I hope describing it to you in detail will help draw us together. It was nevertheless hard without you there as my guide. Maybe it will help us both to revisit in our minds those days we shared together in London.

As I approached the cathedral, I was overcome by the sheer size of this place. This town is nowhere near the size of London but has a cathedral that is enormous. I first of all wandered around the outside before venturing inside. It was extremely high, and I later learned from the guide, who spoke very good English, that it is 159 feet high. This is a skyscraper compared to the tallest buildings back home, which are no more than fifteen to nineteen feet high including the chimney; this one is ten times higher. I thought as I looked up at the narrow, ornate columns that they seemed to completely surround the basic structure and hide what would be the interior shape of the church.

My mind was full of questions to ask when a chance came along. When I visited other cathedrals on my own in the past, such as the

Amiens Cathedral, I did not have the same interest in the history of such places. This new interest has been awakened within me as a result of the places such as Westminster Abbey and the houses of Parliament in London; you're to blame, darling.

When I first ventured inside the large doors, my breath was taken away by the sheer beauty before me. The sunlight was streaming in through the magnificent stained-glass windows, highlighting the high arches, the astronomical clock, and the most elaborate of tapestries. Then there was the ornate marbled floor and the elaborate timberwork, which is always of special interest to me as a timber cutter.

I wished at the time there was some way of capturing such beauty to show to you, but I do not believe even the newest camera's available could do justice to such a huge building. I had to stand in the middle of the church, enabling me to see such beauty all around for 360 degrees from floor to ceiling. The ceiling was so far above that it was hard to pick out the detail. The usual thoughts were going over and over in my mind. How did they build it? How did they get the stone arches to stay in place and for so long?

I listened to the guide as best I could and learned that they started to construct the cathedral in 1226. The building suffered tragedy on two occasions when the tower, still under construction, collapsed, once on top of the congregation. Such was the destruction that they decided not to continue with the tower, and that was the reason the building looks so different on the outside compared to all of the other cathedrals I've seen. I also learned that the cathedral was considered to never have been completed because it has no naïve. I'm not sure what part that is because where I come from in the bush, the only church of any size I'm acquainted with is a little wooden Baptist church, built in 1859 in the small community of Thalabah where I was born, close to Dungog. It's not even big enough to be called a village. It holds 160 people, including those sitting on the windowsills for special occasions.

This Cathedral is only about sixty kilometres from the Amiens Cathedral and was built about the same time. I kept asking myself the same question: how did the people afford to build such massive churches so many years ago? I can't imagine any government today paying such a bill. This cathedral is considered to be in some respects the most daring achievement of Gothic architecture in the world. The choir is referred to as the Pantheon of French Gothic architecture. I don't recall from my history lessons anything about the Pantheon, but the guide said it was one of the oldest buildings in Rome, predating the time of Christ.

The builders of this cathedral were unable to continue with this much-too-ambitious cathedral design in 1573 after the tower collapsed. The planned tower height of 502 feet would have made the cathedral the second tallest building in the world at that time, second only to St. Olaf's Church in Tallinn, Estonia.

I made a lot of notes while the tour guide was speaking. I will keep them and send some of the details home to family. I wish there was some easy way of making extra copies for my family and friends.

This cathedral is the main attraction in town but not the only cathedral. I did wander around to see what else made up such a town, but couldn't help thinking how many other towns must have had such grand buildings before the war started. Many are now piles of rubble, some never to be rebuilt. What a tragedy to see buildings like these completely destroyed by this senseless war.

Ann continued to read Wilf's long letter; she was so thrilled with the trouble Wilf had taken to share his visit to the cathedral with her. She returned to the kitchen and handed the middle four pages to her mother and said, "You should read this, Mother, while I read the next one."

Ann moved back to the lounge room to read over the special pages once again before opening the next envelope. There was some more personal content, just for Ann to read. As she finished reading, Mrs. Davis came in with the tea.

Ann said, "You will be very interested in this part also, Mother. He has gone to lot of trouble with his explanation about those words in 'Waltzing Matilda' that we talked about."

Wilf's letter read in part:

> *I told you when I first went to your home that I would explain to you some time the meaning of the words of the Australian song "Waltzing Matilda." Well now I have the time, so I will do my best.*
>
> *First of all, Matilda is a common girl's name in Germany. It is also the name given to a gadget-cupboard in a German kitchen. In the last century, Australia received many German immigrants who were good engineering tradesmen. They didn't speak very good English, and things were tough, and they found it hard to get a regular job. So they carried their tools in a bag and walked from farm to farm looking for odd jobs, sharpening saws, axes, scissors, knives, and the like.*
>
> *Men who walk around the bush looking for work in Australia usually carry over their shoulder a tightly rolled piece of waterproof canvas and a blanket which they use for bedding. In Australia, this roll is called a swag; hence the man is called a swagman.*
>
> *Over the swagman's other shoulder is slung a sugar bag containing maybe some food (tucker), so that is called his tucker-bag.*
>
> *I've underlined the important words for you because they are all used in this Australian song.*

Now because this bag of tools was quite heavy, some of the German swagmen used their brains to save their backs and made a tool-box on wheels for their tools and called it their Matilda, like the gadget cupboard back home. They added a handle or strap and pulled it behind them on the dusty outback roads.

In the German language, a roller is called a walz, so when the roller or wheel is rolling, they say it's walzen. The song says "you'll come a waltzing Matilda with me." A lot of people even in Australia can't understand why a swagman would have a dancing partner out in the bush with him; well he didn't. It was his toolbox Matilda that went rolling with him along the road.

This gets quite complicated, so I hope you hang in there and understand.

The song says, "He stuffed a jumbuck in his tucker bag." A jumbuck is a small sheep; he was stealing his next meal. The song also says he went down and jumped into the billabong. That's a stagnant pool in the bend of the river that only flows in the wet season. He was running away from the trooper (policeman) with his stolen jumbuck.

Now I think I've covered all of the strange words in the song. If you understand all of this you'll know more about the song than the average Australian.

When Mrs. Davis finished reading the explanation, she handed it back to Ann saying, "It certainly makes a lot more sense than before. I'll need to read it over again some time to fully understand all of those Australian words."

Chapter 13

Wilf returned from Paris with a book full of notes about the places he had seen. He needed a couple of days just to put into writing to Ann and the folks at home some of the sights he had seen in Paris. The architecture of the government buildings was outstanding and very clean. Wilf also learned that Paris was virtually unscathed from the German bombs, not like the damage inflicted on London.

He had also been told that there were over twenty-five thousand monuments in Paris. He had only seen a minute fraction of the total number, but what he had seen was impressive nevertheless.

There was insufficient time to start describing Paris in the few brief letters he now had time to write, on this his last day of leave at the YMCA. In the late afternoon, he rested a little and spent time thinking about his future life together with Ann. Tomorrow it would be off once again to his unit and then back to the front for another of many stunts.

He lay there on his bunk, his head flooded with thoughts of Ann, wondering what she was doing right now. He wished he was back at Whidbourne Street. Even being close together with Ann in the shelter would be better than separated from her by this dreadful war that was destined to continue—for how long, he had no idea.

Wilf returned to the line once more, and the cold conditions were unbearable. Word was going around that this was the coldest winter in these parts for fifty years. Some handled the freezing conditions of winter better than others.

Now they were nearly through winter, but the cold had weakened so many, and some were shipped out to hospitals with pneumonia. Wilf was one of them. His condition was pretty bad, and the doctor decided to ship him back to Blighty again.

Wilf was in a bad state all of the way and was oblivious as to his surroundings a lot of the time. He did wake a couple of times and knew there was a train journey because he remembered being carried by stretcher over some rail tracks before being loaded onto a train. He also recalled waiting in the sun before being hauled up high on some sort of platform with other sick soldiers, onto the deck of a boat. After three days of travelling, he eventually arrived, completely unaware of his surroundings at the King's College Hospital at Denmark Hill; he was checked into ward seven on the second floor.

Ann was still working her usual ward number three on the ground floor and had no idea Wilf was in the hospital until his second day, when she saw his name on the admissions list. Her heart skipped many beats as she bounded up the stairs to make sure it was her Wilf. As soon as she entered the ward, she could see it was and came to his bedside. Before making any attempt to communicate, she read the doctor's report hanging on the foot rail. She studied it carefully to find the reason for his admission was pneumonia; she was immediately concerned to find that his condition was quite serious.

After advising the head nurse of the ward the reason for her being there, Ann came again to the side of the bed and very gently lifted his hand into hers. She considered just how lucky she was to have him back in one piece, even though in a very bad state. She soon had to return to her ward but planned to make regular visits until Wilf awoke.

It wasn't until late on the third day when Ann came to the bed that she again took his hand and brushed his cheek with the back of her other hand. She sensed a slight stirring, and after checking that there were no other nurses in the ward, she leaned over and kissed his forehead. As she did, Wilf opened his eyes.

Ann whispered, "You're not seeing an angel, Wilf. It's me, Ann."

He open and closed his eyes a few times. It took some time before he fully understood who it was; a look of peace came over his face.

Ann whispered again, "Please continue to rest. If you wake and don't see me around, just remember I won't be far away. I'll keep checking on you."

She was due to finish her shift soon and called around again when finished. Wilf was sleeping peacefully. Ann went to see the nurse in charge and told her the story. She wrote down her room number in the nurse's quarters, saying, "I want to be contacted during the night should there be any change for the worse."

"I'll take good care of him, Ann. you go and get some sleep."

Ann was bubbling over with excitement and found it very difficult to get to sleep. Her mind was working overtime planning how to make the most of his stay in the hospital. She needed to get a message to her mother quickly. Of course there was also the period of convalescence to think about after he was discharged from the hospital. Ann knew she needed the rest due to the very long hours she had been working and eventually drifted off into a deep sleep filled with nice dreams.

The next morning, Ann was up earlier than usual. She dressed and went straight to the second floor. As she entered the doorway, she looked directly to his bed to see that he was already awake. He still wasn't in good shape, but the look on his face said everything as he saw Ann coming to his bedside. Ann gave him a gentle hug saying, "You have no idea how thrilled I am to see you again, my love, even in spite of the circumstances."

Wilf looked long into her eyes and slowly said, "It's great for me too," as his emotions got control of his lips.

Ann kept fussing over him, his pillow, and his bedclothes, in between kissing his hand. Ann left him in no doubt that he was back again in her heaven.

Ann stayed for half an hour doing most of the chatting, before reporting for duty back in ward three. After going through the normal transfer procedures with the finishing nurse, she hurried through the urgent duties and then slipped out to visit the registrar.

She explained the situation and said, "I'm looking for a favour. Could Wilf be transferred down to ward three where I can take care of him myself? It would be better than ducking up the stairs all of the time."

The registrar replied, "It would be an honour for me to help you under these circumstances." The swap was arranged for later that day. Ann found it hard to contain her excitement and hurriedly went to tell Wilf the news.

She approached his bed with a glow on her face and lifted his hand, saying, "I've got some good news. They're going to transfer you down to my ward this afternoon for me to take care of you." Wilf nodded his head. It didn't matter what Ann was saying; he was so happy to have her taking care of him. "Now you will be my patient."

Ann returned to her own ward and advised the other girls what was happening. They were all aware of the relationship when Wilf returned to the front and kept a keen interest in Ann's regular news stories. Now he was back here again, and there was heightened interest. The girls on the other shift also needed to be advised of the change.

After Wilf arrived in ward three, things got very busy. Sometimes Ann found it hard to give him the extra attention she had promised. There were other times when things slowed a little, so she took advantage of those slack periods.

Wilf was slowly improving, so after a few days when Ann came on duty, she said, "The other nurses tell me you are doing so well that I think you should be making your own bed."

Wilf detected the light-hearted humour in her approach and replied, "I would love nothing better than to do that. Thanks again for your loving care."

Ann took a glance around the ward and saw she was the only staff member in the ward. She leaned over and kissed him for longer than she knew she should and said, "I love you, my darling."

Ann was already planning to take some time off when he was to be discharged. Each time she had even a minute to spare, she would call by his bed. They would exchange little pieces of stories as they had on Wilf's previous stay, but now they were not as formal as before. From her experience, it would probably be a total of ten days before Wilf would be well enough to be discharged. If he had been a civilian patient, he would probably be out within the week, but because he was a foreign soldier without proper care at home, he would be kept longer.

Ann took the risk and made an application for leave to coincide with his expected release. She had already asked Hazel to drop by her home and tell her mother the latest news. She said, "Tell Mother I will be taking two weeks off when Wilf is discharged, but I will stay at the hospital in the meantime." Normally she would go home for one evening to tell her mother any good news, but she did not want to leave Wilf. All of her off-duty time was spent sitting alongside his bed chatting.

Hazel came back the next day to say, "Mr. and Mrs. Davis will come and visit Wilf on Sunday afternoon." Both Ann and Wilf were pleased to hear the news; he had a lot of warm affection for both of them, even though they had only had a short time to get to know each other on his last visit.

On Sunday afternoon, the Davises arrived as planned, and after the welcome back and the usual small talk, Mrs. Davis said, "When you are released, Wilf, I understand from talking to Hazel that you will need a week or two to recuperate. We want you to stay with us. We also have a nice surprise for the two of you."

Wilf said, "What you have just told me I think is pretty special, Mrs. Davis. Thank you so much."

"No, we have something extra for you. Because of the great job you made of the shelter ensuring our safety, which thankfully has only been used once, we want to do something extra-special for you. We want to give you both a trip down to Devon with accommodation at the Headland Hotel in Torquay for a couple of nights."

Ann was so excited as she threw her arms first around her mother then her father. She kissed them on the cheeks, saying, "Thank you, Mother. Thank you, Father. This is so exciting."

Mr. Davis said, "The Headland Hotel is where we spent our honeymoon, and as it was such a special place for us, we want you both to enjoy the first-class experience the hotel provides."

Wilf was speechless. When Ann finished expressing her appreciation, Wilf said, "I really don't know how to say thank you because I've never had such a generous offer presented to me before. I'm really grateful to you both, and I promise to take good care of your daughter."

Mr. Davis said, "This hotel was built for the Romanovs, the Russian Royal Family back in the mid-1800s as a private holiday home, but it was turned into a hotel not long before we were married. Somebody did tell us that it was then turned into a hospital for a period, but it is back as a hotel now. We thought the sea air would be good for Wilf's recovery."

"I'm sure it will be," said Ann.

Mrs. Davis added, "Can I also suggest that you go to Glastonbury, which Ann knows we also visited on our honeymoon. It's not far out of the way, and it is a very special place. Bath is also very interesting."

"I will leave all of those details to Ann," said Wilf.

After the Davises left the hospital, Ann was so excited she did a little jig around the bed. This was not her normal way of expressing her excitement. Wilf too was excited, but as yet, he knew very little about these places, only what he had learned in the last hour.

Ann said, "I will start planning how we will get there and what other places we could visit on the way. I will speak to one of the other nurses in one of the other wards who grew up in Devon. She should know what else to visit while down that way."

Wilf said, "The names of the places mentioned are completely new to me, but I trust you completely to make the arrangements."

"I do know that it would be less than a day's travel by train, so I will get some information together and start planning."

"It sounds awfully exciting to me," he said.

"As soon as it is confirmed when you are to be released, I will make the booking. In the meantime, I will visit an agency near the station to get all the travel information."

Wilf made good progress under Ann's personal care, and the doctor confirmed to Ann that as Wilf was already up and walking he could see no reason why he could not be discharged on the following Saturday.

Ann was already thinking ahead and did not want to be trapped like on the last occasion when Wilf made such rapid progress. She knew the doctor very well and explained her involvement and what they proposed to do. He then put on his report that the patient would require a further minimum of fourteen days convalescence after discharge before reporting back to the barracks.

Ann said to the doctor, "Thanks for the special favour. I plan for Wilf to come home to our place for a week after he is discharged before we set off for Devon."

"I'm only too glad to help you, Nurse Davis, because you have been of great help to me on so many occasions."

Wilf continued to make excellent progress and was discharged on Saturday as planned. Ann had succeeded in obtaining the next two weeks off, which still left some leave up her sleeve if needed later. Ann arranged for a taxi to pick them up at the hospital. Wilf was still a little wonky, and Ann did not want to overdo things.

When they arrived home, Mrs. Davis gave Wilf a big hug and a cool drink before bringing in a tray with a cake she had baked especially for his homecoming. While she was out of earshot, Wilf said to Ann, "Your mother is such a darling, and you are so much like her in many ways."

"Thank you for the compliment." They all sat in the living room and chatted for hours, catching up on all of the news, but more importantly about the places they would visit down south.

Mr. Davis arrived home and could not wait to tell Wilf, "Gooch's have sold your shelter kit and plan to over 140 customers, both for domestic and commercial shelters. We could have sold more, but getting enough materials in this time of restrictions is very difficult."

"I'm glad it has been successful for the store," said Wilf.

"I even have a copy of the construction sheet for you to see. You can keep it as a souvenir."

"Maybe Wilf could take it back to the front to show his mates how his little project to help this family has progressed as a nice little extra business for Gooch's Hardware Store," commented Mrs. Davis.

Ann opened up her folder of plans for the next week, including timetables and pictures of attractions and places to stay. The Davises made comments about the different places Ann planned to visit. She had lots of questions; Wilf mostly just listened.

Ann said, "I need to check on what clothes to get ready during this coming week."

Mrs. Davis said, "I'm one step in front of you and have been doing some sewing for you in anticipation."

"Oh, thank you, Mother. You are so sweet. I'll take Wilf up to the spare room."

As they entered the room, Ann said, "Mother has rearranged the room, I see."

The oak cupboard, designated as a shelter in case of an air raid, had been removed and recently replaced by a smaller and more practical low chest of draws.

Wilf said, "They have gone to a lot of trouble for me; they didn't need to do that."

"They must have thought you were worth it. Besides, now with the new shelter, they didn't need that heavy, old cupboard anyway."

Wilf and Ann enjoyed a lazy week around the house, plus some progressively longer walks as the week progressed. At the end of the week, Ann said to her mother, "I'm amazed how well Wilf is. I think he is back to normal already."

Mrs. Davis replied, "Well it will be good to get away from here and keep him away from those army doctors. We don't want a repeat of the last visit."

"You don't need to remind me of that, Mother. Wilf and I will be going to church in the morning. After church, I want him to meet some of the soldiers you will be providing lunch for, as well of some of our regulars."

"That will be nice. We will be leaving at ten o'clock. I don't need to be there early in the morning."

Most of the folk at church knew about Wilf from the stories Mr. Davis had told about the shelter and were very warm towards Wilf. Mr. Davis introduced Wilf to their services coordinator, who knew a lot of the troops and in turn introduced Wilf to them. Wilf was able to listen to their experiences as well as share some of his own stories with many of the men. Most of them were Tommies (British Army) with some having served close to the same area of Ypres where Wilf had spent so much time.

They all wanted to know why he and the other Australians would come so far to fight for England, and especially for France. Wilf explained that the AIF (Australian Infantry Forces) men were all volunteers. The money they were paid by the government was so much better than they could earn back home. Back home, most men would only receive about eight shillings per week for labouring jobs. But in the army, privates received six shillings per day.

One of the fellows who hadn't said a word so far piped up, saying, "Six shillings per day? It's more than we get, too bloomin' right it is. I think we get robbed, and we don't have a choice about volunteering either."

Wilf learned that the Aussie Diggers were paid much better than any of the other countries involved on the side of the Allies. Nobody had any idea how it compared with what the Germans and Austrians were paid.

Wilf said, "Now that the Americans are finally getting into war, maybe they will be paid more."

One Tommy said, "The only reason the Americans are entering the war is because of that telegram intercepted between the German and Mexican governments recently."

"What was that about? I haven't heard about that," said Wilf.

"From what I read, Germany wanted to make an alliance with Mexico guaranteeing to help Mexico regain Texas, New Mexico, and Arizona. America panicked and decided they should get involved against Germany."

"I can understand them doing that," said Wilf as he noticed Ann signalling in the other corner. "Well, chaps, I've appreciated the chat. I'm being signalled that it is time to go. Keep safe. I hope to meet you again some time."

Mid-afternoon, they made their way home.

They had a light tea, and Ann helped with the dishes. Mr. Davis, as usual, wanted to know more from Wilf about the front. They chatted for a little while, discussing some of the fellows they met that day.

Mrs. Davis said to Ann, "Why don't you and Wilf take a short walk together, but remember not too far. You've got an early start tomorrow."

Ann replied with her good-natured humour, "Maybe we could go and sit in the shelter; it would be quite cosy."

Ann broke up the discussion and took Wilf by the hand, saying, "Time to go; the war cabinet meeting will have to wait. You fellows have had all afternoon to sort out this war."

They walked out the door into what was a clear moonlit night. They finished up in Argyle Square, which Ann often jokingly referred to as her own neighbourhood shrine of remembrance.

During their time of chatting, Wilf said, "I've really loved getting to know your parents better this week; they're truly lovely people."

"Don't worry; they think you are pretty special too." The evening was quite warm; no need for overcoats like last time. Ann threw her arms around Wilf, and they kissed and hugged for quite some time before returning home.

As they approached the front door, Ann said, "I'm so excited about this trip. I keep thinking I must be dreaming."

"How do you think I feel to have such a wonderful experience bestowed upon me? Nobody will believe me back home when I try and explain. There's no way the boys in the unit will believe me either, that's for sure. I had enough trouble trying to convince them last time how you looked after me; they reckoned I was making it up about you."

The house was all quiet. Ann locked the door, saying quietly, "We need to be up at five for breakfast in order to catch the train at around seven to Waterloo station. Our train south from Waterloo leaves at eight fifteen and arrives at Torquay after lunch. Mum said she would pack us a lunch."

Wilf picked up the lamp and led the way up the stairs, whispering, "I think we still have time for one more cuddle, don't we?" He felt Ann's hand give a little squeeze; he took that for a yes.

Chapter 14

They boarded the train to Exeter and took their choice of seats on the right-hand side. Ann had never been southwest to Exeter before, so she was not sure which would be the sunny side during the morning. Wilf, being from the bush, always knew where the sun would be.

He said, "I think you have done well. The sun should be on the eastern side, providing the train is always heading south." As it turned out, the train was heading southwest, so it was perfect to keep the sun off the window most of the time.

"I've had a good teacher, don't you think?" Ann said, looking up as Wilf stored the bags in the racks above.

Ann pointed out the various towns and anything of significance she knew about them.

Wilf said, "Our early training was at Salisbury, and I noticed today some signs pointing south in that direction."

"You probably know more about this part of England than I do. I've never been west of Brighton."

Ann and Wilf were entwined as one as the train swayed from side to side, twisting its way along the tracks. After what Wilf had been through and what Ann witnessed constantly at the King's, with shattered bodies and lives from the front, this was a delightful experience for both of them. They didn't need to talk, just to enjoy this magical experience together.

At about the halfway mark of their journey, they pulled into Westbury Station. There were a lot of Australian soldiers on the platform, probably on route to or from the training camp on the Salisbury Plains. As the train pulled out, a group of Aussie soldiers was singing "Waltzing Matilda."

"There's your song," said Ann. "I'm so glad you went to the trouble of explaining about 'Waltzing Matilda' in one of your letters." Mum and Dad were intrigued with the explanation."

"I'm pleased about that. I learned that from my friend Frank Baldwin, the schoolmaster I told you about. He was a wealth of knowledge on just about any subject. I spent a lot of time with him coming over on the boat."

"I was telling one of the doctors at King's about it, and he was interested, so I loaned him the pages from your letter, and it then did the rounds of the hospital."

Ann snuggled into Wilf's shoulder for some time, thinking about the next few days. Wilf broke the silence, saying, "This trip through the countryside of England is a very interesting for me. It shows me a totally different view of your farms and fields. I can't get over the lush green pastures divided by either hedgerows or stone-wall fences. The lush green countryside is so much different here from the land back home, or for that matter the brown, muddy fields of France. Although the further I travelled away from the front in France, the greener the fields became—but nothing like this."

The neatly defined fields blended into small villages and sometimes into larger towns and cities. Ann said, "I would like to stop at Westbury on the way back and get a bus to Stonehenge if we have time."

"I'm not aware of the history of Stonehenge, but I'm happy to go anywhere you choose. The one place I particularly want to see is Glastonbury. Your dad has sold me on that place."

"I'll make sure we don't miss it."

They pulled into Exeter Station as Ann commented, "I think Torquay is the next stop." They alighted at Torquay Station, and Ann headed for the city map next to the notice board to find that their Headland Hotel was only a few streets away.

"Let's take that taxi." Wilf Pointed to the taxi waiting just outside the exit.

They managed to put their small amount of luggage on the backseat with them.

Wilf told the driver, "The Headland Hotel please." The driver frowned.

As the taxi moved away, Ann whispered to Wilf, saying, "That's the sort of look taxi drivers give you when they think you should have walked the short distance."

The taxi turned down Beacon Hill Road, and the Headland Hotel appeared ahead in brilliant sunshine. It was a huge, white, three-story building set in well-manicured gardens. Neither of them spoke, not wanting to display their exuberance to the driver.

The taxi pulled up at the entrance door to the reception area. Wilf paid the driver, who avoided any eye contact. Wilf turned to Ann and said, "This is really something; it's more grand than anything I could have even imagined."

They walked inside through the huge doors into a large reception area. Ann said, "I have the booking receipts, so I will go see them at the desk. Wait for me by that column."

Wilf tried not to look too amazed as he cast his eyes around this magnificent building. The ceilings were extremely high with domed arches separating the different sections of the reception-office area and adjoining rooms. He immediately noticed the ornate, oak wood panelling on most walls of this large entry room. The windows were draped with heavy crimson curtains from floor to ceiling, tied back with heavy, golden-coloured, soft ropes.

There was a huge, black marble fireplace off to the left, set into a heavily panelled wall. Ornate brass lampstands with beautifully stitched coverings stood on carved timber tables on either side. A large painting of royalty was set in a wooden frame and mounted over the fireplace. It did seem to Wilf that the beauty of the heavily carved wooden frame covered in gold leaf took something away from the subjects in the painting.

Wilf was taking it all in as he moved to one of the square wooden columns. He was admiring the workmanship of the grooved fluting in the timber when Ann returned, saying, "Wilf, this kind man will take care of our bags." The porter picked up their bags and asked them to follow him to their rooms on the western side of the building's ground floor.

Once they dropped off their luggage, Ann glanced out of the window and then headed for the printed literature on the table to learn about the history of the hotel.

She read to Wilf, "The hotel was built in the 1850s for the Romanov family as a holiday home." This much had been told them by Mr. Davis.

Wilf said, "That must have been the Romanovs in that picture over the fireplace. I wonder where the Romanov family is hiding now. Things are not going so good in Russia since the revolution last year."

"There are stories about the family being missing, but nobody knows for sure where they are," said Ann. "If the truth is to be known, the Romanovs would give their right arms to be staying at this hotel right now."

"They would probably be happy in the lower rooms on the western wing, Ann, rather than wherever they're now hiding in their troubled country."

"I think this western wing was probably the servant's quarters when the Romanovs were in residence." The needlework in the bedspread caught Ann's eye.

"What else does it say?" Wilf continued to check out the different pieces of cedar furniture in the room.

"The family holiday home was turned into a hotel in 1890 and then into a hospital for Boer War Veterans for a short time, then back into a hotel for all those people who liked to play the royalty thing."

"Your father was right about it being used for a hospital."

"Yes, he was. It says here the rooms on the western wing are large and well-appointed, but then according to these photos, they're nothing compared to the premium rooms on the top floors of the main building; they have facilities included for their servants as well."

Wilf said, "Let' take a short walk around the hotel, especially the swimming pool that I notice is on the south-eastern side." On their way out, they walked through the Grand Lounge Room. Wilf stopped to look around the room.

Ann said, "You certainly know how to appreciate beautiful timberwork, don't you?"

"I've never seen such beautiful work as here in these walls and cabinets, and even the ceilings." Once outside, Wilf could see just how big the place was and said, "It's easy to understand how the brochures refer to 189 bedrooms."

Ann said, "The gardens are really beautiful, with the flowers in full bloom coming into summer. Hey, have a look at this pool; it's larger than any I've seen before. And I like the sandstone pavers around the pool; they look really good."

"This is the only pool of this kind I've ever seen. Back home, the only place to swim is in the creeks or in the Avon River." Wilf was having difficulty taking it all in. "How can I describe this to my sisters and brother, Ned? They were always my companions back home in the creek, on those hot days at Kimberly."

They walked back out of the grounds towards the west along the Daddyhole Road, past what appeared to be some type of sporting field. Wilf said, "That looks like a pretty big field. I wonder what sort of games they play here."

"The field's too big for a football field. Maybe it's a polo field. It's right next-door to the hotel; maybe the kings played here in earlier days."

When they reached Collingwood Close, Wilf said, "I wonder what prompted somebody to name this place Daddyhole Road. Maybe the 'daddy' of the day had his own one-hole golf course somewhere along here?"

"That sounds possible," said Ann. "We have a couple of days to explore down this way, so how about we head back now. I'd like to have a nice leisurely bath, then sit around that nice lounge room, playing royalty before dinner."

Feeling refreshed after bathing and then chatting to a stylish couple in the lounge room, Ann said to Wilf, "I think it's time to eat."

They said good-bye to the couple and moved towards the dining room. Wilf said as she took his arm, "Did I hear that lady say they stay here at the hotel regularly?"

"Yes, you did, at least once a month, even though they only live a couple of miles away. He must have a lot of money. I think she just likes to live it up here and throw his money around."

As they approached the end of the hallway, the sign over the top of the double doors stated Romanov Room. Wilf said, "Wait a little. Did you see what I just saw?" He gestured to a painting on the wall to their left.

Ann's mouth dropped in disbelief as she looked at a painting of a single red rose. She looked straight into his eyes and said, "Did you write to the hotel and ask them to do that?"

"No, I did not, but it couldn't be more perfect for both of us. Don't you think so?" They studied the rose briefly, and then Ann squeezed his hand as she guided him through the double doors to be welcomed by the maître de. He showed them to a table in the middle of the room.

Each table had at least one flickering candle to add sparkle to the glassware. Wilf looked apprehensively at the range of cutlery before him and said, "You will need to tell me which ones to use. I have no idea."

"That's easy; always start with the outside pieces and work inward with each new course."

Ann pointed to the long french doors with white see-through curtains along two sides of the large room. "We must remember to step out onto the balcony after dinner to check out the moon. Isn't this a lovely room, Wilf?"

"It is. I've been admiring the large timber beams overhead."

"I think you had better look at the menu. The waitress will be here soon, and you won't know what to order."

"I probably still won't know after I read it."

"You being an Aussie, I know you like lamb, but I remember you telling me that you've never tasted lobster. That's on the menu. Why not try that?"

"That sounds great. Are you going to have the same thing?"

Ann nodded. "What about an entrée? Can I pick something for you? You don't need more soup; you get plenty of that. There's a salmon dish there that should be nice, and what about an apple-strudel slice for dessert?"

"You have chosen well. I couldn't have done better myself," he said as he gave a little wink, knowing he was out of his depth in these things.

When they finished eating, Wilf said, "I suppose this is how royalty would have eaten every night, served with all the refinements to befit a king of the day along with his family, entertaining his special guests from abroad."

"I don't think so. For a start, there would only be one long table in the middle of the room. It would be set with a lot more candles and more sparkling glasses than I saw you trying to fathom, plus all the fancy silverware. Is this according to the same standard fare they serve you in the front line?"

"You must be kidding," he said with a smile. "Bully beef and dog biscuits are the best we can hope for there, although the water's usually cold, providing it's not frozen in the bottle."

A porter came around to each table with a nicely printed message card. He leaned over and said very quietly, as if the invitation was for them only, "Tomorrow evening there is to be a famous Maori pianist from New Zealand in the Concert Lounge between eight and ten o'clock. This man is very talented, and you should not miss him."

Wilf noticed the look of approval on Ann's face and said, "We would love to be there, thank you."

As the porter moved away to the next table, Ann said, "That's for tomorrow night. Remember we have something special planned for ourselves tonight." She gave him a special look that nearly melted him onto the fabric of the chair.

Chapter 15

The next morning, Ann arranged to take a local buggy ride around town through the Botanical Gardens, and then on the same buggy in the afternoon, a visit to the Kent's Cavern Prehistoric Caves. The buggy was small and capable of holding only four tourists and the driver of the two white horses.

Ann said, "I can see that you have a special interest in the horses."

"Yes, I do. They're quite old. There were over two million horses conscripted for the Western Front, and the only thing that saves horses like these is if they're considered to be too old and not worth the transport cost of getting them to the front."

"Oh that's awful," said Ann. "These ones don't look that old."

"They're quite old, and believe me, horses do a terrific job at the front, blindly pushing ahead with enormous loads without being distracted by the noises all around them." He concealed from Ann the real truth of how many of the horses were blown to pieces for just being good horses. There were no medals awarded to horses, but in fact most of them were eligible for the highest award. As a horseman, he knew their value.

The Botanical Gardens were a blaze of colour, and as the driver approached the entrance, Ann said, "Oh, Wilf, we must stop here for a while so I can find the rose gardens. I want to enjoy the smell that is so special to me."

"I think you will be here for a long time; they seem to have every flower known to mankind. It will be hard to find the roses."

The driver waited while they walked around for a short while. Ann found the roses displayed in myriad colours. Wilf pointed to one red rose close to the garden edge. She bent low, and with her eyes closed, she inhaled the fragrance of that one selected rose; her sense of smell was now satisfied.

Ann said, "I would like to have picked that lovely red rose, but there were signs everywhere telling us not to touch the flowers."

Wilf gave her a special look and a squeeze of the hand. They returned to the carriage and proceeded to the Prehistoric Caves.

The popular caves were something that neither Wilf nor Ann had seen in any form previously. Lamps were set throughout the caves to highlight the myriad colours shining through the lime-carbon crystals formed over thousands of years by the constant dripping of water.

"Oh, Wilf, aren't the colours beautiful? I've never seen such colours. Look how they hang down in long, thin pointers."

Wilf said, "They have some fancy names for the icicles, but I can never remember which ones are which."

"Oh, we were told at school an easy way to remember the difference between stalagmites and stalactites. 'When the mites go up, the pants come down.' I never forget that way."

"That's a good one to remember. We certainly have plenty of mites in the trenches. Now I've certainly got a lot more information for my letters to the family at home after seeing this."

At the end of an eventful day, they again prepared for dinner and enjoyed another delightful meal together. Most food was rationed, but the hotel staff did a wonderful job serving great meals.

After the meal, they followed the sound of the piano music coming from the Concert Lounge. "Looks like we're just in nice time," said Ann, and chose two seats in the front row. She looked around the room as she sat down. "I notice a few other military uniforms in the crowd."

"Yes. I noticed too. It's hard to believe this room used to be the coach house before automobiles took over," he said as he studied the improvements.

The Maori stood and introduced himself as Arapeta from New Zealand. A couple of cheers went up from the rear. He was a short, nuggetty man with a mouth full of gleaming white teeth, highlighting a great smile. He was dressed in a black dinner suit with bowtie. He looked more like a wrestler than a pianist. He played lots of popular songs from all over the world, and he sang the words to some of them as well. From time to time, he encouraged everyone, including those who filled the extra seating out in the hallway, to join with him on some of the very well-known songs.

He asked for special requests, and it seemed like there was not a song written that he didn't know. There was not a sheet of written music anywhere to be seen.

He included some Maori songs, and to finish off the evening, he said, "I want to sing a new Maori love song that has only recently been written, actually since this war started. It is a love song about a warrior going off to war, and his lover is saying good-bye but please come back soon. I see some servicemen here and, in particular, a few of my Aussie Digger mates also."

There were more cheers, this time louder.

"I believe it is very appropriate to sing this song, especially in this time of war when so many warriors do not return to their lovers. The name of the song is 'Pokarekare Ana.' I suggest you try and remember the name because I believe this song will become one of the greatest Maori love songs of all time."

He turned around and wrote the name on a blackboard behind him.

He turned back and said, "Tonight I have a very special guest who is a real Maori princess. She will join me to sing this special love song." Chairs moved over to the right as this most beautiful lady made her way onto the raised platform. "Let me introduce you to Princess Ariki Tapaira." Arapeta took her hand as the guests admiring her beauty showed their appreciation.

She was a petite girl of about nineteen or twenty, Ann thought, with the soft, olive skin and jet-black hair of the Maori that she had read much about. She was of extraordinary beauty.

Arapeta first played a long introduction, and then they harmonised together in what was a most beautiful rendition. The princess had a very strong but smooth voice that blended beautifully with the voice of Arapeta. Though the words were sung in their native Maori tongue, the sheer emotion of the presentation could be understood by such a powerful release. The song came to an end as the guests gave a thunderous applause. Arapeta joined hands with the princess, and together they made a low bow.

As the applause died, Ann rose to her feet and said, "That was the most beautiful song I've ever heard. Is it possible for one of you to interpret the words into English and then sing the song again, please?"

Arapeta said, "Thank you for your encouragement. It is not possible to sing the words in English because they don't fit very well. I will try and recite the words first before singing the song once again. I'm so glad you enjoyed this love song."

Ann noticed the silence that came over the room. She could have heard a pin drop; such was the expectation from the guests.

Arapeta pulled a small paper from his coat pocket and said: "These are the best I can do for you." He read:

> The waves are breaking against the shores of Waiapu.
>
> My heart is aching for the return of my love.
>
> Oh, my beloved, come back to me, my heart is breaking for the love of you.
>
> If your people should see it, then trouble will begin.
>
> Oh, my love, come back to me, my heart is breaking for you.
>
> My poor pen is broken, my paper is spent, but my love for you endures and remains for evermore. The sun's hot sheen won't scorch my love, being kept evergreen by the falling of my tears. Oh, my love, come back to me, I could die for love of you.

"Now we will sing this beautiful song for you again."

The princess sang with the same emotion, but this time Ann was captivated by the hand and body movements made to complement the words being expressed.

Ann didn't want the song to come to an end as she gripped Wilf's hand and looked up into his face. She could tell that he was also affected by this beautiful song. The hushed audience rose to their feet as one and gave a prolonged and more subdued applause than the first time. Arapeta closed the lid on the piano and slowly twisted around on the seat before rising to take the hand of the princess again, which they then lifted in a salute to the guests.

Ann couldn't help notice the number of white handkerchiefs dabbing at the wet eyes of the ladies near the front. She assumed it would be the same at the back of the room.

A boisterous applause was not needed. It was obvious to Ann that the appreciation of the guests assembled could be sensed in the subdued atmosphere of the crowded room as they stood for the artists to take their leave. The atmosphere in the room was worth more than applause to Arapeta and Princess Arika. Not many people wanted to move. The song had done all of the moving needed for them, inside their individual thoughts.

The evening air was still warm. Wilf said, "Let's take a walk back the long way through the garden before going to bed." They walked around the darkened pool and stopped at the far end to hug. Ann tried to recall the words of the song. There was no moon as yet, and they kissed in the darkness. After some ten minutes or more, they approached the western wing and heard raised, angry voices, both male and female, coming from the first floor directly above. There were obviously accusations and denials being made by a couple of very agitated people with a third, more subdued male voice trying to calm things down.

Ann didn't like what she was hearing and suggested they walk around to the other side of the hotel.

The next morning, Ann said, "I need to do some washing before going down to the beach a little later as planned."

"That's fine. I'll take a short walk, but not down the way we went the other day. I'll leave that till you're with me, and we'll go down and take a look at the beach together. I've never seen a breaking surf before, so I would like to take a short walk in the opposite direction to the beach wall while you do the washing, if that's okay with you."

"That's fine with me, but don't be away too long. Remember I'm still the nurse in charge here."

Wilf said, "I'll remember that, Nurse. It will only take about twenty minutes. I saw the wall on one of the photographs in the dining hall; it's a large rock wall, so I will go and have a look. I won't be long." He grabbed his hat and started off.

Ann finished the small amount of washing quicker than she anticipated. She walked out to the rear veranda overlooking the garden area, where she thought she would wait for Wilf to return from his walk. As she stepped out of the door, a hysterical female teenager came running up the steps screaming. "An Australian soldier has fallen over the cliff and drowned."

A picture immediately flashed before Ann's eyes with a wave of shock rolling over every part of her body. She felt the strength in her legs turn to jelly. Ann slid to the veranda floor as if watching in slow motion as her dreams were blasted away. Her mind was overtaken by an ever-darkening cloud that slowly turned blacker than midnight.

Chapter 16

Hotel staff were summoned and rushed to Ann's aid. They couldn't bring her around. They picked her up and carried her over to one of the couches on the enclosed veranda. One of the staff arrived with smelling salts. She tipped a little onto a handkerchief and placed it under Ann's nose, which brought her around. Ann realised what had happened and burst into tears; she couldn't be consoled no matter what the staff did for her.

Two policemen had been in the front foyer of the hotel making enquiries about a totally separate matter. They were alerted to this new problem by the hysterical girl running through the hotel and into the foyer.

The policemen immediately came around the outside of the building to the rear. One of them went off through the bottom gate towards the cliff, and the other one asked everyone else to stay inside. He then came inside and approached Ann, who by now was sobbing uncontrollably.

He did his best to help her to regain her composure to some degree and said, "I would like to ask some brief questions that could be helpful to us in our investigations." He proceeded to make copious notes in his black book.

After ten minutes, the hotel manager came in from the bottom of the garden and, not knowing Ann's circumstances, said quietly to the policeman, "Your colleague said it was definitely an Australian soldier's body that was pulled from the water." However, it was loud enough for Ann to hear.

This was enough to cause Ann to again break down into uncontrolled crying. The policeman made some additional notes in his book while the staff did their best to comfort her.

He said, "I understand your situation at this difficult time, madam, but I'm advised that you could possibly know the identity of this soldier pulled from the water at the base of the cliff." Ann could only nod her head to confirm answers to his questions; she could not manage any words.

He had already asked the usual questions about Ann, but he now wanted information about Wilf—his name, age, address or battalion if she knew it, where he was staying, room number, where they had come from that day, where they were planning to go, etc., to which she had great difficulty answering in between sobs. He said, "That will be all for now, but I would like to talk to you again later. Please do not to leave the hotel."

As the constable stood to leave, a police sergeant approached them from the direction of the cliff. He advised the interviewing constable in a loud, monotone voice that the body pulled from the water was now found to have a knife wound to the chest. The matter now was a murder investigation, and nobody would be allowed to leave the hotel. Ann heard quite clearly and nearly passed out for the second time.

The constable instructed the hotel manager to secure all of the outer doors and to advise all guests and staff, both in-house and outdoor gardening staff, to assemble in the Concert Lounge. The manager was asked to quickly provide a list of all staff and guests.

*

While Ann was taking care of the washing, Wilf walked out through the bottom garden gate, down the path towards the cliff, and then east along the SW Coast Path to St. Mark's Road. He found a narrow path leading to the beach wall and walked along the wall until he reached Meadfoot Sea Road.

He gazed out over the breaking sea to the east and thought of home in that direction. He hoped beyond hope that this war would soon end so he could return once again to his family just outside the little hamlet of Craven. He pondered on his thoughts of home for some time, maybe for too long. He thought of his mother, whom he loved dearly. He knew she would be faithfully praying each night for his safe return.

Wilf looked out over the sea towards Australia and felt a little homesick and emotional as a tear ran down his cheek. He decided not to walk further and sat there thinking about the way things had turned in his favour.

He returned along the path, intending to look over the cliff briefly on the way back. A policeman on the path ahead waved his arms and shouted, "Please remain where you are; there has been an accident at the cliff." He offered no further information. It was some time before the officer returned and advised the few who had gathered to return to the hotel immediately.

None of the other walkers were aware of what was going on. Others who had been out walking in the opposite direction or who had been down at the beach were now returning.

As Wilf came through the outer door onto the enclosed veranda, he was intent on finding Ann somewhere ahead, probably near the laundry. There was a bit of a crush ahead with people entering the hallway. He casually looked over to a group gathered around a couch, and he was startled to see that the one on the couch was Ann. He turned and rushed towards the couch and leaned over to speak just as Ann turned her head to see Wilf looking down at her.

Ann nearly fainted for a third time, but this time for the best of reasons. The dark cloud that just a short time ago had turned her brightest day into midnight was washed away as she shot up from the settee, flinging her arms around his neck. She just wouldn't let go, saying, "Thank God you're safe."

"Ann, what on earth is going on?"

Wilf was totally stunned at her response. He could see from the looks on the staff's faces that they were also stunned. Ann blurted out, "We all thought you were the one found murdered at the cliff."

Wilf said, "I didn't even get to see the cliff."

One of the staff said, "They found the body of an Australian soldier with a knife wound in his chest at the bottom of the cliff."

"Well, I can assure you that soldier wasn't me," he said jokingly as he continued to hug Ann, still half-sobbing and laughing at the same time. He wasn't about to complain about the hugs; he could take that anytime.

Ann kept saying over and over, "Thank God you're safe."

Then along came the officer who had interviewed Ann earlier. He said, "I've been informed that your situation now has changed, and I'm very happy for the both of you. However, I do need to get a statement from Wilf." He wanted to know where Wilf had been, what time he left the hotel, did he have any witnesses along the walk after he left the hotel, did he know the other Australian soldier, and so on.

Wilf said, "I don't have any witnesses along the sea wall, nor do I know personally any other Australian soldier at the hotel. I did notice a couple of Diggers seated separately at the back of the Concert Lounge last night, but I didn't see them afterwards."

The constable said to Wilf, "Did you hear any suspicious noises last evening or during the night?"

"There was a bit of shouting in the room above on the western wing just after the concert, but nothing after that."

The constable said, "Thanks for that information."

While they were talking, the sergeant walked around the various lounge rooms saying, "Nobody is allowed out of the hotel until further notice."

Wilf said to the constable, "We will be here for the day, so let us know if you need more information."

"Actually, I would like you to accompany me to your room now please."

"I'm only too happy to be of help," he said as he went with the officer to answer more questions and show the officer where he was outside when he heard the shouting.

When they finished, Wilf expressed his appreciation to the officer for the care he had shown to Ann when things looked bad.

The officer replied, "I'm most definitely pleased to report that we had it all wrong, as far as you being the victim was concerned."

Wilf returned to the Grand Lounge to join Ann, who was surrounded by well-wishing guests expressing their thoughts about the earlier episode. Ann now looked absolutely radiant and back to her best as she clutched his arm tightly in both hands. She looked up into Wilf's face with only slightly still reddened eyes. She snuggled into his shoulder, saying to the small group, "This is my Wilf. He's from Australia."

*

Sergeant Oliver was in charge of five policemen at the hotel conducting interviews for the rest of the day. Their investigations discovered bloodstains had been found in the room above Ann's room, number twenty-eight, both on the rug and around the washbasin. Bloodstains were also found on the external stairs and on the path outside leading around the pool. There was evidence to show where plants were crushed next to the fence where the body had been rested; as the gate at the bottom of the garden was always locked at night. There were lots of footprints in the garden.

There were bloodstains on the fence showing that a body had been lifted with a great struggle over the fence. It was then carried across a narrow path and through a small, curved arch opening in the stone wall opposite. The signs on the other side of the wall showed that a body had been dragged through the bushes and undergrowth for about 150 yards to the top of the cliff. It must have been rested there for some time, probably while the perpetrators decided what to do next. There was a small pool of blood that had soaked into the soil about three feet back from the edge of the cliff top.

Sergeant Oliver let it be known that he was interested for anyone to come forward who believed they had seen an Australian soldier either the previous day or evening. Various guests said they had seen the soldier and the lady during the previous day in various places, casually walking around together. Another mentioned that the dark-haired lady stood out, distinctly different from the other short, blonde lady in the company of another Australian soldier.

The receptionist said, "I recall a very large man in his mid-thirties with an early balding head coming to the desk during the early stages of the concert, asking for a Mrs. Bradford. I told him we didn't have a Mrs. Bradford on our guest list. He then described the lady to me, but I wasn't prepared to discuss other guests with him. He walked away, but he didn't look satisfied with my answer."

"Thank you for that, my lady."

"I didn't tell him that I thought I knew the lady he was looking for. I remembered the lady well. The only tall lady with the dark hair he described, I had noticed was with Cpl Alan Golding, the soldier found down at the bottom of the cliff."

"That's good information. Thank you for that, madam."

The receptionist continued. "When they checked in, she didn't come with him to the desk but preferred to stand some distance away in front of the large wooden column to the right of the desk, facing towards the Concert Lounge. She was smoking a cigarette through an extremely long ivory holder. She stood out as a very stylish lady, wearing an over-large, black, slanted brimmed hat turned up at the front."

Sergeant Oliver thanked her once again. He was keen to learn more about this lady with the long, black hair and hoped other guests had noticed other points of interest that could be helpful to his investigations.

He moved off to talk to another elderly man waiting to pass on some more information. He said, "I left the concert before it finished, visiting the washroom. I was on my way back when I passed a lady with long, black hair and a man with a balding head. It was just near the entrance to the men's lavatories, in the hallway leading to the Romanov Dining Room."

"Is that the hallway behind you?"

"Yes, they looked as if they planned to go up the stairway that leads to the west wing. They looked very excited about something, and I don't think it had anything to do with the singer. I returned to the Concert Lounge just in time to hear the Maori singer announce his last song."

"Thank for that information, sir. I've made a note of your name and room number."

The guests were advised they were now free to leave the hotel just before the evening meal was to be served. Some left the hotel straight away, but most stayed another night, as did Ann and Wilf.

The mood in the hotel was so different from the previous night when Arapeta had sung those songs—especially the love song "Pokarekare Ana," which he and the princess had sung so emotionally. Ann now wished she had asked for a copy of the words, but if Arapeta's prediction was to prove to be correct, the song would soon be available around the music stores. She had made a note of the name and would make a point of keeping an eye out for the song when published. She couldn't get the tune out of her head.

A number of people stopped by to mention they had heard of the trauma caused to Ann when it was believed Wilf had been the victim. They all expressed their happiness for them when it was discovered they had been the victims of mistaken identity.

After tea, they wandered through the halls of the hotel studying the many paintings on display. They read the captions describing the origins of the subject matter. They read the words and discussed some of them lightly.

Ann said, "Wilf, I'm still feeling drained and would like another early night."

"That also suits me. I think we have both had quite a draining time today."

Ann had other thoughts foremost in her mind, romantic thoughts that applied only to the two of them. Before heading off to bed, they once again took a slow walk around the pool and the small garden on the southern side of the building.

The next morning, they walked slowly to the station in time to catch the nine o'clock train heading for Castle Cary. The journey took a little over an hour. Then there was a two-hour bus ride to Glastonbury, arriving just after lunch. The bus dropped them to the George and Pilgrim Hotel on High Street; only a short walk from the Abbey. Ann explained to the lady at the desk about the drama and the subsequent delay at the Headland Hotel.

The lady at the reception table in the stoned passageway said, "Fortunately for you, rooms are still available because the war is having a detrimental effect on the holidaying public in this area. You did want two rooms, didn't you?"

"Yes, thank you," Ann said as the lady handed Ann the large keys and pointed them up the narrow, curving stairs.

"I've given one of you the Henry VIII room. You can decide who gets the four-posted bed with the view towards the Abbey."

After depositing their bags, they headed for the Abbey tea rooms for an early afternoon tea. Mrs. Davis had informed Ann there was a new addition since they had been there, in the form of a large book shop. This was according to some friends who had visited in the last few years. When finished, they headed straight for the Abbey Shop where they purchased some booklets and maps of the ancient Abbey to take back to the boarding house to study at leisure in the afternoon.

Ann had learned a lot about Glastonbury from her mother, but the information Wilf was reading was completely new to him.

Ann interrupted his reading and said, "What do you make of all this information?"

"It's truly amazing. I wonder why all of this historical stuff I'm reading is not taught at school back home. It's so interesting."

"It's not taught in our schools here either."

"I wonder why. Ann, it's all so clear from what I've read so far. It explains how two thousand years ago, a man called Joseph of Arimathaea had a fleet of ships trading tin between the Islands of Britain and the land of Phoenicia. He often visited this area of Cornwell and Somerset, which were considered to have the largest known deposits of tin in the world. Britain was often called the Cassiterides, being the Greek name for tin, the Tin Islands. Did you know that?"

"Only because of what Mum and Dad had learned and told me."

"It appears that Joseph of Arimathaea on one of his voyages to this area, known then as the Isle of Avalon, brought his teenage great-nephew Jesus along with him. After Jesus's crucifixion, his body was buried in Joseph's tomb in Jerusalem. Later on, Joseph brought Jesus's mother, Mary, who was his niece, to Avalon where she spent her last days. A Christian community settled in the area."

"You're a fast learner, Wilf."

"It gets even more interesting. When Empress Helen, the mother of the Emperor Constantine, became a Christian, she sent out her emissaries all over Europe to find the remains of the disciples. She then had them brought here to Avalon for reburial along with Mary in the grounds of what later became the second cathedral."

Ann too had been reading and said, "The ground in this area was often referred to as 'the most-hallowed ground on earth.' All of the legends associated with King Arthur are centred in Glastonbury. Various buildings of worship were built on the site from the fourth century onwards, including the Chapel of St. Joseph with the reburied remains of the disciples in designated places under the floors of the building."

Ann continued, "That Abbey and all of the other buildings were destroyed by fire in 1180. A new cathedral was then built, which was subsequently destroyed during the fifteenth-century dissolution of the monasteries by King Henry VIII, leaving only the walls as they're seen today."

Wilf said, "I'm absolutely amazed at the information we have been reading and cannot wait to visit the old cathedral walls in the morning."

"Do you realise, Wilf, we have been reading for nearly two hours? I think we should take a walk along the High Street to find somewhere to have a meal."

They found a quaint dining room called Esther's Dining Room where they enjoyed the meal before walking back to the hotel. The lady was sitting at her very small desk and looked up when she saw them coming through the archway. She said, "Have you been to the cathedral yet?"

"No, not yet, we only got as far as the bookshop and have been doing a lot of reading. Ann's mother and father were here about thirty years ago and told us we must make sure and take it all in. There is so much to learn."

"There sure is," she replied. "You know the room you have with the four-poster bed is supposed to be the room where King Henry VIII stayed. That's why it is called by that name. History also tells us that there used to be an underground tunnel from this hotel to the cathedral for the exclusive use of the monks of the day. Why they needed the tunnel is anyone's guess."

"That's very interesting," said Ann as she said goodnight and took Wilf by the hand to lead him up the stairs. Wilf took the large key from his pocket and opened the door to this historic room.

As they studied the old furniture closely, Wilf said, "Look at the timber. Even in those days, they knew the value of using cedar timber for their furniture."

"Is there any other timber that resists the beetles and bugs as well as cedar?"

"I don't know, but if there is, I haven't heard of it."

Ann sat on the bed facing the large window. The windowsill was too high to allow her to get any view of the surroundings. She beckoned Wilf without any words, but simply looked at him with that special look of hers that was unmistakable to him. He sat down alongside and put his arm around her shoulders and drew her close. Their lips met for a mini-eternity.

When they parted, Wilf said, "Well, everything you're folks told us about Glastonbury has been spot-on so far."

"When my mother tells you about something special, you can always count on it being very special. But there are some other things about this place that she didn't tell us. I think now is a good time to find out for ourselves. What do you think?"

"Yes, I think you are right. Let's make the most of our time here for just one night. I think it could be very special."

The next morning, they were up early and had breakfast before setting out for the Abbey, a short distance of only two hundred yards away. Ann had all of the maps to show them the points of interest. She said, "I think this will blow you away."

Wilf could not get over how huge this cathedral must have been when first built. The original footprint of the buildings showed the full size, which he believed was larger than Westminster by a long way. It was certainly longer than the Amiens Cathedral, which he had walked around so many times admiring the stained-glass windows and high arches built in the twelfth and thirteenth centuries. But here were the remains of some huge buildings constructed hundreds of years even before that.

"Ann, you read something about the choir last evening; you said to remind you this morning."

"Yes, I read that there was a choir rostered on to provide music twenty four hours per day, every day. If you look down below to the lower level, that is where they would stand, according to this map."

Wilf said, "I read that over the doorways, I suppose you would call them the curved portals, there are illustrations with so much detail for the worshipers of the day. Most people would have been illiterate, so carved images were used to illustrate stories from the Bible."

As they looked up to the tops of the walls, Ann said, "I wonder why all of the grass is growing along the tops of the walls."

"I believe it is because the birds perch up there and their droppings contain grass seeds that eventually germinate and take root. Then the roots travel down into the mortar used in those days, and the roots grow large enough to crack the mortar. Over the centuries, this causes the walls to crumble and fall."

"That's a shame, Wilf; surely something could be done to stop the seeds from growing. I think that would be easier than stopping the birds from squatting along the tops."

As they walked back to the hotel, they marvelled at what they had seen. They didn't have time to waste because they needed to be on the noon bus to Shepton Mallet Station. The train journey was over before it started as they talked about what they had seen that morning. They arrived at Bath Station midafternoon.

Ann said, "I have not made reservations here because I was told there would be lots of good accommodation very close to the station."

After leaving the station, they walked across the wide, cobbled road and found accommodation for one night at Anabelle's Guest House on Manvers Street. As they waited for the receptionist to hand them their keys, a policeman walked up to them. Wilf immediately recognised him as the constable who interviewed Ann and Wilf back at the Headland.

He said, "I noticed you both when you came in the door and thought I should let you know where our investigations have led us. I really shouldn't tell you this, but I think I can trust you. Can I? I would be in a lot of trouble if it gets out, although most of this information will be in tomorrow's papers."

Wilf said, "Yes, you certainly can. It is jolly-decent of you to take the trouble to fill us in."

"Well, we were given information by the station master at the Torquay Railway Station that a man and woman fitting the description of the wanted, tall, dark-haired lady and the heavy-built bald-headed man had boarded the six o'clock train heading north on the morning after the murder. We put out an alert to all stations north and found that the couple had changed at Bristol and then alighted at Bath."

Ann said, "So you think they're here, do you?"

"Just hang on there a little. In the meantime, Sergeant Oliver and I followed on a later train and were advised by our colleagues at Bath that the couple in question had checked into Anabelle's Guest House."

"Right here?" said Ann.

"Yes, right here. Naturally, the couple was taken by surprise when they received a knock on the door with two policemen outside and nowhere for them to run. When interviewed, the women confessed that she was caught by her husband having an affair with the Australian soldier."

"Aha," said Ann. "Caught red handed."

"A fight broke out between the two men, and her husband pulled a knife and stabbed the soldier. Her husband was threatening to expose her deeds to her family unless she helped him dispose of the body and kept her mouth shut. She is the daughter of a well-known London politician."

"Well, what do you know? A London socialite," said Ann as she flicked some hair to one side.

"She helped her husband get the body over the fence and down to the cliff edge. Both have now been arrested, he on a murder charge, and the lady on two charges, one as an accessory after the fact of murder, and the second a charge of conspiracy to subvert the course of justice. They're now locked away in the local cells, awaiting transfer to another secure location."

"No doubt they will be locked up for some time," said Wilf.

"I believe so," said the constable. He wished them an enjoyable stay and apologised for the confusion and subsequent trauma caused in the earlier investigation. He sincerely hoped they had both recovered from their ordeal by now and said good-bye.

By this time, the keys had arrived, and they went off to drop their bags upstairs. There was still plenty of daylight, and they wanted to visit the old roman baths, today if possible. Ann made enquiries at the desk and found the baths were only a few blocks away, so they set off straight away.

Wilf paid for the tickets as Ann went to find some literature. They walked in the main doorway and were immediately confronted by the large bath area. Wilf said, "I cannot believe what we are looking at. You said this place was two thousand years old?"

"Yes, it is. I already had some knowledge of this place, but I'm also amazed to see the bath house is still in such good condition."

They listened to the tour guide saying, "The baths have a lead lining, as was originally installed for the Roman soldiers. The lining was about ten millimetres thick and didn't leak after all that time. The water is supplied continuously by a warm underground stream that never dries up. The underground spring supplies over 250,000 gallons of water each day at a temperature of 115 degrees Fahrenheit, a perfect temperature for bathing."

"Isn't that amazing, Wilf?" Ann said as the guide continued.

"There was only one problem; the Roman centurions who commanded the legions came here for an all-expenses paid holiday break, not knowing that the lead in the water could kill them. The baths were eventually closed down for centuries after the Romans left England."

There was also a lot of information on the walls telling how the baths were also used in sun-worship by the Romans.

Ann said, "We don't have enough time to stand and read all of the signs before closing time. However, we have at least seen the spring. Wasn't that something?"

"I will purchase these brochures, Ann, so we can take them with us." Wilf paid for the extra booklets and then took Ann by the hand and led the way back to Anabelle's for the evening meal before retiring. Tomorrow, there were lots of places Ann wanted to take Wilf, but time would be very short. They were required back at the station to catch the one o'clock train to Paddington.

Ann said, "It's a pity the murder investigations at the Headlands took so much of our time. I don't think there will be enough time to visit Stonehenge."

"I don't think we should be too disappointed about that," said Wilf. "It has been a wonderful few days with some terrifying events thrown in. What a story we will have to tell your parents when we arrive home." They wandered out to the park and found a bench on which to sit close together, going over the events of the week that had been—but nearly had not been.

Wilf said to Ann, "My sisters will find it hard to keep up with the stories when I get time to write about this week. They in turn will tell the stories to the whole school and local community the next day after receiving my letters."

"That should give them quite a buzz and keep them talking for a while. You'll have to tell me more about your sisters some time."

"They all individually write to me on a regular basis, but they must discuss the details with each other beforehand because their letters never tell of the same news from home."

Ann said, "What about your mother? Does she duplicate the same news?"

"No, she doesn't. I have a very close connection with my mother. She always seems to know what to write about, knowing it will give me comfort. How I wish she could have been with us at Glastonbury."

"Do you think she would be interested in all that history stuff?"

"I'm certain that the historical information I learned would have been totally new to her; otherwise I would remember her telling those stories to us as children. It was her mother that started the little Sunday school in her home in Thalabah in 1850. I was born in Thalabah and grew up there before moving to Stroud as an eleven-year-old."

Ann gripped his hand firmly and said, "Every day, I wish I could someday go to Australia and visit with you all of the places you tell me about."

Wilf said, "I hope that will come true someday." They walked back to Anabelle's for a freshen-up before dinner.

There were not many in the dining room, so after the meal, they were able to spread out some of the literature on their large near-empty table.

Ann said, "I think there will be time for us to study the literature in the train tomorrow."

"Yes, I agree. There are more important things to be doing now," Wilf said as he gathered up the literature, put his arm around Ann's waist, and headed upstairs.

Chapter 17

The sun rose the next morning without a cloud in the sky. They had so many places to see, but only one morning before catching the train for home. Another couple at breakfast suggested that they take a taxi up to the Royal Crescent Hotel, which was a landmark in itself. They were then within three or four hundred yards of many other places, such as the Herschel Museum of Astronomy, Royal Victoria Gardens, the Victoria Gallery, and the Circus. Wilf was keen to get moving.

As soon as they finished breakfast and settled the account, they dropped their bags near reception and caught a taxi already waiting out on the front drive. They visited on foot all of the intended places of interest, except the Circus, which the taxi had driven slowly past on their way to the Royal Crescent Hotel. The taxi driver told them it was built in the mid-eighteenth century and was originally known as King's Circus. The architect used the colosseum in Rome for his inspiration.

The Royal Crescent could have occupied most of their morning just walking the corridors and viewing the paintings and works of art. The gardens were absolutely glorious and in full colour at this time of the year.

Ann said, "Time has run away so quickly this morning. We need to head back."

Wilf hailed a taxi, picked up their bags, and asked the waiting driver to drop them to the station.

Fortunately, the train was fairly empty, and they found a cabin all to themselves. Their conversation centred on the places they had visited that morning but had not had time to discuss at the time of their visit.

After making themselves comfortable in the carriage, Ann said, "This has been a wonderful week together, but it is coming to an end. I really don't want to think about you returning to the front. I can't bear the thought of losing you again. I hate the thought." She fumbled for her handkerchief to dab at the tears starting to form in her eyes.

Wilf said, "I'm not keen at all either," but he did not express the thoughts whirling around in his mind of the horrors that lay ahead.

"For a few days, Ann, my mind has been filled with all the wonderful things we have seen. There are so many things to talk about with you by my side, but most of the time, I'm happy just to enjoy your company. Except of course for that horrible one hour at the Headland when I was unaware of what was going on. But for you, my precious one, it must have been the most horrible hour of your life."

"It certainly was," she said.

It was obvious to Wilf that they both knew what the other was thinking as they stared blankly out of the window at the countryside, without seeing a thing. It was that horrible parting again at the barracks behind the King's Hospital. It was now only a matter of days away. He hated the thought but couldn't get rid of it from his mind.

They were the only ones in the carriage, so it was easy for Ann to snuggle into Wilf's chest with his arm around her. Occasionally she would pivot her head, automatically drawing his head downwards towards hers, and then moving her lips upwards to his as they both enjoyed the privacy of the moment. The speeding train caused flashes of sunlight through the gaps in the trees onto their closed eyelids as they kissed for long spells.

Ann said, "This is like snuggling by the fireside with the twisting and swirling of the flames creating changes in brightness through my eyelids."

"I'm enjoying the moment just as much as I think you are." However the flashes of light caused his mind to wander to those bad times that would inevitably come again. Times when he was scared to his very core but still trying to get some sleep in the trenches, with the thunderous rumbling and flaring glow of the explosions all around. The bright flashes turned blackness into daylight and back again in seconds without even opening his eyes. Would he ever be able to block out such thoughts in the future?

He didn't mention to Ann these terrible thoughts swirling around in his head, but he knew she had comforted many troubled souls at the hospital.

The journey was nearly over, and another older couple joined their carriage on the third to last stop.

Once off the train, they made their way through the crowds within the large station. They walked past a group of Tommy soldiers standing outside one of bars. Obviously, they had too much to drink and were making a spirited but awful job of singing together one of their favourites, "Mademoiselle from Armentieres parlez-vous."

Ann said, "Where did that song come from? It seemed to be there at the beginning of the war."

"I think you're right. I'm told it originally was sung by those in the French Army way back in 1830. Some of the words are not real nice."

"Is that right? I didn't know that. I suppose I only get to hear the good parts."

Ann quickly guided them onto the right connections to King's Cross, and it seemed no time had passed before they were turning into Whidbourne Street. Being a warm day, the front door was open, and Mrs. Davis heard them chatting together as they approached the front of the house.

She threw her arms around Ann first and then Wilf, saying, "I can't wait to hear what you both thought of the south. Just leave your bags over there, Wilf, and tell me all about your holiday."

Ann said, "We absolutely adored just about everything we did." Just then, Mr. Davis entered the room, and Ann gave him a big hug as he turned to shake Wilf's hand and welcome them both home.

Mrs. Davis said, "What do you mean by 'just about' everything?"

"You had better sit down while we tell you what happened."

Mrs. Davis happily chimed in with, "Don't tell me you got married?"

"No," said Ann, "but maybe we should have." Then Ann told them what had happened at the Headland Hotel, with tears starting to fall as she relived again the terrifying experience she had been through. Ann told them all the lovely things that happened and especially about Arapeta, the Maori pianist, and the real-life Maori Princess who harmonised so well together with him. Ann was struggling to remember either the tune or the English words of Pokarekare Ana. At least she had remembered the name of the song, because she had written it down.

It took about an hour to go through all of the places they visited, especially Glastonbury. Wilf said, "It was a marvellous experience. How come we have never heard of such an important historical place, especially as far as the Christian Church is concerned?"

Mrs. Davis said, "It is very hard to talk to somebody about Glastonbury unless that person has been there to experience the place. To see the size of the building and to understand just how old were those walls is just so unbelievable."

"People can accept the great buildings still in evidence in Rome or Jerusalem," said Mr. Davis, "but they find it hard to accept that these same people came to our shores and built structures just as big around the same time. Most people think you're exaggerating."

Ann said, "We both want to say thank you for giving us such a wonderful week away together. It was fabulous. Wasn't it, Wilf?"

"It most certainly was, and I don't know how to thank you enough."

Mrs. Davis had prepared a meal for their return, not knowing exactly the time of their arrival. With a little fussing now, she could have it ready in half an hour. They enjoyed the meal and continued to talk about all the places Mr. and Mrs. Davis had enjoyed on their honeymoon so long ago. Ann and Wilf could now share their wonderful memories with them in great detail.

Tomorrow was to be the last free day before Wilf returned to the front. Ann was also required to start the evening shift at King's at three o'clock on Monday. She would have enough time to take Wilf to the barracks again. How she hated that thought. Doing it all over again would be so terrible. They would have all tomorrow to relax and share time with each other. Ann found it difficult to think about the parting again.

Sunday morning broke with a light drizzle. Mr. And Mrs. Davis left early for church and had a big day in front of them preparing hot meals for the troops. Ann and Wilf had a late breakfast before washing some shirts. Ann hung them on a line by the fire to dry in readiness for Wilf to take with him tomorrow.

The rest of the day was spent looking at family photographs and comparing the information Ann' parents had brought back from their honeymoon with her own souvenirs. She found that nothing much had changed, especially at the Headland Hotel. This was probably because it had already been converted into a hotel open to the public when her parents were there.

Wilf said, "I find it hard to understand, as a non-European, how the Royal families were all so closely connected and how they each appeared to holiday in homes they owned outside their own country."

"Maybe it was because they didn't want their subjects knowing how much property they really owned."

"Maybe with all the strife happening now in Russia, the Royal family would prefer to have kept the home so it could still be used as a safe haven. But then, we wouldn't have had such a wonderful week, would we?" he said as he looked at Ann with a glint in his eye.

"With all the power held by the Tsar, it seems highly unlikely that he would not be able to summon enough of his troops to protect his family, wherever he chose to be—at home or abroad, in spite of the revolution."

The Davises came home mid-afternoon, and Mrs. Davis started preparing for the evening farewell meal. Although she had been away all day, she still had made preparations yesterday for this meal.

Wilf said to Ann, "I'm impressed with your mother's ability to organise and make do with the limited variety of food available due to the rationing. I've been watching her working her kitchen." He thought what a lovely person she really was. He could see so much of her in Ann—loving, gentle and thoughtful in every way.

Mrs. Davis said, "I'm pleased and amazed how Wilf's health has improved in such a short time. Maybe the sea air helped after all?"

Wilf said, "I believed it is because of the tender, loving care provided by both you and your daughter, for which I'm very grateful."

They sat down for the meal on the same but differently decorated table and went through the same toasts as on his previous farewell. Mr. Davis spoke for longer this time and said, "I really appreciate how well you, Wilf, have treated our daughter, and I would like to pray again, asking God to keep you safe and return you to us safely." He prayed and then said, "I again want to thank you for the shelter, which we all hope will never need to be used."

Wilf said, "I want to thank you both again for the wonderful few days away that you so generously provided for both Ann and me. I hope someday to be able to repay your generosity. Maybe you can come and visit my family in Australia when this war is over."

"We would love to do that. Wouldn't we, Margaret? It would be a great experience, but maybe we will be too old by then."

After the meal, Mr. Davis said, "I will help clear because it stopped raining quite some time ago, just in case you want to take a walk before retiring."

They did just that and walked to the same spot in Argyle Square and sat on the park bench under the sycamore trees. This time, the birds were quiet as if they knew that this was to be a sad and emotional time for both of them. There was not much conversation from either of them; it was too difficult. They hugged and kissed passionately, knowing that they needed to make an early start in the morning.

The next morning, with hugs and kisses from Mrs. Davis and a warm handshake and a firm embrace from Mr. Davis, Wilf was off again, with Ann by his side for another emotional parting.

Ann said, "I hope you know that my parents think the world of you."

"I also think the world of them; they're wonderful people, with a very special daughter." Ann knew that her parents would be thinking of how another parting would affect her. It had not been easy last time, and she knew they would be very supportive again this time.

They arrived at the barracks with just as many people moving about, and it was no easier this time to get closer to the troops as they lined up ready to go. Their parting would be so much harder because they were so much more involved now with each other than before. She had already told Wilf that she would not prolong the pain, hanging around hoping for a last glance.

Ann knew that Wilf also was very emotional; she could sense it. He was so much more emotional than others around him, but he struggled to keep it under control. Every time they said farewell, the chances of him coming back unscathed were far less than the previous time. These things had been going through her mind all yesterday and this morning, but she said nothing. She understood that two tours of the front was something not many others were lucky enough to survive, but a third completed tour—was it too much to expect? She forced the horrible thought out of her mind.

The bugle sounded for the men to fall in. Wilf pulled Ann so tightly for that one last embrace. Their lips locked together as if glued in one last frantic kiss that would have to last for who knew how long. Ann hugged him so tightly that she was surprised at her own strength.

The bugle continued, and others around them started to move away with their last shouts of good-bye and good luck. Still Ann could not bring herself to make that final separation until some wag moving past said, “Let him go, love. They’re waiting on him.”

Wilf picked up his kitbag and said slowly, “I love you so much.”

“I love you too and always will,” she said as she turned to walk away, not wanting Wilf to see that she had now lost total control of her emotions. She was so proud that Wilf was able to control his emotions. She did not know that he was having one of the greatest battles of his life, walking in the opposite direction.

They were eventually shipped out via Folkestone with a channel crossing to Le Havre. The crossing was much calmer this time but delayed so much longer because of the increased activity of the German submarines. The trains and stoppages were about the same as before, but the cattle trucks were cleaner. They eventually arrived on the outskirts of Amiens at three in the morning on April 1, 1918, April Fool’s Day of all days.

Chapter 18

Casualties from the war had been mounting, and Ann's family had not heard from her brother, Joe, for some time. He was also at the front. Joe had never married; he was too involved with his life as an artillery officer in the permanent army.

It was now August 12, 1918, and the war was not going anywhere. Ann had been receiving irregular letters from Wilf, written whenever he was on leave or away from the front line.

Since she last saw Wilf, he had been up to the lines a number of times. She always looked forward to his letters, which automatically told her immediately upon receipt, without even opening the letter, that he was still alive. How excited she was to come home from the King's to find a letter waiting for her this day. She had asked Wilf to send letters only to her home address so she would know where to expect them.

Wilf wrote:

My dearest Ann,

I could not begin to accurately describe to you my feelings when we had to separate at the parade ground behind King's. I cannot recall such a terrible experience previously occurring in my life. As a matter of fact, I know for certain that there has never been such a time for me. You alone have had such a dramatic effect on my life. The love and care you have shown to me has been quite remarkable.

I was not game to turn around and look at you as I moved away to fall in. I knew I would not be able to control my emotions and probably make a fool of myself. I hope you were able to pull yourself together before reporting for duty.

I want you to understand the broader picture of this war. Forgive me if I get too boring, but this is what we are here for.

The days have gone where the men who set the wheels in motion are themselves caught up in the slaughter. Maybe the likes of Nelson were the last of such leaders. Today the generals enjoy comfortable beds and sumptuous meals many miles behind the lines, issuing instructions to carry out impossible tasks. In most cases, the soldiers are told to do the same thing tomorrow that they had failed to achieve today and yesterday and the day before that.

When will somebody understand this horrible mess and swallow their pride and admit this is not the way to settle petty squabbles about the assassination of some archduke? He was not even connected to Britain. My understanding is that in the middle of 1914 some terrorists, trained and supported by the Serbian government, assassinated Franz Ferdinand

and his wife in Sarajevo. He was the heir to the Austrian-Hungarian throne.

Within one month, Austria, supported by Germany, declared war on Serbia, and five empires gave support to Serbia and are now at war against the Germans and the Austrians.

I understood that before war was declared, Germany demanded that both France and Russia cancel the mobilisation of their armies. When they refused, Germany declared war on both countries and poured one million men into neutral Belgium whose army was outnumbered ten to one.

The many atrocities committed by the Germans hardened the resolve of Britain and France to retaliate, and they subsequently lost 60 per cent of their officers in the first few months of the war.

Forgive me for being so long winded, but this is my understanding of why I'm over here. I'm missing you something terrible.

I long to receive your letters; actually, I can't wait to receive them.

I love you dearly,
Wilf

Having the letters sent to home suited Mrs. Davis because Ann came home to stay more regularly these days, even if it was only for a quick overnight visit. Ann would take the letter straight to her room and read it two or three times before coming out with red eyes. However, there was also a glow to her face that indicated to her mother that everything was all right. Mrs. Davis was just as keen to hear the news, so

Anne was able to read aloud parts of the letter that weren't too personal, or even hand the pages to her.

In another letter, Wilf said:

> *I very much appreciate the hospitality shown by so many of the French families who invite the men into their homes when on leave. They put on parties to share what little they have. Some homes are made available to them by contacts made by the helpers at the YMCA units. There are lots of men who prefer to head straight for the pubs and virtually stay there until their leave is over. Being a non-drinker, I prefer the hospitality shown by grateful families, within their own homes. There are sometimes lots of French girls invited to these parties, but I prefer to be just friendly to everyone. I don't get too involved and prefer to think about you and our wonderful times together in London. How I miss you on such occasions.*

Neither Ann nor Mrs. Davis, were thrilled to hear that Wilf had been taken to a local hospital for medical attention to the back of his left hand. He explained the situation and how fortunate he had been.

He wrote:

> *I have to tell you that I've had some hospital treatment. I was carrying the Lewis gun with my left hand around the barrel, as is the usual procedure, rushing to a new forward position. A bullet knocked the gun from my grasp, shattering part of the wooden hand grip around the barrel, which flew off*

> *and penetrated the back of my hand. The miraculous thing was that the bullet had been heading straight for my heart, and the hit on the barrel stopped the bullet. The hospital staff cleaned the wound, put in some stitches, and told me to report daily for a week, after which time it should heal pretty well.*

Ann looked up at her mother without speaking as they realised how close Wilf was to death at any time.

Ann would later write to Wilf and say how she wished she could have been the nurse in the hospital over there to take care of him. She wanted to tell him how often she thought of joining the Military Nursing Service so she could be closer to him, but thought better of it. Maybe if Wilf had not come onto the scene, she would have already joined the service.

Ann had two days off duty and settled down to answer Wilf's letter. She kept it short, to only five pages, and took it around to the post office on Euston Road. That task took up most of her day.

The next morning, the postman arrived with a letter addressed to Mr. and Mrs. Davis. Ann reluctantly handed the letter to her mother in a very hesitant manner because the letter was edged in black, the customary envelope used to notify of a death. Ann's first reaction was to think of Wilf, but she knew a letter would not be sent to the Davis family, but to his own family in Australia. A look of fear ascended on Mrs. Davis as she slowly eased herself onto the couch to read the letter. Her hands were trembling something terrible. Ann could see how she deliberately delayed opening the letter because she knew what it would say. She eventually withdrew the single page and read the first few lines, collapsing onto Ann's shoulder who was now kneeling in front of her.

They both sobbed for a long time before Ann read the whole letter aloud. It read: *Lieutenant Joseph Davis was involved in a major battle around the town of Passchendaele in Belgium. He has now been missing in action for ten days. There was no positive identification, but many bodies have been recovered. He is now presumed dead.*

After they were able to compose themselves a little, Ann decided Mr. Davis had to be notified at work. It was only just after ten o'clock. Ann went next door to tell Mavis, who offered to catch the bus to Gooch's shop to break the news to Mr. Davis. Ann stayed to comfort her mother.

Mr. Davis arrived home with Mavis at around two, to share this sudden and tragic loss with his remaining family.

The rest of the day was spent making a list of other family members and friends and writing short notes advising them of their loss. There was no funeral for the family to arrange. They just had to get on with life like so many other families in London who received similar letters every day. The Davis family had been shielded from such tragedies in the past, other than grandparents dying of old age, which was going to happen as part of life.

Ann arranged to take an extra two days off to be with her parents. Just as well, because she received another letter from Wilf. He had just returned from leave to be told they were to move out again for the front line. His letter dated August 23, posted from Boves, was received on September 2. All he knew or could say was that there was a lot more activity around the camp and its perimeters this time, so something really big was planned. He expected to be back from the front line around September 5 and would write again as usual.

On September 3, Ann wrote a short letter to Wilf advising details of Joe's death. The two of them had never met. She told him how she was devastated by the news of losing her only brother and was too upset to write in detail as she usually did. She would write again in a couple of days.

Ann signed off saying:

> *I will continue to pray for your safekeeping. Having to wait another ten days or so before hearing from you again will be an extremely painful wait, especially after the death of my dear brother.*

Two days later, the King's Hospital received notice that a bombing had taken place that afternoon in the King's Cross area. Ann was still off duty when the news was received. Bombing raids had not been as frequent as in the past, but Hazel, Ann's closest colleague, discussed the situation with their other colleagues. They were naturally very keen to find out just where the bombs landed this time. Was Ann's home in that area?

Casualties had come from the station area, so Hazel talked tried to find someone who could help her with details. Much to her horror, she found one patient who was still unconscious but had identification showing that he lived on Argyle Street, the street adjacent to Whidbourne Street that Hazel knew well.

Hazel immediately reported her findings to the matron, who also showed her concern for Ann, saying, "I wonder if Ann and her family are safe. Please keep asking questions and keep me informed."

Ann, on her second day off after Joe's death, had chosen to make a trip into town to look around the big stores to find something especially nice to cheer up her mother. She was on her way home in the tube, which came to an unscheduled stop in the tunnel for an unusually long time. Stoppages were caused sometimes because of air raids above. It was natural for most people to think the worst at such times and to hope it would not affect them other than just being late home or some other trivial inconvenience.

The passengers in the train could do nothing but wait in the hot and stuffy conditions. It eventually moved on and arrived at King's Cross Station nearly one hour late. Ann hurried through the station and emerged at street level, fronting onto Euston Road. She could see a lot of activity off to her right and saw smoke rising from the direction of Whidbourne Street. She crossed the road and was now running as quickly as she could. The closer she got to home, the more she started to panic.

There were policemen and military chaps everywhere, but she didn't stop to ask questions. She kept on going, ducking under a barrier rope strung across the street while a policeman was busy looking the other way directing some teenagers to keep away. She rounded the barber's shop corner and the Wellington Pub.

Ann could now see a lot of smoke coming from the left-hand side of the street. As she hurriedly moved out into the middle of the street, she could see wooden houses still burning further along the street. Now worse than that, she could see that her own home had been gutted. The outer stone front and side walls were mostly still standing, the roof and upper floors had collapsed, and smoke and steam were still coming from the inside of the house.

Ann froze on the spot. She could hear shouting from some of the fireman still directing water onto the inside of her home and the other wooden homes. She frantically looked around, but there was no sign of any of the close neighbours; only a few people gathered at the far end of the street past a barricade.

A policeman tried to stop her from proceeding further, but she convinced him that she was one of the residents of that area. The front of her stone home didn't look like it had been completely destroyed. Unlike Mavis's wooden house and the other three adjoining places, which had totally collapsed, there was very little left of them. There were policemen and military men standing around her house, talking in groups and pointing in the air and to the rear of her house. More barriers had been deployed to prevent anyone from entering the smouldering properties.

Ann tried to stay calm and approached one of the military men standing at the front of where Mavis's house had stood only yesterday. She asked in a measured voice, as she would have done in her duty as a nurse, "What happened to the people from the house next door?" pointing to her home.

He replied, "Three people had been sheltering in an air-raid shelter at the rear of the house; it suffered a direct hit. They could not identify the bodies positively, but I'm told it was an elderly man and a lady presumed to be his wife, plus their daughter in her twenties. She had blonde hair."

Ann could not even breathe let alone talk as her legs gave way and she slipped to the ground. The military officer called for the ambulance men waiting next to their vehicle a couple of doors down the street. They tried to help, but they could not revive her. The policemen suggested that she should be taken straight to the hospital. Ann was stretchered into the ambulance and rushed off to the University College Hospital; it was less than a mile from the station straight down Euston Road.

When the ambulance arrived at the hospital, Ann was still unable to communicate. All that the driver could tell the receiving nurse was that she was somehow involved in the bombing attack near King's Cross Station, but nobody at the scene knew her name. They checked her into the emergency ward, and a couple of nurses and a doctor carried out various tests and procedures to bring her around, but to no avail. The nurse went through Ann's bag, which was at the end of the bed, and found a nursing certificate from the University of Worcester issued in the name of Ann Davis. They assumed this to be the name of the patient but did not have an address for her.

The doctor decided that complete rest was the best treatment for this patient who was obviously in deep shock.

After three days of not being able to communicate, Ann finally came around. The nurses brought her food and water. After she was able to finish the sandwich and the water, she started putting together the pieces of what had happened. There were so many things going around in her mind—the death of Joe, the bombing raid, losing her mother and father and Mavis. She still had difficulty talking properly. She lay there thinking about Wilf and her future.

When taking the required amounts of food and liquid offered to her by the nurses, she said very little. When questioned by the doctor, she haltingly said, "Both of my parents and friend next door were killed in the bombing raid at King's Cross." She also told him about news the previous day regarding her brother's death on the Western Front.

The doctor said, "Well, I certainly understand your situation. You need to rest for a few more days." He moved on to make his report to the sister in charge.

All the time Ann lay there, she considered the possibility of joining the military nurses, just as her cousin from Brighton had done. She decided not to contact the King's until she made up her mind about enlisting.

On day five, Ann was up and walking a little. She asked one of the nurses if she knew anything about the bomb attack near King's Cross Station last week. The nurse said they had been so dreadfully busy over the last week since the bombing that they had little time to learn of any details to pass on. On day six, Ann was up and walking much better, so she found her way to the lounge room to look for some newspapers that could give her more information.

The only paper available there was yesterday's, which she hunted through. She found a very small article headed "Three people killed in shelter." It was about one of the senior men from Gooch's Hardware Store who was one of three killed by a direct hit during the King's Cross air raid. He had been sheltering in an air-raid shelter with his wife and another female, as yet unidentified.

The shelter had been built for his family by an Australian soldier using material supplied by Gooch's Store. The article was not complete because somebody had torn out an article on the back of the page, and a few lines were missing at the bottom of the article. Then at the top of the next column it continued and said a funeral service was held at the Anglican church on the High Street the previous day.

Ann tried to cry, but tears would not come.

On day seven, Ann checked herself out and walked directly across Euston Road to the Warren Street underground station. Her mind was still pretty numb as she tried to understand what was happening to her.

Ann took the first train to come along—to where she did not know, nor did she care. She just wanted to get as far away from King's Cross as was possible. Her brain was still not functioning well; she sat and stared into space as the train stopped at station after station until it reached the end of the line at Brixton. That was as far south as the Victoria Line travelled.

Ann remained slumped in the seat as the train reversed direction and headed north. Although she was staring into space, she could not help notice the banner on the carriage wall encouraging nurses to serve their country in the military. As the train approached the central city stations, Ann knew what she now had to do. She would get off the train in the city and go to the recruiting office to check things out.

The only family she had left were her aunt and uncle in Brighton and her cousin, Heather, who had already joined the Military Nursing Service. Now she was an orphan with no immediate family left; Ann felt that she needed to make a new start in life. She had been contemplating for some time the possibility of joining the Queen Alexandra's Imperial Military Nursing Service (QAIMNS).

Her brain was still much in shock, but her inner spirit was telling her to join up. What did she have left to stay for here in London? The only thing that stopped her from joining up previously was that she didn't want to put more strain on her parents, especially with Joe away at the front. Now with Joe's death and this terrible and tragic upheaval in her life over the last week, her mind was made up. Besides, she could be closer to Wilf on the other side of the channel. She didn't think clearly about the communication problems there would be on the vast Western Front.

The armed services were always calling for trained nurses, so when the train arrived back into the city, Ann knew exactly where to go. She alighted at the Oxford Circus Station and headed straight for the QAIMNS Recruiting Office. Fortunately, as it turned out, she had only the previous week put into her purse her nursing certificate, which had previously been kept in her locker at King's. At that time, she decided it would be better kept at home. The certificate was still in her purse.

The recruitment nurses and volunteer staff were very friendly and helpful when answering the few questions Ann had and the many questions that needed to be asked of all applicants. Of course the applicants basically needed only two qualifications, a nursing certificate and a willingness to go.

The question was asked, "When would you be available and be willing to go?"

Ann said, "I've just lost my home and family in a bombing raid last week, so I'm ready to go anytime."

The recruitment sister said, "You may be aware that we are desperate for nurses to go right now; as a matter of fact, we have a group leaving for France tomorrow."

Ann said, "I've no home to go to. All of my possessions have been destroyed. Why should I wait?"

"Very good," said the sister.

"I'm willing to go tomorrow, but I have nowhere to sleep tonight."

The sister said, "That's not a problem because we have spare beds right here, just for that purpose."

Ann signed the necessary documentation and was immediately assigned to one of the assistants, who took her to the store for a full fit-out and issue of clothing, sleeping attire, and shoes, plus the necessary bathroom essentials. The assistant then showed her to a dormitory occupied by other nurses also being shipped out tomorrow.

"No time for introductions now," she said, "other than a brief announcement to the other girls."

She raised her voice and said to the girls, "Listen up, ladies, this is Nurse Davis. You will have plenty of time in the morning to get acquainted."

Before departing, Ann said, "Where can I get some postage stamps to post some letters?"

"Stamps are available from the young volunteer lady in the writing room, and there is a Royal Mail post-box right outside the front door to the left."

Ann was reminded that they would all receive a wake-up call at six for breakfast and to be ready to leave at eight o'clock sharp.

Ann was now in Queen Alexandra's Imperial Nursing Service; the recruitment and induction had all been so surprisingly fast and efficient.

Ann followed her out of the room and went straight to the writing room. On QAIMN's embossed paper, Ann wrote her first letter to the matron of King's College Hospital. She tendered her sudden resignation with an explanation for her sudden departure, brought about by the sudden loss of both parents in the bombing raid and her brother's death. She then slipped the letter into the supplied envelope and paid the girl at the desk for the stamp, as she had been advised earlier. On second thoughts, she bought another two stamps and returned to the writing desk.

She wrote a second letter to her best friend, Hazel, asking her to spread the word to her other friends at the hospital and those at the Church of England on the High Street. They would no doubt be aware of the tragedy that took the lives of her parents and her next-door neighbour and good friend, Mavis. She also mentioned the loss of her brother, Joe, and explained how she had suffered shock and was admitted to the University Collage Hospital. She explained how she was not known at that hospital and was not aware of the memorial for her parents until the day after it took place. She said how she had been in shock for a week and unable to communicate.

She wrote:

> *Please tell them I was so devastated after the news of Joseph's death and then this terrible tragedy right on top. My whole world collapsed, and I'm still unable to face anyone at all, hence the reason for my sudden disappearance and subsequent joining of QAIMNS. You have no idea how quickly it all happened. My acceptance and deployment overseas literally happened overnight. Maybe that was for the best, because I had no clothing left at all, save what I was wearing, and no home to go to.*

The third letter she addressed to the postmaster at King's Cross on Euston Road. Ann knew him quite well and explained about her sudden decision to join QAIMNS and her imminent deployment overseas. She asked for all mail for her and the Davis family to be forwarded to her new address, care of QAIMNS. She provided her new enrolment number and the address for the delivery of mail.

Ann addressed the envelopes, fixed the stamps, and walked slowly down the stairs. She told the security guard stationed at the front door that she was only slipping just outside to post some letters. He held the door open for her return after she dropped the letters in the box.

With weary legs, she climbed the stairs and returned to the appointed dorm, where the other girls were already fast asleep. She half-heartedly checked out the new clothing issued in the dim light available, before undressing. She then dragged herself into bed, buried her face in the pillow, and cried herself to sleep.

The next morning promptly at eight o'clock, they were marshalled for what was to be, for most of her new colleagues, their first journey in a military vehicle. The girls all got to know each other as the vehicle proceeded to the wharf for embarkation. This was to be for most of them their first adventure abroad.

*

A Royal Postal driver collected the mail from the box for delivery to the central sorting depot. Less than half a mile after the pickup and directly ahead on the street corner, the driver saw two men detonating a sound rocket; it went off with a boom and rose some three hundred feet into the air, exploding with another deafening boom. This was the method used in the inner city with unmistakable sound to warn the people of an imminent air raid. He had never been this close to one of these rockets previously. It jolted him into reality as he panicked into hurriedly searching for somewhere to find cover.

Hand-cranked claxons started to sound in the distance as people scurried in all directions to seek cover wherever it could be found. The driver made a sudden turn down a narrow lane for protection between two large, three-story wooden buildings. He stopped his van close against one of the buildings so as not to block emergency traffic, as they had been trained to do in such an emergency. He hurriedly abandoned his van to seek cover for himself. He ran down the lane until he found an entrance to an underground warehouse where he could shelter.

Whilst under cover, he heard another large explosion, which sounded quite near, but he was unsure of the direction of the blast. He listened for the council vehicle driving through the streets with one of the local members of the Boy Scouts aboard, sounding the traditional all-clear on his bugle.

After some twenty minutes, he heard the bugle sounding the all-clear. He left the safety of his shelter and returned to the place where he had left his van. To his horror, he found that one of the buildings had been hit by a bomb, setting it on fire. The fire quickly spread to the other wooden building across the lane. The Royal Mail delivery van was caught in the middle, with the swirling flames totally destroying it, including the mail within.

Without the driver or Ann knowing, all trace of Nurse Davis had suddenly and totally vanished from London.

Chapter 19

Wilf returned to France from Blighty after the most wonderful week with Ann, staying at the Headland Hotel in Torquay and the other special places they had visited. He'd had a great time away from the sounds and smells of war, away from the terrible mud and blood that was everywhere around him in this part of the world.

Not only was mud on the battlefields, but the mud was also in the billets, in the camps, and even in the villages that had so far escaped the devastation that shelling brought to so many towns. The transports moving through the un-shelled towns brought the mud and left it as a permanent reminder of a war taking place not far away. The only redeeming feature about its deep brown colour was its ability to camouflage the rich crimson colour of blood—blood spilt by the millions of soldiers, only to be absorbed and buried out of sight forever.

When he arrived back to his battalion, he found the numbers had again been decimated, with no extra reinforcements coming in to fill the many vacancies. The boys in B Company were also just back from leave.

A few of the boys were standing in a group and saw Wilf approach. Jack Donaldson was the first to see him and said, "Hey, look who's back!" The boys all turned and gave a cheer.

Bob Edwards said, "When we saw you taken away by the ambulance, Wilf, we weren't sure if you would return. You were pretty much gone, mate. There were some others who had the same problem that didn't seem to be as bad; they haven't returned, and we hear that they won't be back."

Wilf said, "Well, I again had the personal services of the same prettiest blonde nurse in the whole of England to take care of me. That's what makes the difference."

One of the boys said, "How come you managed to get the same nurse? There's something fishy about this."

Lieutenant Maxwell heard the commotion and the early remarks from nearby. He walked over, saying, "Good to have you back, mate," as he joined the group.

They all wanted to speak at once, trying to find out the name of this nurse in case they too were shipped out to Blighty.

Wilf said, "That's for me to know and for you not to find out until I'm ready. There are plenty more nurses where this one comes from, but none could ever be considered in the same class."

"Why do you get the special treatment?" quipped one. "Do you know the king or someone up top?"

They probed him for more information and were extremely jealous when he told them of the places he had been.

"You blokes would never believe the places I've been to and seen, so I won't bore you with the details."

"We can stand it for a while, so try us," said Fred as he stomped out his cigarette with his muddy boot.

"Well, I stayed with my nurse-friend in a hotel at Torquay; all expenses were paid by her parents. The hotel used to be the holiday home of the Russian royal family, the Romanovs. While staying there, I was mistakenly listed as missing, believed murdered."

"You're kidding us, mate. We aren't that gullible," said Bob.

"No, I'm not kidding you at all. I'll tell you more at another time. We also visited the historical town of Bath, built by the Romans as a rest resort for their officers. There were so many places, but I'll tell you about them all at some other time."

George said, "We know you're a bullock driver, mate, but we didn't know you were a dreamer also. You must do a lot of that sleeping under the stars back home."

Wilf knew they found it hard to believe he could have so many experiences to tell about.

Joe Maxwell said, "For a bullock driver, you certainly know how to find your way around to some interesting places. I'm intrigued by the wide variety of places you have visited, not only on this trip to Blighty but the earlier one as well."

Wilf said, "That's one of the advantages of being a non-drinker; it's easier to remember the details."

"Don't you worry—I've had some good times too," said Joe.

"Yes, but most of those activities were inside a bar, and you couldn't remember much about them the next morning, let alone a week later."

"You may have a point there. Maybe it's the truth. I'm envious of your ability to have a good time without the need for grog." He turned to leave the group but turned back and said, "Thanks, Wilf, for coming back. We desperately need every extra man we can get."

Wilf enquired after a number of the boys who were not amongst the group, to find that he had lost a number of good mates. He could see that his mates had been through a very rough time while he was away. Some of them had been to Blighty over the last couple of years, including Maxwell, but none had the good fortune he had been blessed to receive, and he knew it.

The first time Wilf got a chance to talk with Burt, he asked him to fill him in with details of what had happened while he was away. Burt had a close cousin who was an officer in the Eighteenth Battalion. They always managed to spend time together drinking together whilst on leave. Often Burt would be told things that he was not supposed to know, so he was always good for information.

Burt said, "I'll try and fill you in the best I can. You won't be surprised to know that constant attacks by the Allies and counterattacks by the Huns continued through the spring and summer of 1918, around the time you were away.

"There appeared to be some major achievements by the Second Division as well as the other Australian divisions under the command of General Monash."

"Good to see them giving an Aussie a go," Wilf interrupted.

"Yes it is, not before time. The battle for Amiens in early August produced nearly six thousand casualties, although these were much lighter than similar-sized battles in previous years. This new strategy required that the attack be properly coordinated along a twenty-kilometre front. They used over four hundred tanks, plus another one hundred supply tanks. The tanks moved first, followed by the infantry, armoured cars, and then the cavalry, without the customary shelling beforehand."

"That makes a lot of sense," said Wilf as he shifted his position to get more comfortable on the bunk. "I think it does anyway because the shelling sometimes lasts for three days or more and destroys the ground over which we chaps have to travel forward. Keep going, Burt, you're doing well."

"Many times, the tanks emerged out of the fog and took the Huns by surprise. This has brought about a totally new form of warfare."

"I can see that, and better for us, I hope?"

"The battle for Albert by the Thirty-Second Division was considered a real success. The New Zealanders are making good progress towards Bapaume. The problem is, Wilf, the Australian units have been virtually winning every ridge but killing off a little of themselves each time they make an advance."

"That's obviously why our numbers are down," said Wilf.

"You're dead right, mate, but the primary objective now is to take the town of Peronne, an old fortress town. It cannot be taken until the artillery and machine guns positioned on Mont St. Quentin are destroyed because they have a commanding view down over the town of Peronne. This makes it impossible to advance."

A bugle sounded for the evening meal, so the conversation was interrupted as they both moved off to the canteen.

Wilf had been in and out of the line a few times since returning after his bout of pneumonia at King's College Hospital. He had a lot of mail to catch up on when he first returned, but since then, there was a regular stream of letters from home and of course from Ann.

The letter from Ann written after their second parting in London was very special to him. By now, it was rather tattered due to the number of times he had read it. He pulled it out to read it once more

> *My dearest Wilf,*
>
> *How my heart broke as I waited in vain to get one more glimpse of you before I returned to the King's. I couldn't bring myself to face any of the staff, so I found a log under a shady tree behind King's and sat and cried for an awfully long time until there were no tears left to cry.*
>
> *Wilf, I hope you don't get sick of me saying so, but I really love you so much. I can't bear the thought of you over there amongst all that terrible uncertainty. I would do absolutely anything to be near you even if I was also in danger; my love for you is so strong. There is something I haven't been able to put into words in person, but I will tell you now in written words…*

Wilf finished the letter again and folded it away for safekeeping.

He only just managed to keep up with his replies because he was now receiving letters from additional friends. They believed he had been away from home for so long that he would be grateful for another letter from home, which he certainly was. However, the time required to answer all of his mail kept him busy when not at the front.

Wilf's Eighteenth Battalion had been waiting in the supports for four days before being put on standby to move up to the lines, just like thousands of other Australian troops. It was here while waiting that Wilf learned that his good friend Roy Brewer had been killed only a couple of miles away and awarded the Military Cross five days after he died. Wilf had learned before he enlisted that Roy's brother, Ira, from Dungog, who was engaged to his sister, Vera Yates, had been seriously wounded at the waterline on the beach of Gallipoli at dawn on April, 25, 1915, ANZAC Day.

Ira was left to die in the shallow water with the stretcher bearers believing he was already dead. Finding him still alive after nightfall but with his neck badly shot away, they transferred him to an aid post where he was left for another two days, giving preference to others they believed could be saved. Three days after he was wounded, they found him still alive, so they patched him up and evacuated him for a long stay in a hospital in Egypt. Ira survived and was sent home for a further long stay in another hospital.

This death of Ira's brother would be an added blow to his mother and family that Wilf knew well.

Wilf's battalion received orders to move out on August 27 and again made their way to the lines as they had done so many times before in the darkness. They were under gas attack most of the way. Sticking to the duckboards was near impossible. Their job was to relieve the other units currently in the trenches.

In some places alongside the duckboards, the rats were having a party, feeding off the dead horses and donkeys as well as soldiers' bodies or body parts. Most of the soldiers' bodies were still half buried in the mud, awaiting the overworked stretcher-bearers.

The fighting was ferocious, to say the least. The smell of the explosive chemicals tore away at Wilf's throat. The continuous flashes and the never-ending thunderous roar from the exploding shells mixed with the rattle of the machine guns from both sides; it set off hammering inside his brain that wouldn't stop. It was near impossible to get through the narrow saps carrying shovels, sandbags, rolls of barbed wire, Mills bombs, ammunition, and weapons, sometimes weighing more than fifty pounds per man. It was especially difficult moving against the outward flow of those being relieved, trying to make it out before their luck ran out.

The medics were already under enormous pressure to respond to the never-ending cries of "Medic!" or "Stretcher-bearer!" from somewhere out there in the impenetrable blackness all around them. The wounded men were somewhere out there, hoping someone would get to them before they died in this godforsaken place called the Somme. Hundreds of bodies were strewn everywhere along the trenches and in no-man's-land. Corpses were often heaved over the parapet from the trenches to make more room for the men doing the fighting.

The men were already exhausted from the move up to the lines, but orders were orders, and tiredness didn't seem to be a consideration anymore. It wasn't long before the orders came to "get ready." The plan was to hop over the bags at 0400 hours. Waiting those last fifteen minutes was one of the worst parts of the trench warfare. Men smoked nonstop, with the glow of the cigarette seen by all in the trench as a string of dancing glow worms. This was the time men discussed all kinds of religion and death without much real knowledge of the former. They were experts in the latter, nevertheless.

Wilf had only taken up smoking since being at the front. Every soldier received a ration, which he had previously given away to his smoking mates. Now at the front, he considered there were much worse chemicals to be breathed in to his body regularly than what they said was in tobacco. It was at times like this that he found a cigarette to be helpful. It helped to calm down the frayed nerves from such relentless tension and exhaustion.

Who knew how many of the enemy were already out there with their rifles already loaded? Their guns would be aimed at the top of their bags, waiting for the first heads to appear over the parapet after the whistle sounded. Once over the parapet, the next challenge would be getting through the rusted belts of tangled barbed wire. Wilf could see here and there what looked like heavy bundles of wet, brown cloth draped over the wire with red arms hanging limp. These were bodies still awaiting recovery by the stretcher-bearers after the last stunt. He knew that the moment he reached the first gap in the wire, he would be subjected to a withering rattle of machine-gun fire both from the right and the left flank.

At four in the morning, the whistles sounded, and up the ladders they went with far too many of them falling back, as always happened.

It was an absolute nightmare. Wilf could not remember seeing so many of his mates in the unit being knocked. He could see them falling in the darkness, silhouetted against the flash of the artillery shells exploding. It was raining constantly, and he couldn't see very far to the right or the left. From the information they were given before leaving the supports, the total number of troops engaged in this push would be larger than any previous battle for the Australians.

Wilf could only imagine what was happening all around him. What he did know was that after they left their trenches, the artillery barrage from the enemy was far in excess of anything he had previously witnessed. Now the artillery from their own boys up the back thundered into action, and shells whistled overhead. Unfortunately, the barrels had been in continuous use for three years or more and were in terrible condition and not capable of accuracy. This resulted in more and more of their own shells dropping short behind and amongst their own lines.

The craters left by the exploding shells were joined closely together like the dimples on a golf ball. Each hole was filled with poisonous chemicals and water from the constant rain. To Wilf, it looked like a field of freshly ploughed soil constantly bubbling with each new shell burst. The upheavals appeared to be generated by an enormous volcano underneath the surface that could not totally break out. This force continued to heave the field up and down in an irregular pattern.

None of the field was left at its original height, but with an ugly pockmarked face of craters full of poisonous liquid. The volcano finally settled down for a short rest, only to rebuild newfound energy for another breakout.

Wilf and his Lewis gun mate, Burt, miraculously made it through the wire. They needed to stay close together as a team. The shells were exploding all around them with machine-gun bullets whipping up the mud in a continuous pattern of dancing pimples wherever they could see. There was nowhere to move without inviting certain death.

They were pinned down in an impossible situation. The mud was so sloppy that it sucked him down two feet deep, making any forward progress impossible. He peered over the rim of the crater where they were sheltered and had nearly been entombed. All that could be seen in the dim light provided by the continuous flashes of exploding shells was a sea of devastation that could not be described rationally.

Explosions were becoming more frequent and closer all the time. The only way forward was around the rim of each crater until that also became impossible to negotiate. They couldn't go forward and couldn't go back, so they decided through sign language to dig deeper into one of the mud craters and stay down.

Wilf sometimes felt a little safer inside one of the craters, believing that lightning never strikes twice in the same place. Hopefully that theory also applied to shells.

Because of the heavy rain, the Germans had stopped firing the gas canisters so they could remove their masks and eat some of their dry rations. Although they were called dry rations, often they were badly baked and shipped soggy, or they became soggy during transport.

Burt drew close and tried to speak above the din, saying, "I cannot remember the last time I enjoyed a hot meal from the mobile cookers."

"I've no idea when we'll get the next one." Wilf tucked into the hard biscuits and water.

Dawn broke, but the rain and artillery bombardment continued. Wilf reckoned that if it were not for their ability to bury themselves in the mud, they would be dead. He calculated that six shells were exploding each minute within a radius of about twenty-five yards. He assumed this would be the same for every other man involved in this Allied attack. The noise was absolutely unbelievable and terrifying, with the scream of shells bursting in every direction.

The terrifying flood light from the flares constantly sent aloft by the Huns showed the tenseness and terror on men's faces. Sometimes in green, now blue, now fiery red, illuminating and pinpointing the Australians' position. The enemy made frenzied attempts to give directions to their men on the artillery located maybe a mile behind the line, to direct even closer bombardment of the Australian troops. After each flare was sent aloft, the chances were the next shells would land even closer.

The exploding shells would spread their flying steel splinters in every direction until stopped by flesh and bone, or penetrate into the soft mud to lay buried for a long time, only to be found by some destitute farmer in the future ploughing his field. Wilf thought this could continue to happen over many years, long after this awful, wretched, and forlorn war had finally concluded.

At the first flush of dawn, Wilf and Burt peered through the grey light across the valley of agony and saw terror born out of the darkness, the battlefield. Wilf could see that the whole army that was supposed to be advancing on the enemy was pinned down in the Flanders mud and couldn't move in any direction. By noon, the rain stopped, but the bombardment continued. *How long can the Germans keep this up?* he thought to himself. *They must run out of shells soon.* That was not to be the case, and the bombardment continued after dark and for a total of three days and nights.

Eventually the bombardment lifted a little, either because of a shortage of shells on the other side, or Fritz was planning something different.

Wilf wondered about the various names given to the enemy. Sometimes they were called the Huns, and at other times Fritz. He worked it out that Fritz was used as a less aggressive, humane term, if that was possible, whilst the Hun was the worst description one could think of when describing someone wanting to kill you.

Soon the Australian officers extracted themselves out of the mud. They were unrecognisable because of the thick mud that slammed into their body from each bursting shell that landed nearby. Now with the whipped-mud covering their clothing and faces, these officers moved around, motivating their men to climb out of the holes of unutterable slush and bubbling ooze and to push ahead.

Wilf believed the men would fall asleep if left in the holes any longer.

For some reason unknown at the time, Fritz was thought to be pulling back from his earlier position on the higher ground. This allowed Wilf and Burt along with the other Australians to extract themselves from the muddy plains where they had been pinned down for three days. It allowed them to move ahead with their own shells lobbing as close as sixty yards ahead of their line, kicking up a wall of earth and smoke that also protected them from the enemy machine-gunner's eyes, searching for their targets.

As the Diggers gave pursuit, so did the Australian artillery, lifting forward of the men as they advanced. Wilf passed hundreds of stinking corpses now covered in thousands of flies that had previously been sheltering from the rain. The flies were back doing the only thing they knew, hunting and devouring rotting food.

Wilf and Burt and the rest of their unit were on the move, lunging from one stinking shell hole to another, keeping close behind their own artillery advancing just in front of their line. As they crossed temporary bridges over low marshes, Wilf could see in the early morning light the exploding shells on either side producing large geysers of dirty muddy water rising high in the early-morning grey sky.

The men moved forward to the bend in the river where they could now see Mont St. Quentin ahead, about one mile. The Mont rose out of the plains to a summit of about one hundred metres. It wasn't a high mountain by any means, but due to the flatness of the surrounding plains, it gave a commanding view for many miles, allowing the Hun to closely watch the advancing Australians.

"Monument erected on Mont St Quentin to honour the men of Aust. 2nd Div."

The Diggers continued their advance towards the Mont with newfound energy—energy mixed with adrenalin coming from a source that Wilf did not understand, but it was real.

Fritz had been taken by surprise. Wilf could now see them scurrying around the lower slopes trying to move their equipment higher up the Mount.

The Diggers rushed the lower trenches with so much shouting that it sounded more like thousands rather than hundreds, causing Fritz to take flight. The attacking Diggers were now completely out of breath, stumbling down into the newly captured empty trenches. They dropped onto anything above water level and drew deep on their newly lit cigarettes and let their own artillery continue to fire low overhead at the retreating Huns.

The Allied armies were now moving forward in a tidal wave that Fritz was unable to stem. They were in retreat back past the Beaurevoir Line. This allowed the Australian troops to gain more ground than at any previous time since arriving on the Somme, over three years.

Wilf didn't have the energy himself, but he saw two diggers with newfound energy jogging along out in front of the rest of the men, stopping occasionally to throw themselves down to the firing position, to discharge another drum from their Lewis gun. They raked the moving targets ahead before jumping up to continue the chase of breathless Fritz franticly trying to haul away heavy equipment.

The Australians continued the pursuit with a new vengeance. Many prisoners were taken, and word spread around that their officers were not keen to face more Australian advances.

The Australians quickly advanced a further two miles past the summit before being relieved by the American Expeditionary Force under General Pershing. Although it was now seventeen months since the Americans had declared war on the Central powers, they were only just getting into the action. In this case, they had fresh troops and hundreds of planes at their command.

"Troops under attack on Mont St Quentin."

The Eighteenth Battalion boys were too exhausted to move out straightaway; all they wanted was something to fill their empty bellies and to lie about. Besides, the enemy was now running away from them, not attacking them, so they lay around to watch the Americans at war.

Wilf thought that the Americans' enthusiasm and dash of courage was outweighed by their lack of battle experience. They were well equipped but sadly deficient in the essentials of war.

Now that the battalion had been relieved at long last, it was their job to find their way back to the supports, wherever that was now. Because they had advanced so far in such a short time, there was no transport available immediately to take the men back. They had to foot-slog it for hours until the struggling rabble of weary men were eventually picked up. Wilf was totally exhausted, but he wasn't alone. The unit had been on the go for what seemed to Wilf like months; he hadn't kept a record.

The men were so tired they struggled to climb up into the back of the trucks. Wilf, like many others, fell asleep standing while swaying to and fro as the transport vehicle bumped and lurched around the twisting, greasy tracks on way back to the supports. He woke up on a couple of occasions when the transport column stopped for some delay up ahead.

On one of those occasions, he heard someone say, "Well, look where we are, right outside the Corbie Town Hall."

Wilf lifted his sagging head and peered through bleary eyes to see a temporary sign attached over the main entrance door, which read: Corbie Casualty Clearing Station. He could not help notice the large number of wounded soldiers waiting outside, leaning against the wall, sitting down on the ground, or lying on stretchers. They were already covered in bloodied field dressings, waiting for their chance to be taken inside for further treatment, in what appeared to be a very busy hospital.

When they eventually arrived back at the supports camp, the men crashed, even before getting out of their stinking clothes and having a bath.

They had been in the same stinking, rotten clothes for over fifty days. Not only stinking because of the mud, but also from their body waste, released while trapped in the mud for days on end. It was a total of nearly eight weeks since they were ordered to move up to the supports until they got back to base for a proper scrub down.

During the battles, Wilf had little time to dwell on his memories of Ann. His time had been fully occupied encouraging every ounce of his strength and mind to stay alive. When he crashed on the bunk, he slept for who knows how long. The next day, he woke and had a bath and cleaned everything in his possession.

Despite the exhausted state of the men, their Aussie humour could not be completely suppressed. One wag made the comment returning from the wash house that he needed a half an hour in the tub before he could find his missing singlet.

Trucks were provided again to transport the men back to base camp. Wilf was anxious on arrival to collect mail that would be waiting for him. They arrived at base in time for a late lunch.

Wilf had a clear plan in his mind of what he would do for the next week. He would spend the next day reading all of the news received and then a couple of days answering the letters.

However, that wasn't Maxwell's plan. Burt told him that Maxwell was looking for him.

Maxwell wasn't hard to find and said, "I'm recommending you for a promotion. You are to be shipped out in two days to NCO's Training School at Amiens. If you need to know more, contact your sergeant; he will have all of the details."

Wilf understood why he was being promoted, simply because there were few others left to fill the positions, experienced or not.

Wilf said, "Thank you, sir. By the way, sir, I understand you acquired another Luger pistol. I was wondering if you planned to get rid of it."

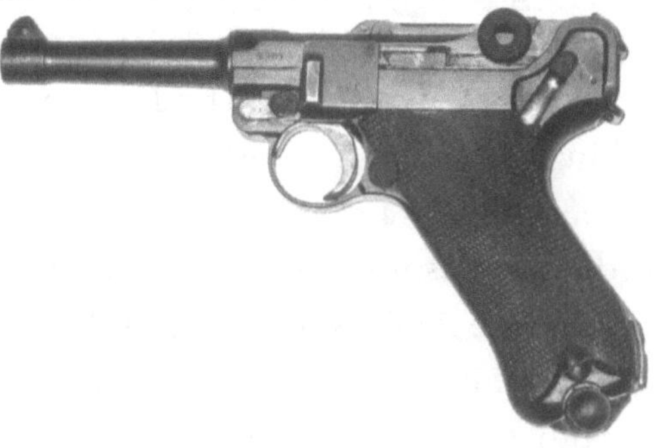

The Luger pistol captured by
Lt. Joe Maxwell and given to Wilf Yates

"Yes, I am. I already have one or two, as you know. Would you like it? I would be glad to give it to you as a reminder of your promotion. I'll let my batman know, and he will get it for you," he said as he walked off.

Wilf had been nearby in the enemy trench when Joe acquired the Luger. He had already won two First Class Medals and Bar and was being recommended for another medal because of this action. During the assault on the Mont, Joe and some other Diggers were in the process of capturing a group of Germans. One of those was a Prussian colonel in one of the fortified trenches. The colonel was immaculately dressed, complete with eye monocle. He strutted over the torn ground towards Maxwell like he was having a Sunday stroll, demanding that he be treated like an officer by another officer. Joe said, "Well, this is where you get off, old man," and proceeded to relieve him of his field glasses and Luger pistol.

Maxwell could not be suppressed and later that day carried out another action in which he personally shot dead three Huns in a trench and captured four more prisoners. He also captured their machine gun and another Luger as a bonus.

There were not many of the original No 8 Platoon, B Company left to share the spoils. Ratting the Hun, as it was called, was like a national sport to the Diggers. This resulted in many trophies of war finding the way home in the bottom of a kitbag.

Wilf managed to get to the Postal Department and collected his bundle of mail. He flicked through the envelopes searching for those with British stamps and was devastated to find not one letter from Ann. *Why?* he kept asking himself. Why? What could possibly have gone wrong? He could not think of a reason.

Fortunately, the sun was now shining, so his washing should dry in time for the journey to Amiens. He went to the canteen, planning to have a big meal, but his appetite was not there. He left most of his meal uneaten and proceeded straight back to his tent. He lay down on his bunk with a heavy heart and fell fast asleep.

He didn't wake till lunchtime the next day, after which he reluctantly opened the mail from home. As usual, there were letters from Mother, but the only letter he really wanted was one from Ann, but there wasn't even one. Even while he was reading the mail from home, his mind kept wandering back to Ann, searching for a possible reason why there was no letter.

Chapter 20

The new recruits were ready early to board the bus from the QAIMNS Recruiting Office near Oxford Circus in the heart of London. For these girls, this would be the start of their big adventure across the channel. Ann noticed how the other nurses were so excited about leaving for the Western Front.

Ann learned from one of the girls that there had been a farewell party with family members the previous day. Family members were not permitted inside the rear courtyard this morning.

The bus arrived, and they all boarded for the journey to the wharf, for embarkation to cross the channel. The girls had met each other yesterday at the party, so they were now keen to meet the new girl who arrived late last night. While waiting around to leave the compound, they came one by one and introduced themselves. Some told why they were there. Mostly it was because of a fight with their boyfriend or family, a new challenge, or just wanting to see the other side of the channel, which was a far-off place for most of them.

Ann gravitated to a small group of four girls as they discussed excitedly their new venture. Ann said, "I've been interested to hear the various reasons why each one has joined up, so I will explain my situation."

"Please do," one of them said, "We would love to hear."

"Well, it's a sad story, starting with the notice of my brother's death at the front."

"Oh, we are sorry to hear that," another girl said.

"But that is not all. I then lost my mother, father, and best friend within two days in the air raid at King's Cross last week." Her tears started to flow as they showed their support and hugged Ann, which made things easier for her.

They loaded onto the military bus and travelled through the streets. There were a little bit like royalty, she thought, because of all the cheers they received from the people on the streets and from the many other vehicles going their way.

They eventually arrived at Folkestone. Ann was so excited when she realised that Folkestone was also the place where Wilf had embarked for his last two trips to the front. This made her feel like she was on the same route and hoped it would lead to the place where she could be close to him. She knew that was expecting a lot because the Western Front was such a vast area.

The crossing was rough, and a journey that should have taken three hours actually took about eight. This was because the captain was under strict instructions to keep altering course to avoid submarines. Ann, like most of the nurses, was very seasick and pleased to eventually arrive at the port of Calais.

They immediately boarded another military bus; this one was not as flash as the previous one in London. The bus took them to the railway station where they were given a cup of tea and a biscuit before being entrained, for where they knew not.

Ann was seated next to Mary, and they chatted easily together.

Ann said, "I cannot help thinking about another nurse who left the comforts of home to serve her country. I read a lot about Florence Nightingale as a young girl, and her story had a major influence on my decision to become a nurse."

"Oh, that's very interesting because I also read about her short life, but not until after I joined nursing."

Prior to them boarding the train, the rumour had gone around that they were headed south for a place called Albert, which was past Amiens and quite a long journey.

Ann said, "I was quite excited about Amiens because I know Wilf, my Australian soldier friend, has been fighting there and could still be close by."

"Is this a serious friend?" said Mary.

"Yes. I've nursed him twice at the King's, and we clicked right from the first moment. He is the most wonderful man I've ever known."

"Well good for you, Ann. I'm sure I will hear more about him over the next few weeks or more."

"I'll keep you posted," said Ann as she turned her head away to the window to hide the tears she could feel building.

"We were told at the get-together before leaving that the war had swung away from Amiens towards Albert. They're currently evacuating the patients further west. That's why all this hurry."

Whilst at the station, their accompanying military officer received orders to change over to a different train again. This one was heading towards the east.

The train journey was nowhere near as long or as bad as Wilf had explained to her, but she supposed that the nurses were desperately needed and did get some priority. The journey was only about eight hours and, from what was being told to them, a distance of about seventy kilometres.

At two in the morning, they arrived at a station without any signage, where they boarded another bus for a short distance to their final destination: Poperinge Military Hospital, about twenty kilometres west of Ypres.

When Ann found out, her heart missed a few beats. She said to Mary, "Ypres is where Wilf has spent most of his time over here. Wouldn't it be unreal if we finish up close to each other?"

"I hope you do, but I should imagine it will take some time to find out."

On arrival, they were shown to their quarters. Ann slept for about twelve hours before being woken and shown around the hospital with the other new nurses. They were due to start their shift at six that evening.

Ann settled in at the hospital very quickly, better than some of the other nurses who had great difficulty adapting to the major injuries being treating at this forward hospital. Many of the soldiers were so bad it was impossible to transport them back to Britain without causing further major complications. The doctors were a very special dedicated lot who had been here on duty for many months without any leave. The hospital had suffered some heavy shelling the previous year, with some patients and staff killed.

The current young Matron Edwards at the hospital became a very close mentor to Ann, having noticed her dedication and skills when she first arrived. Ann was given some special cases to look after and received very close attention from this young matron. They sometimes chatted over a meal, and she also told Ann some of the recent history of the area.

"I was a very close friend to Nurse Nellie Spindler of the Forty-Fourth Clearing Station. Nurse Spindler was killed in an artillery bombardment on the hospital on August 21 last year and is buried in the Military Cemetery close by. She is buried with only one other female in a cemetery of over ten thousand men. Over one hundred officers, four generals, and a surgeon general attended the funeral of this QAIMNS nurse. She was only twenty-four years old."

Ann said, "I'm sorry to hear that." She could see how it still affected Matron Edwards, telling her about the loss of her very close friend.

The matron said, "Fortunately for us, the war has moved further east at this stage, but no one can guarantee if and when it might shift back towards Ypres or even further west. A lot of the major attacks are now centred further south in the area of Albert and Miramont."

Ann went silent because she knew Wilf's last letter dated August 23 was posted from Albert; things must be very bad in that area now. She was very concerned because she had not heard from Wilf since that letter, and it was now nearly one month on.

They assured Ann at the recruiting office that all mail would immediately be redirected to her hospital with a maximum delay of only one week. Her letter to the postmaster at King's Cross advising of her new address would certainly ensure her letters would be redirected to QAIMNS Office in the city, so she should have already received more of Wilf's letters.

Every day, she went to the office to check but was disappointed. All of the other nurses who came over with her had been receiving mail for the last week or two.

By early October, it was nearly six weeks since Ann had received a letter from Wilf. This was much longer than any previous wait. Ann wrote every day now in desperation, to let him know how close she was to him, just in case some of her other letters did not get through. She was desperately worried but could not bring herself to think for one moment that she had already or was going to lose Wilf, as well as her family. She already had her share of recent tragedies and did not deserve more.

She had shared with many of her new friends about her relationship with Wilf, and they too asked every day if she had received mail. It seemed that when the mail arrived each day, the other nurses were more interested to see if Ann's mail had arrived.

One busy morning, the new nurses were called together. Matron Edwards said, "The casualty clearing stations down south at Amiens and Peronne are in desperate need of more nurses, more so than here at this hospital." To Ann, this didn't seem possible.

She continued, "They're asking for eight volunteers to transfer. It is in a much more dangerous area than here at Poperinge, and no guarantees can be given for your safety."

Ann immediately raised her hand and said, "I'm prepared to volunteer with one proviso, that my mail can be transferred to the new location without it going back to headquarters."

The matron said, "I can assure you there will be no additional delay because there is a daily transport between the two places. As a matter of fact, if you decide to go, you will arrive at Amiens tomorrow afternoon, which would be the same time as the mail arrives from here."

After Ann volunteered, another seven girls also raised their hands, so it was all done. They would leave tomorrow morning at six sharp.

The military bus was waiting for the eight girls plus one of the doctors. The trip to the station was only about fifteen minutes, and the train pulled in within half an hour. The journey comprised of many stops and was slow-going, but they still made the sixty-five-kilometre journey in seven hours to a station called Corbie.

Once again, there were no signs on the station, which they were told was to confuse the Germans if they got this far.

Ann could hear the sound of war not too far away; she had no idea how many miles that could be.

The bus was not waiting for them this time but turned up about twenty minutes later for a very slow but short trip over totally destroyed roads. They eventually arrived at the casualty clearing station, which was inside what had previously been the Corbie Town Hall. They were shown to their sleeping quarters, a group of tents at the rear of the hall. It was already close to midnight. They were served some late tea by the local volunteer ladies and told to be prepared for an early start at six in the morning. Ann learned from one of the ladies that regular food supplies were virtually non-existent in Corbie.

The sound of battle was quite loud. Ann could not sleep at all, and when they all gathered together the next morning, she learned that none of the others had slept well either.

Nothing in their training or in their recent experience at Poperinge Hospital could have prepared them for what confronted them that first morning. There were soldiers in great pain all over the large interior of the hall. Others not so critical were on stretchers outside, sometimes forced to wait in the rain.

There were no special rooms for operating; it all happened in the one open area of the large hall. The nurses from the nightshift, although obviously exhausted, were not planning on knocking off as would normally be the case in a regular hospital. Ann noticed that they just wanted to keep at their job, as well as to show the new girls where to find things in between emergencies.

When being shown around by one of the nurses called Elaine, Ann said, "What is the chain of command here?"

Elaine replied, "We don't worry about that; everybody just gets stuck into the task at hand and takes control of each situation as needed.

The doctors decide which patient is to receive immediate attention as they arrive, and then it all just happens from there."

Ann said, "Things appear to be all over the place."

"Yes, you're right, because as yet there are no special cupboards available for the equipment. The equipment is just spread around on any shelf, table, chair, or hook available at the time. What you must remember is this was the Corbie Town Hall two weeks ago, with many large paintings on the walls and plenty of chairs for meetings, but that's about all. The military commandeered the building, left the paintings on the walls as you can see, moved the chairs up onto the stage, put a sign over the door, and they call it a hospital. We arrive with not much more than bandages, bunks, and lamps, and the wounded start pouring through the door. The hospital has been in operation for less than a week."

"That must make it very difficult," said Ann as she dropped her head. "I should have known better than to comment."

"But we are close to the river, and there is plenty of water available, so that's a plus."

Ann observed that every nurse and doctor appeared to be up to their elbows in blood continuously. Their uniforms were covered in blood.

There were piles of blood-soaked sheets and clothing in heaps on the floor. She asked Mary, "Who takes care of the soiled clothing and sheets?"

"We have some local volunteer ladies who help out and take the clothing away. I assume they wash them the best way they can. They have no proper facilities either, so how they manage nobody seems to know. Maybe they take the sheets and the salvageable clothing down to the river to wash them and burn the rest; I really don't know."

Ann noticed some large drums filled with arms and legs. She was reluctant to ask but said, "Do you want to tell me about them?" pointing to the drums as a shudder went through her body.

"Mostly they have been nearly blown off before they arrive. If beyond saving, the limbs are cut off, in some cases with little more than razor blades."

It was a terrible sight to Ann in the dim morning glow of the kerosene lamps. She was used to seeing body parts covered in blood, but with Wilf on her mind continuously, she wondered how she was going to handle this nightmare.

Most of the new nurses got straight into the job as if they had worked under these conditions previously; some handled it better than others.

At ten o'clock, the nightshift staffs were still hard at it with no sign of new patient arrivals slowing down; they just kept on coming. Ann learned that most of the casualties were coming from the area of Mont St. Quentin, which was about forty-five kilometres to the east. The Allies had made some swift advances in the last week on the north side of the river Somme. There were no aid stations in between until they reached Corbie.

There were aid stations on the south side of the river, but it was too difficult to get the stretchers back over the low marshes or the partly repaired bridges. These bridges were in heavy demand, keeping up supplies to the men who were advancing rapidly on the Mont and beyond.

Ann learned from one of the coherent wounded officers that the problem was that none of the top brass believed it possible for such a rapid advance to take place in this area. They were caught off-guard with no casualty stations or food supplies planned for the north side of the river.

They certainly did not believe that Mont St. Quentin could be wrested from one of the crack Prussian Guard units. The thing that terrified Ann so much was that most of the soldiers being treated were Australians. It got even worse when she was able to question some of the wounded, in between cries of pain. She found that the troops who had made the initial attack on Mont St. Quentin were from the Second Division, including the Eighteenth Battalion. She also learned that the Eighteenth had been absolutely decimated over the last few weeks. She looked for the purple and green diamond patch of the battalion that she knew so well, hoping that someone might know if Wilf was still alive. She could not find even one of the Eighteenth colour patches, because of the mud soaked condition of the tunics arriving. Ann kept her problems to herself and did not let on to the other nurses what she was going through that day in Corbie.

Amongst the soldiers treated by Ann was an Australia officer from the Twenty-Third Battalion. He was missing a few toes but otherwise all right to discuss the war. She was anxious to question him about Wilf's unit and said, "I have a very close friend in the Eighteenth Battalion that I'm concerned about. I normally get regular letters from him, but I'm worried stiff because I haven't heard from him for many weeks."

He said, "The Eighteenth has done a magnificent job, but they have taken a caning. I'm sorry, but I don't know any more than that."

"Thanks," Ann replied as she continued to dress his wounds.

"However," he said, "I did hear some good news about the Red Barron. I'm sure you have heard about him and his skill in shooting down our planes."

"Yes, I have. I read about him in the paper back home."

"Well, this Baron Von Richthofen, he was shot down by an Australian Lewis gunner, and they found his plane very near here on the Corbie-Bray Road."

"That's great news," was her reply, but Ann could not help making the connection between Lewis gunner and Wilf, although she understood there were thousands of Lewis gunners.

"I also heard some information from another wounded Tommy officer while waiting out front here. He told me about some German message-runner who was somewhere close to here, delivering documents to the front line. He was badly wounded either by shrapnel or Aussie gunfire. One Tommy private had him in his line of fire and took aim but couldn't pull the trigger because he was already wounded."

"That was decent of him," said Ann.

"Some Aussie medics later patched him up on the spot but left him there for his own blokes to find and take care of him. Before leaving him, they recorded his name, Cpl Adolph Hitler of the list Regiment. We've since heard from a captured German officer that their blokes took him off to the hospital at Pasewalk. He has been recommended for the Iron Cross First Class, for capturing some French soldiers and his heroics amongst the Aussie lines. I think our blokes should have left him there to die like they do to us."

"Oh you couldn't do that, could you?" Ann turned to dispose of some bloodied bandages.

"Too blooming' right I could," was his quick reply.

One thing was for certain; although Wilf was continually on her mind, Ann did not have time to worry about not receiving letters. At Corbie, every minute of her long days were totally submerged under a sea of blood, trying to keep mostly Australian soldiers alive. When finally she was relieved and told to take some well-earned rest, she would collapse into her bunk and fall asleep believing that Wilf could be very close by. But there was also that added uncertainty even if he was close by. Was he still on top of the ground or buried under this terrible mud that continuously found its way into this hall? Mostly it was that slimy mud covering the uniforms of these poor wretches whose lives they desperately tried to save.

Ann no longer had any time to write letters. She had written so many letters that surely one would find Wilf, providing he was still alive. The chances of that seemed to lengthen each day. There were no such things as shift changes here. All of the nurses just worked until they dropped, and sometimes that meant they were on their feet for more than twenty-four hours straight. Sometimes there was not even time to wind the clocks. Besides, time no longer mattered in this inexhaustible struggle to keep men alive; the wounded men just kept coming.

Ann had been in Corbie for three weeks, and the constant stream of wounded had slowed a little as the Australians, or what was left of them, had been relieved by the fresh Americans who had recently entered the war; they had their own field hospitals.

The Americans kept up the pressure and advanced further still into the German's territory. According to all the regular reports coming into the hospital, the front line was extending kilometres further away each day. The Allies looked to be winning, and the Germans were now definitely on the run. This was taken as being a good sign that the Germans were about to give up.

Then out of the blue, that is if there was any blue sky left, it happened. Early in the morning of November 11, a British colonel bounced into the hospital and asked for everyone's attention.

Standing on a chair near the door, he said. "I'm instructed to advise you that an agreement has been made between the Allied Forces and the German authorities. At 1100 hours today, all guns are to remain silent, all fighting is to cease, and an armistice will be signed. Thank you, ladies and gentlemen."

As he stepped down off the chair, the hall erupted. Nobody seemed sure of what an armistice was, but it sounded good. Ann, with scissors and bandage in hand, froze; she thought she was dreaming. She couldn't move. The Aussie soldier she had been treating on the bed suddenly came alive from his comatose state. He heard the announcement and now saw the euphoric outbreak of joy around him. He sat up and threw his arms around Ann's neck and yelled, "I've made it!" and then kissed her.

Ann moved over towards the door and sat on the chair used by the British colonel for the announcement. Nobody else wanted to sit down; they had all rushed out of the door. She dropped her head into her open hands and cried.

By the time Ann made it out the door, everything that could make a noise was being used, from the blowing of whistles and bugles, to the ringing of distant bells in church towers if they were still standing. There was much banging of pots and pans, making an unholy din, not to mention the shouts of joy echoing all over town. There was dancing and hugging in the streets by those still able to stand on their feet and lots of hugs and kisses by everyone both in the street and inside the hospital, staff and patients alike.

Sadly, there were still soldiers dying in the hall who never heard the bells toll. Sadder still were those who heard the bells ringing but could not pay the heavy toll of continuing to breath. They slipped silently away into total darkness and relief from pain as the celebrations continued.

Ann still had many things to do before her day was over, caring for her constant trickle of new patients still arriving. She was in a daze;

her mind was mostly elsewhere. She picked up two sleeping tablets, the ones she gave out so liberally to the injured, and slipped them in her pocket for later.

Had she come all of this way to be near Wilf, only to be beaten by the final bell? Was joining the medical corps a total waste of effort? Was this to be the cruellest blow of all, so close but losing Wilf? When would she know?

When Ann finished for the day, she fell into her bed, put her head under the pillow, and cried like she had never cried before. Eventually, exhaustion overtook her; she was totally drained. She fell fast asleep.

Chapter 21

Wilf arrived at the NCO Training School in Amiens on November 3 for what was to be a ten-day course. Immediately upon arrival, he went to the postal hut to make sure his mail would be redirected to the Training School. They assured him it would be taken care of as a matter of procedure. He checked again the next day, and although there were six letters from home, including two from Mother, there was still no mail from Ann.

The NCO Training School was full-on, even though it was generally expected that the war would not last more than a few more months, considering the way the Allies appeared to be gaining an upper hand on many fronts. As soon as Wilf got a chance, he wrote letters to Ann, his mother, Teen, and short letters to a few others who had been faithfully writing to him. His mind was naturally always thinking about Ann and trying to come up with reasons why he had not received any mail since her short note telling about Joe's death. That letter was dated September 3. It was now two months since he had heard from her.

One of the letters he received was from his younger brother, Ned. Ned had written a few times previously, but this time he wanted to know what it was really like at war. Wilf decided to tell him more than he had told others.

Wilf wrote:

Dear Ned,

Thanks for your letter just received. I'm currently at the NCO school in Amiens. Because of your deafness, you don't know how lucky you are not to be acceptable for army service. Up until now, you have probably heard bits and pieces from the others about the wonderful places I've been fortunate to visit. But there is also the not-so-good side that is hard to write about. Let me give you a picture of things over the last couple of months.

Mont St. Quentin was a heavily fortified position by the Germans on the summit of gradual sloping ground, giving them a commanding view of any army that dared to challenge them. They had an elaborate network of dry tunnels with sleeping benches along the inside walls. They had dry duckboard flooring, meal areas, and even electric lights throughout. There were many concrete pillboxes at regular intervals along the trenches. The Fritz had never planned to leave this fortress.

No military strategist on either side believed it possible for the Germans to lose control of this elevated position. They were all wrong and underestimated the sheer tenacity, raw perseverance, and unflinching courage of the Australian Diggers of our Second Division. We emerged from the mud without proper canteen support or backup and toppled this well-balanced German Army off the hilltop.

We only had eight real tanks to support our push forward. We were on the plains approaching the summit. The Australian Corps Commander General Monash, the master tactician and commander of this attack, used for the first time, dummy wooden tanks. The tanks were placed in position on the plains under cover of darkness, and when sighted by the Huns at daybreak (that's the Germans), the dummy tanks added to their fear of a huge attacking force coming their way.

For me or for any other Allied soldier in the field, we could not imagine taking this fortress. Everyone knew it was protected by a crack unit of the Prussian Guards, one of the most feared units in the German Army. One Digger made the comment that our effort would have the same effect against the Huns as firing peas at a whale. On that one day, six Victoria Crosses were awarded to Australian Diggers. This supreme effort was only exceeded by the seven VCs awarded at Lone Pine Gallipoli; but those seven medals were won over a number of days. One of those killed on the Mont that day was an Australian gold medallist at the 1912 Olympic Games, Lt. Cecil Healy. He won the two-hundred-metre freestyle event.

Amongst the trenches of broken timber, smashed dugouts, and riven-concrete were men that became twisted, broken corpses in an instant of time. There were some incredible acts of bravery during these days with reports of fifty Huns being captured single handed by one Digger. On another occasion, two hundred Huns were captured by five soldiers. In one case, two hundred Huns were handed over to two Aussie privates for escort back to the cages used to lock up the prisoners. The Huns felt insulted that their collective strength was considered so poor by these weary but fearless Australians that an officer could direct two privates to keep two hundred Germans under their control.

The Australian Second Division had been in the thick of battle for five months. We had been unable to change our clothes for sixty days, and many had not slept for the last eighty hours. You would like this bit. Some riders on the horses pulling the artillery with the limber attached behind were observed to be asleep as they moved forward. Sometimes they were woken suddenly by unbridled horses moving so fast with heavy pieces of artillery bouncing over mounds, four or five feet high into the air. Nevertheless, in spite of the men being sometimes outnumbered ten-to-one, we succeeded in achieving the impossible.

Unfortunately, only one day after the summit was taken by a dog-tired-force of Diggers, the Huns counterattacked and regained the hilltop position for just one day. Then the

Twenty-Third and Twenty-Fourth Battalions retook the position on Mont St. Quentin, never again to be lost. Some airman reported that the khaki uniforms of the Diggers could be seen further ahead than any official report stated. These Diggers were already in new advanced positions. One pilot described the scene as "beyond belief."

In spite of the pressure we were under, the Australian humour still shone through. One farm house we captured had a piano in good working order. One of the boys, who is an excellent pianist, continued to rattle out well-known Australian tunes to spur the boys on as they stopped at the house for a drink of water and a dry biscuit from their rations.

According to what we have been told by our officers, Mont St. Quentin was considered the biggest obstacle faced by the Allies during this war, and its capture is the most important achievement by the Australians in the war so far. None of us were aware at the time of its great importance. Australia suffered three thousand casualties just in the last three days to capture Mont St. Quentin. All we were doing for the last fifty days was keeping our heads down and trying to stay alive whilst pushing for the top of the Mont. We have to leave it to the generals to decide the strategies. We are just the bunnies who carry it out.

The Diggers lived up to their name of Digger, by digging into the mud and withstanding the greatest artillery barrage of the war with some five thousand pieces of artillery arranged against us. We have been told that the Diggers performed the impossible, so much so that the rest of the army coming behind, supposedly to support us, could not keep up.

The support troops were not used to such a pace going forward. After the Second Division was withdrawn from the Mont, some were immediately directed east to support the Battle of Peronne. Fortunately, they were only required there for two days of fighting before being withdrawn again from the battle. This was for them a new type of war being fought, house to house and cellar to cellar.

Our Eighteenth Battalion was completely done, so we were relieved by the Americans who had just arrived to play war. We were so grateful, let me tell you. But they were not experienced in this type of warfare.

They were very enthusiastic, but they repeatedly overran enemy positions with hundreds slaughtered from behind by the Huns. Someone amongst our top brass said, "Many good soldiers were wantonly sacrificed at the monument of incompetence." This resulted from a lack of foresight by the American high command. I personally think, from the little I observed, that there seemed to be no liaison between the infantry and other branches of the American Army. However, their enthusiasm to get into the fight was greatly welcomed by all of us Aussies.

The mobile field cookers eventually arrived, enabling us to have a hot meal. This was our first decent meal since leaving the supports. We survived a total of nearly fifty days under heavy attack, eventually driving the Germans back.

Our ranks have been decimated, and our Eighteenth Battalion was reduced down to little more than forty persons entitled to the description of able-bodied men. This number was down from our original strength of 960 back in 1916. The number of us left in number 8 Platoon B Company can be counted on two hands, with some fingers spare.

You will remember me writing to you previously about our fearless leader Joe Maxwell. I think when I wrote last he was a sergeant. Now he is a lieutenant with a string of medals. He has been awarded the VC for his actions on the capture of Mont St. Quentin to add to his MC and Bar, plus his DCM. Of the nearly three hundred men who left Australia with Maxwell in B Company, less than half a dozen of them remain. Of the original ninety nine men who hopped over the bags for this latest attack on the Mont, only nineteen remain fit for duty. So you can see that things have been pretty tough.

I hope the above (sorry it took me so long) has given you a good insight over what you have missed, thank God.

Hope you are well and looking after those bullocks.

Love from your brother, Wilf

Training was almost finished, and the officers appeared to be taking things easy. Then on the evening of November 10, the place was abuzz with activity, which was unexplained to those there for the training.

The next morning at early parade, an announcement was made by Captain Williams, saying, "All guns are to become silent at 1100 hours today, and an armistice is to be signed. The Germans were as good as accepting defeat, and the war is basically over."

The strict regimen of the parade was overlooked when the men let out with lots of cheering and throwing of their hats in the air. After things settled down, the captain said, "The training school is basically finished except for an official parade to take place tomorrow at 1100 hours when stripes will be awarded. Transport will be available today at 1000 hours for those who wish to go into town to celebrate."

The men were immediately dismissed for the rest of the day. As Wilf was about to enter the barracks, he suddenly stopped to think about how good it was to be alive and with excellent prospects of staying alive. He silently thanked God that he had made it through and remembered the promise his mother made on his departure that she would pray every night for his safe return. He was keen to get to a table to write a short letter to his mother to express his thanks for her faithfulness.

Wilf checked with one of the officers as to where his battalion was now located. After some checking, the officer said. "The Eighteenth has already been in Vignacourt for four days. They're still there but are about to be taken to Charleroi in the next few days for extended leave. However, don't make any decisions just yet because special plans are being made now, and an announcement will be made at the parade in the morning."

"Thank you for the advice, Officer. I will take your advice and wait until the morning."

Naturally all of the men wanted a lift into town to join in what would be unbelievable celebrations of the town's people and allied soldiers. Wilf arrived in town to find crowds of people surging wildly into the square where the whole place was already going mad. It seemed like every able-bodied person and their dog were already there dancing and singing in the streets. Bands had hurriedly come together, playing the national anthems and songs of the respective countries involved on the Allied side. The crowds rocked and swayed to the sound of delirious rejoicing.

Restraint was thrown to the wind as rockets flared and bands clashed with thousands singing both in and out of tune. War-weary soldiers grabbed bright-eyed mademoiselles in an endless whirl of gaiety as they embraced and surged wildly though this rejuvenated city from one end to the other, and back again in a frenzy of liberated atmosphere.

Wilf was caught up in this never-before-experienced feeling of relief and exhilaration, with every mother and daughter in town wanting to be his best friend. He was naturally enjoying the feeling of uncontrolled excitement that this news brought to everyone, for the first time in years. However, his mind was also focused on how he could best get to Ann as quickly as possible.

The next day, all of the men were on parade. However, most of them were feeling a little worse for the effects of their all-night celebrations. They were there to receive their well-earned stripes. The colonel making the presentations said, "Each one of you men has been selected for this special honour. These stripes are not only in recognition of the special qualities shown by each one of you, but for the tenacity shown by each man to make it this far. You have come through what is being referred to as the greatest war known to mankind."

Wilf marched out like the others to individually receive his stripes, as proud as the best of them.

The colonel said, "Before being dismissed, I wish to tell you that each one has to make a choice about your departure. You have one of three options. Either you can return to your own battalion tomorrow, or you can stay here at the barracks at the king's expense with all of the privileges, including free accommodation and sustenance for a further ten days, to come and go at your own choosing. Or you can board a train leaving for the coast this afternoon for a border crossing to Britain in the morning."

All of the men except Wilf chose to stay there and continue celebrating with the local girls they had met yesterday. For Wilf, of course, there was no decision to be made; it was mandatory that he go back to London to find Ann as quickly as possible.

The journey was much quicker than any of his previous trips, simply because most of the inward journeys by both troops and armaments had virtually stopped overnight. Food was still moving. Once he arrived at the wharf, he was informed of an earlier departure leaving within the hour. Now that there were no threats of submarine attacks, the channel crossing was also very quick, arriving at Folkestone in less than five hours. After disembarking, they were loaded onto a bus and then a train to arrive at Waterloo Station, with the sun already up. He had slept well on both trains and the boat, so he was feeling refreshed. He needed a wash and shave, which he accomplished with some difficulty at the station.

There were troops everywhere, with many asleep around the station either from sheer exhaustion or too much celebrating. London was still in a party mood, and most soldiers had already found company and were enjoying a new way of living.

Wilf had the privilege in the past of Ann doing the railway navigating, but now he had to find his own way. All servicemen had been granted free travel anywhere on the trains, which made it much easier. All he had to do was find his way to King's Cross Station. He remembered that he needed the Piccadilly Blue Line, so asked one of the ticket attendants. She told him to take the District Blue Line and change at Earls Court.

Inside the carriage, he consulted the wall chart and worked out that he should get off at the next station after Russell Square. He double checked with a nice young lady next to him for confirmation.

Once at the King's Cross Station, he knew where he was. He walked outside and headed across Euston Road and left into Argyle Street. He had been walking eagerly with his kitbag bumping against his buttocks, but now his pace quickened a little more as he crossed the Argyle Walkway and past Ann's personal shrine of remembrance. He could see the undertaker's warehouse and shopfront ahead as he turned the corner around the barber shop into Whidbourne Street. His heart quickened; his journey was nearly over. He hurried past the Wellington Pub, and then unimaginable fear overtook him.

Empty land confronted him where the Davis home had stood; the adjoining wooden houses next door were also gone. There was now only a vast silent space; the street was also silent.

A giant weight descended onto Wilf as his mind could no longer handle this situation; his legs slowly gave way and collapsed beneath him. His mind was going around in a whirl at a hundred miles per hour. He had no idea what was happening to him and had no control over this thing; it wasn't supposed to end like this.

Chapter 22

Wilf lay on the footpath of Whidbourne Street, unable to move. He was aware he was laying there but had no control over his body. After a few minutes, he found the strength to sit up; he half lay across his kitbag that went down under him as he collapsed.

He trembled uncontrollably. This was worse than any feeling he had known during his early experiences of fear in the trenches.

It took him many minutes more before he could muster enough control to stand and walk across the street to knock on any door. An elderly man opened the door to a terrible, trembling excuse for a soldier in uniform. Wilf struggled to get the words out but eventually said, "I'm looking for the Davis family."

The man explained, "I'm fairly new to the area. I came to live with my daughter after her husband was killed in Palestine. My daughter will be back in about one hour. I didn't know the Davis family, but I was told that three of them had been sheltering in a dugout at the rear of the house when it received a direct hit during an air raid. None of them survived."

Before the man finished speaking, Wilf collapsed to the ground and sobbed. While on the ground, his body went into shock, causing him to bite his tongue and cheeks badly. The old fellow was unable to lift Wilf, who lay there for nearly half an hour. Eventually, with the help of another neighbour, they helped Wilf to his feet and invited him inside. The man introduced himself as Barney Ward.

Wilf was totally speechless and could not even manage the cup of tea offered. He did, however, accept a glass of water. Eventually Wilf expressed his thanks without words and left the house. He was still very unsteady but made his way slowly back to the station.

By the time he arrived back at the station, he was able to make some words and enquired at the station where the closest YMCA was located. He was given a slip with the address written in large letters. It was only one station back at Russell Square.

He arrived at the Y and was made most welcome and offered a meal. He couldn't even think of eating and was shown to a room. After lying on the bed for a few hours, he sought out one of the chaplains and poured out his heart to him as best he could.

After Wilf explained what had happened on Whidbourne Street, the chaplain wanted Wilf to see a doctor. Wilf said he was now feeling a lot better and declined the offer. The chaplain was very supportive of Wilf and kept him company for a couple of hours. He suggested that Wilf should take a taxi to the King's Hospital the next day and speak to the matron. He then arranged a sandwich for Wilf. He ate the sandwich and then headed for bed and fell fast asleep.

The next morning after arising around eight, he had some breakfast and arranged to stay a few more days. He caught a taxi to the King's with a heavy heart. As he paid the driver and approached the steps to the main entrance, his steps were sluggish. He wasn't carrying his kitbag this time, but it seemed like he had more than the weight of his kitbag to carry. How was he going to handle talking to the matron?

Wilf went to the main desk and asked to see the matron. He sat and waited for about ten minutes. The matron appeared, and he was surprised that she recognised him. He explained why he was there, finding it hard to manage the lump that threatened to rise in his throat.

The matron said, "I can see you're having some difficulty still, and I understand that, because I'm still trying to accept the loss of Ann Davis also. She was a wonderful nurse. Would you like to come into my office, Mr. Yates?"

Wilf followed her in and sat down on the chair offered. The matron slowly walked around the desk to her chair, looking the other way.

She did not sit down but faced away to hide her tears before turning around.

She said, with a slight trembling in her voice, "Unfortunately, I know little more than you do. It was a terrible tragedy for all of the staff to lose such a wonderful nurse. Ann's best friend, Hazel, has explained to me about the close relationship that developed between Ann and you over those two visits to this hospital. I'm also well aware of the death of her brother, Joe, only days before the bombing."

Wilf knew how badly this conversation was affecting him. The matron said, "Mr. Yates, can I get you a cup of tea?" Wilf could not get any words out but shook his head slowly. He felt a strange feeling come over him that he had never before experienced. He eventually was able to indicate that he would prefer a glass of water, which was arranged for him. The water helped him a little.

The matron said, "All of Ann's personal belongings are still in her locker, and you are welcome to them if you would like them; she has no other family member."

Wilf could do nothing other than move his head slowly from side to side in very short movements; she understood perfectly. He stood up to leave but could not get the words of thanks out that he wanted to express. The matron said, "I must thank you for coming from so far away to help our country."

Wilf managed to get out a soft "Thanks."

She said, "Now that the war is over, it is hoped that everyone can get back to their normal lives once more." She helped him to the front door and turned to shake his hand, which she held for some time before Wilf, still unable to speak, turned to leave.

He walked ever so slowly towards Vauxhall Station. Tears streamed down his face as each step reminded him of those first steps he took side by side with Ann just eighteen months ago. He could not overcome the thoughts of his hand brushing the back of her hand and the sparks of electricity-like tingles that shot up his arm each time they accidently touched. Life had been unbelievably good that day and full of so much promise.

As he approached the station, he could not bring himself to go in but walked on to the embankment, past the flower market to the same spot where they had sat that day and learned so much about each other for the first time. They shared the curried egg sandwiches, and Ann had explained the great houses of interest on the other side of the river.

A ferry, similar to the one on which they travelled to Greenwich, went past. It was probably doing the same trip. On board were lots of partying servicemen and girls having a noisy time, obviously celebrating the end of the hostilities. His thoughts went back to the motor bike accident when Ann helped the rider who was badly injured at Greenwich. Thinking of her caring for the rider took him back to the tender care that she provided for him both times he was her patient.

He started to sob and continued until two ladies walking past noticed his predicament and stopped to ask if he needed help. He indicated no, and they moved on. They probably found it hard to understand why everyone else in London was happy and so full of life celebrating the end of four years of war while this one soldier was so terribly distressed.

Wilf realised he needed to pull himself together but still chose to sit and recollect his thoughts about the great times they shared together.

He wandered over to the fence where a red rose was protruding through the wire, just as it did the last time he was here. He picked the rose and walked back to the seat and studied the perfect, rich red in the petals. The shapes of the petals were soft as his finger gently stroked the inside of the petals.

He remembered presenting the rose to Ann in appreciation of how well she had looked after him whilst in her care at the King's. He had asked her to remember this rose forever, which she had promised to do, with that special look of appreciation that only Ann was able to do. Just like the look she had given him in the dining room of the Headland Hotel. He recalled how her special look made him feel like he was melting into the fabric of the chair.

His thoughts went back to the Maori singer. How Ann stood up at the end of his performance and asked him to sing that beautiful love song again. Wilf was not in any condition now to remember the name of the song. He could, however, remember how Ann so loved that song.

His eyes were then drawn down to the prickly thorns, which reminded him of the trials and troubles one sometimes encounters in the journey of life. These trials besetting him now were such that nobody should be asked to endure.

Besides, this brief season of their lives had not been long enough. This small portion of life, although at the time seemed such a precious part of his life, now seemed so futile and pointless. The tears started to run down his cheeks once more. Whilst he would have many wonderful memories to remind him of Ann, right now it seemed that it would have been better if they had never met. The pain was too great for his broken heart to bear.

Chapter 23

Wilf stayed at the flower market until he was absolutely and totally drained. Eventually he made a Herculean effort, one that he so desperately did not want to make, and walked up the embankment and hailed a taxi. He arrived at the YMCA just as they were serving tea.

The next morning after enquiring at the help desk for directions, he made his way to the closest Australian Army Barracks. He wanted to find out how fast he could get a ship home. He elected to take another taxi.

The officer at the table said, "You'll have to get on the end of the queue in order to be considered for early departure. Why don't you take the opportunity while waiting for a boat to see London or even England for that matter, at His Majesty's expense?"

He was talking much better and said to the officer, "The very last thing I want to do is become a tourist hanging around London to celebrate my birthday in two days' time. I would like to get a ship as early as possible."

The officer said, "I sense your earnestness. I will do my best for you."

As Wilf was about to walk away, the officer called him back and said, "I can see by your face that it's very important for you to get away. Would you be prepared to leave tomorrow?"

"Of course," replied Wilf, "of course."

"I've just noticed one spot now vacant due to the sudden sickness of one of the boys on a vessel called the *Plassy*, due to leave tomorrow, the fourteenth of December, from the Tilbury Docks on the Thames at 1400 hours. Would you take that one?"

Wilf said, "That would be wonderful. Yes, I'll take that one." He supplied his name and number to the officer and stood silently as the papers were completed to allow him to board the *Plassy*.

When complete, he handed Wilf the papers and said, "Good luck, mate. You can stay here at the barracks tonight if you have nowhere else to stay."

"Thank you for your help, sir. I really appreciate it, but I do need to return to the YMCA for the night. As a matter of fact, I would sleep on top of one of the wharf bollards if necessary if there was nowhere else to sleep.

The officer said, "I've never known another soldier so keen to get out of London, especially when he could celebrate his birthday here in London. Not every soldier gets that opportunity."

"I appreciate your concern, sir."

"There must be a big reason to get home so quickly." Wilf didn't make any attempt to explain but just slowly nodded his head.

The last thing Wilf wanted was to be somewhere in England on his own with all of the memories he and Ann had shared together. It was going to be hard enough blotting out such wonderful memories.

Those experiences would flood his mind like rolling surf breaking one painful memory after another—only to be dashed upon the rocks where they would lie exposed forever. He actually believed he would be better off on the rolling ship, seasick enough to drown his memories.

Wilf went back to the Y and advised them he would be staying one more night and would be sailing out tomorrow. The clerk said, "That will be fine. We're so pleased you got a voyage so quickly."

Wilf had a lot of letters to write to his mother, sister, Teen, and many others who had been so faithful in writing to him since leaving home. The message to all of them was the same.

I've survived and am on my way home.

What more did they need to know? Yes, there was one very important extra thing to tell them, especially Teen and her sisters, who hopefully would come to greet him at the wharf where they had left him all those many, long months ago.

I'm arriving on the *Plassy*. Sailing tomorrow 14th December. Don't know when we will arrive Sydney. Check the papers.

The *Plassy* sailed as planned on December 14, loaded up with over a thousand excited troops. These soldiers were some of the first to leave the Tilbury Docks since the fighting stopped, now free from all of that terrible mud and blood of the Western Front. They were now on their way home to the welcoming arms of family and loved ones.

Wilf thought to himself that not all of the men would get the same welcome home from previous loved ones. He was aware of some of the men in his unit who received letters from home bearing bad news. Whilst some of them were away, their wife or girlfriend had found someone else. He realised that although his burden was heavy, there were many others with burdens of a different kind. He would have to think less of his own problems and spare a thought for others.

The troops were not accustomed to any form of transport leaving on time. This time it was different. The tugs were already hitched, and the ropes were cast off from the wharf bollards as they departed right on time. There was only a limited number of people on the dock to see them off. Most of the soldiers had come directly from France to the boat and had little chance to make friends in London; besides, the weather was bitterly cold.

Wilf couldn't help his mind flashing back to the tens of thousands gathered on the wharf in Sydney to farewell the *Suevic*. It seemed such a long time ago. He couldn't stop thinking of how different things could have been, but for that shelter he built at King's Cross. Most probably, he would be right now planning a future life together with Ann in London or enjoying an extended stay in England. Or maybe planning a return trip to England at a later date? Or even better still, for Ann to join him in Australia.

The most frequent and graphic picture that kept flashing through his mind was that shelter. It penetrated into every sluggish, vacant compartment of his thoughts. Would he ever be able to get that out of his mind? How could such a labour of love become such a horrible, never-ending nightmare?

The ship was spotlessly clean with an all Indian crew, a little different from the *Suevic* on the way over. Although it was cold, he chose to sleep on the deck wrapped up in his great-coat to keep warm. He slept soundly only to be woken at six by a crew member preparing to hose down the deck.

Wilf realised it was his twenty-seventh birthday today as he made his way inside to see if he could get some breakfast. Once inside, he stopped short of the galley for a little while to ponder where life had taken him since he had left Sydney Heads. He hoped that his mind would be able to leave behind the tragic events of the last three years and make a new start.

Wilf found it difficult to share his experiences of the past and his hopes for the future with the other men on board, preferring to keep to himself. He noticed that most others appeared to feel the same.

A fight broke out during that first breakfast between two of the men. Apparently one was mouthing off about one of his own heroic experiences during battle. Others around him weren't interested; they wanted a peaceful breakfast. One of the chaps couldn't stand it anymore and gave him a heavy push with one hand to shut him up; it turned into an all-out brawl.

After the brawl, the mood generally turned rather sombre. For Wilf, it developed into a sad and reflective day. It was the first birthday of his life where no one wished him a happy birthday. His attitude was, *Who amongst all these men with home on their minds would really want to know it was his birthday anyway?*

The voyage home was a totally different experience from the one going over. The seas were generally much calmer. Or maybe the events of the last few years had not only toughened him up on the outside but also on the inside.

Wilf's mind went back to the constant upheaval of the earth as shells exploded around him on the battlefield. This caused the ground around him to burst forth into new mounds of broken earth, virtually under his feet as they charged forward over the barbed wire. He thought how the turbulence on land must have prepared him well for the rise and fall of the ocean swells. The swells were peaceful by comparison because there was nobody out there in the darkness trying their best to kill you, so they themselves could live.

Either the quality of the food on the boat had improved or the men had become used to eating whatever food they could get hold of, without question. At times the food at the front line was rotten, but few took any notice. Wilf believed this was because constant hunger was something most men had never before experienced. Maybe it combined with the gut-wrenching fear not only within your stomach, but throughout the whole body.

At the front, Wilf had learned to sleep on anything horizontal, or even standing upright for that matter. He could sleep on anything that was wet or dry, prickly or hard, rough or lumpy; very rarely did he find something soft. Now there were soft bunks or even gently swinging hammocks to lull him to sleep; it was a nice feeling.

The ship called into many of the same ports as they did on the way over, but everything then was a new and exciting experience for him. Now he was no longer in tourist mode. The excitement was gone, and all he wanted was to get home in the shortest time possible.

Wilf not only tried hard to blot out of his mind the horrors of war, but also the memories of the direct hit on that bomb shelter. He couldn't clear his mind of the regrets he had of building the shelter. From what he had learned from Barney Ward, the elderly neighbour across the street, the Davis house was not hit directly, only the shelter. The house caught fire only after the wooden house next door burned and collapsed onto the stone house. This caused the roof to burn, followed by the rest of the house.

Maybe if he had not built the backyard shelter, they would have sheltered in the second-floor bedroom under the up-ended empty cupboard, as was proposed by Mr. Davis. Maybe if they had sheltered there, they'd have had time to escape the fire and still be alive today.

The days dragged on as Wilf found every day to be much the same: nothing to do, nothing new to see, nothing to learn or practice, no drill exercises, just the same old heartache and regrets running around in his mind

How things could have been so different. Ann desperately wanted them to make a trip down to Brighton to visit her aunt and uncle. He tried not to dwell on the wonderful memories he had of all the places he visited with Ann and the special moments they enjoyed together.

How would he be able to recall or share with others back home his memories of those places? Just the mention of Ann would bring him unstuck. Places like the Headland Hotel and Buckingham Palace. Would he be able to hide his inner emotions?

His family and friends already knew he had been to these places because he had written about them in such glowing terms. Would he be able to even talk to others about those places without choking up?

The mood on board gradually improved during the last week of the voyage, but it improved dramatically on the last full day at sea as they headed north up the coast of New South Wales. There were great celebrations on board the ship the night before they were due to dock in Sydney.

It was summer in Australia, and the weather was fine with another clear day forecast for their arrival. This was to be the only night where very few were able to sleep because of the excitement. Most men were excited because of two things. First, the thrill of seeing family and loved ones who they expected would greet them on the wharf. Second and more important was the fact that they had made it home in one piece, against all odds. There were times at the front when none of them expected to make it home again.

This was a huge achievement for all of them, especially those on board who were coming home with limbs missing. Because Wilf was from Craven, about 180 miles north of Sydney, he was not expecting any family to be there to see the ship come in. He was hoping that some of the Bisset sisters who had befriended him would be there, especially Teen, his faithful penfriend.

One of the crew members by the name of Vijay became friendly with Wilf during the journey and kept him up to date, pointing out places of interest along the way. Vijay had made this same voyage many times and was studying navigation on the side.

On this last night, Vijay said to Wilf, "Keep your eye out for the Macquarie Lighthouse on the portside. The lighthouse is located on the top of the hill overlooking Watsons Bay on the inside of the harbour, but it's very high and also quite visible from the sea."

"I'll keep a look out," said Wilf.

"Then there will be a second lighthouse right on the tip of the south head. That one is called Hornby Lighthouse. It's located below the North Head Army Base, and we will swing left around that lighthouse into the harbour."

Wilf, who was always good with his directions, said, "Vijay, I don't understand. How can we turn left around north head if we're approaching from the south? Don't you mean south head?"

"I know what you mean, Wilf, but according to the map, there's an army base on that headland, and it's called North Head Army Base. Yes, it's a little confusing, isn't it?"

Wilf nodded in agreement and then excitedly said, "I can see a light flashing up ahead now. Is that it?"

Vijay turned around to get a better look and said, "That's Macquarie Lighthouse, my boy. You are nearly home. Congratulations."

"It's almost too good to believe," said Wilf with some emotion in his voice. "There were so many times I didn't think I would make it."

Wilf wanted to say more, but that lump came up in his throat again, causing his lips to quiver; the emotion of the moment was more than he could handle.

Vijay noticed this and said, "Let me assure you, Wilf, it's true, you are really home. After we enter the harbour, why don't you go down to the galley and have some breakfast. Who knows how long it will be before you eat again. We will be delayed quite some time once the quarantine people come on board and carry out their inspections. You will have plenty of time before the ship starts moving again. I'm told we will head for the wharf at Woolloomooloo."

"Thank you, Vijay."

The *Plassy* slowed right down to take on board the pilot as it drew level with Macquarie Lighthouse. The pilot would take command of the ship and guide it safely into the harbour. After a short delay, they were underway again and rounded South Head on the southern side of Sydney Heads, just as the sun peeped above the horizon behind them. The vessel slowed once more and dropped anchor in Watson's Bay.

Wilf looked around once more for Vijay, and on finding him said, "Thanks, Vijay, for all the help you've provided. I will say good-bye now and take your advice." He shook the hand of Vijay warmly and left for the galley. He didn't really feel like eating because of his excitement. He managed to force down half the meal and then proceeded to collect his kitbag and head back to the deck.

Many of the soldiers had now gathered on the deck. Others were either still in the galley or scrambling to do a last-minute pack of their belongings.

Soon the entire ship's passenger list was assembled on deck to witness this most unbelievable and exciting day ahead. Every man wanted to be in a good position close to the rail. Word had already spread around that the port side of the ship would come alongside the wharf. Wilf wasn't near the rail or even close. His emotions were already welling up inside him as he thanked God for his safe return to the land that he had thought so many times he would never see again.

Now all he could do was stand in the crowd of men and wait. His memory went back to those awful last two months near Mont St. Quentin when it seemed none of them could survive this hellhole in the mud of the Somme. It didn't matter to him so much that none of his family would be there on the wharf; he was prepared for that. All that really mattered to him now was to get both of his feet back onto Australian soil, from which he promised himself he would never leave again. Of course, he hoped Teen and her sisters would be there.

The tugboats approached, ready to do their job as hundreds of small vessels with added colour were moving around in endless circles, promoting their support to the homecoming troops. The water looked so clear and fresh with pure, white fluffy caps dancing excitedly on the blue waves, the opposite of the murky water in the Thames when they left London.

The quarantine men had now completed their inspection and were climbing down the ladders. The *Plassy* crew threw the hawser lines to the men waiting on the tugboats. Once attached, they hauled the heavy ropes on board, enabling the tug to tow the *Plassy* to its allocated berth for a well-earned rest. The anchor was hauled up, and with little discernible effort, the ship moved slowly but graciously through the harbour and past Shark Island.

With the massive power of the little tugboats, the *Plassy* needed very little steam to keep moving ahead. Instead it diverted every spare cubic inch of steam along the endless lines of insulated pipes to continuously sound the loud foghorns high above them.

Every ship in the harbour sounded their horns also, making a cacophony of discordant sound to welcome home one of the first troop ships to have left England after the fighting ended, now arriving in the harbour. For those with discerning ears, the sound could have been interpreted as *"Good on you, boys, you have done a great job and made us proud."*

It was now daylight as Wilf stared over the water towards the shore thinking about all these men who had left family and friends years before, sacrificing everything sacred and precious to them, especially their family. They had departed from these same shores to serve, as they were told, God, king, and country.

He knew what most of these men had been through and survived, an indescribable living hell. Each one learned very quickly that at any moment night or day, they could be catapulted with unimaginable swiftness into that lurking blackness of death. Now these same men had aged more years than the departure and returning dates showed on their paperwork. Wilf knew they were returning not only in sadly diminished numbers but as triumphant and victorious warriors from the long battle now behind them. Wilf felt for the first time that he was a special part of this Aussie brotherhood of men.

The emotion kept building within him as he saw flags and streamers decorating every vessel that floated in the waters of Sydney Harbour.

Overhead was a cloudless blue sky, promising brilliant summer sunshine for the rest of the day. Every conceivable building along the harbour shores expressed the appreciation of everyone gathered on this beautiful day, just for the Diggers.

In every direction along the shore, Wilf could see coloured flags and banners gently moving in the breeze. The crowd was there in great strength to show how much was owed to the boys returning home and for their sacrifices made. Tens of thousands of people were crammed along every available piece of land, building, wall, pole, and vehicle, waving anything coloured they could find in this war-rationed but now reinvigorated city full of grateful hearts.

Wilf had difficulty controlling the emotion within and knew most of the others would be feeling the same way. There were those times in the past when the sheer terror from the rattle of the enemy's machine guns made it impossible to breathe properly. Especially during those moments before the whistle blew, directing them to scale the parapet of the trench. At such times, darkness hid from their mates their own frozen, breath-starved, blue faces.

Today Wilf had difficulty breathing for a different reason; it was pure emotion. He was not the only one of the thousand or so soldiers on board unable to control his emotions; soldiers all over the ship found it impossible to utter any words at all. The silence from the troops transcended the noise coming from the waiting crowds on the dock.

These battle-toughened warriors had kept control of their emotions during many a hopeless situation in a dugout or when pinned down in no-man's-land, but now they were unable to hold back any longer. Tears streamed down Wilf's cheeks unashamedly as some hugged their mates in silence. Others gave up completely, slinking down against anything upright and stationary on the deck to bury their face in their open hands. Many sobbed uncontrollably at the sheer joy of being home at last. The voyage had been a very long, agonising eight weeks for each one of them.

The *Plassy* was manoeuvred to the dockside as the noise rose from families and friends on the dock. Now that the ship was in place, it trapped and amplified the constant roar of excitement from the crowd waiting. Thousands of streamers were thrown upwards, but few reached the height of the waiting hands stretching down over the rail. The pressure from the boys behind pushed hard against those in front, forcing them onto the narrow wooden rail. Compared to the times when required to throw themselves onto the wire in no-man's-land so others could trample over their backs, this was nothing; they could take it, and they did. The pressure was so great it would have cut lesser men in two.

Then, one of the soldiers would recognise a family member in the crowd waving a cardboard sheet with a single name printed in big letters. The excitement of that soldier was instantly contagious as other mates around him joined in the frantic waving and shouting in recognition of their mate's loved ones below. The only thing that stopped the boys from throwing their mate overboard into the waiting arms of family was the impossibility of withdrawing this one squashed sardine out of the tightly packed can.

As the gang plank was lowered, Wilf wasn't one of the first off the ship. In time, he was herded down the gangway under pressure by the excited men coming behind. None of the men could wait any longer to get off the boat. Wilf likened it to cattle being herded into sale yard ramps as he descended the gangway.

Just like the others, Wilf had an unmistakeable look of excitement and sheer joy written all over his face, that look said, "I've made it home." His shoulders were held back, with pride welling up in his chest, as was the case with every other soldier who had voluntarily answered the call of his country.

Wilf didn't know if he would recognise the Bisset sisters if they were there. He'd only seen them briefly on that one dark night as he marched to the wharf. He shuffled forward the last few restricted steps down the gangway.

Suddenly he heard the cry in unison, "Wilf!" He looked towards the back of the crowd and saw a group of excited girls holding a sign with his name. They were screaming and jumping up and down, frantically trying to climb over the crowd in front, just like sheep dogs running over the backs of sheep to get to him. The Bisset girls were there in force. His emotions let go; they were now totally out of control.

The crowd, realising this soldier had been recognised from the girls at the rear, let him through as they slapped him on the back with lots of *"Good on-ya, Digger."* The girls forced their way through the crowd with Teen managing to hold her position at the front of the pack. He was literally smothered with an all-embracing plethora of arms, hugs, kisses, and tears on everyone's faces, as if he had been their one and only lifelong friend in the whole world.

The words, "Welcome home, Wilf," seemed to repeat nonstop. The lump was in his throat again; he couldn't get a word out. Only his thoughts were working, saying, *Am I really home or am I dreaming?*

The welcome just didn't stop. Nor did he want it to; this welcome home by a family of girls, seemed to wipe away all of the horrible memories and make it all worthwhile.

All the horrors of war, the mud and the blood, the flies and the lice, the rain and the ice, the hardships and tragedies, the deafening sound of the never-ending shells exploding, combined with the continuous rattle of the machine guns, all disappeared instantly. Those haunting thoughts retreated from his mind in an instant. He was now in the midst of this unimaginable excitement of a welcome-home harbour-regatta; it was so unexpected by him.

Back on Australian Soil.

Chapter 24

On the wharf at Woolloomooloo, the Bisset sisters fought in jest for the right to carry Wilf's Kitbag, just as they did on that night so long ago. They moved away from the wharf at Woolloomooloo to find a tram to get them through the city to their home across the harbour in Jones Street, Pyrmont. Teen held Wilf's hand all the way home to show that she had won the right to do so competitively against the other sisters. This was her own battle, well-won. Although Teen had only been a penfriend up to this point, the situation seemed to change dramatically now that Wilf was here in the flesh. Wilf was so thrilled to be home. It was like he had escaped the horrors of hell and without dying, gone straight to heaven.

They reached the Bisset home, and it was decked out with colour, inside and out to welcome Wilf home. He met Mrs. Bisset, who he had learned from Teen's letters was a large, upright woman of strong character; she needed to bring up the seven girls on her own.

Mrs. Bisset said to Wilf, "I'm well aware from Teens constant news updates that you come from the country and probably have nowhere to stay tonight. So we have reorganised a spare room, and you will be staying here tonight."

Wilf said, "Thank you very much for the offer, but—"

"I won't discuss it, Wilf. You're staying here."

It wasn't long before the house was packed with others from their church to welcome home the one they had heard so much about. There had been a total of five boys from their church to enlist; two had been killed, and the other three had not yet returned home.

Wilf was required to report to Victoria Barracks the next day, so Teen volunteered to take him there; he had no idea where to go.

She said, "I would still have taken you to the barracks myself, even if you had wheels fitted to your shoes to run on a pair of rails leading from our front door to the adjutant's office at the barracks."

"I'm not sure how to thank you."

"I don't care how long it takes, I just want to take you there myself."

Still feeling a little strange in this new company, Wilf said to Teen, "I'm so pleased about the way you want to help me. It will only be a brief visit to the barracks to receive information about my upcoming discharge in a few weeks."

Wilf was thrilled at the warm reception being afforded to him by Teen and her family. He was still feeling a little stiff and awkward with his newfound friends, considering what he had been going through. He enjoyed the relationship as Teen's penfriend, but now in the flesh if was different. He was absolutely thrilled how Teen was taking such good care of him. Nevertheless, only a few days ago, he was still going through the depths of depression thinking of the past and his uncertain future.

Teen was such a sweet, caring personality that Wilf's mind was struggling with this unexpected and dramatic change of direction, although he felt so relaxed in Teen's company.

He said to Teen, "According to the information we were given on the boat about my discharge, I should be notified in writing telling me when to be back in Sydney."

Teen said, "If that's going to be weeks away, I don't think I can wait that long."

The next day after leaving the barracks, Teen walked Wilf around the harbour foreshore to show him the sights. They had a lovely, relaxed afternoon getting to know each other.

He said, "You know, my only previous trip to Sydney was to enlist."

"I know that. Well, there are a lot of other places to see; this is just a small part of a big city. I'd love to show you more of our city."

"I'll take you up on that offer some time."

"When are you planning to go back to Craven?"

"Your mother suggested I stay over for a second night and leave early the next morning. My mother and family are anxiously awaiting my return." Wilf had a devotion to his mother greater than most men his age.

The next morning, Teen took him to the station and said, "Wilf, when you come down for your discharge, how about staying a little longer?"

"I would love to do that." he said. Teen kissed him, and Wilf waved good-bye from the window of the carriage as the train pulled out from the station. He was now on his final leg home, a journey of about seven or eight hours, and it took an eternity, or so it seemed. With nothing else to do on the train, all he could do was sit and think. He tried not to think about the past; his mind was now on Teen. Was this lovely lady capable of soaking up those thoughts from the past like a big sponge and wringing the sponge dry into a bottomless well, never to surface again?

Wilf didn't know the answer to that question, but he felt very relaxed thinking about Teen. While he kept his mind on Teen, the past seemed to fade into the background.

Teen had arranged for one of her sisters the previous day to send a telegram to his mother to let her know he would be home the next day sometime in the mid-afternoon.

He arrived at the Craven station at three o'clock and was given a welcome home and job well-done by the station master who said, "I've been instructed to tell you to proceed directly to cousins Alf's place where your family is waiting."

"Thanks a lot Jack," said Wilf. "It's good to see you again; believe me."

"Don't worry, mate. We're all proud of you."

Alf lived just a quarter of a mile from the station. Wilf set off with a real spring in his step and was less than one hundred yards from the house when first spotted by his youngest sister, Millie, who yelled, "Mum, Wilf's home."

His mother was a very staid and normally unexcitable, stoic woman. She rushed from the house and vaulted the low fence with ankle-length dress in tact to throw her arms around her eldest son, saying, "I thought you would never get here." They hugged, and the tears flowed freely for a long time as his four younger sisters also tried to get their arms around him and find a piece of his face on which to plant a kiss. The garbled noise of everyone wanting to add their own welcome made it impossible for him to hear anyone in particular. Mum's eldest son and the big brother to the rest of the family was home at last. This was a very special day for Craven. Wilf was back with all of his family present; now he was definitely home.

Craven was a small village of some fifty houses, including the surrounding properties that extended up to four miles away. It was predominantly a timber-cutting area with four sawmills, cutting the timber into sizes demanded at that time. A lot of the hardwood was for building houses, but the softwood timber that Wilf and his father cut was mostly cedar and white beech used for interior walls and furniture. The outer properties were farmed for dairying on a small scale.

On this day, the whole village knew that Wilf was coming home, so every family was represented in the celebrations at cousin Alf's home. This was probably the biggest event ever to take place in Craven, since the first homes were built there around 1900. Everyone was so pleased that he had returned safely. He was the only man from Craven to enlist for the war. There were many who enlisted from the surrounding districts of Stratford, Gloucester, Stroud, and Dungog; most had not been as fortunate as Wilf getting an early boat home. Some others would not be returning at all.

The celebrations went on until tea time, but Wilf and his family had another four-mile journey by horse and sulky to their home on Glen Road known as Kimberly. Their home was on the banks of Ward's River close to the Craven State Forest. They arrived home after dark, which was not a problem for them because the whole family knew every foot of the road day or night, and so did the horses.

The house was given the name of Kimberly because during construction, one of Wilf's sisters, Vera, found what she believed to be a diamond when helping to dig the footings. She had been reading a book about the Kimberly mines in South Africa so thought it fitting to name the house Kimberly.

Wilf's father purchased five hundred acres of virgin timber land and cleared a portion on which to build their home. The family travelled the twenty-five miles from Stroud with their mother and the four girls in the sulky. The two boys rode on horseback with their dad driving the bullock team. All of their household furniture was loaded onto the bullock wagon.

The house had a tin roof with vertical slab walls. Newspapers were glued to the inside walls to keep out the drafts from the living area. Weather boards were nailed onto the outside walls of the bedrooms. The flooring was made of twelve-inch-wide thin slabs of hardwood butted closely together. Not always close enough to stop the crumbs and sweepings from falling through the cracks and the draft coming up.

One of the modern conveniences Wilf's mother said she would like some day was a new type of floor covering called linoleum. She had heard that some new homes in the district were boasting this new product in their kitchens. It was a mixture of powdered cork, linseed oil, and pine rosin, which was coated onto hessian under pressure.

The house when completed in 1911 was not quite large enough for a family of eight, but they all fit, and it was a very happy home. Two of Wilf's sisters were now married and had moved away, so there was now plenty of room for the family.

For this special occasion of Wilf's homecoming, they were all there together.

Wilf spent his time answering questions about his general experiences at war and the cities he had been privileged to see both in France and London. He was very hesitant and guarded when mentioning the wonderful sights he had seen. He couldn't bring himself to describe the horrors he had been through, nor could he tell of the heartache he had experienced when he lost Ann.

However, he did tell his sisters how lovely the nurses were at the hospital in London and how they took such good care of him. Wilf knew that he couldn't keep secrets from his mother. He knew that she sensed something was wrong because she noticed his difficulty telling the stories. He knew his mother only too well. She would await her opportunity at a later time to probe further.

Wilf wanted to get back to work with the bullocks, but his dad told him that his brother, Ned, was handling things quite well so to take more time to get himself fit and well after the terrible time he had been through.

Wilf was very restless after a couple of days, so he sat down with pen and paper and wrote to Teen. She had given him such a wonderful time in Sydney. He was missing Teen because she helped him wipe a lot of bad memories from his mind, even if only for the short time.

He wrote:

I would like to accept your offer to stay for more than just a couple of days when I come to Sydney to be discharged in about three or four weeks' time. As yet, I still don't know the exact date. I will let you know as soon as I receive the letter.

However, by the time he got to the end of the letter, he realised what an effect Teen was having on him. Before sealing the envelope, he added a PS to say:

I would like to take you up on your offer earlier than planned and come to Sydney for a weekend, even before I come down to be discharged, if that suits you?

The next day, he rode the four miles into Craven on horseback just to post the letter.

To his surprise, there was already a letter awaiting him at the post office from Teen. He was excited to read the letter as he stood there on the spot to read the three pages from Teen's hand. She also expressed the excitement she felt during their time together, after having only met him once previously and exchanging letters for three long years.

Teen finished her letter with:

If you have nothing to do back home, why wait for another four weeks to come back to Sydney? Mother said you are welcome to stay any time.

He immediately purchased some writing paper, an envelope, and stamp to write a short note.

He said:

I've just received your wonderful letter inviting me down for a weekend and have decided to come down next Friday.

Wilf rode home on the same horse, but it now felt like the horse was twelve feet tall.

Chapter 25

The war was over, but Wilf found it difficult to change his way of life overnight. After living in fear of death on a daily basis for so long, it was now hard to turn off the horror tap and pretend it had not happened. His thoughts constantly returned to the horrors of war. Things were very quiet out in the bush away from the crowds he had become accustomed to over the last few years. It wasn't easy to keep his mind focussed; he needed help.

He was so grateful for his supportive family and the knowledge that Teen was just as keen to see him again as he was to see her. He couldn't wait to see her again.

On the following Thursday, Wilf packed his bag. He left home by horse at four the next morning, riding through heavy rain all the way to the station. He caught the early six o'clock train to Sydney. This time he wasn't wearing his uniform; he had very little in the way of civilian clothes from which to choose. He was grateful for the heavy raincoat he was wearing that had hung on the hook for the last three-some years.

Wilf had not yet been into Gloucester, a fifteen-mile ride on horseback, to do some shopping. Gloucester was the closest town with a clothing store. He hoped instead that he could purchase some new clothes whilst in Sydney.

Teen was scheduled to work all day but would be off tomorrow and Sunday. She had arranged for her closest sister, Alma, to meet him at Central Station. The train arrived right on time at 1:40 p.m. Wilf had no trouble identifying Alma, but he could tell she was taken back a little with what appeared to be, and was very much, an out-of-fashion country boy from the bush.

When Alma had seen Wilf previously, he had been up to date with the same fashion as every other soldier in town, wearing the latest army issue. Now, she was looking at a totally different man.

Wilf explained, "I'm in a bit of a predicament. The only respectable gear I had to wear is my army uniform; there are no clothing stores close to home in the bush. I'm hoping you have a little time to spare to show me where I can buy some new clothes."

Alma raised one eyebrow as she often did and said, "Not a problem. I can take you there right now. I can see that you need a complete new fit-out. There's a men's store in George Street, near to where we're meeting Teen."

The store was a real eye opener to Wilf, even though it was only moderately stocked after the rationing period. This exercise filled in the afternoon nicely before meeting Teen when she finished work.

It wasn't far to the clothing factory in Sussex Street where Teen worked along with hundreds of other girls. They watched as the girls streamed out the door. Teen was one of the first girls out and headed straight for Wilf. She kissed him on the cheek, saying, "I'm so happy to see you, Wilf."

"Even the full strength of my bullock team could not have held me back from seeing you again."

Alma said, "Now that I can see you are in good hands, I will leave you two together to get into your own mischief. I need to hurry off and meet some other friends as planned."

Wilf said, "Thanks, Alma, for your expert advice."

Teen said, looking at his brown paper-wrapped packages, "Did you buy all this new clothing here in Sydney?"

"Yes, I did, with the help of your sister, and I'm wearing every piece of it. By-Jove, she knew what she was doing."

"You're right, she did a very good job; you look very smart. I want to take you to a place for dinner up in George Street; it's only recently been opened."

"It sounds good to me."

Teen clasped his hand tightly and led him off towards George Street, saying, "I would prefer to walk around a little first before we have dinner, if that suits you, Wilf?"

"I suppose you'd like to walk a little after sitting down at that machine all day."

Even though Wilf had been feeling quite hungry, having not had a good meal since the snack his mother had prepared for him to eat on the train, he was still happy to walk a little.

Teen took him down past one of the most popular meeting places in Sydney, under the Post Office Clock in George Street, into Martin Place and back up Pitt Street, all the time asking more and more questions about his time away. They enjoyed each other's company more with each step before turning back to the new café.

The tables were arranged as bay-nooks down both walls of this long, narrow café. Each table seated four people, with two fixed bench seats, one on each side of the table. They were both seated on the same side of the table. Teen had never been on a dinner date like this before, so it was all very new to her.

Teen said, "You have no idea how much I enjoyed walking around the city with you by my side. Receiving your letters was exciting, but having you here in person is so much better."

"I also enjoyed it more than I can tell you. Teen, I want you to know that each time I'm with you, it helps to clear away a lot of cobwebs out of my mind. The last three years have filled my mind with so much stuff that's hard to shake." He didn't plan to tell her what those problems were—well, not yet.

After the meal, they made their way to catch the tram to Pyrmont and then walked with arms linked together under overcast skies in the pitch darkness to Teen's home in Jones Street.

Wilf was greeted very warmly by everyone in this obviously loving home of mother and seven daughters. They all sat around to ask Wilf more questions about both the war London and the bush that they had missed asking on his first visit. Wilf was shown to the same room as previously, and they all turned in just at midnight.

The next day was Saturday, which Teen normally worked, but she had arranged for the day off and had pre-planned their day. They set off early for a day at the beach. She had chosen Manly Beach, which required a trip on the ferry to cross the harbour.

Teen kept busy pointing out all of the places of interest around the harbour as Wilf tried to explain how beautiful the harbour was, so different from the crossing of the English Channel.

Teen said, "The ferry crossing to Manly could also be quite a challenge sometimes, especially crossing the harbour entrance when big seas are rolling in."

"I think I can handle the big seas in the harbour after going across the Great Australian Bight, especially with you by my side."

She gave him one of those special smiles and said, "I've been looking at the maps and cannot understand why it's called the English Channel when it looks like France has a lot more coast facing the channel than does Britain. Why wasn't it called the French Channel?"

Wilf said, "I have no idea. I wondered the same thing myself."

The ferry slowed down to approach the dock. Teen said, "This pier was basically a cargo wharf, but since the ferries have become popular, a special spot was allocated for a shelter from the weather for waiting passengers. It's not yet finished, but it's a lot better than it was."

"We didn't have shelters on the Somme, so this looks jolly good to me."

They moved from the wharf to the main street, which ran directly to the surfing beach, a distance of less than a quarter of mile away. There were a few entrepreneurs with small stalls along the street. One man was offering to make pencil sketches of those willing to pay three pence for his services. There was another who made paper cut-outs in a similar manner. Others sold lollies and drinks. They stopped at a bakery and bought some sandwiches to have for lunch.

They did not come prepared to swim, only to get to know each other better and enjoy each other's company. They simply planned to walk along the beach on this lovely late-February day, enjoying this glorious sunshine. They stopped under one of the huge pine trees and spread out the rug Teen brought with her, just for this occasion.

While Teen was fussing with the food, Wilf gazed out across the sea he had only recently travelled. At times like this, Wilf struggled in his mind with the constant flashbacks; he could not suppress thoughts of Ann and the shelter.

He said, "Teen, you have no idea how different is this world from the one I've experienced for the last few years. This is absolutely wonderful."

"I'm so glad it is, and I want to help you to enjoy it even better. I think I can tell when you're struggling sometimes; I want to be there for you."

Australia seemed so far removed from the strife in Europe, from the mud and slush of the battlefields, from the constant sound of war with all of the ghastly images that flashed before him, which could not easily be erased from his mind. It was so good to be home in Australia, enjoying the sand of Manly Beach for the very first time in the company of this lovely lady. The gentle sea breeze from the ocean was cooling things down to a pleasant temperature.

Wilf was silently looking out to sea. Teen said, "I don't think I need to pay a penny for your thoughts, do I? I think I can guess them."

He said, "I'm sure you can." However, he knew there were thoughts she didn't know at all as he turned and took her hand in his and looked into her eyes. "I don't think I've thanked you for all of those letters you wrote to me. It's hard to describe to someone back here just how much it means to receive letters from home when you're so far away. Whether they're from your mother, your sisters, or your old friends, or very new friends like you, they're all so very important; they kept me sane."

"I enjoyed writing letters to you also," she said, "but as time went by, even though only penfriends, we became more familiar with each other, and towards the end, I longed to receive your letters."

Wilf said, "That's nice to hear."

"Let me tell you, my life just about fell apart when I didn't hear from you for that period of three months just before the war ended. You wrote late August telling me you were about to go into the line, and then I heard nothing from you again until the end of the war. That was a terrible time for me."

"It was a real terrible time for me also, let me assure you."

"Wilf, I was sure something terrible had happened to you; I cried myself to sleep many times."

"Maybe one day I will be able to tell you the full story," he said as he started to choke up. The reminder of that period was enough to make Wilf swallow hard and go silent as Teen rested her head on his shoulder.

"I think I understand," said Teen, and then they remained silent for quite a long time, letting the gentle breeze do the talking for them.

After a long period of silence, she said, "I want to tell you how wonderful it was to receive that very special letter written from the NCO Training School telling me that you would not be returning to the front and the war was all over."

"Believe me when I say it was one of the best days of my life."

"It was also one of the best days of my life, Wilf. I hugged all of my sisters and mother one by one, telling them the good news of how you had survived and were coming home in one piece. I told the good news to my friends at church and to all of my workmates and anybody else that would listen. Especially Linda, she is my closest friend at work, I shared with Linda all the news from your letters."

"It's good to have someone special you can share your feelings that you keep from others around you," said Wilf.

"As a matter of fact," she said, "what a pity it is Saturday and not Sunday. Otherwise we could go and visit Linda, who lives up the hill from here at Balgowlah."

"Does she always work Saturdays?"

"Usually she does. We'll do that another time. In the meantime, we'll stay under the shade of this tree and get to know each other better; we've got so much to talk about."

On Sunday, they attended church and then did some more touring around Sydney. It was easy for Teen to choose new places to visit because Wilf knew nothing about Sydney other than what she had already shown him.

On Monday, Wilf returned to his home at Kimberly, but he was unsettled. He couldn't wait until he received mail to advise him the day he was to return to Sydney to be discharged. To receive a discharge from the army in which he had served over the last three years would be an important step for him; at this stage, they were still in control of his life.

Each day around noon, he rode his horse into Craven to check his mail. He was anxious for that special envelope to arrive. It was not so much the discharge he was awaiting but for another excuse to see Teen. She was like a soothing balm that smoothed out the rough patches for him.

Eventually one morning around ten o'clock, one of the forestry workers riding by called out from the gate, "Are you there, Wilf?"

Wilf heard him and moved to the doorway where he could be seen and said, "Yes, Frank."

"The lady in the post office asked me to relay a message to you. There's an envelope from the army, which you've been expecting."

"Thanks, Frank. I'll go straight away."

Wilf immediately saddled up his horse and rode to Craven to collect his mail. He opened the envelope in the store to find he was required to report to Victoria Barracks at 1000 hours the following Monday. He rode home to prepare for another trip down on Friday to surprise Teen with an unannounced early visit. He could get there quicker in person than sending a letter.

Wilf was waiting outside the factory door in full uniform when Teen finished work. On seeing him, she looked twice and then rushed into his waiting arms. This was much to the surprise of her workmates who knew of the relationship but had never seen her showing this sort of affection before.

They hopped onto a Pyrmont tram to surprise her mother and sisters. On the tram, Wilf said, "I have a special request to make. Would you be prepared to take a few days off work and come with me to Craven to meet my family after I'm discharged?"

Teen said, "I would love to come, but I will have to run it past Mother first and then my boss."

Mrs. Bisset was excited about the trip and gave her approval. Wilf's plan was to leave Sydney on the coming Wednesday and return on Saturday. He had already discussed this possibility with his mother before leaving Kimberly. He needed to send a telegram to let her know

Teen was arriving on the three o'clock train on Wednesday afternoon. He would send the telegram once Teen confirmed she was successful in getting the week off.

On Saturday, Teen was scheduled to work. She went straight to her boss to ask for the following week off. She told him she wanted to go with Wilf to see him discharged with full military honours along with thousands of others. She would then travel with him to his family's home at Craven for a few days.

Her boss said, "I would count it a privilege to honour your friend by giving you the day off and most definitely the latter part of the week as well. There is one condition, providing you can come into work on Tuesday before you go. I need your help with a big order that needs to be shipped urgently."

Teen said, "I will be happy to help out."

He said, "I'm disappointed our old friend John Ridley has not yet returned from England. I was advised of his life-threatening injury suffered at the Battle of Fromelles and his subsequent recovery in England. We understand that a bullet shattered his mouth and went out the back of his neck."

Teen said, "Yes, I also heard of his slow progress, but he then volunteered to return to his unit in France."

Teen left his office and told Wilf the good news before returning to her machine for the rest of the day.

Wilf went to the post office to send the telegram to his mother. He then made his way to the same men's clothing store in George Street to deck himself out with more clothes and boots. This time, he didn't have Alma's help. After purchasing his new clothes, he still had some time to spare so made his way, with the directions of one of the store assistants, to the State Library just to kill time.

He found it easily, and once inside, he was taken aback with the size of the library and the thousands of books on the shelves. He felt totally helpless not knowing the procedure.

After some time aimlessly wondering around, he decided to try out this new experience and look up some information. He approached one of the assistants at the desk and asked how he could find information about the different colours of one's eyes. She was most helpful and took him straight to a section on that subject. She expertly pulled out a couple of books and showed him to a seat at a table where he could spend however much time he needed.

He didn't need the second book because he found all the information needed to answer his questions about grey-green eyes. Wilf had been fascinated the first time he looked into Teen's eyes and wanted to learn more. The thing that intrigued him was that he was interested enough to want to learn more. First he read about grey eyes, which said: *Grey eyes, usually a wise and gentle person, known for their sensitivity, flexible attitude with great inner strength, least aggressive, with rational and clear thoughts.*

He could not believe what he was reading but thought he should also read about green eyes because that may provide a balance. It said: *Green eyes contain a certain mystery, curious and intelligent. Mostly they make good relationships with an incredible zest and passion for life.* Wilf was absolutely stunned.

All that her sisters said about Teen, what he had observed in her letters and in person since being home for such a short time, was written here in this library book. He copied the details onto a sheet of paper and slipped it into the back of his diary. He didn't need to know more, so he returned the two books to the lass at the desk.

She noticed the changed, excited look on his face compared to when he had first approached her and said, "I can see by the look on your face that you were able to find what you wanted."

"Yes, I certainly did," he said. "Thank you for your help."

He floated out the door thinking about what he had just learned. The day looked like the most beautiful day he had ever known. Actually, it was drizzling a little, but to Wilf, the grey clouds actually looked white against a blue sky, and it was a most glorious day for him.

On Sunday, he wanted to wear some of his new clothes, but he was officially still in the army, and that would be frowned on if caught. He would go to the Congregational church at Pyrmont with Teen and then take a stroll down to the docks at Walsh bay where they had first met, and also witness another troop ship due to arrive at one o'clock.

Troop ships were now arriving back on a regular basis, and the variety of streamers available were greater than when he returned. This was because restrictions were being lifted regularly now that the war was over. The manufacturing of streamers in Sydney had become a very profitable business, virtually overnight.

The next morning, they arrived at Victoria Barracks early like thousands of other excited soldiers and their families to witness a spectacle that they hoped would never need to be repeated on this scale. Wilf made his way to the designated place to fall in with the rest of the soldiers. He struggled to stop thinking back to the other parade ground behind King's. Teen had a good spot up close where she could see all the happenings.

The prime minister was there on this occasion to say thank you to the many who had voluntarily enlisted to serve their country, defending free peoples from the tyrants who started this war.

There were other speeches, but the sad time came when the numbers were read out of those who had not made it back.

When each soldier's name was called out, they individually marched to the front and received their discharge papers. The marching out parade was completed, and the soldiers were dismissed for the last time, with lots of hats thrown into the air. Whistles and horns continuously sounded with huge shouts of joy seeking escape from within each one present either in or out of uniform.

Teen and Wilf walked with arms around each other, ending up down at Circular Quay. They boarded whatever ferry happened to be going somewhere to celebrate this special day; the place didn't matter. This was to be the last day that Wilf would need to wear his uniform, ever. Or so he thought. He was no longer a member of the Australian Imperial Forces, and it felt so good.

Teen said, "I have a special request to make. I would like you to wear your uniform just once more on Wednesday as we journey to Craven." Wilf's puzzled look said it all, but Teen explained, "I've never had the honour of travelling any distance with you in uniform, and I want that special privilege, especially when first meeting your family, because I'm so proud of you, and I want to see their pride in you as well."

Wilf said, "That's fine with me."

They journeyed around the harbour, with Teen giving the usual commentary. They also talked about how they both had difficulty over the past three years believing that the day would come when the war would be over completely.

Ann said, "The newspapers are already talking about *The Great War to end all wars.*"

Wilf said he certainly hoped it would be the last. Teen and Wilf both realised they were falling in love and talked a lot about the prospect of peace for the future in which children could be brought into a world where they would not be caught up in this sheer stupidity of war.

Now that Wilf was no longer in the army, it seemed to have a psychological effect on his thoughts. Those dreaded flashes did not seem to be as frequent or oppressive now; he hoped it would stay that way.

When they arrived home, the place had again been decorated by Teen's sisters who, being such a close-knit, fun-loving-family, needed very little excuse for a party. The sisters invited many of their friends over to celebrate Wilf's return to society without the need of a uniform. There were offers from some of the sisters to souvenir parts of Wilf's uniform, but he wouldn't have any part of that.

He said, "Teen has asked me to wear it one more time back to Craven on Wednesday." Anyway, he was keen to keep it all intact, though for what reason he wasn't sure.

The next day, Teen had to return to work, so Wilf sat around talking most of the day to Mrs. Bisset. She told him how she, as a young twenty-year-old Agnes Spence, had emigrated from Aberdeen in Scotland, arriving on the *Liguana* in October of 1887 to marry Alexander Bisset, a seaman also from Scotland.

"We had seven beautiful daughters before his problem with alcohol became too much and he left me alone to raise the seven girls."

"That would have been a difficult time for you, Mrs. Bisset."

"It certainly was. Fortunately for us, William, who was Alexander's brother, lived right here next door to us and was a totally different man. He has been of enormous help to us as we struggled to make ends meet."

"I'm so glad to hear that you have had that help close by. Teen has mentioned his name many times."

She said, "All of our family, like so many other Scots, were seamen. My uncle went down with the *Dunbar* when it hit the rocks off Watsons Bay on the twentieth of August 1857. Let me get you a picture." She went off to bring in a framed copy of the article.

Mrs. Bisset produced a framed copy from the *Sydney Herald* with the front-page story of the sinking when 121 men and women lost their lives. She handed it to him, saying, "Those lost included my Uncle John Spence, who was the second officer. You should remind Teenie to take you out to Watson's Bay sometime where there is a memorial stone to commemorate the sinking. The ship's anchor is half lodged in the concrete on the cliff top as a memorial to those who lost their lives. I'll let you read it for yourself, Wilf."

The story in the paper told how the ship was involved in bringing more immigrants to the colony to hopefully strike it rich in the gold rush happening in Victoria at the time. The only survivor of the tragedy was James Johnson, who was on deck at the time; he was thrust overboard by the jolt of the ship hitting the rocks. He lay on the rocks for two days before being found.

Mrs. Bisset, pointing to the section about the lone survivor, said, "He eventually became the Nobby's Lighthouse keeper at the entrance to Newcastle Harbour. He was also the coxswain of the lifeboat that saved the only survivor of the *Cawarra* in 1866."

Wilf said, "I've heard of the *Cawarra*—tragedy, because it was the worst loss of life in Newcastle Harbour with over three hundred witnesses standing on the sandy hilltops nearby in the mid-afternoon. They watched the ship break up only three hundred yards away and saw over sixty souls lost in the boiling surf at the harbour entrance."

"So you know it well."

"I've read somewhere that the lifeboats that were close by were not launched in time to save those in the water because of men procrastinating for some two hours over who should man the boats."

"Your memory is pretty good," she said, "because that is exactly what happened."

Mrs. Bisset also brought out her most treasured piece of crockery she had brought with her from Scotland, saying, "This is a plate I purchased on my one and only trip to Arbroath south of Aberdeen, not long before leaving home. We journeyed south about one hundred miles to visit this beautiful town on the coast, just to visit the old abbey. This abbey and the declaration that was signed there are as important to us Scots as the Declaration of Independence is to the Americans."

Wilf listened carefully.

She explained, "Arbroath Abbey was where the Scottish Declaration of Independence was signed on April 6, 1320 by the fifty-one magnates, nobles, barons, and earls, including the king of the Scot's, Robert the Bruce, and four bishops. They wrote beseeching Pope John XXII to come to their aid against the horrible British who were trying to overrun them and rob them of their independence, which they had enjoyed for a much longer time than the British. The Declaration made particular mention of how they had survived captivity and journeyed through the Red Sea as Israelites."

Wilf said, "This is very interesting especially when added to the information I learned when I visited the old remains of the Glastonbury Cathedral. Those people also believed they were Israelites."

"That could be right," she said.

They discussed this topic and others for hours. Mrs. Bisset said, "I firmly believe that you are a kindred spirit, Wilf, and a great catch for Teenie, especially since you are a non-drinker. From my sad experience, that means a lot."

"Thank you, Mrs. Bisset. I appreciate your approval."

"Well I'm very pleased that you are taking good care of my daughter. She has confided in me so much."

The discussion brought other thoughts to Wilf's mind. He said, "There is a very nicely carved headstone belonging to one of my ancestors in the small cemetery alongside the church at Thalabah. This is a small bush community not large enough even to be called a village, where I was born. The inscription says, *In loving memory of Mary Ann Yates, Mother in Israel.*"

"That's very interesting, Wilf."

"I've looked at the inscription many times but never understood what those words meant. Now I'm starting to think more broadly and filling in some of the gaps."

Wilf reluctantly ended the discussion as it was time to go meet Teen when she finished work for the day. He was keen to continue the conversation at another time and hoped there would be many future opportunities. He left the house and, with clear instructions, caught the right tram and alighted at the right stop, arriving just in time to see Teen come out the door with the other girls.

Their embrace had moved up a notch or two, and this was noticed by the cheers of the other girls. Teen needed to go straight home to pack, to get ready for their early departure the next morning.

On the tram, Wilf said, "I had a great time today discussing many things with your mother."

"What were you talking about for so long?"

He filled Teen in with details of the long conversation and said, "I have so many unanswered questions to explore. I hope you will help me find the answers."

"Wilf, I would love to do that."

At the next tram stop, a number of elderly ladies came on board. Wilf immediately stood to his feet and offered his seat. The rest of the journey, he stood and swayed with the movement of the tram, silently thinking about his new situation. Ann had been a huge part of his life for the last few years; actually, his whole future had been about being with Ann.

He found it extremely difficult to accept Ann's death, leaving so many unanswered questions. But now he was on home soil and away from the battlefront, he was starting to pull himself together slowly. Of course, the reason for the change was undoubtedly Teen.

This gentle lady was so caring and understanding of his situation, especially when he seemed thousands of miles away with his silence and his thoughts. It was as if she knew of his relationship with another person whilst away. He knew that was not possible, but Teen was so special.

His deep thoughts were interrupted when Teen said, "This is our stop."

Chapter 26

They were both up before daybreak to catch an early tram. Wilf was intrigued to learn that the trams ran all night. When they reached Central Railway Station, Wilf purchased first-class tickets with Teen's help and proceeded to the waiting train. They found a six-door dog-box compartment on the train that at this stage was empty, and they hoped it would stay that way for the whole trip, but that was not to be.

They were called dog-box carriages because they consisted of six isolated compartments per carriage. Each compartment had two fixed, padded seats facing each other, the full width of the train. The other special feature was the dog-box only had one door on each side, which opened directly to the outside and hence to the station platform on that side. There was no access between each of the boxes.

There was one lift-up seat adjacent to the window, which allowed the backrest to swing away from the wall to become a doorway into a WC. Naturally, the person occupying that seat, before being interrupted, was required to stand or use the missing person's seat, awaiting their return.

Two other couples joined them, and they proved to be good company for the trip. One of the men, Mr. Lewis, had already been to Newcastle a number of times during the construction of the new steelworks. He was moving his wife to Newcastle permanently to complement his management position at the recently opened BHP-Steelworks. He had arrived from Scotland with his wife a few years previously, but Mrs.

Lewis had chosen to live in Sydney until construction was completed and a company house was also completed for them to move into.

Then another couple joined them, Mr. and Mrs. Evans from Melbourne. They were coming to Newcastle to spend time with her parents.

Teen was able to answer most of the questions asked by both parties. Wilf had been away since the steelworks was started and really knew nothing about Newcastle from a personal point of view. On the other hand, he was able to answer many questions about the bush and timber cutting and especially the war.

Mrs. Evans had lost her brother on the Western Front. They were very interested to learn that the places her brother wrote about were the same places Wilf had been. Her brother was in the Fifth Division.

Mr. Lewis said, "I'd like to know what you think the average Digger thought of Monash."

Wilf said, "Well, if the average Digger knew the facts, I think they would approve."

"Why is that, Wilf?"

"Well, let me give you some background. The Australian troops had mostly been deployed in the same small area around the Ypres Salient and the Somme in general, for most of the time. There had been very little forward or backward movement for the first three or so years. Then the greatest leap forward came about only in the last few months before the war ended, when the Australian divisions captured Mont St. Quentin under the leadership of General Monash."

Mr. Lewis said, "I understand that prior to this, the Australian troops had been commanded by British generals."

"Yes, that's absolutely right, both British and French," said Wilf. "The only reason Mrs. Evans's brother mentioned so many of these places in his letters was because when a soldier was withdrawn from the front at place A, they went on leave to place B, and then when they returned to the front again, it would not be at the same point A, but a new place C, where it was considered he was most needed at that time. This may be one hundred miles away from where he had been fighting earlier."

Mr. Evans, said, "Thank you, Wilf, for that simple explanation because I could never understand why they were in so many places, according to his letters. They seemed to be hopping all over the place from one town to another but never made any progress against the Germans."

Wilf had noticed a change come over Mrs. Evans's face when he mentioned Mont St. Quentin, and he ventured to ask where her brother was killed.

She replied, "St. Quentin area, I'm told."

Wilf said, "It would have probably been in the last four months or so. Am I correct?" She could only nod in agreement in between little dabs at the tears now appearing.

Wilf was also now having trouble with that big lump welling up in his throat. However, before turning the conversation to another subject, he said to Mrs. Evans, "I can assure you that your brother would have done great credit to his unit and his country. Those men who gave their lives were all part of what will become known by historians as one of Australia's finest moments of sacrifice and achievement. The capture of Mont St. Quentin helped bring the war to an early and unpredicted end."

All the time Wilf was speaking, Teen held his hand and, almost unnoticeably to the others, moved her ever-so-gentle fingers against his skin to let him know she was with him all the way. Wilf was very much aware of the special way Teen had of providing strength to him when needed.

The conversation went quiet for some time, and then Teen said, "I'm enjoying for the first time these special views around the Hawkesbury River. It's nice how the train follows the water's edge as it makes its way under the high sandstone cliffs. I've never been this far north previously."

Wilf was aware of the constant and tender touch of Teen's body sitting next to him. He thought about the information he had obtained from the library about her eyes and marvelled at how this wonderful, caring lady next to him so closely matched what was written probably hundreds of years ago.

As the train emerged from the tunnel, they all took time to capture the beautiful views of the long train curving ahead around the Brisbane Waters. The smoke from the engine was flowing back over the carriages, making a postcard picture. Mrs. Lewis took out her new camera to take some photos.

The last couple of hours passed with all of them trying to get some rest as the train made its way around the western side of Lake Macquarie and into Newcastle. Both couples said their farewells to Teen and Wilf and left the small carriage at Broadmeadow Station; they were now on their own.

Wilf said, "I really appreciated the gentle touch of your hand when I was having difficulty expressing words about the war." She gave him one of those special looks as he gently caressed the little finger on her right hand. It had been cut badly by a broken bottle when she was a girl. It now tended to stand out straight when holding a cup of tea, making it look like she was putting on the airs of those in high society. They sat looking out of the window as the train wound its way through farming land and around the mountains through Dungog and eventually to Craven Station, arriving about half an hour late.

Wilf and Teen were the only ones to alight from the train at this small village station. They walked to the end of the platform and were greeted by Ned, one half of the family welcoming committee. Ned was aged twenty-one. He was waiting with a borrowed and decorated horse and carriage to take Teen for her first carriage ride to Kimberly, just over four miles from the station.

The other half of the welcoming committee waiting in the shade was Wilf's youngest sister, Millie, aged eighteen. She was keen to come along for the ride and to be one of the first in the family to meet this splendid city lady Wilf had told them so much about. Wilf introduced Teen to them both and lifted the bags on board. He then helped Teen up to take the seat facing the front. Fortunately, this four-wheeled carriage that Wilf had never seen before had a good shade cover for the ride home. It was larger than a traditional wagonette and had been built specially for one of the dairy farmers out of town to transport his entire family to church every Sunday—rain, hail, or shine.

Ned, who had lost most of his hearing when he was ten years old, had taken it upon himself to attach a couple of small bells to the harness of the two horses. The people in the village of Craven could hear of their approach and come out to welcome Teen. They had all heard about this very special occasion and knew she was coming; secrets could not be easily kept in this small village.

This journey was something special for Teen as they travelled along a narrow dirt road that never seemed to get there. The road wound hard to the right and then hard back to the left around the many sharp cuttings. This road was mostly cut by Wilf and his father's bullock team winding around deep ravines from the heights overlooking the river.

Ned did an excellent job as they traversed over the hills and eventually down the last long slope to the sharp bend in Wards River below. He guided the horses over the river crossing in their slackened stride and then up the sharp bank on the other side to the Kimberly homestead. The gate had already been opened in anticipation, with a large welcome sign on each post saying Welcome, Teen.

Ned pulled up the carriage right outside the front veranda. The family, three more sisters plus mother and father, came out to greet Teen.

Mrs. Yates was a tall and serious type who didn't mince words but normally knew exactly the right words to say at any time; this time was one of those exceptions. She was known around town as a smart dresser, always with black, full-length frocks to the ankles, long sleeves, and high-neck collar. She tentatively hugged Teen and said she was looking forward to get to know her over the next few days.

Mr. Yates was shorter than his wife and had a white beard that had never been totally shaved. He was a man of very few words. The other sisters welcomed Teen warmly and gave her a good old country hug. Wilf's eldest sister, Leila, had married just before he went to war and now had two nieces and one nephew for him to meet for the first time. Leila had come back to Kimberly for a visit to welcome Teen.

Teen was taken inside this quaint country home, the likes of which she had never seen before, and shown around by Millie. Teen was a city girl through and through, and most of the homes she visited were made primarily of stone, with maybe horizontal weather boards at the back or sides. The interiors were usually lined inside with lime and cement, exposed boards, or boards plastered over.

This home was a definitely a self-built home elevated on a foundation of uncut river rocks joined together with a form of lime-cement mix under the outer walls. The walls were vertical split timber slabs around the living area and horizontal weather boards around the bedrooms. There were hinged, galvanised iron swing shutters for windows cut into the upright slabs and glass windows in the sleeping area.

The swing shutters were open most days to let in light and air. Inside the house, there were no ceilings, just an exposed, corrugated iron, gabled roof rising to an apex of about fifteen feet. The interior dividing walls were made of hessian about eight feet high. The kitchen was spotlessly clean, fitted out with craftsman-built furniture made from white beech timber.

Teen said, "The white timber in the furniture looks very nice."

Millie replied, "That's because we scrub the table and crockery cabinet with sand-soap every day to keep it that way. Dad cut the timber and had it made by a cabinet maker in Gloucester."

Although the house was completely different from what Teen was accustomed to in Sydney, she could see that all of the handmade covers for the chairs and bedding had been lovingly and painstakingly crafted by someone very talented with a needle and thread. Teen, being a dressmaker herself, could instantly recognise the high quality of the work and the fancy embroidering on every piece of material in this home.

Teen asked, "Who makes all of the coverings? They're beautifully done."

Millie replied, "They're mostly made by Mum, but she has taught us girls, so there is some of our work mixed in there also."

Teen was particularly drawn to the handmade clothes worn by Mrs. Yates and the girls. The skirts were all high-waisted, and the blouses had lots of fine embroidery to show off the skill of the seamstress. Wilf had already told Teen that his mother would never be found sitting around doing nothing. She was always busy with her needle and threads, making or mending some item of clothing or furnishing.

Teen also made her own clothes and for this special occasion wore a full-length, dark skirt with broad waistband high under the breast. She wore a light beige blouse with long sleeves and large lapels to complement the central broach and string of pearls hanging around her neck. She wore a large-brimmed hat with short, hanging tassels around the outer edge, which was ideal for the expected hot days in the bush.

Ned had borrowed a camera from a friend, so he wanted them all outside for a family photo, with Wilf holding his youngest niece, Mavis, who was nearly two.

It took a little time to arrange the photo with everyone, including the three children wearing their broad-brimmed hats. Ned managed eventually to get them all in place, saying in his deep, monotone voice, "I hope my first attempt at photography turns out all right. I have no idea how it all works."

Teen said, "I'm sure you'll do fine, Ned, but where is your father?" not realising that Ned couldn't hear her.

Vera said, "He makes himself scarce every time a camera shows up. He's not into this photo nonsense, to use his own words."

Ned completed his first stint at photography, and Wilf brought in Teen's bag as Millie led her outside to the wash-house to suggest that Teen may need to freshen up a little. The wash-house was just outside the back door with a common roof cover over the space between the two buildings, with a wall at one end. It consisted of a wash bench and basin, a concrete washing tub and a fuel copper in the corner. There were also some internal lines in place to dry clothes with the heat from the fire under the copper, for when there was no sunshine to dry the clothes on the outside lines.

An outdoor lavatory was located at the other end of the outside clothes line.

Mr. Yates retuned from the direction of the river, whistling the only tune he knew to announce that everything was ready down on the bank by the willows for a picnic tea.

It was a beautiful place for a picnic on the lush green grass located on the inside bend of the river. There was a background orchestra of the never-ending noise of the rushing water as it emerged from the deeper water on the far side of the bend over the many steps in the rock floor, making its way to the lower levels of the river downstream.

Rugs had been set in place under the willows. A smoking fire was already cooking the meat down on the pebbled area of the lower bank of the river. The sun was about to go behind the hill across the river, making it a perfect evening for them to eat and get to know Teen.

The whole family had taken an instant liking to Teen, maybe with some reservation from Mrs. Yates. She had been hoping one of the local girls awaiting Wilf's return would make a good wife for her son. She was not sure if a city girl could fit into this sort of life, and she most certainly did not want her eldest son running off to live in the city. Leila left early with the little ones while there was still light, with Ned taking them back in the borrowed carriage into Craven.

They had all enjoyed a wonderful meal together, getting to know Teen. When the light started to fail, they packed up and headed back to the house where Mr. Yates had already lit some kerosene lamps inside.

It was customary in the bush to go to bed when it became dark and get up at sunrise. As darkness descended, they all said their goodnights and headed off to bed, except Wilf and Teen.

Wilf walked Teen down by the river in the opposite direction to where they had picnicked, for a short way where the water was much deeper and quieter.

He said, "I hope you have not been too shocked by the simple lifestyle my family lives."

Teen said, "No, not at all. As a matter of fact, I'm very impressed by the tidiness and comfortable furnishings throughout the house. It is quite obvious to me that you have a very loving family and a well-kept home."

Wilf wrapped his arms around Teen in the coolness of the country evening. The moon appeared ever so slowly over the top of the hill as they heard the hushed sound of water gently rippling over the smooth stones on the river's edge. They listened to the continuous backing-chorus of the crickets singing their well-rehearsed hometown anthem. In the distance was the sound of frogs expressing their own happy welcome to a stranger in their midst.

Wilf wished there was enough light to see Teen's eyes as he kissed her softly for the first time on home ground, saying, "I don't think you quite understand what it's like for me to have you here with my family, Teen. Thanks for coming. You've made my day."

"I'm so thrilled to be here with you too, Wilf. I really didn't know what to expect." They hugged for some time in the moonlight before they made their way back to the house for an early night, after a very long day. Millie had been very thoughtful and left a candle burning for Teen to find her way around.

Chapter 27

The next day, Wilf was up early to try out some more of his new civvies; it was time to say good-bye forever to the khakis. They all had to be washed and stored away—for what, he didn't know. Teen also woke early when everyone else stirred because, with only hessian walls, there was no way to disguise the sounds of getting up. Mr. Yates scraped out the cold ashes from the fireplace and lit a new fire. Normally there would be some hot ashes on which to re-establish the fire, but because they had used the picnic fire last night, this one was cold.

There were the heavy iron pots and kettles on the stove that Teen hadn't seen for some time. Mrs. Yates was busy getting the food ready to prepare breakfast, and Wilf's sisters were either preparing the table or milking their cow to provide fresh milk for breakfast.

They all sat down to breakfast together and planned the day.

Teen said, "I'm keen to see how the men make their living in the bush by felling trees and driving their bullock team."

Ilma said, "Wilf will be the one to show you; he certainly knows how it's done."

After breakfast, Mr. Yates said, "Well, we had better go and get things started." Ned was always attentive to lip movements and understood that his father was ready to go. He arrived back after dark last evening and now set off with his father to round up the bullocks and yoke them up, ready for work.

Wilf said, "Bullocks need to graze in the early morning, so the team will be ready to go around ten o'clock."

Teen said, "I don't think I have suitable clothes for the bush."

Vera said, "That's okay. We anticipated this. We can loan you some for your first horse-riding lesson."

"That's very thoughtful of you, Vera, thank you."

"Where the bullock team is working is only accessible by either horseback or lots of very difficult walking. It would be totally unsuitable to walk, and besides, I hear you're keen to try riding," said Vera.

"Yes, I am. Everyone up here rides horses, so it shouldn't be that difficult, I hope."

Wilf said, "Every member of the family has a horse, but Millie's is the quietest, so that's the one for you to ride."

"Thank you, Millie. I hope I can look after it for you. What's its name?"

"Bonnie," said Millie. "She's getting a bit old these days, but she will be good for you."

"That sounds good to me," said Teen as she went to change into her riding gear.

After getting Teen onto the horse and some short walks around the perimeter of the house, things went very well. Teen felt she was ready to attempt the journey up along the creek to see the team in action. Mrs. Yates had prepared a lunch and bottles of water to take with them. They would only be walking the horses, so it would take them the best part of one hour or so to reach the work area, arriving just before lunch according to Millie.

Teen proved to be a very competent learner and had no trouble along the way, although her rear end was feeling a little sore from sitting in this unusual position for so long. Before crossing the creek and making the steep climb away from the creek to where they would find the team, Wilf called for a short rest to allow the horses to drink.

He said, "When approaching water on horseback, you should be prepared to lean backwards over the rump of the horse."

Teen said, "Why is that?"

"Because the horse will drop its head quickly to get water, and you will fall forward if not prepared in advance."

They mounted up again after a short break, and Teen was prepared in advance and held the reins firmly and allowed the horse to approach the creek slowly.

Wilf said, "You did very well for a new chum, and I'm very proud of you."

"Thank you. I was very pleased with myself as well."

They made the final slow climb up the winding hill to where Ned's axe could be heard cutting the tree. Although Teen had handled the horse very well for a novice, she was glad to arrive and sit down on a log for a rest.

Wilf took Teen over to where Ned was cutting and said, "Ned knew you were coming to see them working and had half-prepared a tree to be felled a couple of days earlier. He had already set his planks and cut some of the way through the trunk."

"What do you mean, 'set his planks'?"

"You see the slots cut into the tree trunk? They're used to insert the end of the planks to get up to the correct height, like steps. The two planks you see are about six inches wide and are locked in position at the right height and angle for Ned to stand on while cutting."

"But why doesn't he stand on both of them for better balance?"

"He doesn't need better balance. He only stands on one at a time. When he needs to swing from a different angle, he steps over onto the other plank already set in the right place."

"How does he know where the tree is going to fall?"

"Before Ned starts cutting, he marks the trunk with chalk where he needs to cut and then follows his plan. If his plan is right, and if he follows the plan correctly, the tree will fall according to his plan."

"How do you learn to mark the tree right in the first place?"

"By making mistakes," said Wilf.

"Wouldn't it be better if you didn't make mistakes? Because it could be dangerous, couldn't it?"

"Yes, it could be very dangerous, but you try not to make that same mistake again. Isn't that the same way you learned to make shirts?"

"Yes, I suppose so, but we have a supervisor watching us."

"The only supervisor out here is your father or your brother. Or you learn the hard way, and that takes longer."

My Yates was working the team a couple of hundred yards further on, so Wilf decided that Ned should show his skills with the axe before stopping for lunch. He indicated that to Ned, so he climbed up onto the planks again, a distance of only about eight feet because this was a relatively small tree.

Wilf said, "A larger tree would take too long to cut through and could take most of the day or two or even longer with one person working on his own."

Ned cut into the tree with accurately aimed, powerful swings. Teen said, "How is Ned able to keep his balance for such a long time whilst still swinging the axe?"

"It all comes with lots of practice. On many of the large cedar trees we cut, it requires the planks to be set up to twenty feet high, and that requires good balance for obvious reasons."

"That's a long way up," she said. "Why do you need to go so high? Why not cut the tree closer to ground level where it would be safer?"

"There are two reasons why not. The first reason is that the timber is not as good lower down and would be wasted. The second reason is that the girth of the trunk is much larger closer to the ground and therefore could take two or three times longer to cut through."

Ned had been using a lot of energy swinging the axe for quite some time, without much obvious progress being made from what Teen could see. A fire had already been lit earlier, so Wilf prepared to boil the billy for a cup of tea, just as his father arrived back through the scrub for lunch. Ned looked down and said, "I'll come down and join you. My stomach is rumbling. I can't hear it, but I can feel it."

It was another beautiful day to enjoy as they sat on a log in the shade to eat the sandwiches prepared by Wilf's mother. Teen had lots of questions to ask about various things and said, "How do you get on when it rains and what happens if someone gets hurt in the bush?"

Wilf replied, "Well as for the weather, one must become a good judge of the weather and not start out for the day if bad weather is expected. You must remember that the bullocks can't get traction if it's too wet underfoot."

Teen didn't want the second part of her question ignored and said, "And what about if there is an accident?"

"We haven't had a bad accident yet, but we always take great care."

Ned unknowingly saved the situation and said, "I still have about another hour of cutting before the tree will be close to falling, so why don't you take Teen over to see the team working?"

The team was about two or three hundred yards away in the opposite direction from the way they came in. Wilf said, "We'll do that, so give us a yell when you're ready."

As they approached the team, Teen marvelled at the size of these beasts; they were huge. William and Wilf were known as two of the best bullock drivers in the district, and to everyone's amazement, neither of them swore at the bullocks. This was very unusual because bullock drivers had a reputation of having the most flamboyant variety of foul expressions to keep the team working. William didn't need to curb his language just because Teen was there, and the bullocks responded to his every command with everyday language.

As the team came close alongside Teen, she paid close attention to the lead bullock's large, brown, disinterested eyes as they looked steadfastly straight ahead. It seemed they were not interested in anything off to the side. It was as if the beast had been programmed just to do that one thing. It seemed that the harder the sweating bullocks pulled, the longer became their necks, and the closer to the ground the head reached. Both lead bullocks slowly swayed their heads together from side to side in perfect unison to match their steps.

Wilf said, "They're a real good pair and work well together as a unit."

Teen was intrigued to find that every beast had a name and responded quickly to any commands when his name was called. She said, "How do they know what to do?"

Wilf said, "When my father says, 'Wee-back, Rowdy,' that requires the lead bullock on the right to pull his partner to the right for a right turn. If the command is 'Wee-back, Number,' that requires the other lead bullock to pull to the left for a left turn. That's a ninety-degree turn by the leader."

"That's amazing. Is that all they know?"

"No, there's more. If the command given is 'Wee-back gee-back, Number,' the bullock knows that a complete wheel about is required to lead the team to the left and back alongside the team in the opposite direction."

Teen asked, "How do you get the bullocks to stop?"

"The command is just 'woo-back,' nothing else."

"I find all of this so fascinating that the teamster can have the entire team working according to his commands."

"That right; otherwise, you don't have a team."

"How do they know their names?"

"Well, you need to start talking to them up close when they're young so they get used to the name."

"How do you teach them the commands?"

"You must teach them when they're young. It's not that much different from the army."

"I'm impressed, but I have another question. Why is it necessary to constantly use the long bullock whip on the rump of the bullocks?"

Wilf explained, "Each beast has a special position and job to do on the team, dependant on that bullock's strength or weaknesses. For instance, the biggest bullocks are usually positioned at the rear because of their ability to add extra pull when required. Extra pull may be needed to pull the log across a sharp, narrow dip in the land, such as a creek. This is to stop the log from becoming wedged into the forward sharp bank. These bullocks are generally lazy and don't pull consistently all the time, but they respond to a sharp crack on the rump to pull harder just at the right time."

He continued, "The lead bullocks are usually more intelligent and capable of obeying instant commands without the need of the whip. Most lead bullocks are also much leaner than their opposite numbers at the rear. The bullocks in the middle of the team also have special tasks when needed but are generally prepared to pull consistently and just follow the leader."

Teen said, "Can you pick an intelligent beast by its looks?"

"No, I don't think so, but there's an old saying amongst bullock drivers, that unless you're a leader, the view never changes."

It took a little time for Teen to grasp the significance of that saying, but with a little help, she understood and then said, "You know, I like that; it's quite profound. I like the saying so much I'm determined to remember it and apply it to life in general."

Teen thought long before asking the next question. "How do you tie them up into a team? I'm sure you don't have some team specialist who comes out here when needed to catch them and tie them all together."

Wilf explained, "You yoke up a team; you do not tie them together. This is actually the toughest part of the day, especially if doing it alone."

"Is it really?"

"And it needs to be done every morning."

Teen said, "I would like to see how it's done some time."

"The bullocks are allowed to graze in the morning in a restricted paddock before we herd them into a smaller yard. In that paddock, the yoke and chains, etc., are still lying on the ground from where they fell the previous evening. The bullocks are then moved up in their pairs as required, starting with the lead pair, to the exact position where the bow is located on the ground. With the front pair in place, the heavy bow has to be lifted and placed across the necks of the two beasts. Then the long, steel bows are lifted up from under their necks and inserted through the holes in the yoke; the nuts are screwed on to hold them in place."

"It sounds dangerous to me."

He replied, "All of this has to be accomplished while avoiding the long horns waving around. The bullocks don't necessarily like the idea of being yoked up, knowing that a hard day ahead is expected of them. It is this procedure that causes many injuries to the teamsters. The bullocks throw their heads about as the teamster duck underneath, in between, and around the bullocks' heads to secure the bows."

"I'm not so sure that I still want to see how it's done now."

Wilf continued, "After each pair is locked into the yoke, a heavy chain is then attached to the underside centre of the yoke and extended along the ground, ready to be connected to the next pair of bullocks when they're prepared. Of course, another problem is to keep the first pair standing in one place until all of the other pairs are prepared and connected. This is not always easy. However, the fact that bullocks, like cows, have four parts to their stomach, this allows them to regurgitate the grass that they ate earlier. If they get plenty of sweet grass before being yoked up, this tends to keep them content to some extent."

"Do they make much noise during this time?"

"No," said Wilf. "It is during this extended period of preparation where communication between the teamster and the bullocks become very important. This part of the day's work with the bullocks helps them to hear and respond to their individual names. You keep using their name when close, and they become familiar with their name and the teamster's voice.

"To yoke up a large team could take the best part of two hours' work each morning. The unyoking each evening doesn't take quite the same time because the bow, chains, and yokes can just fall to the ground in place, ready for the next morning."

Teen felt tired already after listening to all the work required to prepare the team before the real productive work started each day.

Mr. Yates stopped by at this point and said, "A good bullock team works like a well-oiled sewing machine. The machine responds to the commands given by Teen's feet and fingers in the shirt shop where you work. The sewing machine goes backward and forward or to the left or right according to your command. I've never seen one of those machines working, but Wilf explained the movements to me."

"I don't know how he knows because I don't think he has ever seen one working either."

"You don't know what I've seen, do you?" he said as he looked at Teen with real affection. "We will follow the team on the next pass down to the log dump to see how a teamster can load even the largest log onto a bullock wagon without anyone else's help."

They followed the team, and Teen watched as the large log, about six feet in diameter, was taken along the top side of the dump and unhitched. The team was then brought around to a stop at right angles to and facing downhill away from the middle of the log. A chain was slung over and around the middle of the log and attached to the chain at the rear of the team.

When everything was ready, the team was moved forward in very small movements to drag the log over the edge of the dump onto the waiting wagon.

Wild said, "If the team does not stop exactly on command, a large log could overshoot the end of the dump and either crush the wagon or tip it over. It is a very delicate manoeuvre and not to be attempted by novices."

Teen said, "I wish Ned had brought the camera with him so I could take some photos to show the girls at work. They wouldn't believe just how big these logs are."

Having watched the loading of the log onto the wagon, Wilf said, "I just heard Ned sing out that the tree is ready to come down, so we'll make our way back to where we had lunch."

Ned was sitting on the log in his own silent world, taking a swig of water and having a rest awaiting their return. He didn't hear them approaching, but when they stopped in front of him, he looked up and said, "Righto, I will cut through the last section for Teen to watch it fall."

He then expertly climbed the planks wedged into the pre-cut slots in the side of the tree and proceeded to complete the cut. Ned swung the axe with great force and accuracy to make the chips fly. Teen was amazed to see that there were not many small chips flying. Because of the accuracy of the blows, the chunks of wood falling to the ground were not small but mostly chunks weighing a couple of pounds each or more. First he would swing horizontally with a couple of cuts and then would change to a downward angled cut from a higher swing start. This would splinter off the large chunks, all the while keeping his balance on that narrow plank.

Ned, being totally deaf, couldn't hear the creaking of the timber. He had to rely on a vibration that he could detect through the trunk to warn him that the tree was ready to fall.

It still took another fifteen to twenty minutes before the tree started to creak. Ned clamoured quickly down the planks to await the tree falling exactly as he planned with expertly directed cuts to the trunk. Teen watched in awe as this tall tree, very slowly at first started, to fall in silence, finishing with a thunderous roar as it crashed through many smaller trees and hit the ground. Although Ned had lost most of his hearing, he sometimes still heard the roar of the falling trees when they crashed. He also heard the crack of thunder sometimes if it was close.

Teen turned to Wilf and said, "Do you mean to tell me this is what you are coming back from a dangerous war to do? Surely there has to be a safer way to earn a living than doing this every day for the rest of your life?"

"I know nothing else, and I don't think it's that dangerous anyway." He went off to gather the horses that had been standing patiently off to one side where there was some sweet, green grass to keep them happy.

They mounted up and made for home, stopping once along the way, not only to relieve Teen's sore rear end, but also to enjoy a little snuggle along the bank of the creek in the cool of the afternoon. The horses also enjoyed a well-earned drink before being mounted up again for the remainder of the ride home.

Wilf said, "We will continue on past the house a little and across the river. I have something I want to show you." They rode past the house, and at the same time Wilf sang out to let his mother to let her know they would be another half an hour.

Before crossing the river, Wilf said, "Don't forget to be ready as you approach the water for when the horse drops its head." They crossed the river without incident at the bend and climbed to the top of a steep pinch that overlooked the homestead and everything else in all directions.

Teen was impressed with the location and asked, "Why did your father not build his home on top of the hill here instead of down below closer to the river?"

"I don't really know the answer, but maybe he had intentions of building a second house here at a later stage. My father is not one to talk much but spends a lot of his time thinking and whistling. He's not one to waste time with idle chatter, so if he had chosen the wrong place to build his house, he would not be one to bemoan the fact by talking about it."

"This is an absolutely glorious spot for a house."

"Take a good look, Teen, in every direction and remember this position because I want to talk to you about this view at a later stage." They turned the horses back down the hill, over the river, and arrived just in time to wash before tea. Teen was relieved to be off the horse, free from that rear-end feeling, which she was told by Millie would be worse tomorrow.

The next morning, the sky was overcast but suitable for what Wilf had planned. Teen had never seen cows milked, so the plan was to visit the Blanch family who had a herd of some forty cows. They had breakfast, and Wilf harnessed up the horses to the borrowed carriage and set off before seven. This would give them enough time to see the latter part of the herd being milked.

When they arrived at the dairy, Teen looked over the cows released from the bails and the other lot still to be milked. She wasn't too fussed about the smell emanating from wet manure on the ground in the yard where the cows waited to be milked. Wilf guided Teen into the milking shed and did the introductions. They were glad to see both of them.

The Blanch family had, like every other family in the district, kept up to date with Wilf's involvement in the war effort. They had not seen him since he returned. They kept milking away whilst keeping the questions coming for both Wilf and Teen to answer.

Teen was fascinated with the milking process but declined, when offered, to have a go herself. This was normal procedure to make such an offer to all new chums, or townies as they were called when from the city. They continued talking until the milking was finished for the morning, looked around the dairy, and then went over to the house for some morning tea with the family before setting off for a journey into Gloucester, a distance of eleven miles. To Wilf, this was the big town, but to Teen, it was nothing compared to the shopping available in Sydney.

Everywhere they went, people rushed up to Wilf to welcome him home and to meet the lovely Teen by his side. Most people in Gloucester knew Wilf and everyone else in the district. They all expressed relief that he had returned in one piece. Teen couldn't get over how everyone knew each other and how friendly they were, especially towards her.

They set off for Kimberly sometime after three, arriving in time for the evening meal.

The next morning, they were up early to leave on the six o'clock train. Ned had arranged to drive them into the station in the borrowed carriage before returning it to the generous friend who had loaned it for this special occasion to welcome Teen. Wilf planned to return to Sydney with Teen, over her protestations that she would be all right returning on her own. Wilf had no intention of giving in, knowing that he would stay in Sydney for a few more days and be with Teen.

The return journey was much quicker, or so it seemed, but they enjoyed the train journey together just as much. Lots of discussion took place about living in the country so far removed from the city. Obviously Teen was looking at the pros and cons for that day when Wilf hopefully would ask for her hand in marriage. Wilf, on the other hand, was trying to put positive spin on the lifestyle to which Teen would need to become accustomed if that day arrived.

There would be a number of trips for Wilf back and forth to Sydney, including the wedding of Minnie, one of Teen's sisters.

"Wilf and Teen's wedding."

Wilf had been home from the war for six months when the day came for him to ask Teen for her hand in marriage. By this time, they were both comfortable with the plan to marry, so it was not a big surprise for Teen. Nor was it for Mrs. Bisset, who had grown very fond of Wilf and agreed to the marriage with her very special blessing. They travelled into the city and purchased a wedding ring that thrilled Teen to pieces.

Wilf told Teen, "Cast your mind back to that first day on the hilltop overlooking the Kimberly homestead. I've made arrangements to purchase a portion of father's land, which includes the whole of that hilltop on which to build a new home."

Teen said, "That would be fabulous."

He said, "I've already talked to Jack Peacock, a builder in Stroud, who has agreed to build a new house right on the part of the hill where we stopped that day. It can be started immediately when I give him the okay and a deposit. It can be completed in time for our wedding on December 11." Teen threw her arms around Wilf's neck to seal the deal.

Plans were put in place for the wedding, with the church to be booked and suits to be hired. Teen would make her own dress and accessories, plus the same for her sister Vera who was to be the bridesmaid. Because Teen's father was no longer around, they asked Uncle William next door to give the bride away. Invitations were sent out to Teen's workmates and family, plus all of Wilf's family. Most of them had never been outside of the Stroud, Dungog, and Gloucester district, let alone to visit Sydney.

The big day arrived, which was more significant and full of adventure than for most brides. After the wedding, Teen would be leaving all of her friends and family to journey to a far-off bush location, four miles from her nearest neighbour, with the exception of her in-laws across the other side of the river. Her husband-to-be would be away in the bush all day, six days a week, and she would be all alone in a completely new environment, without any means of communication.

This new venture would be so different from what she had been used to, with daily connectivity with her workmates and family. She had a close social involvement with her friends from church at night and on weekends. Her family and workmates expressed amazement at her sense of adventure. They all said, without exception, that they could not do the same thing. Teen was being held up as a real pioneer-adventurer by her family and friends.

One week before the wedding, Teen finished her last day at the shirt factory. All of the girls took her out for dinner on Saturday night, and for Teen it was an extremely tearful experience. This was the first of many friendships that would be interrupted for some indeterminate time as Teen moved to the country.

Teen had a very busy week ahead to complete the wedding dresses and other clothing Teen would be taking on the honeymoon.

Teen looked absolutely stunning as a bride on her wedding day in the gown of her own creation. Teen's dress was three-quarter length with unique and intricate stitching down each side to match the slightly shorter veil. The lacework of the veil had beautiful needlework over the top of and attached to a floral head piece, like an ancient Greek Olympian's olive wreath, known as a *kotinos*. The *kotinos* sat upon Teen's beautiful, silky-fine, brown hair that was the envy of all her sisters. She carried a pastel-coloured bouquet of flowers with a broad, white bow. The bow had long tails to match the wedding gown, pointing down to the white stockings and shoes. Teen made a most beautiful bride that day in the Congregational church at Pyrmont.

Wilf and Ned, along with Uncle William, were decked out in their hired wedding suits. They wore waistcoats to match, with gold chains across the front to hold their fob watch in the pocket. The white, silk shirts with high collars, white bow ties, white gloves, and polished lace-up ankle boots all looked the part. The men looked very smart but nothing like their normal selves, especially Wilf and Ned.

The church was filled to overflowing with a dinner afterwards in the hall behind for all the invited guests. The wedding was a real success, with so many of Wilf's family coming to Sydney for the first time. Most had arrived the day before, and one of Wilf's sisters said, "We had our eyes opened staring out the train windows approaching the city, not to mention the tram ride coming into our hotel from the train."

"You shouldn't have been so surprised," Wilf said. "I've been telling you about Sydney for a long time."

Some of the country folk were planning to stay a few more days to see more of the sights. Everything was so amazing to them, and this became the major topic of conversation at the reception. Naturally, with their style of clothing, they stood out as country hicks, but all, including Wilf's mother and father, were made to feel welcome by the Bisset family. The contingent of men from the country was keen to provide a noisy send-off for this very special couple, and so they did.

The newly marrieds planned to travel by train and stay in a honeymoon suite, pre-booked by Teen in a small seaside holiday village on the south coast of NSW, at the Thirroul Guesthouse.

After the reception, they stayed for one night in a small hotel in George St, close to Central Station. The next morning, they left on the ten o'clock train for Thirroul. Thirroul was located about seven or eight miles north of the city of Wollongong. After they arrived at the Thirroul Station, it was less than a fifteen-minute walk down Moore St. to the guesthouse on Ocean Drive.

The guesthouse overlooked the rocky headland and the ocean baths below. Upon arriving at the hotel, they checked in just in time for lunch to be served in the dining room. Their room had a magnificent view of the coast, and they had a wonderful week with perfect weather. They had lots of walks along the sandy beaches and rocky headlands, exploring all of the sea creatures in the rock pools that Wilf had not seen before.

On one occasion, Wilf caught himself making comparisons with the site of this guesthouse and the Headland Hotel at Torquay. He was ever so grateful that Teen had helped him wipe away most of those thoughts of that awful time, now so far behind. The week at Thirroul was filled with excitement as they learned more about each other. Life was so good and exciting.

At the week's end, they journeyed back to Sydney by train and arrived at Teen's home late on Saturday afternoon. Teen had a lot of packing to do before leaving on the following Wednesday for her new life at Kimberly-Two. Lots of friends called to wish her well, and most promised to pay her a visit sometime.

It was another emotional time for Teen with so many well-wishers stopping by. In between visitors, she continued packing all of her worldly possessions into a number of wooded crates, as well as a steel trunk that had been used by her father when he was at sea.

Mrs. Bisset said she wanted Teen to take with her the souvenir plate from Arbroath that she had shown to Wilf and discussed in great detail.

There were other precious souvenirs that Teen's mother wanted her to take with her to decorate her new home, such as some rare, large seashells. Teen felt extremely honoured to think her mother wanted her to have them. These shells had always been highly prized items in their house from when Teen was tiny. They were admired by so many people, and now they were to be hers.

A taxi truck was arranged to pick up the boxes for consignment to Craven; they would be there waiting for them on their arrival.

With lots of teary farewells from family and friends on Tuesday night, they went to bed in what had been Wilf's room on previous visits. They had to be ready for the early departure in the morning, for a whole new life ahead at Kimberly-Two, as Teen liked to call the new home she had not yet seen. Wilf had made sure that everything was finished and paid for before leaving for the wedding. Because of his careful handling of his army pay, which had been mostly transferred directly into his mother's care, he had been able to pay cash for the new home.

The train left the station at six o'clock. They had not planned for anyone to be there to see them off.

They had company in the dog-box as far as Broadmeadow, and then they had it all to themselves until Craven. A lot of the journey was spent in silence with both contemplating their lives together into the future. The silence was interspersed with the occasional questions, mostly from Teen about Kimberly and her new home.

Wilf said, "I'm very much aware of what you are giving up to spend your life with me in the bush. I myself am not making any significant lifestyle change at all, but I realise the many sacrifices you're making."

Teen replied, "It's not that I haven't had a lot of time to consider the changes, but I'm totally prepared to do whatever it takes to become accustomed to a different life, working together for a happy marriage."

"I'm committed to making things as easy as possible for you, Teen, and am prepared to make whatever sacrifices are required to achieve that end. The very nature of this unique situation will not always be easy, especially for you."

Kimberly 2 built for Teen in 1920 as it stands today.

Chapter 28

They arrived at Craven Station, and as planned, Ned was early and had already loaded the boxes of Teen's goods, which had arrived overnight onto the carriage. Overhead was wall-to-wall blue skies, which Wilf pointed out to Teen, saying, "The blue skies are a good indication of our future life together."

"I hope so too," said Teen as she looked lovingly into her husband's eyes.

It was a picture-perfect ride to Kimberly, a beautiful bride being driven to her new home for the first time on such a glorious day. As Ned turned the horses towards what the family all called "the bend in the river," Teen was quick to notice the new home. It was on the hill exactly where Wilf had taken her by horse on that first trip, where had told her to "remember this spot."

She turned to Wilf, showing the love that reflected so easily from her eyes, and said, "It looks beautiful, Wilf, it really does." She was so excited to see her new home for the first time. It stood out with its shiny, new galvanised roof and natural weather boards.

Wilf said, "I'm glad you like it. Everything has been planned with you in mind."

Teen could see it had a veranda around two sides, so she assumed it had another veranda out the back because Wilf had promised her verandas on three sides.

Ned stayed the reins, and the horses slowed a little, swinging up into the gateway approach that had also been recently added since she was last there. Ned hopped down and opened the gate while Wilf pointed out various features with the new house. Ned took the carriage through the gate and stopped right alongside the main entrance steps leading up to the full-width front veranda. Wilf stepped down first to assist Teen, who was still not looking at what she was doing but gazing around at her new home.

Wilf said, "Your new home, madam?"

Teen didn't reply immediately as she stepped down. Then she threw her arms around his neck and said, "Thank you, Wilf, for such a beautiful house," and kissed him a number of times.

"Wait till you see inside," said Wilf as Teen did a little, fancy skip, wanting to be the first one inside the house. Once inside, Teen's eyes needed a little time to allow the transition from brilliant sunshine to the dim light inside. All the things in her new house that she had hoped for, such as floor coverings and big windows, were instantly noticed.

Large, glass curtain-less windows were featured in every room. Teen went to each window to take in the spectacular view, different from every window. In one direction, she could see the rolling hills away in the distance or the foliage of the trees running away towards the river, then the long road up the hill towards Craven.

Better still on the other side, she could look down and see the water as it babbled over the smooth rocks down the mini-rapids in the river. On the other side of the river, she could see the home of her in-laws, and above that, she could see cattle grazing along the fence line of the road, winding far out to the State Forest.

Wilf said, "Do you like the view?"

"Of course I like it. I love it. Who wouldn't?"

Now that Teen's eyes were accustomed to the lesser light, she turned her attention to inside. With the exception of the kitchen, all rooms had stained cypress pine flooring boards, with large carpet squares in the middle.

The walls were lined with vertical bevelled-edge beech boards upwards from the chair rail, with diagonal boards stained a little darker below. In the dining room was a heavy oak dining room table with chairs and crockery cabinet to match.

Wilf said, "I had the dining room suite made to order by a professional cabinet maker in Dungog."

Teen said, "I like the side board with the round mirror and the two glass doors at the sides. That will be perfect because, as you know, I've been collecting my glory-box for some time, in anticipation of our wedding. My treasured pieces will complement this furniture."

Wilf said, "All of the beech timber and cypress pine I cut myself and sent to the mill to be either tongue and grooved for the flooring or double-bevel-edged for the ceiling and walls. Beech timber is the most scarce and sought after of all the timber used for interior finishing of large, stately homes, both in the city and the country. I hope you like it. The cypress pine flooring will resist the termites."

"Oh this is so exciting, Wilf. You have done just great. Have I told you today how much I love you?"

"I don't think so, not today, but come out and see the kitchen."

The kitchen floor was covered with modern linoleum and featured a large kitchen bench with a fresh water tap over a sunken sink. The bench and crockery cabinet were also white beech timber, with a meat safe hanging nearby. On the far wall was a large fuel stove with a black kettle and large pot already in place.

Teen said, "I remember your mother telling me she would like linoleum on the kitchen floor. She said it's soft enough to protect crockery when dropped."

The only exception to the white beech timber furniture was the red cedar kitchen table that Wilf had proudly made himself from timber he cut. He bought the wooden chairs with rounded backrests set around the table. It was a well-built, sizable table meant to last well into the future for a large family still to come.

They walked into the main bedroom, and Teen said, "I like the way you have done the walls and floors the same in all the rooms; it' so unusual, but it looks really nice."

"I thought you'd like it."

There was a large, four-posted brass bed and a marble-topped wash-stand with dainty tiled flash-back. It had a recessed bowl and matching white water jug with roses decorating the sides. "Oh," said Teen, "that's nice. Did you pick out the basin and jug with the red roses?"

"No, Vera picked them out for me; I had nothing to do with that purchase."

Teen inspected the large cedar wardrobe, saying, "I love the full-length mirror in the centre, and with a dressing table to match, I see."

"I didn't get a cover for the bed because I knew you would want to make your own."

Again Teen wrapped her hands around his neck and said over and over, "Thank you, thank you, I'm so happy with everything you have done."

"There are other things to be added," said Wilf, "but I want you to choose them."

"I will have plenty of time to make curtains for all of the windows and bed covers on my new Singer." The machine was still on the carriage outside; Ned needed help with that heavy box.

Teen expressed her special thanks to Ned, who read lips very well, providing he was watching. He had developed a loud monotone voice, speaking each of his words very slowly.

Ned popped his head around the door before leaving and said, "Don't forget Mother has prepared tea for you both, so there's no need to start thinking about what you're going to have for tea."

After the meal, they made their way back in the dark to their beautiful new home across the river, thinking they would be able to have an early night. They were preparing for bed when both were startled by an unbelievable racket that broke the silence outside the house.

"What on earth is that?" said Teen, with real fear showing in her face as she sought protection in Wilf's arms.

The racket continued unabated as Wilf said, "I forgot to warn you and had even forgotten myself. There's an old tradition in this part of the bush called a tin kettle-ing."

Teen said, "What on earth is that?"

"It's the banging on tins, saucepans or anything else that can make a loud noise under a new couple's bedroom window. It's a special treat for all the local young men to arrive unannounced and create a racket on the first night when a couple moves into their new home. The only way it can be stopped is to invite them in for a cup of tea."

"I don't know how you can call it a special treat, but you had better invite them in."

Wilf said, "There is only one problem. They won't leave till they get a cup of tea, and we don't have any hot water or even a fire going to boil the water."

However, Ned had known of these plans and arrived in time at the back door with a large billy-can of hot water.

Ned Said, "There are supplies of tea, sugar, and milk already placed in the cupboard, in readiness for the boys."

Wilf went out onto the front veranda and invited in a total of fifteen blokes and introduced them all to his new wife. Fortunately, they were all very considerate and left as soon as they had their cup of tea.

Teen and Wilf were tired after their long journey and the added excitement of their first day in their new house.

Teen said, "I don't think I will need much rocking tonight; I think we should both sleep well." The next morning was to be the beginning of the rest of their lives together.

Chapter 29

Meanwhile back in Europe, shortly after the armistice had been signed and the troops were withdrawn from the front, the Casualty Station at Corbie Town Hall was no longer required. However, there were many soldiers to be moved back to other hospitals for ongoing treatment. So many of them had major problems, such as serious head injuries, blindness, burned-out lung problems from the gas, huge stomach wounds, and the lesser problem it seemed of limbs having been removed.

The removal of limbs was usually a fairly clinical procedure that took some time to heal, but it usually did. The other injuries needed very special care for many months on end, even for many years to come for some poor wretches.

Ann had become a totally different and subdued person after she accepted that Wilf was no longer around and part of her life. She had nothing to go home for, so she agreed to stay in France to care for the soldiers who were too critically ill or injured to ship home. She signed on to stay for one year at the Central Medical Hospital on Rue Jean Catelas in Amiens.

At this hospital, they specialised in psychological help for the soldiers who were seriously affected from their grotesque injuries. Some were so bad that they would spend not years but the rest of their life in the hospital. Over the first twelve months, less than 10 per cent were able to be repatriated back to Britain, and over 50 per cent eventually died as a direct result of their injuries.

So it was a particularly sad time for Ann, who was thankfully kept busy most of the time. This was the way she preferred it, as she had little spare time to think of what could have been a very different life together with Wilf. Every day in the quietness of her room, she succumbed to tears, but when on duty, she could cope. To her colleagues around her, she was a most dedicated, caring, and efficient nurse doing a great job under the most trying circumstances. The hospital was known as having some of the worst war cases in Europe.

After the war ended, troops were relocated without notice, and the military postal system in Europe descended into chaos. Some units, even whole battalions, were being transferred daily without notice. They moved them from one place to the next as well as back across the channel at short notice. With so many dead, missing, and wounded soldiers in hospitals spread all over France, Holland, Belgium, and Luxemburg, as well as back in the hospitals of the British Isles, it became literally impossible to deliver letters with any certainty.

Even the healthy, able-bodied soldiers did not always receive their mail in reasonable time. In addition to their regular problems, there were exceptional circumstances where literally millions of pieces of mail disappeared.

One of those occasions took place on November 13, 1918. The Military Postal Department had accumulated over eight hundred thousand pieces of mail addressed to Australian soldiers fighting on the Southern Front around the Amiens and Peronne areas. The troops were in the front line, advancing continuously during September through to when the armistice was signed; they had no access to their mail.

As soon as the war was over, troops were moving fast in the opposite direction back across the channel. This made it even more difficult to accurately direct the mail. The postal department made the decision on November 13 to ship all of this accumulated mail back to Britain where it could be resorted according to their most up-to-date records and redelivered.

In the absolute chaos within the Harbour of Le Havre, literally hundreds of boats of all sizes were used, trying to get troops onto the transports to get the men back across the channel. The logistical effort to get the men home as quickly as possible resulted in many minor collisions. An accident occurred at night on November 14 when a postal barge was taking the mail out to one of the larger transport vessels in the harbour. The small postal barge collided with a coal carrier, resulting in the sinking of the postal barge, along with its full cargo of mail.

Amongst the cargo were the eight hundred thousand pieces of bottled-up mail addressed to the Australian Diggers. These were the Diggers who had fought so hard and in effect brought about the first major retreat of the enemy. They helped bring the war to a faster end than any strategist had even dared to hope. Among those letters were all of the frantic letters Ann had written to Wilf daily to let him know she was so close to him at the front.

All of that mail was lost in some thirty metres of water along with the intimate dreams and feelings that Ann expressed with such loving detail in those many hours of writings.

Ann's letters would never reach Wilf to tell him she was now so near to him in Corbie. He would never know it wasn't Ann's life that was snatched away so suddenly in that dreadful direct hit on the shelter; it was Mavis Buckley from next door who died with Mr. and Mrs. Davis.

Mavis's estranged husband was also listed as missing after one of his dangerous missions as an officer on the minesweeper. Neither Mavis nor her husband would ever learn the fate of their partner.

After Ann's one-year contract was up, she decided to return to Britain, but not to London. It would still be too painful for her to even contemplate. She had written a few letters to her cousin, Heather Williams, in Brighton, so she decided to go and see her first.

Ann knew she had to get a ship to Eastbourne and a train to Brighton. She arrived at Brighton Station and had all of the address details so was able to catch a bus for the short journey to the Williams home. She arrived unannounced, not having been able to advise when the boat would arrive at Eastbourne.

Ann was given a great welcome by her remaining family as afternoon tea was served and enjoyed by all. The subject of her losing her family was naturally the major topic and discussed in light detail, as all four of them had difficulty controlling their emotions on such a sensitive subject. At that stage, nothing was discussed in detail about Wilf, although the Williams family knew of the relationship.

Mrs. Williams asked Heather to show Ann into the guestroom. Once inside, they both sat on the bed as Ann poured out her heart to Heather. Ann could see that it was a bit of a shock for Heather to learn just how closely she had become involved with Wilf in a relatively short time.

Heather said to Ann, "Did you ever write to Wilf's family in Australia?"

"No, I didn't. I pondered over that question so many times, but the silly thing was that at no time did I ever record Wilf's home address. I only had his unit address. I know it was on the note that Wilf gave to Mum with his details, but that was always kept in the writing bureau; it was destroyed in the fire."

"That's a pity," said Heather.

"I know it was somewhere in the country hundreds of miles north of Sydney, but the town never seemed relevant to me because we were both so positive about our future together; nothing would happen to keep us apart."

Heather then asked, "Did you ever contact the Australian Army to seek details of his address?"

Ann said, "No, I didn't. Our involvement together was so strong that if Wilf had survived those last couple of months on that dreadful battlefield, he would have left no stone unturned to make contact with me."

"Yes," said Heather, "from what you have told me, I'm also sure he would have made some contact with you or those staff he knew at the hospital."

"He was with the Australian Second Division, Eighteenth Battalion, and they played a key role in the overthrow of Mont St. Quentin."

"I remember Mont St. Quentin," said Heather. "That action has been credited with having brought the war to a swift conclusion; it was horrific and with so many deaths. There has been much said in the papers about the high casualty rate in that region."

After such a long trip and the outpouring of emotions, Ann decided to head straight for bed rather than have tea and face the others in her present state. Heather was able to explain to her mother and father all of the new information she had learned from Ann.

The next morning, Heather explained to Ann that she had told her family the full story. Ann felt better knowing this, and they all discussed together Ann's future plans.

Ann said, "I enjoy nursing and am not qualified to do anything else, so I will look for a position somewhere."

Heather said, "I know they're looking for specialised people at the Brighton General Hospital where I work, and they have a vacancy for a senior nursing sister of your experience. I believe you would have no trouble obtaining the position."

The next day, Ann made a visit to the hospital and secured the position without any trouble at all. When she arrived home and broke the news, Mr. Williams said, "It would be a great privilege for us if you would like to use the spare room for however long you need it. We would love to think of Ann Davis as another member of our small family."

Ann said, "I'm most grateful for your offer and would love to accept. You tell me the cost, and I will be more than happy to pay my share, whatever it is."

The hospital worked out well for Ann, allowing her to use some of the new skills she had learned during her stay at the hospital in France. The staff members at the hospital were all very nice to Ann and soon included her in their social activities. Between the social life of the hospital staff and the large circle of Heather's friends, life became quite busy for Ann. The busy life helped wipe away some of the memories that constantly haunted her sleeping and waking moments.

After some six months of hectic life, Heather introduced Ann to one of her new friends who had recently moved into Brighton from London. His name was Spencer Watford-Smith, the eligible new manager of the Scottish National Bank in Brighton. It wasn't long before Spencer asked Ann out on their first date, and things moved along nicely from there. Ann found that gradually some of the memories of her family's tragic death and the loss of Wilf were able to be pushed further into the past. Life was once again a joyful experience as it had been pre-war and during her time with Wilf.

Two years after the war ended, Spencer asked Ann to marry him, and plans were made for a new house to be built. Spencer took Ann to see the old house he had purchased for demolition. This was to make way for their new home that the architect was already planning. It was a beautiful spot on the seafront looking south across the channel.

Ann felt a little apprehensive about the thought of looking across the channel but convinced herself in the end that it was foolish to keep looking back. Ann had only told Spencer a limited version of her involvement with an Australian soldier killed in action, but she hoped the outlook from her new home, looking across the channel, would not be a constant reminder. She would, however, forever wonder how he had met his death on that now well-documented great advance by the Australian soldiers to capture Mont St. Quentin.

Ann wasn't quite sure of what part of France was directly opposite Brighton so took an opportunity one night to check in an atlas. She discovered that the front door of her house looked directly south to Le Havre Harbour in France. If she turned her gaze maybe just a few degrees to the east, there would be Amiens and Ypres, but a little back the other way to the west was Mont St. Quentin.

Ann was well aware that on both occasions when Wilf had returned to the front, it was across the channel to Le Havre and from there into the battle. For days, Ann found it difficult to get these thoughts out of her mind. Could she ever look out the front of her new home without bring back those memories to spoil her day?

Ann had never been made aware of the fact that her many letters written to Wilf towards the end of the war had all finished up in the depths of Le Havre Harbour. This information may have presented her with additional memories to confront, memories she may not have been able to handle.

Ann married Spencer on November 10, 1921 and became Mrs. Watford-Smith. The house was completed in time for them to move in after their honeymoon to Scotland.

From day one, Ann always made sure she had either a single red rose or a bunch of roses in a vase on the mantle over the fireplace in the lounge room of her new home.

Chapter 30

Married life at Kimberly for Wilf and Teen had been full of challenges, especially for Teen. Having come from the centre of Sydney, snakes were something she had only read of or heard about. One of the things she had heard was that snakes didn't die until sunset.

After a week of settling in, Wilf started back driving the bullock team. He had left home around nine o'clock so he could be home before dark.

Not long after Wilf left the house, Teen was washing the dishes at her kitchen sink. The builder had made a larger hole than necessary to fit the water pipe from the water tank outside to the sink. A six-foot-long, black, red-bellied snake, one of Australia's deadliest, decided to try out this hole right in front of Teen.

She sprang into action, and the weapon closest to hand was a carving fork, which she expertly thrust into the neck of the snake. However, although the snake looked dead, Teen decided to be on the safe side; she needed to keep the fork firmly buried in the neck of the snake until Wilf returned at sunset. It was her longest day.

There were to come many lonely days where Teen took on the role of homemaker with her sewing machine. The machine was an attractive extra piece of furniture in their home with three rounded draws down either side, a lift-up lid to cover the drop-down head, the treadle plate underneath. Wilf thought this surely was the most wonderful, technologically-advanced piece of machinery ever made by man. He marvelled how the little bobbin twisted and turned and danced so fast to produce a methodical row of even stitches.

Teen kept herself busy making bedspreads, curtains, clothing, and anything else that could be made for themselves and others on this piece of modern equipment. She was expertly able to use her machine to the utter amazement of so many who had not seen this sort of technology in action. None more so than her mother-in-law across the river who was extremely skilled in the handiwork of her own needle and thread. Wilf soon had more beautifully crafted shirts than he had ever noticed in any store he had visited. Teen transformed Kimberly-Two with her own hands and artistic flare into a beautifully kept home.

Teen's family never had access to holidays in the bush, so all of her sisters travelled by train to Craven and were picked up by their now country-sister and brother-in-law, in the horse and sulky that Wilf had purchased soon after the wedding. They were each treated to the four-mile trip along the winding road just as Teen had experienced the first time she came to Kimberly.

Of course, the family was all anxious to do the same things like riding a horse for the first time, watching Wilf fall huge trees, and seeing firsthand a working bullock team in action in the bush.

On one such occasion, her sister Alma came to stay for two weeks. Alma was Teen's closest sister but was so different in many ways. She was the tomboy of the family and always the life of the party.

On the sulky ride out to Kimberly, Alma said, "Wilf, driving this sulky doesn't look that difficult. Can I have a go?"

"Sure you can have a go, but I'll take over again around the cuttings."

"You don't trust me, I can see, do you, Wilf?"

"No, I don't. Teen has told me too much about you."

Teen said, "If Alma is going to drive around the cuttings, you can let me out now. I don't want to finish down the gully and in the creek."

They all arrived home safely, and the next day, Alma said, "When do I get to ride a horse? Driving the sulky was pretty easy, so riding a horse can't be too difficult, can it?"

Wilf said, "I want you to enjoy at least one day of your holiday first; then we'll see."

Teen showed Alma around the first day and even had her trying to milk a cow in between fits of laughter and falling off the milking stool. Day two was a scream for everyone from early morning till late afternoon, with Wilf trying to sit Alma on the horse, with Teen on the other side, repeatedly catching her on the way down.

Alma's greatest problem was her laughter; it became infectious with those around her and made others incapable of normal procedure. She eventually mastered sitting on the horse and after many false starts was able to walk the horse slowly.

The next day with her first horse-riding lesson now mastered, they set off to see the bullock team in action.

They eventually reached the team, and the men had the task of lifting a saddle-sore Alma down off the horse; it was not really that difficult, but it was highly entertaining.

After staring at the team in disbelief for some minutes, Alma said, "When does all the swearing start? Isn't that what all bullockies do?"

Wilf's simple answer was always the same, "Why would you need to use that sort of language in front of these bullocks? They wouldn't know what you were talking about, and they understand well enough with normal, everyday language. Besides, they may be offended."

Alma didn't have one of her normal, quick answers ready and after a pause said, "Sounds good to me."

Alma produced the same types of question that Teen had asked on her first day with the team. Now Teen was able to answer most of Alma's questions herself.

Wilf felt pleased with himself that he was able to get Alma back to the house at the end of the day in one piece.

Teen had such a great time with her closest sister and was sad to see her go at the end of Alma's two-week stay.

Teen had the new home looking great, and they both decided that the home needed children. Good news in the bush always spreads quickly, not only in the bush, but also amongst Teen's family when she fell pregnant.

Being four miles out in the bush and fifteen miles from the closest hospital at Gloucester, Kimberly was not considered the best place for babies to be born. Teen had developed a friendship with a midwife in Dungog, so it was decided that she should go to stay with Bessie in Dungog for the four weeks before the baby was due, just to be on the safe side. Teen was to repeat this same process for her next two children.

The first baby was a girl who they named Jessie Agnes, the middle name being an old Scottish name. It was also the name of Teen's mother, who came to pay a visit and stayed for a few weeks after the new baby arrived home. Teen now had plenty of extra chores to keep her busy. She also had a beautiful baby daughter to keep her company each day while Wilf was out in the bush making a living to support the enlarged family.

Within a couple of years, a second baby arrived, this time a boy; they called him William Alexander after both Wilf's father and Teen's father Alexander. Billy (William) was a beautiful little boy, and Jessie became Teen's little helper.

However, tragedy struck when Teen and Wilf took the two little ones on the train to Sydney to spend time with her family. On the first night after arriving at the home of her eldest sister, Ollie, in Marrickville where her mother also now lived, Teen awoke during the night to find her nine-month-old William dead alongside her in the bed.

Chapter 31

To lose such a healthy little baby boy that showed no signs of sickness was extremely hard to accept for both Teen and Wilf. Teen's family was on the spot and did their best to comfort them.

Teen was distraught and kept asking Wilf, "Was there something I did that caused Billy's death? Did I have him too close to the window in the train coming down? Did he catch pneumonia? Did I feed him something that caused it? Is there something wrong with my milk?"

"No, Teen, the doctor said it was none of those things; he said it was totally unexplainable. He has known of similar cases, but nobody has an answer."

Teen kept asking the same questions over and over. It was a terrible time for both Teen and Wilf to go through in Sydney, but nothing as bad as going home to Kimberly without their darling little boy. The trip home to Craven seemed more like seven days rather than the normal seven hours.

Ned picked up Wilf, Teen, and Jessie at the station and drove the sulky all the way to Kimberly, most of the way without a word being spoken by anyone. Teen was already pregnant with the third child and was extremely fortunate that she didn't lose that baby due to the shock. Wilf didn't return to work straight away but stayed with Teen to comfort her for some ten days. In due course, a healthy baby arrived, and they called her Dorothy Alma, after Teen's sister.

“Wilf and brother Ned cutting a cedar tree.”

"Wilf's bullock teem with Jessie and Dorothy as his helpers."

After another couple of years, another baby boy arrived while they were still at Kimberly; he was named Ronald Allen. Wilf now realised how vulnerable his family was out there in the bush without support during a medical emergency. He worked hard and provided well for his family and purchased a brand-new 1927 Model-T Ford Tourer; it was the first one in the local district. He was then able to do away with the horse and sulky; it was now too small for the enlarged family.

To enable the children to have better access to schooling, and to start a new life for the family, Wilf and Teen decided they needed to relocate. After nine years in the home he built for Teen when first married, they sold the house at Kimberly to Wilf's brother, Ned, and bought another home in the village of Craven, nice and handy to the school.

"Wilf and Teen's family in 1939 with Model T Ford."

He also started his own dairy farm on the new property. The house was situated on eighty acres of land, set back two hundred yards from the Pacific Hwy on the front side. There was a similar distance at the rear to the main northern railway line.

Craven was a thriving town of some fifty houses, including the outlying farms, which supported four saw mills, a railway station, a one-teacher school, and a church. Compared to the two houses at Kimberly, Craven was like the big city to his family.

Apart from the obvious reasons for moving to Craven, such as a new lifestyle and school, there was another reason. Wilf was now suffering from periodical, uncontrollable attacks to his nervous system. These were believed to be stress-related to his war service and often referred to as War Neurosis or the Jelly Shakes, similar to the one he suffered when he learned of Ann's death. Being alone in the bush when these attacks happened was not ideal for him or his family.

The house at Craven was adequate for the family when first purchased but soon became quite small.

Wilf had accidently managed to start off his children's middle names with the letter A, meaning that all of the children's initials spelt a word ending in AY. He decided to keep the tradition going. By this time, more of Teen and Wilf's children had arrived, to which he also gave a middle name starting with A. Beryl Athol, Margaret Ann, and John Arthur. All of these new babies were born at the Gloucester Hospital, which was now only an eleven-mile road trip from Craven in the Model-T Ford.

When Margaret Ann was born, Wilf couldn't help naming her with Ann Davis in mind because she too was a beautiful little blonde. He had never forgotten how Ann's name was actually Margaret Ann, but it had been shortened to just Ann by her older brother, Joe. Also, the shortened name avoided confusion with her mother's name.

Sleeping arrangements became quite tight in the new house. There were only two bedrooms, with four girls in the second room, and the two boys in the bathroom, with one single bed and the youngest sleeping alongside in the bath, converted to a bed.

There was a lounge-dining room at the front and a large kitchen at the rear. The kitchen was equipped with a fuel stove, but there were few cupboards or benches to suit a large family. The kitchen converted into a bathroom every Saturday when a large, galvanised tub was placed in the middle of the kitchen floor. Water was carried from the dam over one hundred yards away, heated in the fuel copper in the laundry, and carried by kerosene-tin come-bucket to the tub for all to use, after which it was used sparingly on the garden.

After a number of years, Wilf and Teen purchased the general store in Craven to supplement their meagre income from dairying.

In 1939, the Second World War broke out in Europe. Wilf and Teen decided in 1941, after eleven years at Craven, to sell the house and shop and move to the city of Newcastle, halfway between both families. They believed jobs would be more plentiful in the city for their growing family, three of whom had already left school.

The war was making it difficult to obtain enough stock to make the shop viable. All of their supplies came from the wholesale grocer in Newcastle, R. Hall & Sons, who had in the past made weekly road deliveries to their many country customers. Now that petrol was restricted, the company installed gas bags to most of their delivery vehicles. However, gas was only suitable for short runs, so country deliveries were restricted to fortnightly and then deteriorated to monthly deliveries instead.

Many products readily available before the war were now missing from the monthly price list R. Hall & Sons provided to their customers. One such product was toilet rolls. This had been a new growth product, which now because of the shortage of paper was impossible to buy. The restrictions also had an impact on the local store because Wilf had built a business out of personal service to his customers in the outlying farms. Now he could not get enough petrol to service his customers.

Wilf also needed a stable income to support his large family. He made a trip to Newcastle to pay a visit to an old Gloucester mate that was in his unit during the war. Arthur Williams lived at Waratah and worked in the Army Inspection Branch at the Stewarts and Lloyd's plant at Mayfield, making shells for the army.

Because of Wilf's war service, he was assured of a job as an inspector once he relocated to Newcastle. He applied for the position and was successful. Arthur offered him lodging whilst looking for a suitable home.

Wilf caught the train back to Craven to break the news. He was met by Teen at the station in the Model-T. He hugged Teen and said, "I've got great news for you, and I know you are going to be real happy."

Teen said, "That sounds like a nice surprise. Tell me?"

Wilf hesitated a little before saying, "I already have a new permanent job in Newcastle working as an inspector for the army and can start next week. We can sell everything here and move to Newcastle. I've already contacted a real estate agent and asked him to find us a big house."

Teen was over-the-moon because she was still a city girl at heart, despite having lived in the bush for nearly half of her life. She said, "I don't think I've been so happy in a long time. This will be great for the kids. I can't wait to tell them," as a little tear fell down onto her soft cheek.

Wilf realised again just what a sacrifice Teen had made by giving up her city life to move to the bush. He had appreciated this from the beginning, but right now it hit him pretty hard. He said, "I don't really know what to say other than I'm sorry for all of the stress it has caused you and the hard work you did to make wonderful homes for our family."

"You don't have to apologise because it has been a great experience to share with you and the kids."

Wilf kissed her whilst standing there on the empty station platform.

Teen and the older family members looked after the selling of the house, shop, and the Model-T, plus the packing and moving details at the Craven end. Wilf found a very large home opposite the Mater Hospital in Lorna St. Waratah and moved the family of eight into this modern home.

Their new home was full of surprises for each one of them. There were electric lights in every room, totally unknown to all except for Teen. Her home in Pyrmont had electricity before she was married.

Now at Waratah, the lights simply turned on or off at the flick of a switch. The kitchen was equipped with both a gas stove and a separate fuel stove. The bathroom had a white cast-iron bath with gas heater-over. The lounge-room had a power-point into which could be plugged a wireless that no longer needed a battery. At Craven, the battery always seemed to go flat at the wrong time.

Now the whole family became mesmerised by the array of serials proceeding forth from the wireless in the corner of the spacious lounge-room. In those days, the radio brought into many homes a continuous bevy of serials starting with "Yes What" and the schoolboy antics of Green-bottle before the evening news at six o'clock.

After the evening meal was over and the dishes done, ears strained to hear the Australian classic of "Dad and Dave" heralded by the theme music known as "The Road to Gundagai." This song was written by Jack O'Hagan MBE, who became an institution throughout Australia because of this song. This prolific Australian songwriter wrote over six hundred songs, all played on radio around that time. "The Road to Gundagai" was the best-known song throughout Australia for many years and was sung by all from when they were knee-high. Then followed other programs in succession: "Hagen's Circus," "When a Girl Marries," and finishing with "Courtship and Marriage" to end the evening's entertainment. Then the girls dispersed to do individual chores of homework, washing, ironing, or hair preparation for the next day.

Without a doubt, the best new feature for Teen was the gas stove, controlled heat at the strike of a match. To the family, it was the cast-iron bath with a gas heater-over that could be run at any time, not just on Saturdays in the old, galvanised round-tub at Craven. This new bath, with heater-over, was a good example of real modern-day living at Waratah for this family.

The timing of the move from Craven to Waratah in the last week of November 1941 could not have been better because WW2 was now intensifying. It would have made things so much harder to sell the house even just a few months later. As the clouds of war rolled nearer, Wilf was very concerned about the bleak outlook on the horizon. Japan was now showing up as a real threat to Australia, more so than the old foe, the Huns, which he knew only too well, or the Krauts as the Germans were now called in this war.

Wilf liked to read out the headlines to Teen as she prepared meals in the kitchen. He also liked to cut out pieces of interest and read them over at a later date. On one such day, he read aloud some of his cuttings to Teen, mostly from *Smith's Weekly*. He read:

Submarines attack Sydney Harbour.

Sydney experienced an attack by three Japanese midget submarines inside the harbour on 31st May 1942, two of which were damaged and captured, with the other one escaping out to sea.

Teen interrupted and said, "That was on John's birthday."

Wilf said, "I didn't realise that. You know, I'm not good remembering birthdays." He read on:

The US Navy suffered a huge blow when the Japanese attacked Pearl Harbour on December 7. This was a devastating blow to the Americans, but on the other hand was a blessing in other ways because it forced the Americans into the war immediately. Previously, the Americans refused to be committed. Shortly after Pearl Harbour was attacked, the Japanese invaded the Philippines and North Borneo as a forerunner of much worse to come.

Teen said, "I remember you telling me in one of your letters something about America being forced into the war because of something to do with a pact signed between Mexico and Germany."

Wilf said, "By-Jove, your memory's pretty good."

The month of December was described as the blackest month in the history of the British peoples. On December 10, literally eight hours after Pearl Harbour was attacked, the first casualty for the British Royal Navy in the Asia Pacific Region was the sinking of their two largest battleships. *The Prince of Wales* and *Repulse* were sunk with a loss of 840 men. Without these two ships, it put in danger the defence of Singapore, Britain's Gibraltar of the East. On the same day, Kowloon was invaded by over 50,000 Japanese troops who breached the recently completed Gin Drinker's Line, bringing about the evacuation of British troops in Kowloon to the Island of Hong Kong. This resulted in the surrender of Hong Kong to the Japanese on Christmas Day.

Even worse came the attack on Singapore by General Yamashita, who became known as The Tiger of Malaya. The Allied forces surrendered after only seven days of fighting, with 138,000 troops lost for the loss of only 10,000 Japanese.

Winston Churchill described the loss of Singapore as the "worst disaster in British history."

Teen said, "It must be pretty bad for Churchill to say that. The news is terrible. I thought after what you and the others did in the last war that there was never going to be another war."

"That's what they told us, but here we are just twenty-four years later, and it's on all over again."

Wilf enjoyed his relatively easy job as an army inspector at Stewarts and Lloyds. It certainly was easy work compared to life in the bush. Once settled in, he recognised the need for older men like himself with war experience to serve as air raid wardens. Most WWI men were too old to enlist again but could provide a valuable service in another way. The wardens could utilise Wilf's experience gained during WWI.

Wilf said to Teen, "I believe I should join the wardens and do my bit to help the war effort."

Teen said, "I think that would be a great idea especially as it won't be as dangerous for you as it was in WWI."

"I certainly hope not." He went the next day to offer his services and joined up.

One of the routine tasks performed by the wardens at that time was to patrol the streets in their designated area at night, to make sure all windows were covered with black-out paper. This was to ensure that light could not be seen escaping from windows and doors and seen by enemy aircraft overhead. This service required three nights per week on duty for three hours each night.

The threat of a Japanese invasion of Australia was being seriously considered and appeared imminent. The roll of the warden was being taken to a much higher level, and training was required for the new leaders. This was to cover activities such as casualty direction, crowd control, evacuations, fire drills mobilisation of civilian men able to carry weapons, and many other facets of the defence of civilian peoples when under enemy attack.

News about the war occupied the newspapers daily. The annual Anzac Day Parade through the streets of Sydney and most cities took on new importance. The parade was held each year on April 25 to honour those who served in WWI.

Wilf had enlisted for WWI in Sydney, and most of the other chaps in his unit did likewise. As a result, he didn't get to catch up with his Digger-mates at the annual Newcastle parade. He decided to take Teen and his younger family to Sydney for a special treat, which would enable him to attend the ANZAC Parade. His family could also catch up with Teen's family, who all lived in Sydney.

Wilf attended the Sydney march and located his Eighteenth Battalion meeting point prior to the step-off. The men were all looking very old. The celebrated Lt. Joe Maxwell was there marshalling his men as he had done so many times before. On seeing Wilf, he turned in surprise and said, "Well if it isn't my old bullocky mate, good to see you, Wilf. I haven't seen you since the war ended; I'll catch up with you later."

A march these days was always a challenge for Wilf's bad football-knee, whether in Newcastle or Sydney. After the march was over, the men all gathered at the RSL hall to reminisce about those terrifying days they shared together. Many of the chaps had not kept well since the war, and some had died; the numbers were thin.

Joe had suffered badly, and it showed. Alcohol had destroyed Joe, who found it hard to handle life after the war. Whilst at the front, his skills had been in demand. Soon after his return, he had a top celebrity wedding but could not keep the marriage together. Wilf learned the marriage fell apart within a year.

In the early post-war years, Joe was in demand as a war hero, spinning his sometimes exaggerated but always highly entertaining yarns at special events. The events were organised by the RSL or Joe's publisher to remember the sacrifices made by those at the war.

He was a colourful character but wandered around from town to town trying to get work, especially during the depression days. Moving from town to town was not unlike his days at the front, moving from trench, to leave towns, back to another trench, and repeated so many times.

Joe didn't have many skills outside of the army, other than spinning his yarns. Wilf bumped into him spinning one such yarn to some of the boys.

Joe saw him approach and interrupted his story, saying, "Join in here, Wilf. I've often wondered what happened to you because you weren't there with us when the armistice was announced, were you?"

"No," said Wilf, "you sent me off to NCO School at Amiens just days before, and then I shipped directly back to London from there."

"You probably went chasing that blonde nurse in London you told us about. Did you marry her?"

"No, I didn't, Joe, but now's not the time to tell you the full story; the boys are waiting to hear you finish your story."

Joe said, "You know, mate, I can spin a good yarn or two, don't you."

"I certainly do, Joe. I think I can recall you holding the floor on more than one occasion, standing in mud with a bottle in your hand."

Joe said, "You're right there, mate, but since then I've had a journalist mate in Melbourne who took me under his wing and encouraged me to write a book about our exploits at the front. I called it *Hells Bells and Mademoiselles*."

"I read your book, Joe. You were certainly well qualified with your subjects, especially the mademoiselles."

Joe rolled his eyes as only he could do, saying, "Where did you hear that?"

Wilf knew that the book had earlier become a best seller within Australia, but he also knew that the best jobs Joe could get now were part-time gardening jobs. On days like this, the men could talk openly together about their experiences, the same experiences they found hard to share with their families.

Wilf said to Joe, "I see you're wearing your VC medal but not your other medals. Why is that?"

"That's a long story, mate. Back in 1927, I was living at Belmont, Lake Macquarie, and had trouble paying the rent. I was moving all of my stuff in a small boat to a new flat I had arranged on the other side of the bay. A stiff southerly came up, as it can in Belmont, and caught me unexpectedly; it swamped the boat in Belmont Bay, and I lost everything. I was lucky to get away with my life. I was closer to death there than anything I experienced at the front. Fortunately the VC was in safekeeping with my mum."

"I'm disappointed to hear that, Joe. I hadn't had a chance to tell you, but I moved down from the bush and now live in Newcastle working as an inspector in the Army Inspection Branch at Stewarts and Lloyds. As a matter of fact, we have booked a holiday home on the waterfront in Belmont Bay for next summer."

Joe said, "Don't bother looking for the medals, mate. They're probably buried under a couple of feet of sand by now."

"Have you applied to get new medals?"

"Yes, Wilf, I have, but believe me there was so much red tape involved that I gave up. Maybe I'll try again someday."

Wilf left Joe to return to his family at Marrickville and did a lot of thinking as he sat in the swaying tram. He could not help notice the difference in the man who once had nerves of steel at the front compared to the poor, trembling excuse for a human being he had degenerated into. The ravages of war, combined with the grip of alcohol, had destroyed Joe. Wilf silently gave thanks to God for his own safekeeping, bringing him home, giving him a wonderful family, and sparing him from the same destruction that had befallen Joe and others in similar circumstances.

Chapter 32

Wilf had been selected to do a Senior Air Raid Warden's course, the equivalent of an NCO's course in the military. He was advised to report on June 7, 1942 for an overnight, two-day course at the Fort Scratchley Battery on Flagstaff Hill.

This hill, located at the eastern end of Newcastle overlooking Nobbys and the Pacific Ocean, was where coal was first discovered in 1791 by some escaping convicts from Sydney. The potential of the resource was realised by Lieutenant John Shortland in 1797, who noticed the coal while chasing another group of escaping convicts and gave the Hunter River its name in honour of Governor Hunter.

Fort Scratchley was constructed in 1882 to defend the city against a possible attack by the Russians, they being the perceived enemy of the day. It was equipped with two case-mounted 6" BL Mark V11 guns, plus an extremely rare gun called an Eight-Inch BL Disappearing gun. This gun was loaded and aimed from a position out of sight below ground. Then when ready for firing, it was hydraulically raised and fired in the one action, with the force of the discharge repelling the gun back below ground level, ready for reloading and aiming.

The fort was also equipped with a number of Vickers machine guns, plus an observation post with one searchlight located below the fort but above the esplanade. Another two lights were located nearby in Parnell Place and Nobbys.

The underground caverns at the fort were quite extensive, covering an area nearly the size of a football field. There were also accommodation blocks to house quite a large contingent of troops.

Wilf reported at the main gate shortly before eight in the morning for the course as required. The day was to be spent in lectures with twelve other men. All were veterans of WWI and selected from around Hunter Valley and Newcastle.

The lecturer was the equivalent of a colonel in the regular army; he was from Sydney. He said, "The war has now entered a new phase. In the past, wardens have been primarily trained to monitor black-out regulations on the home front, allowing younger men to be deployed overseas. However, now we have the situation developing where we may have to face the enemy on our home territory. This is being considered as real possibility."

Wilf said, "I assume that wardens will only be needed to fill the gap until regular troops can be deployed on home soil."

"Yes and no," replied the lecturer, "because we are dealing with so many unknowns. The major unknown is the length of time needed to deploy regular troops. Therefore, wardens must now be trained in so many different facets, such as crowd control, civil unrest, intelligence gathering, pinpoint enemy positions, and notification to the military headquarters via Air Raid Wardens Control Office. Then there are other matters, such as being on the spot to issue armaments and ammunition and in a worst-case scenario, to confront the enemy until the army arrives and takes control."

Another fellow asked, "Will this be a full-time or part-time position?"

"At this stage, it will be only part-time, but there will be a small amount paid to cover the essentials," he replied. "Of course that could change at any time."

The fellow next to Wilf said, "We did our share of that sort of thing in the last bash, and it looks like we might have to do it all over again."

"Well, we most certainly hope it won't come to that, but we must be prepared, and that's why you're here. We need men with war experience that can be trained to take leadership positions and train the rest of the wardens and new recruits. You must get into your minds that this is a very serious business. Australia is vulnerable to attack by the Japanese at any time. Now this is where we must start."

He continued on as Wilf's mind drifted back to events that he would prefer to forget. After the long day of lectures, the evening meal was provided by the army. They were then taken to see a demonstration of the recently installed searchlight before being directed to their sleeping quarters for the night.

Wilf, like the other wardens, knew nothing of the alarm code in operation at the fort. At 12:45 a.m., they were awoken by sirens blaring and red lights flashing outside in the yard. One of the regulars said, "Not to worry, chaps; it's a Red Warning, which happens from time to time when one of the lookouts reports some activity out at sea. Soon you will probably see the white lights flashing; that's the all-clear."

The white lights flashed after a short while, and they had just about settled down from that excitement and were ready to go back to bed when the sirens sounded again, and red and yellow lights flashed outside. This time an officer came and said, "One of the lookouts reported a submarine in the Stockton Bight, about five to six miles out to the northeast; this is a Yellow Warning and is a serious alarm. However, there is nothing for you fellows to do, as it is already being taken care of by the regulars."

Soon afterward, the all-clear White Warning lights flashed again, and Wilf and the other new chaps returned to their bunks.

At 2:15 a.m., they all bounced out of their bunks once again as sirens sounded continuously right throughout the fort, with both the yellow and red lights flashing.

The frenzied rush by the men to bounce out of their bunk again for the third time caused quite a deal of stress. Wilf, while scrambling to dress, said to Frank in the next bunk, "I must say with all of the experience we had in France, it doesn't make it any easier now, does it?"

"You're absolutely right. I feel the same way. I'm not sure what I'm getting myself into."

Wilf was shaking as he finished dressing but like most others kept his fears in check. There was one poor fellow at the other end of the dorm who collapsed when the sirens sounded the third time. It took two of the other chaps plus a regular officer to get him under control. The effects of those days on the Somme were still being secretly suppressed by these men who had been through so much.

The Japanese sub was now firing shells nearly directly over the fort. Everyone was outside the barracks and could clearly see the flashes and hear the shells going over. This was a sound that Wilf did not ever want to hear again. He believed after WWI was labelled The War to End All Wars that he would not have to hear that sound again, but here it was happening again right here in his hometown.

The first shells fired by the Japs were star shells that illuminated the sky. Nobody was quite sure where the shells were being aimed. Were the Japs aiming for the BHP Steelworks, Fort Scratchley, the shipyards at Carrington, or the ships in the harbour? One shell landed nearby on the tram depot on Wharf Road, one landed nearby on the northern wall of the ocean baths, and another landed even closer and demolished a couple of terrace houses in Parnell Place. According to one of the wireless operators, another shell was reported to have landed on a warehouse at BHP, while others landed harmlessly in the harbour.

After the sub had been firing for some thirteen minutes, the two large fort guns opened fire on the sub without success. The noise from these guns was deafening within the confines of the fort walls. Once again, the sound took Wilf back to the trenches, even though the scenery here was so different from the muddy craters of the Somme battlefield.

After a couple of hours of unwelcome excitement, the wardens were told to turn in; none of them slept a wink.

The next morning, the remainder of the Senior Air Raid Wardens Course was postponed until the following Saturday.

The *Newcastle Herald* reported the next day that the submarine in question, number 1-21, was pointing out to sea and fired a total of thirty-four five-and-a-half-inch shells directly over the stern. This made for a very small target to be picked up by the searchlights at five thousand yards.

The only injuries inflicted by the sub were minor shrapnel wounds to two army men racing back to the fort across Parnell Place. They were caught by flying debris when the two terrace houses were hit in Parnell Place. Another soldier twisted his ankle when he sprung out of his bunk in the fort when the sirens sounded.

The *Herald* article concluded saying, *Some of the shells did not explode, one of which landed just outside the main office at Stewarts and Lloyds. After it was found to be safe, it was placed as a door stop at the main office as a memento.* Wilf made a point of having a look at this dummy shell the next time he passed the main office on his way into the plant.

The following Saturday didn't turn out to be much better to complete the training course. A machine gunner at the fort, who had authority to open fire if needed, did so when he believed he saw another sub entering the harbour. He was quickly joined by a second gunner plus the two captured German WWI Hotchkiss 2 pounders, followed by the HMAS *Minesweeper Cowra* already in the harbour. The *Cowra* proceeded to lay down a carpet of charges as it left the port.

One of the things being emphasised at the course was to encourage as many people as possible in their area to be prepared. They could best be prepared by digging a small shelter in their own yard. Copies of plans were made available for distribution to those prepared to take up the challenge to first dig the hole and then build a satisfactory shelter. The thing that surprised Wilf was that the plans provided were for a shelter very similar in size and design to the one he had built for the Davis family back at King's Cross all of those years ago.

Each senior warden was told he should set an example by being the first in his area to build a shelter. The following Saturday, Wilf was not scheduled to work, so he planned to dig his shelter. He found enough materials stored under his house.

Saturday came, and Wilf was up early as usual and marked out the area in the front lawn to dig for the shelter, preferably in their front yard for others to see. He had made some preliminary plans during the week but had some premonitions about the effect this job could have on him. He thought he would be able to brush the thoughts aside, but the closer he got, the less sure he became. He could not erase from his mind what had happened the last and only time he had built a shelter away from the front line. He dug out the buffalo grass in the lawn and proceeded to a depth of about nine inches. The emotion for him was so great he could not continue.

For some strange reason, he felt exhausted, which for such a small hole was very unusual for him. He sat down on a wooden box nearby and looked at the shallow trench. His heart started to pound, and his hands trembled. This was so unusual for a man used to hard work all of his life. No matter how he tried, he could not clear his mind of that other shelter so long ago.

To have lost Ann the way he did was just so horrible, a memory he could not wipe away. But if the same thing happened again to his wife or family, he would not be able to bear such a tragedy. He told himself that he would be able to come back to the job at a later time. His family was not used to seeing him leave a job half finished. The next week, he still could not bring himself to proceed further with the shelter.

He explained to his family, saying, "No amateur-built, non-concrete shelter could survive a direct hit. This is not a bomb shelter as such, but simply a shallow trench where a few people could lie face down below the ground surface during an attack. They would be safe from flying shrapnel or debris from a shell bursting elsewhere." The unfinished, open trench stayed that way.

Not many months after the attack on Newcastle, Wilf suffered a serious injury at work. His job as an inspector required him to examine various components being manufactured on the plant for the army. Shells had a brass outer shell, but in the back end of the shell was a machined steel cap to be pressed inside the casing. This cap was heavy and had an extremely sharp edge around the rim.

As he was selecting for inspection a casing from the stack of shells on the bench, one of the workers carelessly threw another casing, which hit Wilf's right hand, nearly severing it. He was off work for three months during the healing process.

He explained to his children, "That was the second time my right hand has been injured by a shell or bullet. The first occasion was in Ypres. If it had not been for me holding the Lewis gun in the carry position, I would be dead. I was holding the gun in such a way that the barrel protected my heart from the projectile that struck the barrel.

A piece of the wooden hand-grip on the barrel splintered off into the back of my hand. If the bullet hadn't hit the barrel, none of you would be here today either."

Whilst Wilf was serving in WWI, he was always grateful to people who opened up their homes to the soldiers from distant lands when on leave. They put on dinners and parties for the troops and invited in the local girls to make them feel welcome. Wilf made himself a promise that if ever he was in a reverse situation where there were soldiers away from home and on leave in his home territory, he would do the same for them. As a non-drinker, he always appreciated the hospitality when he was in Europe and now wanted to do the same for others.

He made arrangements with the padre at the large army camp at Greta about thirty miles away to provide four soldiers as guests for lunch every Sunday at Wilf's home. Mostly they would come to church first and then come home for lunch. This was no mean task for Teen to cater for so many extras. She usually prepared a baked dinner for Sunday lunch before going to church. But it was not just for the four soldiers, because the family of eight would also be there, plus the two borders they had to supplement their income. So Teen provided a meal not only for fourteen people for lunch every Sunday, but the soldiers usually stayed for tea also.

With four daughters in the house, there was usually a waiting list of soldiers at the camp wanting to make this dinner list each Sunday. Wilf had a very large, enclosed veranda at the front of the house, measuring about twenty-five by twenty-eight feet, which was ideal for parties. From time to time, Wilf arranged a party on the Saturday night made up from the list of soldiers who had been visiting on Sundays along with the eligible girls from the church. Party games were all the rage at the time, and the parties were a great success.

Teen's hospitality extended into other areas, especially with people from the bush visiting family at the hospital across the road. It became well known that the Yates family had a large home, and Teen was always able to make a meal go a little further to handle a couple of unexpected strangers visiting family at the hospital. There were no cafés serving meals anywhere close to the hospital, so for people from the bush, Wilf and Teen's home became a real haven. Many people, stressed by having family members at the hospital with a range of illnesses or injuries, found hospitality at the Yates home.

In 1945, the war ended first in Europe, and later the same year, two atomic bombs were dropped on Japan, bringing peace to the Western world. The day the war ended in Europe, Victory in Europe (VE Day), May 1945, was a big day for celebrations, with the Yates family amongst those cerebrating in Newcastle with a large parade down Hunter Street. This was nothing compared to the celebrations for the end of the war in the Pacific in August of the same year, known as VP Day (Victory in the Pacific). Both Wilf and Teen were very keen to take the younger members of their family into Newcastle for the parade and celebrations. They were always conscious of the fact that they themselves were brought together amidst the celebrations at the end of WWI.

The aerodrome for training pilots was located close by at Broadmeadow, and most people in the area were accustomed to seeing low-flying Tiger Moths doing practice runs over the houses all the time, but today was to be something else.

The neighbour's son-in-law was a B24 Liberator pilot temporarily stationed at Williamtown. He phoned them to say he would be flying low over the house at exactly 9:08 a.m. from a northerly direction on his way to Sydney for a fly-past over the city. Word spread quickly amongst the neighbours, and at exactly 9:08 a.m., with most of the people in surrounding houses out to watch, this huge monster approached at great speed and extremely low, thundering right over the open space in front of the hospital. For that brief moment, the outline of the pilot could be seen waving out the window to the residents gathered in the street below.

For the fraction of a second the giant plane was overhead, its shadow seemed to darken the sky, and then the thunderous noise caught up and enveloped all those out to watch.

"Wow, what a sight," said Wilf. "I thought I had seen some large planes, but I never imagined they could be so big. I did read that the wingspan of the B.29 is nearly wide enough to cover the width of a football field." Nobody was listening; they were still staring in disbelief with mouths open as the plane zoomed off to the south.

The same day, Wilf and Teen took the younger children to the parade in Newcastle where nearly everyone in the city turned out to celebrate the end of all hostilities. Hunter Street was awash from end to end with people dancing and celebrating after the main military parade passed by.

The older girls of the family were regular volunteer workers at the Armed Force's Canteen in town. They were on duty that day to cater for the overwhelming numbers expected at the canteen on this long-hoped-for but never-to-be-repeated occasion.

With the war now over, production of shells ceased immediately, and Wilf was no longer needed by the army as an inspector. He had to look for another job. Bullock drivers and timber cutters were not needed in the city, and Wilf had no other skills. With so many younger men being discharged immediately from the armed services, jobs were hard to come by.

Wilf's eldest son, Allen, worked as a tire-fitter-moulder in a tire retreading factory in Newcastle. With Allen's help, Wilf secured a job as a sweeper and general labourer. The wage was very low, but Wilf was able to secure a second job in the evenings as a security guard, after finishing his day job. He also took on another job on Saturdays, gardening and general odd jobs around the gardens of the highest building in Newcastle called Jesmond House in Barker Street on The Hill.

This was a very large, stately home on the hill, built during the last century for one of the wealthiest, early families in the district. It had a commanding view right along the coast. So good was the position that the American forces commandeered the building during the war and used it as their headquarters in Newcastle. After the war ended, Jesmond House was left derelict for some time, and the large yard deteriorated into a big mess. Wilf's job was to clean it up.

It was heavy work for a man in his midfifties, especially when he already had two other jobs. Still, he had a large family to care for and a large mortgage on the house, so he needed all the money he could get. He was very grateful for the work even though he had a difficult time with his old football-knee; it had suffered more damage during the war.

Some twelve months after the war ended, many businesses were struggling to retain employees, and Wilf found it necessary to find a new job in an engineering company at Broadmeadow as a boilermaker's labourer.

Teen was a loving, caring, and affectionate person who never complained about anything but just got on with things. To Wilf, she had always been the perfect partner. When travelling in a bus, the gentle, affectionate touch of her fingers on his hand always gave him the utmost assurance that she was with him all the way, whatever the situation. Even when sitting on their lounge entertaining visitors, she would sit close to him just to make sure Wilf knew of her affection, love, and devotion to him.

However, Teen was not well, and her health started to go downhill in 1948. A simple task like walking less than one hundred yards to the local store became too much for her. The housework needed to be shared amongst the girls still at home. Teen was reduced to bed for much of her time, with Wilf sitting by her side when not at work.

Doctor Henry made one of his regular visits and told Teen that he wanted her in the hospital for an exploratory operation. Teen took the news bravely, and so did Wilf in Teen's presence.

After leaving Teen's bedside, the doctor drew Wilf to the lounge room and said, "Mr. Yates, your wife is not in good shape. In fact, she has a growth in the bowl and needs an operation as soon as possible. I will make the necessary arrangement to have your wife admitted to the Mater this afternoon. Timing is critical, so I will arrange for surgery early tomorrow morning. I think we can beat it with the knife, but I'm sorry, I cannot give you any guarantees. Make sure the family is there to see your wife during visiting hours tonight."

Wilf couldn't utter a word; he was devastated. He showed the doctor out the door and uttered muffled thanks and then fell apart. He went inside and sat for a few moments to consider this news.

Why was this happening to such a sweet lady? How was he going to break the news to his family? How was he going to handle his job? How would he be able to keep going?

He pulled himself together and returned to comfort Teen, who by this time had tears on her cheeks. Wilf hugged her delicate body close for some time.

Teen was admitted to the Mater Hospital that day, and the family was summoned. They were present to offer their mum encouragement. It wasn't supposed to be to say farewell to such a loving and gentle mother that everyone loved dearly, but the operation was to be a big one with no guarantee.

Teen's bed was located on the left side of the large ward, in the last bed at the end of the ward. Wilf arranged for each member of the family to have a few minutes with their mother, one by one, during the visiting hour, before leaving her to rest ahead of the operation scheduled for early the next morning.

The last one to spend time with his mother was the eleven-year-old, youngest son, John. Oh how he loved his mother. He walked through the ward towards her bed, completely oblivious to the many other patients and visitors watching him. His focus was on his lovely mother at the end of the ward, conscious of the possibility that this may be the last time he would see his mother. He had not been told everything, but he knew things were not good. As he walked away from the bed, he turned repeatedly with tears in his eyes to offer another good-bye wave to his lovely mother.

As visiting hour came to an end, the visitors walked out. Wilf overheard one of the nurses say to the sister in charge, not knowing he was close by, "I've never before witnessed such respect and emotion from the other patients and their visitors, observing such a brave and loving mother saying good-bye to her children. I don't know how she held it together."

That was too much for Wilf as he broke down and slowly followed his family back to his home across the road.

Her eldest son, Ronald Allen, was given special permission to see his mother a little later that night. His work took him out of town each week, and he would not return until after normal visiting hours had finished. Teen always worried about Allen because of his involvement in racing motorbikes in the Speedway each week at Broadmeadow and other places.

In previous years, Wilf had told Teen of the terrible accident he had witnessed close to him when he visited Greenwich in London during his leave. He had never trusted motorbikes, and Teen had the same fear. The noise from the Speedway at Broadmeadow could be heard at their Waratah home, and both would lay awake, unable to sleep until they knew Allen was home safe. This night at the hospital, Teen had a special parting message for Allen, "Please, Allen, give up the motor bikes, just for me."

Chapter 33

Back in Brighton, UK, in the early fifties, Mrs. Ann Watford-Smith enjoyed a very active life with her husband, Spencer, and lacked for nothing, with the exception of more children. Spencer was very successful in his job with the Scottish Bank, and his income could have supported many sisters or brothers for their only daughter, Victoria; that was not to be.

Victoria did very well at school, but unlike her mother, Victoria did not enter the nursing profession; instead she became a secretary to the manager of a finance company. Victoria was very much out of the same mould as her mother, very caring with a happy disposition. She married a talented pilot in the Royal Air Force by the name of Flt. Lieutenant Andrew Moss.

Andrew was stationed at RAF Northolt Base when Victoria first met him. He had been chosen a couple of times to do the fly-past for both the lord mayor of London's Parade and also the Remembrance Day Parade on November 11.

A few years after they were married, he was transferred to the RAF Base at Biggin Hill outside of London. This was very handy to Brighton, which was only a few hours' drive away, allowing Victoria to see her family often.

Biggin Hill was a very exciting base where the original 617 Dam Busters Squadron was located during WWII. This was one of if not the best-known British squadrons of all time. From Biggin Hill, the Lancaster Bombers flew to bomb and successfully destroy the major

German dams of the Ruhr Valley; this hurried up the end of WWII. It was also an exciting base because only the best of the RAF were posted there. In 1950, with two little girls in their family, Andrew was offered a two-year exchange posting to the Royal Australian Air Force base in Williamtown, NSW, Australia.

Andrew and Victoria had reservations about going to Australia because Victoria's father, Spencer, was quite sick. They were not happy about leaving Vickie's mother with the added responsibility of caring for her sick husband.

Ann told them, "I will be fine, and time will fly because it will only be for two years. I don't want you to miss such a golden opportunity to see the other side of the world, and besides, it will also be a promotion for Andrew."

After much discussion and heartache, they decided to move to Australia for the two years before the little girls started schooling. Those two darling little girls would be badly missed by both Ann and Spencer.

Ann decided this was the time to share her well-kept secret with Victoria, saying, "I've never needed to share this story with you in the past, but now is probably the right time seeing that you are going to Australia."

"This sounds as if this could be interesting, Mum. Please go ahead."

"Well, when I was nursing at the King's College Hospital, I twice nursed an Australian soldier, and we became very close. As a matter of fact, he was the reason I signed up with QAIMES and did nursing in France."

"You sneaky old villain, Mum. How come you never told me this before?"

"I didn't tell you because it was always a delicate matter for me after he was killed in the closing days of WWI at the battle of Mont St. Quentin."

"Oh, Mum, how terrible for you! No wonder you didn't want to talk about it."

"Let me assure you, it was so horrible to get through not long after I lost my brother, Joe, and Mother and Father in that dreadful air raid on our home at King's Cross; I've told you all about that."

"Yes, you have a number of times, but with this on top, I don't know how you coped. What part of Australia did he come from?"

"Well, I don't really know because his address and family details were destroyed in the fire. All I know is that it was north of Sydney in New South Wales, somewhere out in the bush as he called it."

"Oh that's a shame. It would have added some extra interest knowing where he came from. The base at Williamtown where Andrew is being posted to is in that general area north of Sydney."

Victoria put her arm around her mother and gave her a hug, saying, "I'm glad you told me, Mum. I only wish you had told me earlier, although there was nothing I could do, naturally. Now with Dad being unwell, it makes me feel awful to be leaving you; you have certainly had your share of traumas in the past."

Spencer lasted only six months after Victoria, Andrew, and the girls left for Australia, before succumbing to cancer of the liver. Victoria did not return for the funeral, on Ann's insistence.

Ann was now alone without family other than her cousin, Heather, who had married and moved to Norfolk, which was on the other side of the country. Ann only received an occasional letter from Heather, and her parents had passed away over three years ago.

Ann had a nice circle of friends, but having family around was what she missed most. She tried to gain strength from her friends and met with them frequently.

On one occasion, Ann decided to make a special trip into London; she had not done this for many years, since the restoration work in London had been carried out after WWII. After looking around at some of the old sights from long ago, she made a snap decision without much thought and took the underground to King's Cross. She crossed Euston Road to visit her old address in Whidbourne Street. As Ann passed the Wardonia Hotel and rounded the corner, she started to feel uneasy. Should she turn back now or proceed? Maybe this was not such a good idea to come here. These were the thoughts running around her mind.

She continued rather reluctantly at a slower pace and noticed that the name of the pub had changed from The Wellington to Mc Glynn's. The undertaker's shop was still directly across the road to the right.

She was not prepared for the sight as she looked left where her house once stood. A four-story block of commercial units extended the full length of the street. Ann stood there for just a few minutes, taking in what was now there. She suddenly realised just how terribly alone she now was—her family and home gone, her husband gone, her daughter and family gone. She couldn't take any more and turned towards the station. Her life was now changed forever, and the past could not be relived.

Victoria, or Vicky as she now preferred to be called in Australia, wrote every week and told how the family was enjoying Australia. They were renting a house at Stockton, only two hundred yards from the surfing beach and located across the narrow harbour looking directly at the City of Newcastle.

Vicky wrote, *We like to take advantage of the sunshine, and we don't miss the cold weather of England at all. We can walk to the harbour foreshore, only seven minutes away, and take a five-minute ferry ride to the Newcastle CBD. We love it so much and think you would too; besides, it would be good for you. Why not fly over and stay with us for a few weeks, or more if you want.*

When Ann read the letter, she realised this was just what she needed and contacted the travel agency straightaway to make the necessary plans.

Ann arrived at Sydney's Kingsford Smith Airport for her holiday with her family. It was the beginning of March, and the weather was just perfect for her. In Australia, it was the beginning of the autumn season when the hot weather was now behind them. Most Australians stopped surfing around this time of year, but Andrew and Vicky, who were used to much colder weather and water, continued to enjoy the beach.

Ann loved the climate also and was reluctant to even think about returning home. She loved being with her little darling girls again and also loved being with Vicky so much. Andrew enjoyed his new administrative roll at the RAAF Base at Williamtown, which was only twelve minutes by car from home. Andrew had purchased one of the new Australian-made Holden motor cars and had taken many trips into the country on the weekends. They took great delight in taking Ann on trips up to the Barrington Tops and the Hunter Valley Vineyards, which were expanding into the traditional farming lands.

Ann knew the time to leave her only family was fast approaching. She was not looking forward to this parting and tried to avoid the subject whenever it came up.

Three days before Ann was due to fly home, Vicky said to her mother, "Andrew has some news for us to discuss over the evening meal."

Vicky prepared a special baked dinner and decorated the table to celebrate this special occasion. The girls' favourite desert was served, fruit salad and ice cream. This desert had actually become a favourite of the whole family and was associated with every special achievement, even at preschool.

Ann said, "This is now my favourite food too because it's not as readily available back home as it is here."

Ann was anxious to hear the important news, so special to have this dinner. She didn't know any details but suspected that Andrew was being offered a promotion or an extension of another year, a change of air base or at worst maybe another two years with the RAAF. She was not prepared for the news when it came.

Andrew said, "I've been offered the chance to transfer permanently to the RAAF with a salary increase of nearly 30 per cent."

There was silence around the table as Ann's mouth dropped, but words didn't come out for some time. She then said with some quivering in her voice, "You mean, to live in Australia permanently?"

"Yes, Mum," said Vicky, "the salary is not the main reason for us considering the change. It is because we have all fallen in love with Australia, the people, the way of life, and the opportunities available." Ann was totally shocked at the prospect of being permanently separated from her only family. She had difficulty holding back the tears and left the room for a little while to sit on the bed and shed some tears.

Ann then started to think about this news and did some serious searching of her own thoughts. After a little while, she returned to the kitchen where Vicky had finished clearing the table and was sitting with red eyes, reading to the girls. Andrew was at the sink doing the last of the dishes.

Ann said, "I was totally shocked at your announcement, believe me, but after thinking through the implications, I understand how you feel about Australia. In the few weeks I've been here, I've also come to realise what a great place this is to bring up a family. I have no real ties back home so I'm prepared to go back home and give long consideration about coming back to join you."

Vicky nearly jumped over the table to get to her mother and to throw her arms around her and smother her with kisses of appreciation, saying, "Oh, Mother, that is so good to hear. I love you for the way you have taken the news."

Andrew also threw his arms around them both as tears of joy appeared on three lots of cheeks. The girls were also very happy but were not really sure why they were happy; it didn't really matter.

For the next two days, every conceivable argument was raised both for and against the idea. Vicky even took her mother down to one of the local real estate agencies to get a handle on approximate house prices in nice areas. The cost of a nice house would not be a problem for Ann because Spencer had left her in a very healthy financial situation.

Then unexpected turmoil struck the home. Sarah, the eldest at four years old, fell awkwardly off a swing at the park and broke her arm. Andrew rushed home to collect Ann and little Suzie to drive them to the Mater Hospital. Vicky had already gone with Sarah in the ambulance to the hospital.

Andrew was already scheduled to drive Ann to the airport in Sydney the next afternoon for her return to England. On the way to the hospital, Ann made the decision not to go back now that this accident had happened. She decided to phone the airline from the hospital and cancel the booking. She was secretly relieved that she had a genuine reason for not leaving Australia right away because she also was getting very fond of the climate and the place in general. She needed more time to plan her future.

Sarah's broken arm healed quickly, and having one arm in plaster was sometimes fun for a little girl. Ann became even closer to the girls, knowing that she wasn't necessarily going to be leaving them for some long, indeterminable period. Now every decision she made was as a possible future resident rather than as the tourist she had been for the first part of her visit to Australia.

Ann stayed another three weeks before the time came to return to her home in Brighton. In those extra three weeks, she had positively made up her mind to sell up everything in England and return to Australia, although she had not yet confirmed this to Vickie. She needed to contact the Australian government office in London to arrange for a visa. This should be easy because Australia was looking for as many emigrants from the UK as possible to move to Australia to fill the many vacancies available in a rapidly expanding country.

As they travelled in Andrew's car to the airport in Sydney, Vickie said, "Mother, since you told us there is a chance that you will be coming back to live in Australia, we have noticed a significant change in your disposition, for the better. I think you have already made up your mind to come back to live in Australia, haven't you?"

"Yes, you are right, my love. I planned to tell you at the airport."

"That's terrific, isn't it, girls?" Vickie encouraged them to agree.

Andrew said, "I want you to know that I'm more than happy; it will be good for all of us."

Ann said, "It will take a few months to organise. The first thing I need to get is a visa, and then I need to sell the house and get rid of what furniture I won't need here."

Vickie said, "Don't make the same mistake we made and bring old furniture with you. There is so much available here and probably cheaper."

Chapter 34

Things were looking a little brighter at Waratah in 1950. Teen came through the operation, and things were looking good for a short time until her health again deteriorated. She was confined to her bed for nearly three years all told as her weight fell away to leave her helpless and unable to even roll over in bed. Margaret Ann, the youngest daughter, was encouraged to leave school after achieving her intermediate certificate at the age of fifteen, to care for her mother while Wilf continued to work to support his home and family.

The cost of the medications required by Teen was very expensive, so Wilf reluctantly also encouraged his youngest son, John, to leave school and get a job to help relieve the cost burden.

After three years of sickness, Wilf was given the worst possible news.

Doctor Henry said, "I'm very sorry to have to give you this news, Mr Yates, but your wife has only about one more week to live." Wilf took the news a little better this time because he had seen his beloved Teen's condition deteriorating over many months and knew this moment was coming. So did the older members of the family. Margaret Ann had been a full-time nurse to her mother for the recent years, and she knew only too well the situation.

Wilf called his youngest son, John, into the lounge and said with breaking voice, "Your mum has suffered so much over the last three years, and she won't last much longer; the doctor tells me about one week." That was all he could manage, but now it was John's turn to choke for want of words. He dropped his head and made his way to his bedroom. He sat on his bed for a long time to think about what life would be like without his mum.

Tragically, Teen passed away in July 1952 after suffering so much. Wilf was absolutely devastated that he had lost his special partner with whom he could not recall ever having rowed with over the years. He was so devoted to Teen, and she to him, and now he was on his own, apart from his supportive family, but that was not quite the same. Wilf had his family around him, but he was still a very lonely man.

As the months went by, Wilf overcame his grief and got his life back in order once more. He remembered in the weeks visiting Teen in the hospital, there were patients who very rarely enjoyed a visit from family or never appeared to have visitors at all. To enable him to get his mind off Teen, he was looking for something else to help keep him occupied. He was very active in his church at Mayfield Baptist, so he decided that he could provide a service to those people by doing the rounds each night, just to say hello to these people. He offered to make phone calls to family on their behalf or make some simple purchases for them at the little shop in the grounds of the hospital, or any other small service that they needed.

This became a real community service for him to do, and he became well-known within the hospital and outside for his dedicated service. He was always made welcome by the nursing staff at any time, either during visiting hours or not, just as they would welcome a visiting clergyman. He became very dedicated to this service, which helped him overcome the void that had been left in his life when he lost Teen.

On one of the regular visits, he sat down and talked to an elderly lady in her early eighties who had a badly broken hip. She had been in the hospital for nearly two months and was known to all as Mabel. She was from up Muswellbrook way, and the only family she had was only able to make the long journey down to see her every two or three weeks.

Mable was a very intelligent person and able to hold a conversation on most subjects. She looked forward to the regular visits from Wilf, and on this particular visit, she was detailing to Wilf the individual reasons for each of the other patients being in that particular ward.

Mable soon learned the background of any new patients arriving and said, "The lady directly opposite only came in during the evening meal. Her name is Ann something, and she has only recently arrived from England. They have sedated her in readiness for an operation tonight for appendicitis."

Wilf said, "Did you talk to her at all?" as he tried to get a better look at a strangely familiar face.

"No, she was in a lot of pain, and they had the curtains around her. The drugs seemed to have an immediate effect on her."

Wilf was only half listening to Mable's answers as his mind was doing mental gymnastics thinking about the lady opposite. He said, "How did you find out about her?"

"Nurse Wilson told me about her when she was checking my blood pressure."

Although the lady was drugged, Wilf thought he knew the lady's face from the distant past; she was strangely familiar. She had very blonde hair for her age, very smooth skin, and high cheekbones. He had nothing else to go on other than the name Ann and the fact that she was from England. His mind was racing, but he brought himself back to reality, saying to himself, *No, it can't be; forget it.*

Mable was still talking, but Wilf was not hearing anything at all. He eventually excused himself from Mable and strolled across to take a look at the patient's identification board hanging on the end of the bed. This was something Wilf often did, and it was not considered unusual at all. He raised the board to read *Margaret Ann Watford-Smith*. She was at this time totally unaware of his or anyone else's presence. Wilf's hand started to shake so badly he could not read more for the moment.

He recovered a little and raised the board again to look for the date of birth line, which read, *Born 29th February 1894 in King's Cross, London*. Wilf's legs began to turn into warm plasticine as he struggled to reach the visitor's chair only four feet away. His whole body was turning to jelly as visions of long-gone days flashed before his mind like a moving film he had seen for the first time in one of the WMCA halls in Amiens.

Before his mind, Wilf saw flashes of the murder scene at the Headland Hotel, the flower garden at Vauxhall, and flashes of sunlight through the trees streaming through the train windows as they returned from Glastonbury. Then there were more flashes from the horrible scene of the bombed house in King's Cross. His frantic mind was in turmoil trying to come to terms with so many thoughts.

He heard the voice of Mable singing out to summon the nurses as he collapsed onto the chair and began to tremble uncontrollably. Tears streamed down his face. There was very little likelihood of there being another Margaret Ann born in King's Cross as a leap-year baby in 1894. Surely this was Ann Davis in the bed in front of him. But how could it be? Ann had been killed by that bomb in 1918.

One of the nurses alerted by Mable's cry quickly came to his aid to support him and to prevent him from collapsing off the chair onto the floor. Another nurse arrived with a glass of water. They had no idea what the problem was and immediately summoned a doctor, who arrived with stethoscope and other aides.

The doctor proceeded to monitor his heart, but Wilf tried to wave him away. He was not able to tell them why he was in this state. He couldn't talk at all until six or seven minuted had passed. Eventually he was able to slowly get out the words, "This lady was a special friend of mine over thirty years ago during the First World War. I was told she had been killed in an air raid on London. I cannot believe she is here right now; it's not possible."

The head nurse said, "Are you absolutely sure?"

"Yes," he said. "I'm positive it's her."

Other nurses arrived to see what all of the commotion was about and to see if their help was needed. After Wilf settled down, he said, "Please go and have a look on your records to see who is listed as her next of kin."

The nurse returned and said, "She has no husband. Her next of kin is her daughter, Vicky Moss of Stockton." Wilf took a deep breath and relaxed a little; he was absolutely sure this was Ann Davis.

Wilf recovered enough for two of the nurses to help him away from the bed as some wards men now arrived to take Ann away to the theatre.

Before leaving the hospital, Wilf enquired from the head nurse, "How long will it be before this lady will be out of the theatre and able to have a visitor?"

The nurse replied, "We think about two o'clock tomorrow will be a good time, just before general visiting hour at three."

"Thank you," he replied, "please don't pass on any information to the incoming nurses or the other patients about my recognition of Ann. I want to surprise her myself."

Wilf sat in the visitors lounge in the foyer for about half an hour, thinking about what had just taken place. He was now feeling much better, so he thanked the nurses for their help and slowly walked out of the ward, took the elevator down to the ground floor, and walked to his home.

Wilf felt as if he was imagining the whole thing. He told his family living with him, who were at home that night, what had happened. Margaret, the second youngest, was still single and worked at a small general store around the corner. Dorothy, the second eldest, was married and worked as a hairdresser at Mayfield. They were intrigued by the meeting but still had not been given the full story. John, the youngest, was at home but showed little interest in the story.

Wilf said to them, "She was one of those wonderful nurses in London who nursed me back to health on two separate occasions. I've spoken about the nurses many times." He had never told them that there was one special nurse who he believed was killed in an air raid shelter he had built for her family; he still didn't tell them now.

"All I can tell you at this stage is that I was told that Ann had been killed in an air raid over London. What happened from there, I still have no idea."

Wilf didn't have any answers at all about Ann's supposed disappearance and her now reappearance, but hopefully he would learn more tomorrow.

Wilf went to bed that night, but his mind was overactive as it raced trying to fabricate answers. Answers to fill the voids left about how Ann survived the bomb attack and reappeared right here in Waratah. He tossed and turned all night and was unable to sleep until nearly daylight.

He stayed in bed until nearly ten o'clock before rising for a very late breakfast. This was completely out of the ordinary for him. He had never experienced such a thing in his life before, and for that matter, not many other people had either. He bathed, shaved, and dressed and was ready to go at one o'clock. He had nearly one hour to kill before leaving. As was his normal custom, he always kept a diary and made notes of his thoughts for his own use. This would help him to ask the right questions of Ann when she was well enough to talk. He needed to fill in the many gaps to complete this unimaginable story.

It then dawned on him that he had a lovely lot of red roses in bloom in the garden, so he decided to cut a large bunch to take them with him. He took great pride in his garden, particularly his many rose bushes. A red rose had been a very important part of this incredible story of long ago.

At two o'clock on the dot, Wilf stopped at the desk of the nurse in charge of the ward to enquire if Ann was up to seeing a visitor.

The nurse said, "The lady is quite well, just sleeping it off after the operation. The doctor visited earlier and said she was doing fine. He said, 'If she is not awake by two, wake her up with a cup of tea and a sandwich.'" Wilf was well-known to both of the nurses on duty, neither of whom knew about the episode last evening.

Neither of the nurses had ever known Wilf to bring flowers to any of the patients before, and one of them said, "This must be a special visit for you, Mr. Yates, to bring in flowers?"

"The roses are from my own garden, and you have a very special lady in your ward."

The sister replied, "Is that so? We should have already woken her, but seeing you have the flowers, why don't you go and wake her by waving the flowers under her nose?"

"I would love to do just that," he said as he turned to go.

Wilf approached the bed where Ann was lying with her eyes closed. He placed the roses on the bedside cabinet and sat down on the chair close to the bed. He gazed upon Ann's face and cast his mind back over all of those years. The more he looked, the more he realised Ann hadn't changed much at all; this was the same Ann Davis of Whidbourne,

St. King's Cross. He was having trouble controlling his emotions but managed to hold himself together. He didn't want to wake her just yet; he was content to sit and gaze at her face.

After some five or six minutes, he noticed Ann's eyelids start to stir. They were flickering just a little. He stood and leaned over towards Ann and whispered, "Hello, Ann Davis, this is Wilf Yates."

Ann opened her eyes just a little and stared at Wilf without any emotion showing on her face at all. Her eyes closed again. He waited another fifteen or twenty seconds and then repeated the words again.

This time, her eyes sprung wide open as she stared at Wilf for a long time before saying, "I thought I was dreaming. Is it really you, Wilf? It can't be."

Wilf took her hand and kissed it on the back, saying, "Yes, Ann Davis, this really is Wilf Yates."

Both Wilf and Ann were speechless for some time before the tears started to flow down Ann's cheeks. Wilf was having trouble also. After some time, she managed the words, "Please don't tell me I'm dreaming and this is not really happening."

After the tears stopped cascading down Ann's cheeks, Wilf lifted the bunch of roses, which had been out of Ann's sight until now, and withdrew the most beautiful rose from the bunch. He handed it to Ann, saying, "Maybe you will believe this is for real and actually happening. Do you recall the red rose I picked for you from the flower market down by the Thames near Vauxhall Train Station?"

Ann stared at the rose as more tears flowed, and she sobbed uncontrollably. Wilf said, "Can you recall me asking you to remember that rose forever as an appreciation of the way you cared for me in King's College Hospital on Denmark Hill?"

"I most certainly can. How could I ever forget?" she managed between sobs as the tears continued to flow down her cheeks and Wilf's also as he leant over and kissed her on the wet cheek.

"I think you should rest before we try to find the answers to so many unanswered questions. I will stay here by your side until you get some more sleep, and later we can have a great conversation."

Ann said, "I have one very important question to ask first."

"What is that?" said Wilf as he gripped her hand.

"Are you married, Wilf?"

"No, Ann, I'm not married."

"How lovely is that? Neither am I."

Wilf sat by the bed for some fifteen minutes waiting for Ann to show signs of sleeping, but sleep was the last thing Ann needed or wanted at this time and regularly opened her eyes.

Ann said, "I need to keep opening my eyes to make sure I'm not dreaming and to make sure you're really there."

The nurse had been keeping an eye on what was happening and came along with a cup of tea and sandwich for Ann.

The nurse said, as nurses do, "Come on, Ann, wakey wakey. I want you to have something to eat. I will help you sit up a little."

The nurse with Wilf's help raised her up and puffed up the pillows underneath to make her more comfortable. While Ann had the sandwich, Wilf attempted to explain briefly to the nurse how they had first known each other in 1917.

The nurse said, "How did you become separated in London?"

Wilf replied, "I don't know the answer to that because I was told that Ann had been killed in an air raid."

Ann, now in the land of the living, said, "I thought Wilf was killed in battle on the Western Front."

The nurse left them for a few minutes and returned with an extra cup of tea for Wilf, saying, "I would really love to hear the full story when you have it all worked out. It sounds like it would make an interesting book to me. I think this ward needs some good news for a change, so I'll let Mable know what happened; she'll spread the story around."

The nurse moved away to take care of other patients and spread the news.

It was now three o'clock and time for visiting hour again. Wilf was still sitting at the bedside when two excited little girls rushed to be first through the door to visit their grandmother. They were followed by their mother. Ann had just finished her tea and sandwich as Vickie lifted the girls up one at a time to kiss Grandma.

Ann was still bamboozled and very shaky as she tried to introduce this stranger to her daughter, saying, "Wilf, this is my daughter, Vickie, and this is Sarah and Suzie, my two lovely granddaughters. And, Vickie love, this is Wilfred Yates who I nursed when he was in London on two separate occasions during WWI."

Vickie said, "Nice to meet you, Mr. Yates, but how did you two meet up again? Was it just now?"

Ann said, "Yes, it was just a short while ago. We really don't know the answer to that question yet, but when we do work it all out, you will be the first to know."

Wilf said with emotion in his voice, "You will not believe what happened because we still don't believe it either."

"For both of us, this is truly an unbelievable story with a chance meeting again. We are both so happy," said Ann as she dabbed at her eyes.

The only Australian soldier Ann had mentioned to Vickie was the one that was killed in action; she told Vickie that story just prior to Vickie leaving for Australia. But Vicky had not been told about any other Australian soldier.

Wilf thought it best to leave them together to talk, as this was a complete shock to Vicky, and it showed. She needed to have some time alone with her mother.

Wilf reluctantly did not make any attempt to kiss Ann. He said good-bye to them all and said he would see Ann tomorrow. He made his way across the ward to Mabel, who had already heard a little of the news and wanted to hear it all. Wilf said, "It is absolutely true, and I promise to tell you more at another time."

"I will keep you to that promise, Mr Yates." Right now he wanted to go home and confirm to his family that it was actually Ann Davis who he had known very well in London during the war.

When he arrived home, the girls were eagerly awaiting his return, to learn the full story. They had so many questions to ask, but he still could not provide all of the answers. One of the first questions Dorothy asked was, "How is she doing after the operation, Dad?"

He said, "I feel like a real goat because I didn't think to ask her in the midst of all that was happening. There were too many other things going on, but I'm certain she is doing fine; she was so happy."

Margaret said, "Did you find out why she's here in Australia?"

"No," he said, "we didn't get around to finding out the answers to those questions. We were just so happy finding each other again. Hopefully tomorrow all will be revealed."

As he sat down in his favourite lounge chair, he somehow believed he wouldn't know all of the answers tomorrow. The questions would roll on for weeks or even months before all of the pieces of the jigsaw would fit together and complete the picture.

Margaret came around and sat on the armrest of the chair. She put her arm around his shoulder and hugged him as his emotions got the better of him. She continued to hug him as he literally fell apart.

She said, "I somehow get the feeling that that this was a huge part in your life that you kept bottled up all those years. This story is probably another one of those periods of war that happened while you were away and you could not speak openly about it."

Wilf delayed responding until he was confident he could control his words. He then said, "Ann was a very important part of my life when I was in England, more than you could possibly imagine. I don't have all the answers yet, but I will tell you the whole story in the next day or two."

Margaret comforted him for quite some time and then said, "This story was obviously something that happened before our mum was really in the picture."

He nodded his head, still unable to talk. Margaret said, "I know what Mum meant to you, there is no doubt about that, but I just want you to know that whatever happened way back there, we will always love you and support you, regardless of the circumstances. I can see that it must have been a very important episode in your life during the war; I can see how it is affecting you now. When you're ready, I want you to share the story with us because I sense it to be a most beautiful story. Will you promise me that?" He nodded his head.

Dorothy said, "I can't wait to hear the whole story either, Dad."

Wilf was encouraged by the support shown to him by his family in this very emotional time and managed a few words, saying, "You don't understand just how much those words mean to me. When I can, I will tell you everything."

The next day, Wilf left it till after lunch before making his way over to the hospital. The nurses were always happy to let him do his rounds at any time and had told him so, but this was different. When he walked into the ward, Ann was already half-sitting up and looking in his direction as he came through the doorway. Her face lit up like a large sunflower welcoming the bright sunshine after long days of rain.

Wilf leant over and kissed Ann as the other patients, or those well enough, looked on. There was even a soft wolf-whistle from the other end of the ward. To many, this story made their stay in hospital easier to endure and added real excitement, which spread further than just this ward.

Ann said, "I've been telling some of the nurses and the ladies on either side of me the background to our story and how we become separated, from my side of the story only at this stage. Because, until you tell me what happened, I still don't know your side of the story."

"Well, I'm in exactly the same boat as you because I don't know your story either."

Ann said, "I'm so happy to see you, Wilf. Thanks for finding me."

"You certainly made it very hard to find you. I'm dying to find out what happened to Ann Davis in King's Cross."

Ann said, "Notice how quiet it is in the ward. The women and the nurses have heard only heard a small part of the story. I think they're hoping to find out right now."

Wilf smiled. "How did you tell them?"

"The story was passed on from bed to bed. It would be interesting to hear the story from the person at the other end of the chain because, like Chinese whispers, the story has probably been embellished a lot, and maybe it bears little resemblance to the real story."

Wilf said, "I've been hauled over the coals by my family for not asking you how you were feeling yesterday after the operation."

"You can tell them I'm feeling super good, but I'm going to get even better. Remember, I have not been out of bed yet."

"Having sorted out that problem, I think it's time to find out what happened to each of us at the end of the war," he suggested.

"Well, I'll go first," said Ann, "but you'll need to sit down. After my parents were killed, I joined the Army Medical Corp to be closer to you in France and finished up at a casualty clearing station at Corbie. Then, when the war was over and I had not heard from you, I was certain you had been killed because there was no communication at all. I signed up for a twelve-month posting at the Central Medical Hospital in Amiens."

Wilf interjected and sat upright. "Corbie? You were at Corbie? I can't believe it. We went right through Corbie after Mont St. Quentin, but I was asleep on my feet in the back of the transport vehicle. The only thing I can remember is seeing all of the injured men on stretchers outside the town hall/field hospital waiting for treatment."

"This is absolutely amazing. You were in Corbie? I was one of the nurses inside the town hall trying to save the lives of those poor boys. It was really terrible. It was a nightmare. I cannot believe we were so close."

"I can't believe it either," he said.

"But before I get too far ahead, how about you tell me your side, Wilf."

"Okay, let me fill you in up to that period. After we were relieved on Mont St. Quentin and returned to base camp, I was immediately sent off to NCO school in Amiens. I was there when the armistice was signed and given the opportunity of returning to my battalion at Vignacourt or returning to London.

"I chose to go back to London and went straight to King's Cross to find you. I went immediately to your home only to be told that you and your parents had been killed in a direct hit on the air raid shelter in your backyard."

"That would have been so terrible. I'm so sorry for you. That was my parents, true, but it wasn't me. I wasn't there."

"Ann, I was so shattered that I wanted to get out of London as quickly as possible and requested an early return. The horrible experience of being told that all three of you had been killed was too much for me to handle. Losing you was bad enough, but I thought the world of your parents also."

"I don't blame you. How long did you have to wait?"

"I was so lucky and got a boat the very next day." Lumps in his throat were now causing Wilf difficulty continuing.

Tears were starting to trickle down Ann's cheeks, but she bravely suggested that she continue with more of her story.

She said, "After one year at Amiens, I returned to England and went to Brighton to work in a hospital there. I met and married Spencer Watford-Smith, a banker. He died of cancer only a couple of years ago."

"I'm sorry to hear about you losing your husband. I also recently lost my wife to cancer."

"Oh, I'm sorry, Wilf. So it's been difficult for you as well." Ann continued, "I then came to Australia to visit my only daughter, Vickie, who you met yesterday. She married an RAF pilot. He then came on loan to the RAAF at Williamtown for two years and liked it so much they decided to stay permanently. I came for a visit and also liked it here. I sold everything and came back here. I bought a house in Regent St. Mayfield only two months ago. Last week, I took sick and finished up here in this hospital with you today."

"What a great day for both of us," he said with a smile.

"Wilf, this is going to be one of those quirky things where I will be able to say how glad I am that I did get sick, because I found you again. But I want you to keep going with the rest of your story."

"I returned to Australia on that first boat and was met at the wharf by Teen Bisset; you will recall that I told you about her."

"Was she the penfriend who wrote to you during the war?"

"Yes, she was waiting for me, and one year later we got married. We lived in the bush at Craven before moving to Waratah, right across the road from this hospital. Teen took sick and died of cancer in 1952, and here I am at this hospital, still in shock, visiting Ann Davis or whatever your new name is?"

"Watford-Smith," Ann said, "I'm sorry to hear about you losing your wife. I know exactly what you must have gone through."

"Yes, I remember now the name Watford-Smith," he said. "I recall seeing your name written on the patient board hanging on the end of your bed, just before I collapsed."

"Oh, you didn't, did you?" She laughed. "You'll have to tell me about that another time."

Wilf said, "I find it interesting that you also lost your soul-mate to cancer."

There were lots of questions still to ask back and forth and for Wilf to explain why he was visiting the hospital. They talked for over an hour with only some of the many questions answered.

Wilf said, "I heard you say you bought a house on Regent Street. I know Regent Street very well because my old boss, who owned a tire retreading factory, lived in a large house on the high side. I often went there to take care of the gardens."

Ann said, "My house is on the high side. Wouldn't it be funny if it's the same house?" They decided they had plenty of time to check that out later.

Wilf said, "You know, I collapsed in the street when I was told by the old guy, Barney, across from your home in Whidbourne Street that you and your parents had been killed in the shelter."

Ann said, "I didn't know any old guy by the name of Barney across the street. He must have moved there after the bombing."

"By the way," said Wilf, "I was thinking about this last night. Who was the other blonde female killed in the shelter with your parents? Was it Mavis from next door?"

"Yes," said Ann, "but I didn't find out about the mistaken identity until long after I returned from France and was nursing at Brighton. All of my friends at the King's and church also believed I was dead. I've been through this experience before."

It was time for visiting hour, and right on time Sarah and Suzie came through the door, followed by both Vickie and Andrew. Vicky was a lot more friendly today after her mother had told her more of the story, after Wilf had left yesterday.

Wilf chatted well with Andrew, asking all sorts of questions about his roll with the RAAF at Williamtown. Andrew, on the other hand, wanted to know more about Wilf's time during WWI. Wilf led Andrew over to the window and pointed out his home directly across the street and said, "Ann has only today explained how she has bought a home in Regent Street, Mayfield." Wilf pointed in the general direction and said, "If you cast your eye along the ridge line over there above that tall stack, that's Regent Street."

Andrew said, "We have quite a commanding view of the district from here on the third floor, don't we."

Wilf said, "On VP Day in 1945, our neighbour's son-in-law, Wing Commander Harold Tapner," he pointed to the florist shop across the road, "flew his Super Fortress low past the hospital, right out the front here. People on the top-floor balcony of the hospital said they were looking straight out into the cockpit as it thundered by. He was on his way to Sydney for the celebration march."

Andrew said, "How things have changed since those times. There are so many restrictions now about flying over built-up areas; it would be a court martial for any pilot doing that sort of thing today, even if he didn't fly that low. During the war, you could get away with anything."

They walked back into the ward, and Wilf said to Vicky, "I will leave your mother to spend the rest of the hour available with family. I'm sure she has a lot to tell you."

Vicky replied, "I'm sure she does, now that both of you have had some time to find out how each other disappeared off the face of the earth."

"I can assure you, it's quite a story. However, before I go, I must be ready for questions at home. Yesterday, my family thought I was terrible for not having asked your mother how she was feeling."

Turning to Ann, he said, "I know you told me when I first came in today that you were feeling absolutely fabulous. Can I assume that is still the case?"

Ann said, "You can tell them I'm now feeling even better than that. As a matter of fact, I don't know why I still need to be here."

Wilf said his good-byes to everyone and assured Ann he would see her again tomorrow. He went home to find he now had most of his family waiting to learn more about this amazing story. He was feeling so much better than he did yesterday when he fell apart. Margaret had given him such wonderful support.

Dorothy took the initiative and phoned the other two sisters and told them what had happened, so now all four of them were waiting for their father to return from the hospital.

Because of all the questions being asked amongst themselves about this mysterious story and in particular Ann, who they still knew so little about, they did not hear their father enter. The lively discussion soon ceased as he went to each of the girls and gave them a hug. He then said, "I think we should sit around the table so I can start this story from the beginning."

"I think that would be a great idea," Dorothy said. "I have the water hot, so how about I get everyone a cup of tea first." They all pitched in and were anxious to learn more.

They sat down at the family table, around which they had all grown up. Beryl, the third daughter, worked in a jewellery shop in Newcastle. She had only recently married. She said, "Right, we're all ears, Dad. Why not start from the beginning."

He started by saying, "I think you will all remember me telling you, probably more times than you wanted to hear, about my first trip to the hospital in London when I was twenty-five years old, suffering with trench foot."

Beryl chipped in, "Dad, you told us so many times we got sick of it. But now, I think for me anyway, I would like to hear it again in great detail."

"I told you how the nurses at the hospital were so wonderful. Well that is where it all started with one particular nurse called Ann Davis." He took a long breath. "She was the most wonderful, caring nurse in England, and she took really good care of me."

The silence around the table was deafening as he continued his amazing story. They had never thought of their father as a storyteller, but few questions needed to be asked because he told them everything. Tears were evident by the constant dabbing of the four pairs of eyes as he told them with great difficulty how he went back to London after the war ended, only to be told that Ann had been killed in the bombing raid.

John had been half-listening from another room. He was only fifteen and at that stage of his life was not interested too much in family matters. He had started his own business repairing and painting bicycles for the other bike shops around town. When he heard the words "bombing raid," he thought he had better join the others; he was always interested in learning about the war.

Beryl, who was sitting next to her father, put her arm around her dad's shoulder and said with tears bursting forth, "This must have been so horrible for you; I don't know how you could even bear to go on."

Wilf was now very emotional but managed to get out the words, "I don't know how I did it either."

After a short break for everyone to recover, Jessie, the eldest who had only recently returned with her husband and two small daughters from living in Adelaide, said, "I don't know how you have been able to keep this story bottled up for so long."

Wilf said, "The only way I was able to go on was because of your mum, who was waiting for me at the wharf in Sydney to welcome me home. She changed my whole world around and got me back on track."

Jessie said, "Were you ever able to tell mum about what happened?"

"No" he said, "I couldn't, knowing that I would become emotional and could cause Mum to think that she was only my second choice. I would never have wanted her to be hurt by hearing this story. Besides, Ann was gone forever. What would be the point?"

Chapter 35

At the hospital, after another three days of catching up with so many until-now unanswered questions, Ann advised Wilf she could go home in the morning. They had another hour to themselves with more questions and answers.

Ann said, "Vicky has planned not to visit today, but she will be here at ten o'clock in the morning to take me home. Vicky won't bring the children with her in the morning, but I would like you to come with me in the car to help me home."

Wilf was glad of this special opportunity and said, "I would love to be there to help you." Naturally, Ann was appreciative of his support.

Both Vicky and Wilf arrived a little before ten. Ann and Wilf both responded to the many well-wishers amongst both patients and staff. One of the patients said, "We like what we have heard; we think it would make a great movie."

One of the nurses arrived with a wheelchair for Ann. "Oh, I don't need that," said Ann. "I can manage with Wilf's help."

"Ann, take advantage of the chair while you can," said Wilf as he helped to set her down into the chair.

They left the ward and proceeded down in the lift to the foyer, where they waited while Vicky went to fetch the car. Wilf helped Ann into the car and returned the chair to the nurse who was waiting. They settled in for the ten-minute trip to Regent Street. Vicky of course knew the house quite well and did not need instructions from Wilf.

"Wilf, whatever happened to that lieutenant in your unit you used to tell me about that thought he was bulletproof? Did he survive?"

"Yes, he did. That was Lt. Joe Maxwell VC, DCM, Military Cross and Bar. He was celebrated all around Australia as one of the great heroes of the war. Then the grog got him. I saw him in Sydney just a few years ago."

"Oh, that's a shame; you always said he was a likeable larrikin."

They turned into Regent Street, and Wilf said, "I hope you didn't buy one of those large homes on the high side; they're too big for you to look after."

"No," she replied, "the small, dark-brown, brick place on the other side of that really large one up ahead is big enough for me." Ann's mind suddenly thought for the first time that just maybe she would soon have someone to help look after her home.

They travelled slowly past the largest house as Vicky prepared to turn up into the drive. Wilf said, "Well what do you know? It's right next door to where I used to look after the gardens."

Really?" she replied. "I've only met the neighbours on one occasion; I think their name is Stead. They seem to be very nice people."

"Yes it is, Ann. Mr. and Mrs. Stead. That's a very lovely little home you have bought, Mrs. Watford-Smith, very nice indeed. I did meet the people who lived there once or twice; I think they took really good care of the house."

"I think so too. Vicky found this one for me."

"We would like to have bought it for ourselves," said Vicky, "but we didn't have that sort of money."

"Don't worry, my dear. The one you bought is very nice, and it's closer to Andrew's work at the base," said Ann as she pointed to the red roses growing alongside the driveway.

"Yes, I noticed them too," said Wilf as he got out of the car and came around to help Ann. "Now take it very steady. I'm here to look after you."

"I feel great," she said. "As a matter of fact, I don't feel like I need any help, but I'm happy to take all the help you want to give me. It may make up for some of the help I needed in 1918, when it wasn't available."

They both helped Ann into her home and sat her down at one end on the long lounge in Ann's spacious lounge room. Wilf sat in the armchair opposite, admiring the lavish furnishings in the home, the picture railing shelf around the room with a few treasured items displayed and the unique glass bricks on the front wall letting in the morning light.

While Vickie was getting the tea ready, Wilf walked back out to the front drive and picked the best red rose from the garden. He returned and placed it on the side table alongside Ann, without saying a word.

Vicky entered with the tea and set the tray on the occasional table in the centre. Vickie said, "I'm not having a cup. I need to get away because I want to do some shopping for myself before collecting the girls from school. I've already done your shopping and put the things away in their usual places."

"Thank you, Vicky. I don't know what I would do without you. This is one of the many good reasons for me coming to Australia."

As Vicky turned to leave, her mother said, "Before you go, Vickie, would you be kind enough to bring me the large, brown-covered photo album in the left-hand drawer of the dressing table, please?"

While Wilf was questioning Ann about the origins of some of the furnishings, Vicky arrived back with the album, saying, "Is this the one?"

"Yes, that's the one."

"Well, I'll be off," Vicky said, and left the room.

Ann listened for the car leaving and said, "Come and sit over here. I have something special to show you."

Wilf got up and walked over to the lounge. As he sat down, Ann said, "Not that end of the lounge. I want you here right next to me."

He moved closer as Ann took his hand and pulled him gently to her and said, "I've been waiting all week for this special moment, to give you a big hug and a kiss."

"I've been waiting also. Just like the ones we had in the shadow of the crumbling walls of Glastonbury?"

"No," she said, "even better."

After they hugged a little, he said, "We still have a lot of catching up to do. I have lots of questions to ask."

"Me too," said Ann.

"I've also been waiting all week to show you this very special surprise. Are you ready?"

"I certainly am."

Ann reached for the album on the armrest and said, "Before we start asking more questions, I want you to see what I have in here." She opened the album and turned straight to the pocket flap inside the back cover and withdrew an old photo.

She studied the photo for a long time before handing it over to Wilf, saying, "I never, ever wanted to get rid of this photo and treasured it all those years."

Wilf took the photo and stared in disbelief, immediately recognising the photo. "This is the photo we had taken in Trafalgar Square in 1917." His hand started to tremble as he said, "My mind goes back as if it was yesterday, back to that very special time."

Ann took hold of both hands as they studied the photo together. She felt a tear starting to run down her cheek. Wilf made an effort to reach for a handkerchief, but Ann wouldn't release his hand.

Ann said, "I'm not ashamed of crying. I've done so much of it in the past. I notice a sweet look of satisfaction on your face also." Then their tears blended together.

Neither of them touched their cup of tea; it went cold.

After some time, Ann said, "Do you remember that last special night in Argyle Square in the moonlight before you returned to the front the next morning for the second time?"

"How could I forget that night and every other night thereafter, waiting for your letters to arrive?" he said. "But they never arrived."

Ann said, "Every fibre within my body also cried out waiting for your letters to arrive telling me you were still alive, especially when we were unknowingly so close to each other in Corbie."

With emotion breaking his voice, he said, "They literally drove our filthy bodies right past that town hall in Corbie. We were in absolutely disgusting and unrecognisable condition, making our way back from

Mont St. Quentin to base camp. I didn't know you were less than fifty feet away, caring for those poor wretches from the Mont."

They continued to hug each other gently with eyes closed as the memories came flooding back. They remembered in silence so many of the wonderful times they had enjoyed together during that catastrophic time of war.

He adjusted his position on the lounge and said, "Can you recall that special time on our first date near the flower markets at Vauxhall?"

"Of course I can. I remember every time I see a red rose."

Wilf stood and picked up the red rose from the side table and sat down next to Ann again. He presented the rose to Ann's waiting hands, saying, "Promise me you will never forget the red rose?"

Ann lifted the rose and slowly inhaled the fragrance that was so familiar to her. "How could I?" she said as she lowered the rose and kissed him ever so gently. "I've never even forgotten the first rose you gave to me."

"I always hoped, Ann, that whatever happened, you'd always remember."

"What about those other special times together in London, in Glastonbury, Bath, and so many other places?"

"I remember those places just like it was yesterday," Wilf replied. "What about Queen Boadicea and of course the merry-go-round and the music machine in St. James Park?"

"What about that awful time when I thought you had been murdered at the Headland Hotel in Torquay? How could I forget that?" She placed the album and the rose on the floor.

Wilf looked into her red eyes and said, "Did you ever get to hear again that song the Maori and his princess sang at the Headland Hotel?"

"I did better than that," she whispered, with a twinkle in her eye. "I bought the record, which is still packed away. I will play it for you sometime. It has always been my favourite song."

"I can recall the name of the song, 'Pokarekare Ana,' but I could never remember the name of the Maori fellow who sang it."

"His name was Arapeta," she replied, "and her name was Princess Ariki Taipaira."

"How in the dickens did you remember that?"

"Because I had a good reason to remember, so I wrote it down and then later wrote it on the record cover," she said. "I've never forgotten your favourite saying, *How in the dickens*?"

He smiled.

They sat there together with closed eyes, thinking about the past.

Many memories both joyful and painful had been deliberately but only temporarily flushed from their active minds after the war ended. Some of those memories lay dormant during the intervening years.

Now those memories came flooding back like printer's type tumbling from the font tray onto the blank pages of their own special book of life. Memories of long ago now to be reprinted in large type, bringing back to life the long-forgotten, intriguing history of their respective stories. The silent pages of their lives kept turning over as they sat together in the quietness and stillness of Ann's lovely home in Mayfield.

www.ingramcontent.com/pod-product-compliance
Lightning Source LLC
Chambersburg PA
CBHW022032120726
47899CB00001BB/93

9781639503599